Acclaim for *The Blood Upon The Rose*

'Heart rending – a tragic historical romance.'
City Limits

'Writes well . . . in the style of Archer, Seymour, Uris.'
Irish Times

'An exciting story of plot and counter-plot, and a doomed love.'
Books

About the Author

Tim Vicary was born in London in 1949. He was educated at Brighton, Hove and Sussex Grammar School and Sidney Sussex College, Cambridge, where he studied English and History. He subsequently trained as a teacher, and is now a Teaching Fellow at the University of York. His second novel, Cat and Mouse, *a story about suffragettes and Ulster Unionists, was published earlier this year by Simon & Schuster Ltd.*

The
Blood
upon the
Rose

A Novel of Ireland

TIM VICARY

POCKET
B O O K S

New York London Toronto Sydney Tokyo Singapore

First published in Great Britain by Simon & Schuster Ltd in 1992
First published in Great Britain by Pocket Books, 1993
An imprint of Simon & Schuster Ltd
A Paramount Communications Company

Copyright © Tim Vicary, 1992

This book is copyright under the Berne Convention.
No reproduction without permission.
All rights reserved.

The right of Tim Vicary to be identified as author of this work has
been asserted in accordance with sections 77 and 78 of the Copyright
Designs and Patents Act 1988

Simon & Schuster Ltd
West Garden Place
Kendal Street
London W2 2AQ

Simon & Schuster of Australia Pty Ltd
Sydney

A CIP catalogue record for this book is available
from the British Library

ISBN 0–671–71528–3

This book is a work of fiction. Names, characters, places and
incidents are either the product of the author's imagination or are
used fictitiously. Any resemblance to actual events or locales or
persons, living or dead, is entirely coincidental.

Typeset by Keyboard Services, Luton

Printed in Great Britain by
Harper*Collins* Manufacturing, Glasgow

To Sue
with love and gratitude

I see His blood upon the rose
And in the stars the glory of His eyes.
His body gleams amid eternal snows
His tears fall from the skies.

Joseph Mary Plunkett, written in
Kilmainham Gaol, 1916

I have been told the new policy and plan, and I am
satisfied, though I doubt its ultimate success in the main
particular — the stamping out of terrorism by secret
murder.

A letter from C. Prescott Decie, a newly appointed
commander of the Royal Irish Constabulary, to the
Assistant Under-Secretary at Dublin Castle, 1 June 1920.

1

THE POLICEMAN CYCLED slowly along the road from Ashtown Station. He was a burly man — too big for the bike, really — and his knees stuck out sideways as he pedalled. He was frowning; partly because of the concentration needed to avoid the potholes in the unmetalled road, and partly because of the importance of the task his sergeant had given him.

As he approached the pub, the Halfway House, a motor car swept round the corner towards him. It was a big car — a huge, gleaming, armour-plated limousine, with a little Union flag fluttering from the bonnet — and it confirmed all the constable's worries about the importance of what was to happen that morning. Awkwardly, he raised his hand to salute. But the car was going very fast, and as it came nearer it swerved into the middle of the road, to avoid the potholes. This flustered him. As he saluted with his right hand he turned the handlebars sideways with his left, and put his front wheel straight into a pothole. The bicycle tipped him forwards, and he grabbed the handlebars and floundered desperately with his legs to stop himself falling into the deep, muddy ditch that gurgled along beside the country lane.

A derisive cheer completed his embarrassment. The armour-plated limousine had rushed past, and behind it came an army lorry, a Crossley tender, with half a dozen tin-helmeted Tommies sitting high up on the back of it. They had had an excellent view of what happened, and roared their appreciation.

'Go on, Paddy, go for a swim!'

'Get off and milk it, flatfoot!'

Flushed with annoyance, the policeman shook his fist at them, and then hurriedly raised his hand in salute again as a third vehicle followed them down the lane. This was another big, armour-plated limousine, going slightly more sedately. Like the first, it was empty apart from the chauffeur, who raised a gloved finger casually from the wheel to acknowledge the constable's salute.

The constable watched them go a couple of hundred yards down the road and over the level crossing to the little country railway station. It was a warm, clear December day, and the wheels threw up a little cloud of dust that irritated his eyes. Through it, he saw them park outside the station, where his sergeant greeted them. An officer got down from the lorry and began to post sentries where they would get a clear view of anyone approaching or leaving the station. Then he went inside, and the soldiers began to chat and smoke, settling in for a long wait.

Cursing the Tommies under his breath, the constable dragged his front wheel out of the pothole and began to pedal on towards the police station at Ashtown Gate, as the sergeant had told him.

Ashtown Gate was one of the northern entrances to Phoenix Park, Dublin, where the Viceroy of Ireland, Field Marshal Sir John French, had his residence. It was the constable's job to guard that gate, and keep it clear of all obstructions when the Viceregal limousine approached it.

Already, looking ahead, he could see that some clod of a farmer had chosen this time of all times to park his horse and cart in the middle of the road. It looked as if the wretched man was getting out a nosebag for his horse, and settling down to have his lunch, right there in the path the Viceroy's car would take!

Swearing softly, the constable stuck out his knees sideways and began to pedal faster.

Outside the Halfway House, Sean Brennan leaned against the wall reading his newspaper. He read with deep interest, hardly glancing up when the military convoy swept past, and apparently not noticing the policeman at all. And so the constable saw only a young man in an old coat and cloth cap, with a half-empty glass of beer on the wall beside him, studiously reading.

Perhaps if he had seen the title of the newspaper, he might have worried. *An tOglach* – The Volunteer – was the journal of the Irish Volunteers, who had now come to call themselves the Irish Republican Army. On 31 January 1919 *An tOglach* had declared that a state of war existed between England and Ireland, and that Irish Volunteers were justified in 'treating the armed forces of the enemy exactly as the National Army would treat the members of an invading army'. And, as the constable knew, policemen like himself were included in the category of 'armed forces of the enemy'. On 21 January 1919, the day on which the elected Sinn Fein MPs had met in the Mansion House in Dublin and declared themselves the Dáil, or Parliament, of an Irish Republic, two police constables – ordinary Irish family men, just like himself – had been ambushed and shot dead while escorting a load of dynamite to a quarry.

Between then and the date on Sean Brennan's new copy of *An tOglach* – 19 December 1919 – eighteen policemen had been shot dead by the IRA. Some of them ordinary police constables, some of them detectives, trying to penetrate the organization of the IRA.

Today, however, Sean was after a bigger target. He waited until the constable had cycled laboriously past, then folded his newspaper quickly and slipped into the pub.

Inside, seven other young men like himself were waiting. Three more, Sean knew, were further up the road, with the horse and cart. Those in the pub were sitting around casually, drinking and talking. They looked like several unconnected groups of friends who had taken advantage of today's fine weather to cycle out the two miles from Dublin in the crisp December air. He joined two of them at the end of the bar, and nodded imperceptibly.

'They've come,' he murmured. 'Just as we thought. Two cars and a tender. The constable's gone up the road.'

The man he had spoken to glanced at his watch. 'Another ten minutes then,' he said. He glanced around the room, conscious that conversation had died, and that many eyes were watching him. Only a group of four farm labourers in the corner carried on happily with some uproarious story about a cow. 'Best get back outside, Sean. Let us know when the train's in sight.'

Sean shook his head. 'I can't see it well from the road,' he said. 'I might not know until it had come. But there's a ladder round the back. If I got up there I could see, I think. Then I could signal, if someone else were outside.'

The other man frowned. 'What would you be doing up the ladder, if anyone asks?'

'Mending the thatch, maybe. It looks pretty leaky up there.'

'All right.' He glanced at the third man in the group, a young lad like Sean. 'Martin, you go with him. I'll stay by the window. We don't want more than two of us where we can be seen.' He left them, and wandered over to join the other two groups.

Outside, the two young men propped the ladder against the back of the house. Sean climbed it, while Martin stood with his foot on the bottom rung. At the top, Sean glanced over his shoulder. He could see the two big cars outside the station, and soldiers lounging in the back of the lorry. He thought one of them looked his way for a moment, and he pretended to busy himself with the thatched roof, examining the reeds. As he faced the wall to do that he could still look to the right, where the railway line disappeared into the green countryside to the west. He could see clearly here, over the deep banks and hedges that bordered the country roads. At first he found it a little hard to make out the line of the railway. There were a number of bare trees in the way, and the railway, too, seemed sunk in a cutting behind hedges.

But then a young horse bolted in a field about half a mile away. Sean watched it, and saw something that brought a tense, boyish smile to his lips. Despite himself he felt his hands clutch the sides of the ladder convulsively. A plume of white smoke was rising into the air above the trees, and moving steadily closer, towards the station.

In the train, Catherine Maeve O'Connell-Gort was hugely embarrassed.

A slim, dark-haired young woman of nineteen, she sat by the window and sulked. The rest of the carriage was full of men, and all of them had tried, in turn, to be gallant and polite with her, but she had rebuffed the lot. She was furious with them all, especially her father, who had tricked her.

When they had left their family home in Galway early that morning to catch a train to Dublin, he had not said there was anything unusual about the train. To Catherine, one train was much like another; she never thought about them. Her father had seemed a little agitated when their car had been blocked on the roads by several donkey carts and then two herds of cows in quick – or rather slow – succession, but there was nothing abnormal about that. People did get agitated when rushing for a train. They caught the train at Galway, and it was only when they reached Athlone, and her father had insisted that they get *off*, that she had begun to smell a rat. On the platform, the stationmaster had appeared in his best uniform to fuss around them and order porters to carry their bags. He had conducted them to another platform which was roped off so that she and her father were the only passengers on it. Then the wretched stationmaster had actually drawn himself up to salute the train which was steaming in there. It was a quite different train from the one they had left. There were little flags fluttering from either side of the locomotive, and there were only two coaches. Two coaches gleaming with bright paint and the imperial coat of arms on every door.

'There you are, Cathy! How's that for a surprise, eh?' Her father had smiled, full of this ridiculous, tasteless joke, and she had wanted to scream. So this was why he had put on his best uniform this morning! But she was too shocked, too well brought up, to let him down at once in public. So he had handed her into the train, and she had curtsied politely to the short, white-haired old soldier with twinkling blue eyes and military moustache who met her. The arch-enemy himself, Field Marshal Sir John Denton Pinkstone French, KCB, KCMG, Viscount of Ypres and High Lake, Viceroy and Lord Lieutenant of His Majesty's Kingdom of Ireland.

'So this is the young lady! Welcome aboard, my dear. I ordered your father to join me this morning, and he said he would not be parted from you on any account. Now I see why. Come in, do. Roger, take the young lady's coat, and get her a drink, will you!'

It all seemed a terrible, nightmarish trick. Instead of being in an ordinary train compartment rubbing shoulders with the common people of Ireland, she was welcomed into a room with comfortable armchairs and chesterfields, low tables, curtains, pictures on the walls. And standing politely in front of the chairs, boots and belts gleaming with polish, the staff officers of Ireland's enemy!

'Tea, my lady? Or something stronger?' A waiter had bowed in front of her and she had felt ashamed of the practical blue dress and bob hat she had chosen that morning; clothes that would not pick her out among a crowd.

'Yes, thank you. Tea will be fine.' She sat in one of the big armchairs, and her father and Lord French sat opposite. She saw the proud, anxious smile on her father's face, and hated it.

'So. What do you do in Dublin, my dear?'

'I am a student. A medical student.'

'I see.' A frown of surprise, perhaps disapproval, crossed the little field marshal's face. 'Going to earn your living, then, as a doctor, what? Lady sawbones, eh?'

'I don't know. Perhaps. There are the examinations, first.'

'Quite. Bit unladylike, that sort of thing, don't you find?'

'No. I like it.'

She could not believe it. Here was she, a girl who longed to identify herself fully with Ireland's struggle for freedom, sitting opposite this crusty old fool who was the epitome of everything that stood in its way. The man who, at the age of sixty-six, had been appointed commander in chief of the

British Expeditionary Force in France, and had had the ultimate responsibility for the fruitless blood bath of Ypres, in which her eldest brother, Richard, had lost his life. The man who had wanted to introduce conscription to Ireland, and had actively recruited thousands of young Irishmen to be slaughtered in the trenches of Flanders. The man who had arrested seventy-three prominent Irish men and women because he thought they were plotting to land German soldiers in Ireland by submarine. The man who had constantly asked for an extension of martial law to suppress and imprison the Sinn Fein volunteers whom Catherine so admired.

'Did I not receive you at the Castle last year, my dear?'

'No, my lord. I'm not a debutante.'

'Really? Why not? You're of an age, surely?'

'Well...' To her intense annoyance, Catherine had actually found herself blushing. Her father had rescued her with a lie.

'It was an illness, my lord. We thought perhaps this year, if there is to be a ceremony.'

'Hope so. Can't be sure. Depends on these damn Shinners, you know. Ideal time for potshots. But I don't want to disappoint the girls.'

Catherine remembered the long, bitter wrangles at home last year, when she had refused to be presented as a debutante at the Viceroy's court. She would have had to parade in Dublin Castle in an elaborate, bridal dress, curtsy to this stupid old man on his foreign throne, and let him kiss her.

It was not the kiss that Catherine would have hated, but

what it stood for. It was a sign, she thought, not only of the power of all men over women, but of this man, the representative of the King of England, over all the defenceless women of Ireland. Both droit de seigneur, and the rule of the English. Over the past few years, she had come to hate both of those things.

And here she was in front of him, making ridiculous polite conversation. What would her heroine, Constance Markievicz, have done? Something, at least. I shall never have such an opportunity again, she thought. I must strike my blow for Ireland – here, now!

For a wild moment she thought of snatching a revolver from one of the officers, and shooting him. That was what a Sinn Feiner would do, if he could. But it was absurd – she was a good shot, but all the revolvers were safely buttoned down in the holsters of big, strong men. No; she would have to use words instead.

For the first time she forced herself to look directly into the eyes of the white-haired old soldier. He looked surprised and pleased; charmed, almost. French was well known to be fond of women but he had been about to give up hope of extracting any conversation from this dark-eyed, rather sulky young girl. The gallant gleam in his eyes annoyed her intensely.

'Viscount French, why don't you leave Ireland?'

'What?' Lord French looked startled. A ripple of interest spread to the officers sitting nearby, rattling their teacups.

'Why don't you leave Ireland and go home? Leave us all in peace?'

French coughed, and sat up in his chair. 'Well, er, as to that, my dear, I couldn't leave Ireland and go home. I have

my own estates here, as you know. In the County
Roscommon. My family have lived here for generations, as
yours have, I believe. At Castle French in Galway. I have
just come from there now.'

'You know what I mean. You are an Englishman, you
represent the English king, the British Empire. You have no
right to be here now, to hold the land in slavery. There has
been a free election and the people have voted for a
republic, for Sinn Fein. You are an invader in a foreign
land!'

It was harder than she had thought. She felt tears in her
eyes – partly from the strength of her own feeling, but also
from a consciousness of the helplessness and absurdity of
her own position. An officer at the end of the carriage
neighed with laughter. She glanced briefly at her father's
face, saw it was bright red, and looked resolutely away
again.

French looked embarrassed; amused and annoyed at
once. 'Nonsense, young woman. Who the devil's been
filling your head with such drivel? This is my country, just
as much as it is yours and your father's. Surely you've been
brought up to know that?'

'I was brought up to know it, yes. But I've taught myself
better. We've been stealing from the people for hundreds
of years. That's why there's so much poverty everywhere –
why so many had to go overseas in the Famine! That's why
people like you and father are rich and have big houses
and estates here – because we stole the land from the
people!'

'Catherine!' Her father put his hand on her arm. 'Please
– stop now! At once!'

'No! I'm sorry, Father. You know how I feel — why shouldn't I say it? I don't want to live the rest of my life like a rich thief, stealing the land from the poor! I'm going to be a doctor, work for the people, serve them! And just because I was born into the same ... class ... as this man, it doesn't mean I support the terror he's waging against the people of Ireland. Arresting them, shooting and torturing them — just because they have voted for freedom!'

French had risen to his feet. His face was bright red and his hands were clasped behind him. He would have stood ramrod stiff, but the train was going over a bumpy patch of line, so he stood with his legs a little apart, rocking slightly to keep his balance. His voice was sharp, hard. It was clear he felt his hospitality had been grievously insulted.

'I do not shoot men and there is no torture that I am aware of. My job is to ensure that the law of this country is upheld — no more and no less. Give me one example of unprovoked shooting or torture, young woman, if you please. One, go on — just one!'

Tears of frustration came into Catherine's eyes. 'You arrest men all the time, and they are beaten and starved in prison. How do I know what happens in all the prisons — I have not been ...'

'You have not been there and you do not know. Men are not tortured. I asked for an example of one man who has been shot without cause.'

'Thomas Clarke, Padraig Pearse, Thomas MacDonagh, James Connolly — you had to tie him to a chair, didn't you, because he was so ill he couldn't stand!'

'Those men were traitors. Tried by court martial in 1916 and found guilty of leading armed rebellion in time of war, with guns obtained from the enemy. They were given every benefit of law. You have a strange idea of justice, young woman, if –'

'Thomas Ashe, then! Was that justice – to arrest a man for nothing, and then kill him because he would not eat? Thrusting a tube down his throat until he was throttled, like the poor suffragettes!'

French's face twitched. 'Clumsy fool of a doctor. It should never have happened; we don't do it now. Anyway, that was two years ago, young lady, before I had this office. I asked you for one example – one – of a man or woman that has been shot without reason since I was Viceroy.'

'Oh, without reason! Well...'

'Unjustly, then. You imply that soldiers – or policemen, is it? Which? – go around this country, with my blessing, shooting men on sight. Tell me one instance, then, and I shall have it investigated.'

The atmosphere in the carriage was electric. No one in it could pretend not to be listening to the extraordinary, shouted argument between His Majesty's Lord Lieutenant of Ireland, and this insolent slip of a girl. The men all stood around, watching, while she unconsciously exercised her woman's privilege to remain seated. Catherine gloried in it. Whatever happened, she was striking her blow! Only... she could not quite remember an actual instance...

'Oh, there have been dozens of cases!'

'So I hear. Tell me one.'

The men waited. Unexpectedly, the train rattled into a tunnel. In the sudden darkness, Catherine was again seized by her wild fantasy of snatching a pistol. But – where?

Then the train came out into the light again, and the men were still in their places, swaying slightly with the movement of the train, waiting for her answer.

'Your police break up election meetings with batons and bayonets! I saw them do it once. They charged an unarmed crowd...'

'Did they shoot anyone?'

'No. But it was only by chance. They raided meetings of the Dáil, with guns and armoured cars!'

'Did they shoot anyone?'

'N-no.' Catherine shook her head angrily. There must be something wrong with her mind. She believed it so strongly, had heard it said so often – why could she not remember an example, now, of all times?

'They did not shoot anyone because they are a disciplined force. Illegal gatherings have been broken up, it is true, men have been arrested, and the law has been enforced. But at no time since I have been Viceroy has any soldier or policeman shot an Irishman, unarmed or not. Whereas, as you surely must know, young woman, there are almost weekly reports of policemen being shot, in the street, by cowardly assassins. If those are the sort of men who represent your noble republic, then God help Ireland, that's all I have to say. Now if you will excuse me, I have work to attend to in the other carriage. Please stay and make yourself comfortable for the rest of the journey, and think about what I have said. Come, gentlemen!'

'They are heroes!' Catherine shouted, to his retreating back. But she was so choked with anger at her defeat that her voice was an awkward squeak rather than a shout, and he ignored it.

Her father had left with the others, and for the rest of the journey she had been alone. She sat in the comfortable flowery overstuffed armchair and stared out at the wintry fields of the country she loved. A surge of conflicting emotions boiled inside her, like the great Atlantic waves she loved to watch when they were forced into a narrow cove under the cliffs, and met the backwash of the one before. Sometimes she felt elated, as she thought how she had seized her moment, and told the Viceroy to his face things he had probably never heard before. She felt fury that she had lost the argument in the end, through a trick, a form of words. Perhaps no one *had* been shot, but the bulk of it was true — the oppression, the provocation, the internment! Then she felt embarrassment, and pain for what she had done to her father. She must have made him look a fool, in front of these men, and she had not meant that. She had often fought him in private, but never in front of others; that was not her way. But he shouldn't have tricked her and brought her here. He knew what she felt, he knew what she was like, surely — what had he thought would happen?

Several officers tried unsuccessfully to talk to her, but her father did not come back into the carriage until the train pulled into Ashtown Station. Then he was quiet, polite.

'We have some unfinished discussions, and Viscount French has offered to drive us both, in his car, to the Viceregal Lodge. I hope you will come.'

She pitied him, and stood up dutifully. 'Yes, Father, of course.'

* * *

Sean Brennan fingered the Mills bombs in his pocket. He had left the pub now and was walking slowly up the road towards Ashtown Gate. In one pocket were two Mills bombs, in the other a revolver. He had fired the gun several times before, but never thrown a bomb. His fingertips traced the criss-cross pattern of indentations in the metal. These were the weak spots in the little steel egg, he thought. The explosion would rupture the egg here first, sending little square shards of the thicker metal whizzing through the air to tear through flesh, cartilage, bone. He could feel the bombs through his coat pocket as he walked, bouncing against his hip. He was a medical student, he knew how bodies worked. He thought of the movement of the hip, the ball and socket joint where the thighbone moved back and forth in his pelvis as he walked; he imagined the tensing and loosening of the ligaments, the flexing of the muscles, the movement of the skin above. All quite painless, effortless. His fingers touched a ring in his pocket. One tug on that, and a few seconds later his hip would be smashed into a red mess, mincemeat pierced by shards of shattered bone...

'There it is, Sean,' muttered his companion, Martin Savage. 'They're coming out.'

Sean turned his head, jerkily, and looked back at the station about half a mile away. The cars had started their engines, and stood there shaking and steaming in a line. Between the two, he saw a police sergeant, like a tiny puppet, saluting, and a number of khaki-clad figures strolling casually out of the station. At a little distance from the two cars was the army lorry, with the rifles of the soldiers bristling above it.

'Don't look so sharp, Sean! We're just out for a walk, for the health of our lungs, remember?'

'That's right. I'm sorry.' He noticed with a slight academic interest that he felt warm. His mouth was dry, slight prickles of sweat formed on his fingers. I wonder what my eyes look like, he thought. I wonder if they widen. He seemed to hear everything very clearly, as one did before a thunderstorm.

Someone was shouting.

'You'll take it away, I tell you! 'Tis the Viceroy himself is coming through here!'

'That we won't, old man!'

The voices came quite clearly to his heightened senses, although the speakers were nearly twenty yards away. At the road junction, the police constable was arguing with the three Volunteers who had control of the farm cart. The unhitched horse munched peacefully beside them. The cart was a vital part of the ambush. It was to be pushed out into the road to block the second car, which would contain the Viceroy. If they could run across the road with it quickly enough, it would cut Lord French off from the first car, and leave him stranded, at the mercy of their bombs and guns. More Volunteers were hidden on the rising ground behind the hedges opposite the pub, watching the argument with the constable.

'They'll have to deal with that fool!' said Sean's companion. 'If he doesn't leave off this instant he's a dead man!'

As he spoke, Sean saw the argument develop into a

tussle. One of the Volunteers grabbed the constable's coat, trying to drag him away. But the constable was a big man, and he threw his attacker off. The man staggered, tripped over a stone, and fell down. The constable stepped back, warily eyeing the other two who were moving towards him. Then all three turned their heads as an engine by the station roared into life and the first car started down the road towards them. The policeman glanced at it, and then stared back at his attackers. His mouth fell open in a wide O as the terrible truth burst like sunlight in his brain. He stepped back, raising one clumsy hand to wave at the car while he fumbled with the other for his whistle.

Sean saw the bomb coming through the air, but his mind did not register what it was. It came slowly, in a high lob from behind the hedge, turning end over end like a tiny rugby ball heading between the posts. It came over the policeman's head, hit the road between him and the cart, and rolled around in a little circle like a stone. Then it exploded.

The blast hit his face like a hurricane. But it was hot, as the Irish wind never is. He threw up his arm to shield his face, and stumbled back, hanging on to his friend, Martin, to stay upright. Then it was gone, and he saw the policeman writhing on the ground, clutching his leg. The three Volunteers were on the ground too, crawling oddly several ways at once.

'For the love of Mary!' shouted Martin. 'Will the fools warn every peeler in the County Dublin?' Then they looked and saw the first car speeding towards them — faster than before, it seemed.

'Come on, Sean!' Martin shouted. 'Get the cart!' One of

the three men around the cart had got to his feet, but the other two were still crawling feebly, like lost animals. The two young men ran to the cart and grabbed its sides, ready to push it out into the road. The car was nearly upon them. Sean heard the crack of gunfire. He heaved at the cart, but the great clumsy wheels wouldn't move.

'We're too late, Martin!' he screamed.

'No! Don't worry about that one!' his friend yelled. 'Get the second car! That's the one the bugger's in! Come on, boy – push!'

But Lord French was in the first car, with Catherine, her father, and two other officers. The rest had stayed on the train. In an attempt, perhaps, to smooth over the quarrel, the Viceroy had insisted that Sir Jonathan O'Connell-Gort and his daughter accompany him, and had, most unusually, got into the first car outside the station, instead of the second. Catherine, trying to make amends to her father, followed in mutinous silence.

The chauffeur, wearing his leather gauntlets, driving helmet and goggles, shut the door on them politely as they climbed into the back. Lord French's personal detective, Detective Sergeant Halley, sat in the front beside the chauffeur. As they moved off, the Viceroy smiled at Catherine rather stiffly, trying to resume their conversation where he had broken it off.

'When you are older, young woman, you will understand that this country needs firm government, like all other parts of the Empire. Firmness and justice, that is what is needed. I am not opposed to Irish people having a say in their own affairs, and neither is Lloyd George. It is my belief that we have held back on Home Rule long enough, and I daresay it is no great secret if I tell you I expect him to bring in a bill to the House this very week. So you will get most of what you want! Read the papers and see, if you don't believe me. But as for this murderous campaign against the police –'

'It won't be enough!' Catherine burst out angrily. 'I do read the papers, my lord; I have read a lot about what Lloyd George has to say. He will never give us enough unless we fight for it!'

Lord French frowned. He flicked his gloves irritably against his thigh. 'Do you really mean to tell me, young lady, that we should give way to a man with a gun, just because he asks us to?'

'You gave way to the men of Ulster when they had guns! When the government was going to give us Home Rule before the war, the Ulstermen faced you with guns, and said they wouldn't have it. You didn't stand up to them then, did you? You gave in to them at the Curragh! Where was your firm government then?'

Lord French's mouth was set in a hard line, and for a moment he said nothing. Catherine noticed, with interest, that his cheek had gone suddenly pale, and then, equally swiftly, was flushing bright red. In a very cold, clipped voice, he said: 'I imagine you were only a child then, Miss Gort, and you are little more than that now. But it may interest you to know that I resigned as Chief of the Imperial General Staff over that affair, and that I in no way endorsed the action of Sir Edward Carson and the Ulster Volunteers. Perhaps you should tell that to your revolutionary friends, if –'

There was a muffled explosion from the front of the car, and a curse from the chauffeur. Catherine thought the car had backfired, but then it suddenly started to go much faster. She peered ahead, over the detective's shoulders, and saw a cart and some figures running around in the road.

'What is it, Sergeant?' asked Lord French.

'Don't know, sir.' Detective Sergeant Halley was pulling his revolver from his pocket. 'I think . . .'

The window beside Catherine exploded. There was a blast of hot wind, glass all over her face and coat, and shouting. Detective Sergeant Halley was shooting out of the window, and there were bangs and rattles along the side of the car, as though someone was throwing stones at it. Lord French and her father had their pistols out, and French was pulling down the window on his side. The car was going very fast, bouncing and swerving wildly.

The sound of pistols being fired from inside the car was much worse than anything from outside. Catherine put her hands over her ears, then took them away again as she realized there was glass on the sleeve of her coat. She stared out of the broken window and saw two young men, a few yards ahead, standing by a farm cart. A revolver jerked in one man's hand, once, twice, three times, a puff of blue-grey smoke coming from it each time. The other young man had a bomb in his hand. She saw him take it out of his pocket, pull out the pin, and bend back his arm to throw.

She saw his face quite clearly. She would never forget it. It was a face that she knew too well.

Sean only saw the car itself, not who was in it. It surged up the road towards him, bouncing and swaying on the rough surface, and he saw a confused blur of faces behind the windows, nothing more. When he had taken the pin from the grenade everything seemed to slow down, and the crack of the pistol shots were pinholes in an eerie silence, waiting for the explosion. Only two or three seconds, but time had slowed down. He swung his arm behind him, thinking only: My hands are too sweaty, it will stick to them like glue, I won't be able to let go! And so he hurled it with extra, vicious force, straight at the goggled, helmeted chauffeur. But at the same moment the car lurched violently to the left, to avoid the still writhing body of the police constable. The bomb, thrown too hard, sailed over the car roof and burst on the road behind. And the car was gone, up the road towards Ashtown Gate and the safety of Phoenix Park.

'Now! Get the second – that's our man!' Martin, Sean and two others seized the great, heavy, lumbering cart and dragged it one, two, three feet further out into the road. Not far, but enough to make the passage between it and the hedge narrow, perilous. The second car was nearly upon them but it was going slower and an appalling hail of bullets was rattling on to it – far, far more than had met the first. Sean felt a rush of fierce, savage pride – they would do it this time, it was stopping, it was caught! He pulled the pin from another bomb and threw it easily this time, with skill and without fear, like a cricket ball. The bomb hit the door pillar, smashing all the windows on one side, and the car lurched feebly, hopelessly, into the right-hand ditch. More bombs were coming now, from the hedges beside the road. They burst all around the car, but none seemed to go inside it. The chauffeur climbed out, his gloved hands above his head.

'We did it!' yelled Martin, his eyes alight with triumph. 'We got the bugger!'

'That's just the chauffeur!' Sean yelled back. 'We've got to be sure of French. Can you not get closer and put a bomb right inside it?'

'Surely.' Martin grinned. Sean had thrown both his Mills bombs but Martin had one ready in his hand. He dashed out from behind the cart into the middle of the road. Sean ran after him, a yard, two yards behind, revolver in hand, thinking to shoot French if he saw him.

Martin was still running when he stumbled and fell, nose down on the hard ground.

Sean had played a lot of Gaelic football but he had never seen anyone fall like that, straight down on his face without trying to break his fall with his hands. And the body was immediately, suddenly limp, like a rag doll. The grenade rolled out of the fingers, round and round in a little circle, like an egg. The pin was still in it.

'Martin!' he yelled. But as he ran forward to his friend the ground began to hop and skip all around him like a cloudburst. There was an enormous noise everywhere. He looked up and saw the army lorry pulled up at an angle across the road, and all the soldiers firing their rifles at him.

He picked up the grenade, bent low, and scurried back behind the cart, where two other Volunteers were shooting at the lorry with their revolvers. There was a great pain in his chest, but he had not been hit at all. 'Martin!' he said. 'They shot him!'

'Don't worry about that, son. We've got French!' said

the man beside him. There was a gleam of exhilaration in the man's eyes. Sean looked past the body of his friend to the shattered car in the ditch. How could they be sure? He pulled the pin from the bomb and hurled it, and this time it went straight and true, end over end through the air and in through the window. There was a huge echoing explosion and blast fragments came out of all the windows. That's for you, Martin, he thought.

The Crossley tender revved up its engine and came straight towards the cart. Sean fired his pistol once, twice, and then it jammed. His companion grabbed his sleeve, dragging him back. 'Get away, boy! Come on, out of this!'

'But what about Martin?' Sean said.

'He's dead, son. There's nothing to be done. But you save yourself and live – live for Ireland!'

Then Sean was running, dodging and swerving from side to side, around the side of the pub to where he had left his bicycle. And so away, pedalling like a lunatic down the long road towards Windy Harbour and normal life in Dublin. Halfway down the road there was a herd of cows, shambling into the dairy on the edge of the city to be milked. Sean and his companions rode straight down upon them screaming like eagles, their coat-tails flapping in the wind behind them, and the cows panicked and began to climb up on each other's backs and push each other into the ditch.

Only when they had the cows between them and any pursuit by the army lorry did Sean begin to laugh, and then for a while he could not stop. He laughed as he pedalled, great long laughs of triumph and exhilaration, with the tears not far behind.

2

THE BULLET-SCARRED limousine pulled up in a spray of gravel outside the Viceregal Lodge. The passengers piled out. Lord French, his revolver smoking in his hand, strode up the steps and barked orders at the astonished sentry. By the time Sir Jonathan, the other ADCs, and Detective Sergeant Halley followed him under the Ionic pillars of the elegant portico, the old general had servants and soldiers scurrying across the vast hall in every direction, their heels clicking urgently on the marble floor.

In all the flurry, Catherine was temporarily forgotten. She sat down, white-faced, stunned, on a little gilt chair in the corner. She was certain it had been Sean. That smooth, boyish face, the wide grin, the silly stick-out ears; there could be no doubt. That one second had burned a picture of him into her mind, as though her eye had been a camera. She could see him still, like a photograph – if only photographs could be in colour. He had been half-smiling, his young face flushed with excitement and determination, his arm bent back to throw the bomb. Like a hero, she thought. It was truly heroic – a young soldier of Ireland in action, taking up arms for the republic against the armed might of the British Empire! A young man in civilian clothes, a cloth cap and long tweed coat, daring to stand out in the middle of the street to attack a convoy of enemy soldiers!

Because of Sean, the Viceroy, that old fool French, was running around like a scalded weasel, his face bright red with indignation above his white moustache. So much for discipline and firmness! Catherine began to laugh. And when she had begun, she found it hard to stop. Her voice echoed in the hall.

A butler spotted her and came over. 'Can I be of assistance, madam? You were in the car, weren't you? I can see you were hurt.'

Catherine controlled herself with an effort. 'What? No, I'm all right.'

'Forgive me, madam, but your face is bleeding.' He turned and clicked his fingers. 'Mrs Boyd! Here, please!'

Catherine touched her cheek hesitantly. It was wet, slippery; her fingertips came away red. A short, middle-aged woman in a housekeeper's cap and apron came up.

'Oh, my dear, that looks nasty! Have they shot you too?'

'No, it's just a cut, I'm sure.' She stood up. 'I'll be all right, if I can just wash it. Don't make a fuss, please.'

'All right, miss. I'll show you.'

Catherine followed the woman down a corridor, past a number of sculptures and paintings, and up a flight of stairs. She opened the door into a large bathroom. In one corner was a bath with a massive oak shower cabinet at its head; there was a window with stained glass in it, a window seat, some cane chairs and stools, and a large basin with a mirror.

'You sit down there, dear,' said the woman, pulling up a stool. 'I'll clean it up for you.'

The sight of her face in the mirror was a shock. Her small bob hat was awry; and under it, ragged fingers of blood trickled down a paper-white skin. She took off the hat, astonished. She didn't feel bad — how could her face be such a mess?

She had a small, delicate face with large deep-set eyes and dark pageboy hair, which her hands tried to pat into place. The overall effect was normally of a sort of elfin beauty. Now she looked as though she had been torn by a cat.

The housekeeper ran some warm water into the basin and began to dab at her forehead gently with a flannel. 'There's a few cuts just under your hair,' she said soothingly, 'but not too bad. Heads always bleed a lot. I remember my son once...'

Catherine did not listen. Sean did this, she thought. Did he see me in the car? Would he still have thrown the bomb if he had? A week ago he kissed this face. She remembered how it had felt...

They had met in her first term at University College, in October. As one of only thirty-two women among some hundred and sixty men studying medicine, she had been plagued by youths inviting her to ceilidhs, picnics, tennis parties — quite enough to satisfy her father, if these had been the sort of young men he had had in mind. But

Catherine, like the other women, had been more serious about her studies than most of the men – predictably, for it had been a hard struggle to get in – and she had rejected most of the invitations as distractions.

Sean had seemed to her one of the more serious students. She remembered the first time they had met. He had sat next to her in a lecture, and afterwards asked if he could buy her a cup of coffee. Then he had started to talk, not about anything trivial or flirtatious, but about the subject of the lecture, the structure of the colon and small intestine.

It was one of many subjects which she found very difficult to discuss with male students. Either they avoided it altogether, because it was indelicate, or they became defensively childish, elaborating on all the most repulsive details to see if she would be embarrassed.

But Sean had been simply interested – and, it turned out, a little confused. After a few minutes' conversation she found herself having to repeat most of the lecture over to him again, illustrating the main points from her notes. There were quite a few things Sean had not taken in, or had misunderstood. And he had not been insulted by this, merely grateful.

'I do take notes,' he said. 'But he goes so fast, don't you think? That's hardly fair, when it's all new stuff.'

'I don't know,' she said. 'I suppose they expect us to read it all ourselves, as well. That's what I do. I look up the titles of the lectures to see what's coming, and then try to read about it beforehand. Then the lecture's clearer; it comes as a sort of revision.'

'Mary and Joseph! Whenever do you find the time?'

'Oh, I don't know. In the evenings.' She realized how priggish her explanation had sounded, and tried to make amends. 'I'm alone a lot. I probably don't have so much to do as you do.'

'No.' He had regarded her with a rather quizzical, fetching grin. Soft hazel eyes, smooth, brown hair, carefully combed back, a little dimple appearing on his cheek. Two months later, in the Viceregal Lodge, she could remember that grin clearly; at the time, it had had a definite unsettling effect on her pulse. 'I've got the books, of course, but I'm afraid I don't have that much time for them. I'm out most evenings.'

'Doing what?'

'Well now.' The grin got wider, and more quizzical. 'For one thing, I go to the Gaelic League. I'm learning the language.' Then he said, in hesitant Irish: '*Do you have the Gaelic?*'

'*Of course I do*,' she answered fluently. '*My nurse spoke it.*'

'But that's tremendous! You must come. You can teach us!'

'Oh, I couldn't do that,' she said. 'It's a long time since I had a nurse, you know. I'm sure there are a lot of things I'd say wrong, or I've forgotten.'

'It doesn't matter!' His face had lit up, in a way quite different from when they had been discussing medicine. 'You've had the Gaelic as a child – I wish I had. We should all learn it, you know! We'll never be a nation if we lose our language.'

And so she had gone along to the Keating branch of the Gaelic League, in 46 Parnell Square, opposite the Rotunda

Lying-in Hospital. It had been a strange experience. There was an odd mixture of people: students like themselves, working men, actors, one who claimed to be a playwright, some intellectuals with wispy beards, and several middle-aged women – including, once, a tall woman in a wide hat and sandals, who was said to be the Viceroy's elder sister. The use of the Irish language was equally varied. One or two spoke it fluently, others contented themselves with writing words down, or speaking about Gaelic enthusiastically in English.

Catherine seemed to be the only one who had learnt the language as a child; and that was not such an advantage here, either, because nearly everyone in Parnell Square wanted to discuss politics, and she had not learnt the vocabulary for that, picking up seashells with her nurse on the beach in Galway.

It was a busy, fascinating place. There were several classes going on every night, and some of these seemed to attract quite a different clientele. There was a group of men who met in a room upstairs, and came and went briskly on bicycles. Some she recognized – elected members of the Dáil, prominent Sinn Feiners. They came down in ones and twos, smoking and talking busily, and rode away again into the night. One or two might look in on the way, and give Sean a friendly wave. She had been impressed, and teased him in Gaelic: '*Is it yourself that's the armed revolutionary, then, a chara? A Fenian with a gun?*'

He had winked at her, his open eyes sparkling above that wide engaging mischievous smile, and said: '*I am that.*' She had only half believed him, then; but today, in the Viceregal Lodge, she saw it was true. It was a thrilling, sobering thought. No wonder his eyes lit up more when he spoke about Ireland than about medicine. He was really at the heart of the movement she admired so much.

Two weeks ago she had been with Sean to a ceilidh. It had been hot, noisy, charged with emotion. Catherine had danced all evening, relishing the sense of being part of a crowd of Irish people, touching, singing, swinging each other round in the dances. Her own life was so intense, so lonely, she had been intoxicated by the sense of together-ness – the sense of touch.

So when at last they had come out into the cold night air she had leant against Sean, naturally, easily, wanting to make the warmth last a little longer.

He had walked her home, one arm round her, wheeling his bicycle with the other. She wondered, now, if she had been a sort of passport for him, for the soldiers and the police were less likely to stop a young couple together. But it had been the natural thing to do, after all.

She could not invite him in and she did not want the servants to see, so she had stopped on the corner of Merrion Square and pointed across the little park to her house.

'That?' he said. 'Sure it's a mansion!'

'A town house. I told you I was an aristocrat.' She tried to make out his expression in the dim gaslight. 'Are you shocked?'

'No. Well, yes, maybe a little.' He glanced at the house again and shook his head. 'To think you live in a place like that and still spend time with me. Do – do you have all of it?'

She laughed. 'Yes. Well, Father has half, and then there's

the servants. We're great employers, you know. There's half a dozen people in there.'

'Is that so?' He took his arm away from her waist, and put both hands on the handlebars.

'Sean.' She had not wanted the contact to end. She had been alone for so much of her life; that was the way of her father's world, the world she had been born into. Sean was at once himself to her, and the spirit of the people, the warmth of the ceilidh. She reached out and held him. 'I know it's unjust, but don't blame me now. It was a grand evening, wasn't it? I don't want it to end.'

When he put the bicycle against the wall and embraced her it had been oddly aggressive, fierce, as though he had to overcome something within himself to do it. But that she only remembered later, when she thought about it carefully, languorously, alone in her bed. For in all her nineteen years, it was the first time she had embraced any boy alone, like this.

She had thought perhaps he would kiss her lips and so he had, but only briefly. Then he had kissed her eyes and her cheeks and her hair, and held her close to him, very hard. They were nearly the same height, and his bristly cheek rubbed against hers. She nuzzled against him like an animal, and he leaned back, his hands clasped behind her, and lifted her off her feet.

'You're a lovely girl for all that,' he said. 'I can carry you – look!' He turned in a circle, whirling her round with her feet in the air, and put her down panting.

'That's a new dance,' she said.

'Yes.' And then they had looked into each other's eyes in the shadows of the gaslight, and their smiles had faded and they had indeed kissed each other's lips, very slowly and long until neither had any breath left; and then they tried again and got the breathing better, and in fact the whole thing was so very much better that they might have gone on, with short pauses, for the rest of the night, had not a policeman scrunched into the square behind them, and coughed discreetly to let them know he was there.

It had been a cold night. But half an hour later, as she climbed shivering into her bed, she wondered how it was that she had never felt warmer in her life than in those few minutes, crushed against his overcoat outside in the square.

A fortnight later, staring at her face in the mirror in the Viceregal Lodge, she wondered what he had been carrying in the pockets of that coat.

Sir Jonathan O'Connell-Gort was in a fine, cold rage. He thought he could not have looked a greater fool if he had tried. Newly appointed Divisional Army Intelligence Officer, he had met Sir John French on the train that morning to brief him on the current reports, and to plan an improvement to the service. He had served briefly under French in France, before Haig took over, and he respected him for a fine officer who did not suffer fools gladly. Sir Jonathan had had a good war, and he had hoped to make a good impression on the little Field Marshal. He felt confident in his local knowledge, and had a report in his pocket suggesting that Michael Collins and his murder gang were short of arms, exhausted, nearly finished. Sir Jonathan agreed. The people of Ireland, he felt, had had enough. The crisis was nearly over.

So he had thought this morning, as he had motored through the cold, crisp air of Galway. And then, in quick succession, he had been humiliated by his daughter, and nearly murdered by Collins and his thugs.

His discussions with French on the train had been polite but frosty. The conference in the Viceregal Lodge, which had just ended, had been tempestuous. The Lord Lieutenant was a brave, choleric soldier, with a great deal of physical courage, as Sir Jonathan had seen in the car. But he also had a strong sense of the dignity of his position. He had not, he told Sir Jonathan, been appointed His Majesty's Viceroy in Ireland in order to indulge in pistol fights with street hooligans. Nor did he expect his Intelligence Officer to feed him pure unadulterated stupidity. Clearly the Irish Republican Army was neither unarmed, nor exhausted, nor finished. If it had been quiet for a couple of weeks, they now knew why – because it had been planning an operation on a rather grander scale than the murder of a few policemen. And it had nearly succeeded. Perhaps the British Army Intelligence service was staffed exclusively by blind deaf morons, but clearly the same could not be said of the IRA. They appeared to have known the exact time and place that his train would arrive, and which car he normally travelled in. If the IRA's Director of Intelligence, Michael Collins, was able to get hold of such facts, then the sooner the man was arrested or shot, the better. Perhaps, Lord French suggested, if Sir Jonathan and his colleagues ever did get hold of Collins, they could ask him to put on a training course, to show them how an intelligence service should be run.

It had been a very painful interview indeed, and Sir Jonathan's temper had not been improved when he came out of the room. Lord French's butler had glided up to inform him, smoothly, that his daughter had been served with tea in a drawing room and would no doubt expect to see him shortly.

'What?' Only his lifelong training had prevented Sir Jonathan from cursing his daughter out loud. 'Yes, thank you, Chitham. I'll see her when I have time.' And more self-control, he thought bitterly, as he strode down the corridor. If I meet that girl now this house will be treated to a family row the like of which hasn't been seen since the Normans!

He had thought she had stopped all that nonsense over the past year. Studying medicine was hardly his idea of a ladylike thing to do, but at least it had seemed to keep her quiet. It was respectable, too, in a bizarre sort of way — better than all that agitation she had made a few years ago about evictions, tenants' rights, and the damned Irish Republic! He had thought she had calmed down, and forgotten all that Sinn Fein nonsense. She hadn't spoken of it to him when he was at home. She had been quiet, polite, friendly, as she had used to be — that was why he had risked inviting her on to the train. It just showed how out of touch one could get, when one was away from home so often.

'Sir Jonathan?'

The voice broke into his thoughts — a strange, rather quiet voice, almost apologetic. He turned, and saw a small, round, inoffensive man, a civilian, looking at him from a doorway. The man wore spectacles, and had a pale, mouselike, bookish air. He recognized him as a sort of civil servant; Harrison, that was the name. An important fellow, he recalled, more imposing than he looked. Had the ear of people in high places in London as well as here.

'Yes. What is it? You know the place is in uproar – there's been an assassination attempt.'

'Yes. It's that I want to talk to you about. If you could spare me two minutes.'

Despite his anger, Sir Jonathan had nowhere precise, at this moment, to use the surplus energy the shock had given him. He had to mobilize an attempt to find the assassins, of course, but that was being done already; and if they had not been caught at Ashtown, nothing he could do would catch them in the next five minutes.

'Yes, of course.'

He strode through the door, into the little man's surprisingly large and comfortable office. There was a Persian carpet on the floor, bookcases round two of the walls, and wide windows giving an impressive view of Phoenix Park. The little man indicated a leather armchair.

'I heard about the shooting. I imagine the Viceroy has ordered you to bring in the assassins without delay. And their leader, Michael Collins, in particular?'

'Something of the sort, yes.' It didn't take a lot of political sense to realize that, Sir Jonathan thought.

Harrison sat down opposite Sir Jonathan and contemplated him carefully. He pressed the tips of his fingers together in front of his mouth, as though he were at prayer.

'You will not find it easy to catch Michael Collins.'

Sir Jonathan realized with a shudder that the man must be half-blind; for his spectacles were so thick that they magnified his eyes to two or three times the normal size.

'No, perhaps not,' he agreed. 'But I'm going to try every method until we do.'

'That's what I thought.' The little man moved his fingers forward from his lips, but kept them pressed together, carefully, in concentration. 'I too have been thinking long and hard about that man, Sir Jonathan, and I have a suggestion which I would like you to consider . . .'

3

'WASTE.'

'Sorry, sir?'

'That.' Kee indicated the body in front of him with a brief movement of his big, flat hand. The body lay face down in the road outside the country pub, where it had fallen. The head was framed by a puddle of clotted blood, like a mockery of a medieval halo. The hair would probably stick to the road, Kee thought, when they moved him. The brains might fall out too, if there was a large exit wound underneath.

Irritably, he explained himself. 'It's a waste, wouldn't you say, Detective Sergeant? A terrible, dreadful waste of a young man's life?'

In the silence that followed, he found he had shouted. The uniformed men, standing at a respectful distance, gazed at him stolidly. Several soldiers and RIC men, combing the road for bombs and bullets, glanced curiously over their shoulders. Get a grip on yourself, Tom, he thought. They're nervous as it is; they look to you for support.

He was conscious of a surge of emotions within himself – revulsion at the sight before him; anger at the men who had caused it; even fear, that one day they might do this to him. He looked at Davis, his detective sergeant, and thought he saw the fear reflected in a face that was unusually closed, stony, grey.

'Come on, Dick,' he said more quietly. 'Let's get it done.' He knelt down, put his arms under the body, and rolled it over. The body was floppy, soft, limp. The bullet hole in the shattered left eye socket had dust and grit in it. There seemed to be no exit wound. A gobbet of still-moist blood leaked out of the mouth and slithered jerkily down the cheek.

'Great God Almighty.' Kee felt his gorge rising and turned away. He saw Davis still standing there, watching, not moving to help. Anger forced down his disgust. 'Come on, Dick, bear a hand, can't you? At least it's one of theirs for a change, for what that's worth.'

Just a young boy, he thought, sitting back on his haunches and holding down his bile. A stupid bloody kid. The body looked oddly small in death, shrunken like a child's. Davis, like the other big men numbly staring at it, was six foot two – all the officers of the Dublin Metropolitan Police had got into the force partly because of their height. A magnificent body of men, they were called. And now they all went in fear of their lives because of an undersized bunch of kids.

The hair, tangled and matted by its halo of blood, stuck up ragged and unruly as an urchin's. The clothes were more respectable – working man's jacket, decent trousers, tie even. Cycle clips on the trousers, and an automatic pistol in the right-hand jacket pocket.

Kee turned the limp head to one side, so that the wound did not gape so directly at him. A uniformed sergeant approached.

'This was on the ground over there, Inspector,' he said. He held out the pin of a hand grenade.

Kee nodded, wiped his sticky hands on the dead man's jacket, and turned back to the gun. German – a Parabellum 9-mm automatic. He opened the grip and checked the magazine. Two rounds still in it. So that's what they use, he thought. He held it out to Davis. 'Look at that, Dick – that was never looted from a landlord's shooting room. Now let them say they didn't get help from the Boche!'

Still Davis hadn't spoken. He just stood, watching, as though struck dumb. Kee felt annoyed and surprised. He had come to Dublin from Belfast six weeks ago, and had begun to respect Dick Davis as one of the most resilient and cheerful officers of the Dublin Metropolitan Police G

Division. And in the past few months they had needed someone cheerful, God knew. G Division was the section of the DMP which dealt with political offenders – at least, that was the theory. But recently it was the political offenders who had been dealing with G Division. In the past six months four G men had been shot dead in the street – one only two weeks ago. Each time, the street had been crowded, but no one had seen or heard anything. Only the shots, and men walking or cycling calmly away, leaving a detective twitching in the gutter. No one recognized the murderers, or could describe them. No one had been arrested or charged.

There were a dozen men in G Division, and most of them had received warning letters. The letters were printed in large, clumsy, childish capitals, quite easy to read and impossible to trace. They warned the recipient that if he did not cease his treacherous activities against the Irish Republic, he could expect the same fate as his colleagues. Two men, pleading the strain on their families, had asked for a transfer to the criminal branch. Several others, Kee was sure, had simply ceased doing the job. In order to keep the Division going at all, a new Assistant Commissioner, William Radford, had been brought in from Belfast, and Kee had come with him.

Kee had not received a threatening letter yet, but Davis had. He had folded it into a paper aeroplane, lit the tail, and flown it out of the window. He had continued to investigate as actively as before. He was unmarried, intelligent, ambitious. In the last few weeks, Kee had come to rely on him more and more. They had got nowhere, but at least he felt they had not stopped trying.

So why was he upset today? Almost certainly, the young man on the road in front of them was one of those who had been waging war upon G Division. Kee knew who their leader was: Michael Collins. Since 1916, Collins had been a member of the Supreme Council of the Irish Republican Brotherhood. Formed in the 1860s, the IRB, the successor to the Fenians, had always been the main target of Dublin Castle's intelligence service. It considered its Supreme Council to be the legitimate government of Ireland, and thus all the established police and government agencies to be its enemies. Which wouldn't have mattered much, if Collins hadn't also been an elected Member of Parliament, the Finance Minister of Dáil Eireann, and the Adjutant-General, Director of Intelligence, and Director of Organization in the Irish Volunteers – the body of armed men who had opposed conscription during the war, risen in 1916, and were now increasingly referring to themselves as the Irish Republican Army.

If there was one man whom Tom Kee wanted to interview more than any other, it was Michael Collins.

But the man was as slippery as Robin Hood. The city was his forest; he could move where he liked in it, safe, invisible. Everyone knew about him, no one had seen him. Kee was not even sure what the man looked like. In weeks of patient investigation he had not come across anyone who could give him a positive lead to Collins, or any of his assassins.

Until today. A dead boy in the road. The sort of boy he saw hundreds of times a day, serving behind counters, cycling from one place to another with deliveries. Only this one had a German automatic pistol in his jacket pocket. If he had been alive, Kee could have questioned him. But bodies could tell stories too. Kee handed the Parabellum to Davis, and started to search the pockets of the pathetic figure in front of him.

In the other pockets he found a handkerchief, clips of cartridges, a cycle-repair kit, and a Mills bomb. Kee took it out carefully and handed it to a uniformed constable. In the inside pocket, a toothbrush, a comb, a packet of cigarettes, a wallet.

Kee opened the wallet. Money, some postage stamps, and a folded letter. He unfolded it. Kee was a highly emotional man, and his job was a constant struggle to hide this, especially when interviewing suspects. When he succeeded he put on a heavy, stolid, uncomprehending look. It helped to let people think he was stupid, and gave him time to evaluate every reaction. But this time, as he read the letter, he could not prevent a slow, deep smile spreading across his face.

The letter appeared to be a receipt. It read:

Mr J. Kirk, Grocer, North Strand, Dublin.
20 October 1919.
Received from my tenant, Mr Martin Savage, the sum of £4 10s 6d, to be held safe by me until such time as he shall demand it.
Signed: J. Kirk.

Kee read it twice, carefully, and then handed it to Davis. 'There you are, my boy. Maybe we've found a clue for once. Will you start up that infernal machine of yours, and we'll go and pay a visit on Mr Kirk right now, shall we?'

* * *

An hour later, as he lit the gas mantle in the second of the two rooms at the top of the grocer Kirk's house in North Strand, Kee felt more disgust than before. The first room, Martin Savage's, had been small, untidy, sparsely furnished as he had expected. An iron bed in the corner, a fireplace, a bucket of coal, two shabby armchairs with some socks drying on them, a desk and chair under the window. A crucifix with a bleeding heart over the mantelpiece, and a photograph of a man and woman standing solemnly outside a rough stonebuilt cottage. The one across the corridor, belonging to the dead boy's friend, was smaller than the first, and tidier. Very tidy indeed, Kee thought, for a young man. The bed was made, and there were no clothes strewn about. A pair of shoes was arranged neatly under the bed, by the chamberpot. Kee would have approved of it, had it not been for the bleeding crucifixion on the wall.

Such things struck him as idolatrous, extravagant, sinful. The son of a staunch Presbyterian docker from north Belfast, Kee had grown up with the idea that beauty existed in much simpler things. A clean, neat house with a warm fire and an honest woman in it. A great factory throbbing with industry. The smooth cover of a well-worn Bible. The clear knowledge of right and wrong. All things that seemed to be missing from Dublin in the winter of 1919.

There were twenty or thirty books in the bookcase by the wall. Kee examined the titles curiously. Several works of history, including Griffith's *The Resurrection of Hungary*, which Kee knew was read as a blueprint for how

Sinn Fein should gain independence in Ireland. Another, entitled *What Germany Could Do for Ireland*, appeared to set out all the advantages to Ireland of Britain losing the war.

There were a few novels, including G. K. Chesterton's *The Man Who Was Thursday*; and a shelf and a half of medical textbooks, most bought second-hand but still quite expensive. What did that mean? Only a medical student would have these, surely?

He turned to the desk, and his suspicions were confirmed. There was a half-finished essay on diseases of the blood, and a file of lecture notes and diagrams. Kee was elated, and puzzled. It should be easy enough to find out the boy's name from these – yes, there it was at the top: Brennan. Sean Brennan. The university should have full details of its students.

But could a medical student be an assassin? Kee had been a policeman long enough to know that anything was possible, but the idea disgusted him. They took an oath to save life, didn't they, not throw Mills bombs into cars?

Kee wondered if he had made a mistake. There was something guileless, innocent, about the room. There were the books, certainly, but books on their own did not kill. There were two photographs on the mantelpiece; one of a middle-aged couple with some children, the other of a young man.

He picked up the second, and showed it to Kirk. 'Is this him? Sean Brennan?'

There was a hesitation, then a sullen nod. Kee studied the photograph. It confirmed the impression of innocence. The face was more like that of a choirboy than a killer.

Clean-cut, with smooth, downy cheeks – Kee glanced towards the washbasin to check that there was shaving tackle there – and short, slicked-back dark hair. A broad forehead, bright, intelligent-looking eyes, stick-out ears, and a wide, cheeky smile. Someone I wouldn't mind for my son-in-law, Kee thought, if he were a bit older.

He handed it to Davis. 'What do you think?' he asked.

'Nice lad.'

'I mean, could he have done it? A boy like that?'

Davis hesitated. 'Why not? Boys like that were dying in the trenches until last year.'

'Yes, but that was a war. This is murder we're talking about, Dick.'

'True.' Davis looked at his boss, thinking how foreign he was to the city. Maybe he came from the same island, but it was from a different culture, a different background altogether. It would be very difficult to enlighten him, even if he wanted to. Davis didn't want to. So he said: 'Some people are just evil.'

A few minutes later, as he went through the neatly folded shirts, vests, and underpants in the chest of drawers, Kee was forced to agree. Underneath the shirts, at the back of the bottom drawer, was a box of German 9-mm ammunition.

The sort that would fit a Parabellum automatic.

4

THE DUBLIN HOUSE of the O'Connell-Gorts was an imposing, four-storey mansion in Merrion Square. As a child, Catherine had regarded it as an Aladdin's cave of pleasure and happiness; as an adolescent, she had hated it as a nest of evil; as a young woman, she had come to be its mistress.

As a child, she had come to the house for Christmas, and for the Dublin season, which lasted for six weeks afterwards. It had belonged to her Gort grandparents then, and she remembered it as a time of parties, treasure hunts, skating in the park, great candle-lit meals, laughter, and music. Always music, and fine, rustling, many-layered dresses, for there were balls in the square nearly every night. The carriages would come rattling into the square, full of gay young debutantes, the windows would be thrown open, and no one would sleep until one or two in the morning. Her grandparents would always throw their own ball, and that would be the grandest of all. Catherine and her brothers would stay up all night, rushing in and out of the ballroom, their eyes wide at the extravagance of gorgeous dresses and uniforms.

She remembered her parents opening the ball, the handsomest couple there. Always her father and grandfather would dance with her, and she would go crimson with the pleasure of it. One night, when she was eleven, the Viceroy's ADC had danced with her, and everyone had clapped because she had done it so well. Afterwards, he had sat her on his knee and fed her bonbons, and she had asked him to wait for her until she was old enough to marry him.

The next year, her grandparents had died, her father had inherited the house, and her mother began to go mad.

Catherine had not understood why, at first. She had been only twelve years old, and thought her mother was the most beautiful woman in the world. Not only beautiful, but powerful, important too, because of her beauty. Artists painted her, poets worshipped her; even the Viceroy bowed his head and kissed her hand. But in that year, 1913, something had happened, and her mother had never gone to Merrion Square again.

It showed itself first as eccentricity and weeping. Her mother had taken to going for long lonely walks across their estate in west Galway, coming home wet and bedraggled and then shutting herself up alone in her room for days on end. The poets and painters were banished, and replaced by doctors. Catherine's brothers went away to boarding school and her father to the army. Only Catherine was left with her governess in the big house by the wide, empty sea, 200 miles from Dublin, to witness the long slow collapse of the mother she had so admired.

Her father said it was a disease, and certainly, Maeve O'Connell-Gort was ill. Her once fine bones became gaunt, skeletal under a paper-fine skin; her eyes wide, dark, haunted. But she would not accept that she was ill. 'The body itself is only an expression of the mind, my dear,' she had whispered to Catherine, one dark winter evening in west Galway, while an Atlantic gale howled around the rafters of their house, Killrath. 'I was beautiful once because I was loved, and you are beautiful because you are a child of that love. Now your father has abandoned me, and there is nothing left. It is not my body, it is my heart that is broken.'

And so Catherine learned of her father's English mistress, Sarah Maidment, who had usurped her mother's place in the Dublin house in Merrion Square. For seven years Catherine had visited the house only once, under duress. Sarah Maidment had put herself out, bringing Catherine dresses from England and arranging visits to the theatre in the hope of winning her over as she had done with her brothers. But Catherine had thanked her, curtsied, and then scarcely spoken again for the whole visit. She had put her foot through the skirts of the dresses so she could not wear them, and then left them behind.

Sarah Maidment was a rather short, round woman with the beginnings of a double chin, which made it easy to despise as well as hate her. She had turned most of the house into a hospital for wounded soldiers, which was very admirable, no doubt; but Catherine had refused to help. Her interest in medicine grew out of a desire to help her mother, not these strangers. So she ignored them, saying the war was against Ireland's interests, anyway, so the soldiers should not have gone.

It had not been a happy visit.

And now her two brothers and her mother were dead, and Mrs Maidment was in a nursing home somewhere in Bournemouth. So Sir Jonathan had asked Catherine to be mistress of the house. It was part of a deal they had made between them. There was little love in it.

They had made the deal ten months ago, in the big dining room where she had once waltzed with her father and the ADC. When Catherine saw it after the war, it was stripped bare. All the paintings had gone, the wallpaper was stained and scribbled on, there was a single dim lightbulb in the chandelier. The last of the wounded had been carried out, but there were still two hospital beds in a corner.

Sir Jonathan had been in his army uniform. His riding boots echoed on the bare floorboards. Catherine had worn a bright, defiant red dress with high button boots. She sat on one of the beds and swung them, looking at him.

He said: 'You know Sarah – Mrs Maidment – is dying. She has cancer of the lungs. She has a few more months, that's all.'

At least she'll be thinner, Catherine thought, viciously. But she said: 'I'm sorry.'

'Are you?' He raised an eyebrow. 'Well. I ... I've thought of marrying her, you know. We've discussed it.' He looked at her for a reaction but there was none visible. 'She has two children, grown-up boys. By her husband, of course, they are no relation of yours. They are all quite poor.'

Catherine looked away from him, out of the window. Her mother had been dead for less than a year. She still loved her father but she despised him, too, for what he had done.

'Mrs Maidment's sons are no responsibility of mine but they are decent fellows. Both did their bit in the war; one lost an arm. Neither has a job yet – *are you listening to me?*'

She had got up and walked to the window. It was so painful to hear. Without turning round she said: 'Yes, Father.'

'If I married Sarah, they could inherit this house, and my part of the estate. It would be a reward for virtue. But they are not my family, and you ... are.'

She turned to face him. 'I see. You think I don't deserve to inherit?'

She was tall, and the lift of her chin made her, though she did not know it, both desirable and terrifying to most young men. To her father, the look reminded him of his wife, as she had been when he loved her. Before she had become ill, and mad, and impossible to live with. Before he had left her for the comfort of Sarah Maidment. Catherine looked to him like Maeve's ghost, come back to haunt him.

'You never expected to become a great heiress, and you never would have done if your brothers had not given their lives for their country. You would not have been poor, but ...'

'Land-owning is for men?'

'Yes.' They looked at each other coldly. He thought how like Catherine's eyes were to her mother's – dark, passionate, compelling. But there was a determination in them too, a strength that Maeve had never had. There was something in them that he saw in the mirror each morning. It unsettled him.

After a long pause he said: 'The fact remains that you are flesh of my flesh. Our family has owned Killrath for three centuries, and this house for half that time. That stability is the whole basis of this country.'

'Still?'

'Still.' He waved a hand dismissively. 'I know you have other ideas, but I hope and pray they will change. Listen, my dear. I want to make a bargain with you.'

It had been a great surprise. For the last year of her mother's life, Catherine and her father had scarcely spoken. She blamed him so much for her mother's death; she did not think he could care for her at all. When the interview had begun, she had been prepared to be disinherited entirely.

'I will not marry Sarah, and I will settle the whole estate on you, on three conditions.'

'I see. And what are they?'

'One: that you help me restore this house, and reside in it for at least half the year. That should not be too hard.'

She looked around the desolate room. 'No. Just wearisome. But worthwhile, I suppose.'

'I'm glad you think so. Second: that you run the Killrath estate in trust for your own children. It will not be yours to sell off in bits and pieces for some mad revolutionary cause. I will not have that. You have the whole thing, or none.'

'It seems you want me to have none of it. Is that legal?'

'I can make it so.'

'And the third condition?'

'That you marry a man of my choice.'

'What? Father, that's absurd!'

'It is not. It is the system that has prevailed for hundreds of generations, and it is a good one, particularly where large estates are concerned. You will need a man to help you, and he should be someone born to the task. I am not a fool, you know – I won't choose a monster.'

'No? Father, you're a monster yourself!' She walked across the room, and her mocking laughter echoed from the bare walls. It sounded hysterical; but then, it was a mad situation. 'You can't just use me to breed, like one of your mares! I'm a woman, you know, a person in my own right! It's a new century, those ideas are gone. I can even vote – do you know that?'

'Not until you're thirty. By then, you may have changed your ideas. If so, I can change my will.'

'And my career? My studies at UCD?' At the time of the conversation she had only just got her place. It was the one thing she had fought for, all those years alone at Killrath. Her career was like a beacon in a storm to her. Something that would give her light to understand the physical side of her mother's illness; and the independence to ensure that such a mental collapse would never happen to her.

'I don't object to that. Though you might be better advised to study economics than medicine. In a way, I . . . I suppose it is an achievement for a young woman to think of such study at all.'

She stared at him. With a shock, she realized there was a hopeful, slightly *appealing* look in his eye. He really meant these things *kindly*. 'Father, you are ... antediluvian! You realize you cannot force me to marry anyone?'

'No. Perhaps I put it badly. Of course you can have a say in the choice.'

'A say in the...'

'But I must give my permission. If you marry without it, you will be disinherited.'

'What about Mother's estates?'

'She died insane. Therefore they are all mine.'

'And if I do not marry, and have no children?'

'That would be a pity. Catherine, you are nineteen now. You cannot marry without my permission until you are twenty-one. I think it is reasonable to say that you *must* be married by then.'

'Reasonable!'

'It is a natural thing; it will happen anyway. As for children, that is in the hands of God.'

'Oh yes? It may have to be, with the husband you choose!'

'That is hardly a ladylike response, Catherine.' He paused. 'Do I take it you refuse my conditions, then?'

There had been a long silence. She had considered him, a grey-haired, slightly stooped figure in his khaki uniform. A pillar of an establishment that was completely out of touch. He was standing in the centre of the room, almost exactly where he had called her out to dance with him, all those years ago. She had worshipped him then. It was hard to make the connection.

She had a choice. To defy him, cut off all connections with her childhood, go out into the world to make her way on her own merit. Part of her believed that was the right thing to do. She believed she would do it, when she was older. As a girl she had dreamed of selling her share of the estate, to build a hospital and work in it as a doctor. But to struggle to qualify as a doctor without money — that was a cold, lonely decision, forced on her like this. For all her idealism she knew little of the world. Only that without wealth, she would have the power to change nothing.

Difficult though her father was, he was her only family now, as she was his. His was an awkwardness she understood, and believed she could work with. The conditions were really a bluff to hide the weakness of his own position. In a few months Sarah Maidment would be dead, and the connection he had with her sons would begin to wither. Besides, whatever he said, he could not *force* her to marry anyone.

And she did want, very much, to restore this house to something of its former position. To reclaim it, in memory of the mother who had danced here, so long ago.

So she had agreed.

And now, ten months later, the dining room was again furnished with a long shining table and carpets. They had taken down the old wallpaper, with its war poems and graffiti, and replaced it with something less grand but serviceable. Several pictures had been brought down out of the loft and rehung. There was a dresser, a silver service, and a black-leaded fireplace. They employed a butler, a cook, three maids, and a manservant.

It was very empty and quiet in the house. The three maids, the butler and the manservant had a room each on the fourth floor, and the cook slept in a room beside the kitchen. The hall, the grand dining room, and a drawing room took up the rest of the ground floor; on the second floor there was a library, a large sitting room, her father's office, dressing room, bedroom and bathroom; and on the floor above, two spare bedrooms and a suite of rooms for Catherine.

To Detective Inspector Kee, as he arrived on the morning of 20 December, it seemed extravagant.

The butler showed him into the dining room, where Catherine was finishing a solitary breakfast. Her father had already left for the Castle.

Catherine rose to welcome him. She was wearing a bright-blue woollen dress with a white lace collar, a few inches below the knee, as the fashion was now. If he had met her in the street he would not have thought her unusual, but her self-assurance in this large room, and her clear resemblance to the woman in the twelve-foot-high oil painting on the wall, slightly unnerved him. He was also puzzled by the odd, incongruous fact that the university lists had revealed her, unlike her father, to be a Catholic. Perhaps that, too, had something to do with the handsome woman in the portrait.

Catherine saw a solid, burly individual in a drab raincoat and heavy boots, with a square determined face and short moustache. A typical stolid policeman, she thought, all method and no imagination. She regarded the interview as an amusement, a formality. She smiled politely, like a good society hostess.

'Can I offer you coffee, Inspector?'

'No, thank you, miss. I've had my breakfast. I've come to ask you some questions about the shooting the other day.'

'Yes? I doubt if I can help very much. It was all a bit of a blur, I'm afraid.'

'Nonetheless, we think we've got some idea who did it. You're a student at University College, I understand.'

'Who told you that?'

'I've been checking the lists there. You're registered as a first-year medical student.'

A feather of fear brushed the soft hairs on the nape of her neck, as though the man's boots had blundered over her grave. Or Sean's. She gazed at him coldly, noticing for the first time the intelligence of the eyes in the solid, square, working man's face.

'That's right.' She sipped her coffee, to give herself time. 'I don't quite see . . .'

He held out a photograph. 'Do you know this fellow?'

It was Sean, of course. She should have known. A fresh-faced, proud smile, collar, tie, very neat slicked-down hair; a photo that might have been taken on prize day at school. This detective was a Belfast man, an outsider – how could he have got hold of Sean's photo so quickly? Her coffee cup rattled in the saucer as she put it down. Kee noted the reaction with interest.

'Yes, I . . . may do.'

'How do you know him?'

'Oh, he's just another student at the faculty, I think. I've seen him there in lectures. I don't know him very well.'

'Did you see him on Friday? At Ashtown Gate?'

'No.' A vehement shake of the head. I'm not Judas, you know.

'What sort of chap is he, this Simon Brennan?'

'Sean. It's ... Sean Brennan, not Simon.' Catherine spoke more slowly, as she saw it had been a trick, and the hairs rose again along her spine. Have I betrayed him already?

Kee said: 'Yes. Sorry. Sean, then.'

'I don't know. I told you. I don't know him very well.'

'Well enough to know his name.'

She sighed. This man must be dismissed before he uncovered more secrets. She made her voice frigid, like that of her mother bored by some tedious tenant. 'Yes, well, that doesn't mean much, does it? Look, Inspector, I don't want to seem rude, but it's not very likely that a medical student would be throwing Mills bombs at the Viceroy, is it? We've got too much reading to do, for a start.'

'I agree it's not likely, miss, but I regret to say we've quite a lot of evidence to show that it happens. Not everyone behaves as they should, these days.' He picked the photograph up, as though to put it back in his pocket. Then he changed his mind, and held it between his fingers on his lap, facing her, so that she had to see it or look away. 'It must have been quite an upsetting experience for you, being in the car. You might easily have been killed. We're very interested to talk to this young lad, you understand. Would you ... be likely to be seeing him again?'

She blushed. There was no disguising it. She could feel the warm flush spreading up from her neck, round behind her ears and into her cheeks and forehead, in a way that it had not done for years. In a hopeless attempt to hide it, she stood up and walked to the door.

'I really couldn't say, Inspector. Certainly not before next term, anyway. It's the vacation now, you know.'

'Yes.' Kee stood up too, intrigued. But he did not immediately accept her implied invitation to leave. 'And of course you don't meet him at any other time?'

'No, I do not. As I say, I hardly know him.'

'Fair enough.' Kee folded the photograph and notebook into his pocket. 'I'm sorry to trouble you, miss. It must be an unpleasant memory. But if you do think of anything more, you'll give me a ring, won't you? Here's my card.'

She took it, and showed him out.

Now isn't that interesting, Kee thought as he walked away. Nothing is what it seems in this godforsaken city. Here's a young woman with more money than a hundred decent families, her father a personal friend of the Viceroy, no less; and she gets shot at and nearly murdered in his lordship's car by a band of bloodthirsty hooligans. Does she show fear? No – that's breeding for you, perhaps; they're used to being sniped at from childhood. Does she show anger, or a desire to know why we haven't caught the devils? No, not a word. Does she show shock when I show her the photograph? Yes – but she's not shocked as she ought to be, because such a nice young man could be suspected of such a thing. Oh no. She was shocked because I knew about him, that's all. She was quite prepared to believe he might have done it.

He thought about the blush. It had been quite charming, quite overwhelming, quite damning. At the very least it meant that she entertained strong feelings for the young man. Of course, the feelings might all be on one side – he might know nothing about them. But on the other hand, she might already be quite involved with him. They were both young, after all, and good-looking, on the same university course. Such things happen all the time.

But if so, young lady, Kee asked himself, why did you not show anger at the thought that he might have been one of the murder gang? Or is that the sort of behaviour you expect from your suitors? Even when you yourself are in the car?

So what happens now, he wondered. Clearly, he was not going to be very popular if he told Sir Jonathan that his own daughter might be involved with one of the suspects. Equally clearly, it would be sensible to put a watch on this young lady, to see where she went in the next day or so, and who she met.

His main problem was to put himself in the mind of a young female Catholic Anglo-Irish aristocrat, who was apparently consorting with militant republicans. For Kee, a middle-aged Protestant Belfast docker's son, that was a little hard to do.

When Kee had gone, Catherine leaned with her back against the solid front door, feeling that dreadful tell-tale blush slowly fade. The butler came into the hall and looked at her questioningly. She came to, and shook her head.

'It's all right, Keneally,' she said. 'I showed him out

myself. It was the police asking about the shooting.'

'Yes, Miss Catherine. Have they caught anyone?'

'No. Not so far as I know.' She walked past him, up the main stairs, which one of the maids was brushing busily. It was hard to know from Keneally's tone what he thought. Would he be glad if some of the Volunteers had been caught — and hanged? For they would surely be hanged, if they were caught and convicted of this. She did not know. As for what he would think if he knew that his young mistress was in love with one of them... well, butlers were paid to be discreet. That would be a test for him, wouldn't it?

Nevertheless, it was not something she wanted her servants to think about. They were all much older than her, and could hardly be expected to approve of a thing like that. She climbed the great staircase under its ornate plaster ceilings to the first floor, and continued up a slightly less grand one to her own rooms. She shut herself in her sitting room to think.

It was a large, comfortable, untidy room. When she had moved back into the house she had chosen it as a retreat, and that was what it still was. The servants were allowed in only to light the fires, and when she specifically asked them. There were two desks on either side of the window, one cluttered with the accounts and papers for running the house, the other with her essays and lecture notes. In between the two was a long green window seat, which was what she had chosen the room for. She could sit here in the sunshine, and read, or gaze out over the little park in the square and remember what it had been like before the war. For this was the room in which she had slept — or stayed awake, entranced – in those magical times of her childhood.

For the rest, there were several glass-fronted bookcases, some lemon-coloured armchairs, an ottoman, and a number of pictures of lakes, beaches, horses and mountains in Galway, to remind her of Killrath, her other home.

But now, she hurried to the window seat, to see if the detective was still in the square.

He had gone, but the confusion he had left behind him remained.

Sean's act – the bullets through the car window, the blood, the headlong flight through Phoenix Park – had been heroic, romantic, exhilarating. She had felt no fear at all then. But the policeman in her own breakfast room this morning, his big hand holding Sean's photo on his knee, made her feel sick inside. This was no game now, it was real. If her republicanism was anything more than fine words, she had to help Sean now – protect him from those big hands that had held his photo so casually.

She had to see Sean, that was clear. As soon as possible. But how? She did not even know his address; and anyway, if the detective had taken the photograph from his flat, Sean could not be staying there any more. If he went there and was caught, he would be in prison.

Perhaps he was already in prison! The thought made her gasp, like a blow. The Inspector hadn't actually said they were still looking for him, had he? Perhaps they had already caught him and he was refusing to talk. The thought of Sean, alone in some stone cell, made her shudder. She wrapped a shawl round her shoulders, and strode up and down thinking back frantically over the interview. No, surely he had said the police were anxious to talk to him, something like that? Sean must still be free then.

Who would know him, to give him a message? Professor O'Connor perhaps, the people from the Gaelic League in Parnell Square. But the classes were closed for Christmas. And anyway, what would she say? The police are after you, they've got your photo, please be careful. That was silly, he must know all that already. Perhaps not about the photo, but all the rest. And then – she remembered her blush – that Inspector was no fool. He might be waiting for her to go to Sean, have her followed, so that she would lead the police to him.

In that case, she must not see him at all.

But the thought of it was so painful, she dug her fingers into the velvet cushions of the window seat in frustration. She wanted to see him, more than anything else. Not because of the police visit, that just made it more urgent. She wanted to see him for herself.

Kee sat together with Radford and Detective Sergeant Davis in DMP headquarters in Brunswick Street.

They were in Radford's office. It was a drab, functional room with a desk, several filing cabinets, and a solid table that was cluttered with papers, dirty teacups, and ashtrays. It was eight o'clock in the evening. The single window, which was slightly open to let out the smoke, looked down on the street two storeys below. The occasional sound of cars, and the clip of hurrying feet or hooves, formed a background to their discussion.

'So that's it, then, Tom, is it?' Radford asked. 'The grocer gave the lad a room and a job, let him take time off whenever he chose, and never asked any questions?'

'That's what he says.'

'And his other tenant was a model university student, only pausing from his studies to help old ladies cross the road.'

'That's the boy.'

Radford sighed. 'Well, I suppose we could intern him on well-founded suspicion of lying through his teeth, and earn ourselves another half-dozen newspaper articles about police insensitivity. But there's another lead, you say.'

'Yes. The girl. Catherine O'Connell-Gort.' Kee pronounced the surname with exaggerated precision, as though it offended him in some way. He got out his notebook, and went carefully through the details of his interview with her. 'She's one possible lead to the boy, Brennan. If she is involved with him in some way, she may lead us to him. I think we should put a watch on her.'

Radford paced up and down, considering the idea. 'It's promising, but there are difficulties. First, the boy, Brennan. We can't prove he was at Ashtown, or even that he's a Shinner. All we know is that he shared lodgings with Martin Savage, who definitely was there, and that he had a clip of German cartridges in his sock drawer. Well, that might not convince a jury, but it should be enough to intern him for a while, if that's what we want to do. Then there's the girl. If anyone ever had the perfect alibi, for God's sake, she has. She was sitting there, squashed up between her father and Johnny French, when the bullets started flying through the window! You're not saying she planned it?'

'No, sir, of course not. I just think she's fond of Brennan.'

'And you base this theory upon a blush?'

'Well, not entirely, sir. Her whole demeanour, more like.'

Radford stopped pacing and sat on his desk. 'I don't know about your experience of the female mind, Tom, but I would have thought the young lady's ardour – if it ever existed – might have received a rather rapid douche of cold water if she really saw her young Lochinvar chucking a Mills bomb at her head, as you say.'

Davis laughed. Kee said: 'She may not have seen him. She may just have believed it was *possible* he was involved. In which case she might run off in desperation to ask him if it was true.'

Radford considered this. 'Possibly. In which case Sod's Law tells us she's with him now, while we're discussing it. But then there's another thing. Her daddy, as you know, is a fairly important man in Dublin Castle, and in the country generally. Have you thought what I'm going to say to him about this, if she complains she's being followed everywhere by men in raincoats?'

Kee sighed. 'We stick to the grocer, then.'

'That's about it, unless you've got any more ideas.' Neither of them had. 'Right, then, I'm going to get a bite to eat. Dick, can you type this up, as usual?'

'Sir.' Davis gathered his notes together, and took them into his office. Kee took his coat off the stand by the door.

As he was leaving, Radford touched his arm. He pushed the door softly to.

'Sorry about that, Tom,' he said quietly. 'It wasn't such a daft idea as I said. But there are other things we can do. Come on back to the hotel. I'll buy you a drink.'

In his office down the corridor, Davis had also closed his door. He sat down at his desk, in front of the big Imperial typewriter. He was a good typist, for a policeman, and a meticulous keeper of records. He arranged his notes carefully on the left of the machine, and took paper, carbons and flimsies from the drawers on the right. He arranged these neatly. A top copy for the Assistant Commissioner, Radford; then a carbon; a second copy for the main files kept in this room; then a second carbon; a third copy for Military Intelligence in Dublin Castle.

Then he added a third sheet of carbon paper, as he always did; and a fourth sheet of flimsy paper.

He looked at his notes, and began to type. If he wasn't interrupted, he would be finished in about half an hour.

Tom Kee was a man of few loyalties, deeply held. His wife, Margaret, was the one he held most dear. Since their marriage he had seldom been away from home for more than a few days, and his transfer to Dublin had caused him much inner distress, because of the separation from her. But they had three sons and a daughter, all at good Protestant schools in Belfast. He wasn't going to risk their education for anything.

He had hoped to travel home at weekends, but had only

managed it once so far. Some of the greatest miseries of this time were the constant train strikes, encouraged by Sinn Fein as a protest against British rule. The one time he had got home, he had had to wait seven hours on Sunday night for the chance to return.

So he was forced to rely on the telephone. He had had one installed in the house before he left; it was only the second private phone in the street, the engineer had told him, and they had put up a special pole to carry the wires. But it was not very satisfactory. Kee was an undemonstrative man, but he loved his wife deeply, in the way the Bible prescribed. He realized now that he loved the warmth of her, the rich full curves of her body in his arms in bed; and he loved her cheerful efficiency, the way she bossed him and the kids around, so that they dared not be lazy or untidy. And he loved the smell of hot stew or fresh bread when he opened the door of the little terrace house in the evening, despite the irregular, unpredictable hours that he worked. None of that came out of the tinny, crackling voice on the telephone; and Kee could not express his feelings towards her, with the thought of the ever-present ear of the operator on the line.

So their phone conversations were inhibited, awkward and increasingly irregular.

His other great loyalty, apart from those to parents, church and Empire, was to William Radford. Indeed, it was only for Radford's sake that he had agreed to come to Dublin at all.

If it had not been for Radford, Kee would probably still have been a uniformed sergeant, patrolling the Shankill

Road on Saturday nights. A docker's son, he had no connections or influence to help him climb to the top. But ten years ago Radford, then a detective inspector, had recognized some traces of ability in the young sergeant, and encouraged him to take the exams for the CID. He had passed, and had worked with Radford during the war on anti-espionage work. They had foiled two attempts by spies to penetrate Belfast's naval dockyards, and their mutual respect had grown and lasted. So when Radford had been made Assistant Commissioner of the DMP, with orders to do something about the demoralized G Division, he had asked for Kee to go with him.

Now they lodged together in the Standard Hotel in Harcourt Street, a few hundred yards from the entrance to Dublin Castle.

Most of the rest of the clientele were army officers. As the two detectives crossed the dining room to a table in the corner, Kee noted with amusement how several had ostentatiously laid a loaded revolver on the table before them, beside the fish knife.

Radford waved greetings to one such officer, a much-decorated major with fine handlebar moustaches.

'What's that for, Tony? Waiters late with the soup again?'

The Major shook his head. 'This is a country in rebellion, Bill – don't you forget it. I remember a chap like you in Simla once. Intelligence officer. Fine fellow, great on the polo field, but refused to believe the natives meant what they said. I had to fish his body out of the river in the end. Nasty business.'

Radford nodded. 'I know. I'll be careful, don't worry.'

Kee admired Radford's assurance. He might be an inspector now, but he wasn't able to relate to men like these. He lacked their sense of ease, of banter, of worldwide social control.

Their table was quite secluded, out of casual earshot for the other customers, away from any door or window. To Kee's surprise it was laid for three. 'Expecting someone, Bill?' he asked.

Radford smiled, and ordered beer. While they waited for it he said: 'That's my surprise. The man we're meeting here tonight is from Military Intelligence. To be precise, that girl's father.'

'What?' Kee spilt some beer on the table, and mopped it with a handkerchief.

'I know, he doesn't look the type. But he must have more between the ears than he lets on, to be where he is.'

'Perhaps; I haven't met him. But if he's in MI, how can he be so daft as to let his daughter run around with the murder gang?'

'You wait till your kids are her age, Tom. They don't always turn out exactly as you'd hope.'

Kee frowned. 'Not my kids. Not a thing like that.'

Radford took another draught of beer, and smiled. It was the thing he liked most about Tom Kee – his utter reliability. For all his intelligence, he never seemed to have any doubts about what was right and what was wrong. Ambiguity, in Kee's view, was a disease that afflicted criminals, not the rest of the world.

'I hope not, for your sake, anyway. But here he is.'

Radford pushed back his chair as a tall, grey-haired colonel made his way towards them across the dining room. As he approached, Kee had the impression of an archetypal soldier: tall, high forehead, long nose, a proud, disdainful chin under the bushy Kitchener moustache. Well-cut khaki uniform with a line of medal ribbons, highly polished Sam Browne belt and cavalry boots, cap crushed under his arm. A man who would be at home leading the King's birthday parade in Phoenix Park, Kee thought; but hopelessly at sea fighting Collins in the back streets of Dublin.

But when Sir Jonathan shook his hand, Kee noticed the eyes. Hard, cold, grey – paler than those of his daughter, Kee thought: the eyes of a man who was no one's fool, and would get what he wanted whatever the cost.

They ordered, and while they were waiting Sir Jonathan asked, crisply, for a report on how far the police had got with the Ashtown incident. Radford told him, giving details of the findings in North Strand. With a warning glance at Kee, he mentioned the interview with Catherine, but omitted his suspicion about her blush. He passed Sean Brennan's photograph across the table.

'Good,' said Sir Jonathan. 'Pity it's not the negative. But we'll try and get some kind of copy made for the troops. There's a young major in the Castle who's hot on that sort of thing.'

The soup came. Radford tucked his napkin under his chin, and said: 'You're off to London tomorrow, Colonel, I hear?'

'That's right. Lloyd George is presenting his bill, and

he'll want up-to-date information on the situation here. That's one reason why I want to talk to you chaps.' He sipped his soup, and dabbed thoughtfully at his moustache with a napkin. 'You've both been in post for over a month now. What's your candid opinion of the ability of the DMP to get to grips with this terror?'

Radford sighed. 'Unfortunately, sir, not high.'

'There are a few leads,' said Kee loyally.

'But not many, Tom. Our problem, Colonel, is that half the experienced Dublin officers, with all their local knowledge and contacts, are dead, and the rest are clinging to their mothers' skirts in fear. In addition to which, I don't know how, I have the impression that Collins knows everything we decide to do five minutes after we've decided it. So I hardly dare trust anyone. In short, the whole of the effective official police force opposed to Collins is sitting right here at this table.'

Kee said: 'There's Davis, too, surely?'

'I hope so. He works hard, I'll give him that. But I've only known him a few weeks. You and me, Tom, we've been together a long time.'

Kee shrugged. He didn't like running down his force, even an adopted one, before a soldier, but the truth was inescapable.

Sir Jonathan glanced from one to the other. 'Anyway, whether it's two or three doesn't make much difference. I get your drift. It's you two against half the city.'

'Right.' They waited while the waiter brought the main course. Kee glanced around the room. Through the open door of the dining room he could see several men, in civilian clothes, come off the street into the foyer. The loaded revolvers beside the soup plates began to seem more of a comfort than an eccentricity.

Sir Jonathan resumed. 'Well, that's pretty bleak, but it's truthful. And the fact is we're dealing with a major political conspiracy here. A threat to destabilize the whole country, by murder if necessary. Agreed?'

Radford nodded. Kee began to eat his food, gloomily. He wondered where all this was leading.

'And you, as the established police force, are in no position to deal with it. You agree to that too?'

'At the moment,' Radford said. 'But if we could just get hold of the ringleaders, the thing would change entirely. There can't be more than five or six at the very top. Put them behind bars and their organization would start to fall apart, and morale in the force would rise. Those men who are just serving out time at the moment would start to put their backs into the job again.'

'Exactly.' Sir Jonathan waved his fork emphatically. 'And as far as I can see there are two ways to do it. Martial law and a curfew would help, and Johnny French has asked for that again. But even if the fools in the Cabinet give it to him, it'll only help if we can lay our hands on these beggars, Collins especially. And to do that, it seems to me, we must fight them at their own game.'

Kee sipped his beer thoughtfully and said: 'What do you mean by that, Colonel?'

The clear grey eyes stared at him coldly. I wouldn't have liked to be up before you for a disciplinary charge, Kee thought.

'What I mean, Detective Inspector, is that when the country is being destabilized by a group of armed thugs who have reduced the police force to a cipher and have attempted to murder the Viceroy himself, it's time we sought out men skilled enough in the same arts of spying and assassination to fight back.'

There was a silence. The conversation in the main dining room seemed to have fallen, but it was unlikely that anyone could have heard them. Kee noted with relief that the group of men in the entrance hall seemed to have gone.

Radford said: 'You mean we should run agents, like we did in Belfast during the war. I agree, but it will take time to set up. We can't tap into the local network yet, because it's all corrupt or terrified. And if we brought in an outsider he'd stand out like a sore thumb. You'd find him lying in a gutter somewhere with a cardboard sign round his neck.'

'Maybe. It'll take guts, I agree to that,' Sir Jonathan said. 'But what alternative have we got? Damn it, man, my own daughter was in that car as well. She'd have been lying in the gutter, too, if those scum had succeeded.'

The waiter cleared their plates again, and brought the dessert. Radford met Kee's eyes across the table. He said: 'In principle you're right, Sir Jonathan. If Military Intelligence can find us such men, then it's our duty to cooperate with them, though what help we can give, I'm not sure. We could provide support if called on, and channel information from G Division, to give them an idea of the layout.'

Kee snorted. 'I'll write the information on a postage stamp.'

Radford smiled. A Kee joke was something rare enough to be savoured. 'Your handwriting must have improved, Tom. Don't forget there's all that stuff Davis keeps so carefully in those files. There must be something useful there.'

'Two postage stamps then. But that's not the point.' Kee put down his spoon carefully and looked Sir Jonathan firmly in the eye. 'You said we should seek out men who are good at spying, Colonel, and I fully agree to that. We'll give them all the help we can. But assassination is another matter. As a policeman I've spent all my adult life upholding the rule of law in a Christian country, and that's how I intend to continue. Secret murder, even of Sinn Feiners, is a thing I'll have nothing to do with.'

Sir Jonathan reddened. For a moment Kee had the odd feeling he was going to be bawled out, publicly, here in the hotel dining room in front of the assembled company. But the blush faded and the cold grey eyes continued to examine him. Quietly, Sir Jonathan said: 'I presume you carry a revolver, Detective Inspector?'

'I do, sir, yes.'

'And if Michael Collins and his thugs walked into this room now, wouldn't you use it?'

'To defend myself or make an arrest, sir, yes, of course. But to kill him without warning? No sir, I would not. That would be to descend to the level of the enemy, and that is not what my God or my conscience would allow me to do.'

There was a further silence. Radford sighed, and Kee wondered how much his old friend agreed with him. They had been colleagues too long for Kee not to realize the embarrassment he was causing. But there were some principles Tom Kee regarded as too important to abandon, whatever embarrassment they caused.

Sir Jonathan said: 'If you had seen as many dead men as I have, Detective Inspector, you would realize that only a fool waits until his enemy fires first.'

'In war, no doubt, sir. But I'm a policeman, not a soldier.'

'This *is* a war, damn it! Ask the Sinn Feiners if you don't believe me! Any man I recruit will risk his life *as a soldier*.'

The waiter was hovering again. He cleared their plates and they ordered coffee. While they were waiting for it Radford spoke hesitantly, like a man trying to throw a rope bridge across a chasm which he knew could never be crossed. 'Naturally most men in G Division would be pleased if some of these Sinn Feiners were dead, Sir Jonathan. But in law and conscience Tom is right, of course. Officially, neither he nor I could do anything to support what would be technically murder, however justified the cause. But if your agents were to act in order to gain information leading to an arrest, then of course we would give our full support. Delighted to, in fact.'

'The full support of the two active officers of G Division. Quite.' Sir Jonathan stood up and pushed in his chair. His eyes held Radford's in a long, careful stare. 'Well, thank you, gentlemen. There may come a time when you will have to choose between your principles and your lives. However, I shall report your views to the Cabinet, if asked. No doubt the politicians will be suitably impressed.'

The waiter brought three coffees but there were only

two men sitting at the table. From which, Radford thought, an astute mind might deduce that the meeting had not been an entire success.

Kee rubbed his cheek with the palm of his hand and looked at Radford across the table. 'Sorry, Bill,' he said. 'If you didn't want to hear it, you shouldn't have asked me.'

Radford stuffed tobacco into his pipe, lit it, and regarded Kee thoughtfully through the clouds of smoke. That simple, undeviating sense of morality was one of the things he most valued about his old friend. Paradoxically, it also came between them. He said: 'You're too good for this world, old son.'

'Maybe. There are times I'd rather not know what the military are thinking.'

Radford shook his head. 'You need to know, Tom. For two reasons. First, because at any time they may be crossing your path. And secondly, because I, Bill Radford, may not always be here. Don't worry, I fully intend to be – I've even ordered one of these steel and silk bullet-proof waistcoats. But I was appointed to free this city of political murderers, and that's what I intend to do, in any way I can. These Sinn Fein bastards are getting very damned efficient, and it can't have escaped their notice that at last there's someone in G Division who intends to carry the fight to them. I know what I'd be thinking, if I were Michael Collins.'

'No, you wouldn't,' Kee said. 'Because you're a policeman, not an assassin. That's what gives us the right to govern the country, and makes him a common murderer.'

Radford sighed. His attitude to the interview with the Colonel had been rather different. He took his pipe out of his mouth and waved it in the direction of the main entrance, where Sir Jonathan had just gone out. 'It's not us who govern the country, Tom,' he said. 'It's men like him.'

5

CATHERINE HAD BEEN looking for Sean for three days. He was not at the university, he did not come to the Irish class in Parnell Square, and Professor O'Connor could tell her nothing. She did not know where else to look.

She began to realize how little she knew about him. She had known he had lodgings somewhere on North Strand, but she had never been there, and clearly there was no point going there now. She had teased him about being a gunman, but never really believed, before Ashtown, that he was actively involved with the Volunteers. She had not realized, until now, that they always met on his terms, when he chose. If he wanted to, he could just completely disappear. It intrigued and annoyed her at the same time.

She had not realized, either, how much she needed to see him. The war, and her isolation at Killrath, had kept her out of the company of young men, and those whom she had met, even at UCH, she had mostly scorned, until now. She felt they were too like pale versions of her brothers, they had no mystery for her. Sean was the first young man she had really kissed; and when she had kissed him once he had got into her system like a drug so that she wanted to do it again and again. The meetings after lectures, the evenings at Parnell Square, the slow walks home after a drink in a pub, had become the high points of her life, with everything in between grey, unsatisfactory. She studied and ran the house in a daze, and lay restless in bed at night, dreaming of him, sometimes kissing the soft parts of her hand as though it were his lips.

And now at a stroke he had become an Irish revolutionary hero, and vanished. She felt like an addict deprived of her drug. It made him more appealing than before, and less attainable. On her way to and from college she found herself scrutinizing every young man, seeking a certain shape of the face, a smile, a turn of the hand, that would be his.

On Sunday she went to a Christmas party at University College Hospital, given in a ward for the incurably shell-shocked. Professor O'Connor had insisted that all his students attend, and Catherine had come because Sean had promised to be there. But that had been before Ashtown. He was not there at the beginning, and she sat for an interminable hour on the bed of a one-armed ex-soldier. The man began by slyly trying to persuade her to diagnose an illness in his lower stomach, and ended by fulminating against his wife who had abandoned him for a cowardly stay-at-home Sinn Feiner. The man in the next bed had his children there, dressed up in beautifully starched and crimped pinafores and ribbons for their father's glazed, unrecognizing eyes to ignore. The nurses in their tall white hats gathered a group around the Christmas tree and crib. A student played the piano and the professor led carol-singing. The male students' voices were loud, defiant, jolly. One of the patients had a fine tenor, three were raucous, and the rest sang like ghosts. Their mouths moved, but the sound that came out was scarcely detectable. Catherine only heard it because the singers sang more slowly than the piano, so that they did not quite finish when everyone else did. She shivered. It was the sort of whispered singing she could imagine hearing alone in a graveyard at night.

She felt irritable and guilty. Professor O'Connor was right. These were the people she was training to serve. This was what it was like, being a doctor. But she could not focus her mind on the patients at all.

Then Sean came in, and the room filled with sunlight.

He sat on the bed, helping her patient unwrap his present, and winked at her. She had thought he would look different, somehow; she found herself looking for lines on his face, or scars. But there were none; only the smooth skin, as though he scarcely shaved; the grin from the wide, cheerful mouth; the smooth, neatly combed hair. The hazel eyes watching her – a little tired perhaps, but happy, unafraid.

For a moment she felt not love as she had expected, but anger. A voice inside her screamed that he should look hard and cold and guilty. If that bomb had come inside the car I would be a broken cripple like these men here. But the voice cried in a wilderness and was forgotten. He could not have meant to hurt her, he hadn't known she was there. He had risked his own life, and he was here, unharmed, at her side!

He smiled at her, and only the smile mattered, not what might have been. She felt oddly light and tender all over, curiously detached from the world.

On the way out of the ward Sean took her hand. 'I was going to Sandymount for a walk. Would you come with me?'

She smiled. 'Is that your idea of an invitation?'

'It is that. I've been wanting to talk to you.'

'Then I might spare you a moment or two, if you're lucky.' But she thought, if he hadn't asked her, she would have hated him for ever.

It was a cold, grey day, hinting at snow but then disappointing, as so often in December. They walked eastwards along Wilton Terrace, with the grey water of the canal on their right. She noticed how Sean looked up and down the road carefully, his eyes never resting in one place for very long. A motor omnibus for Sandymount stopped in front of them, and they boarded it.

On the bus their thighs touched, and she felt every jolt of the road. She said: 'You weren't followed to the hospital?'

Sean's smile faded. 'No. Why do you say that?'

'I'm not stupid, you know, Sean Brennan. I've got a thing or two to tell you, as well.'

They spoke little more on the bus, for people were crowded all round them. When they got off, they walked along the promenade beside the beach. Here, surely, they were safe from pursuit. There were a fair number of people strolling up and down — mostly couples and families, seeking a breath of fresh air before dusk — but not a policeman or soldier in sight. Small children ran after hoops or kicked balls under the eyes of indulgent parents.

Catherine leaned back against a pillar in the low sea wall, taking both Sean's hands in hers and pulling him towards her. She would not let him go now. He looked solemn, and opened his mouth to speak, but she touched a finger to his lips.

'It's all right, I know what you have to tell me. And I'm proud of you, Sean, as any true Irish girl would be. Except for one thing.' She shivered, and felt his fingers between her own. Big, smooth firm fingers, that had pulled the pin from the bomb and thrown it. 'If you'd succeeded, I wouldn't be here today.'

'What do you mean?' He scowled at her, the boyish face slightly flushed, a little angry. He really didn't know, then.

'I was in the Viceroy's car, Sean.'

It is true, she thought. A sudden shock does cause blood to drain from the face. She could see it happening. He stared at her, wide-eyed, then took his hands from hers and turned guiltily away. And she thought, I didn't mean that, don't abandon me now.

She said: 'It's all right, Sean, I told you. I'm not hurt. And I know why you did it. I would do the same, if I dared.' She touched his cheek gently, to comfort him. He shuddered, and jerked his head violently, as though her hand were a wasp.

'What the hell were you doing in the damn car, then? You had no right to be there!'

'It's not a crime, you know! Anyway, I was tricked into it.' She explained the trick her father had played, and her attempts to argue with Lord French on the train. But she could see he was only half listening. He turned away from her, and thrust his hands into his coat pockets angrily.

'You couldn't expect me to know you were there! I'm a soldier, and French is the enemy. You shouldn't go near him!'

Will he reject me for that? She stood quite still, not touching him, waiting to see if he would walk away. When he did not she said gently: 'I know that, Sean. I want him dead too.'

'*You* do?' He turned back, looked in her eyes, surprised.

'Yes. If it will help Ireland, I do.'

It struck him how slender she was; yet very straight-backed too, strong, determined. The delicate beauty of her hurt him. He thought of the way a crocus could be strong enough to burst its way through the tarmac at the side of a road, and then be crushed by any casual passing boot. He might have maimed her for ever.

'I'm sorry, Cathy. It's you that has the right to be angry, not me. I might have killed you.'

'You might have been killed yourself. You took that risk.'

He reached out his arms, and she slipped gladly into his embrace. They held each other very close, very still, while the seagulls screamed on the beach behind them. A mother, passing with two small children, glanced at them nostalgically.

They walked along the promenade, arm in arm for warmth. There were some steps down to the beach. They went down them, and stumbled across the sand to the sea's edge. It was dusk, and a small cold wind was coming off the sea. She told him of the detective who had visited her, and the photo he had shown her. She gave him Kee's card.

'What did you tell him?'

'Nothing. Only that you were a student in my year, but he knew that already. He had searched Martin's room, and yours. He thought I might have seen you at Ashtown.'

'And you told him you didn't?'

'Yes.'

'Martin.' Sean skimmed a stone across the grey water. Its splashes were oddly bright, like snowflakes in gaslight. 'He would have been alive now, if it wasn't for me.'

She had been too bound up in herself; she had never thought of this. 'Why, Sean?'

He picked up another stone, and flung it high in the air with a vicious twist of his arm. It fell into the sea with an odd sucking noise. 'Because I told him to run out and chuck his last bomb, that's why.' It all came back to him: the sudden dash out into the middle of the road, the bullets splattering around them like hailstones, Martin falling on his face like a stuffed doll. 'And the bloody car was empty all the time!'

She linked her arm through his, tentatively, so that he could break free if he wanted. 'You couldn't have known that.'

'No.' He touched her hand and looked round at her. Her face was pale, indistinct in the twilight. 'And if we *had* known it . . . Sweet Mother of Christ!'

'She was watching over me,' Catherine said. 'Will you try to kill French again?'

'If we get the chance, and Mick Collins learns where he plans to go. But he'll be walled in by guards now, more than ever.' Sean gave a short bitter laugh of triumph and frustration. 'The man's a fugitive now. Viceroy, indeed! He's a criminal on the run!'

They stepped back hurriedly to avoid a wave larger than the others. Catherine leaned her head against his shoulder. 'What about you, Sean? Now they've got your photo, what will you do?'

He frowned. 'It's too risky to come to college. I'll have to give up studying for a while. But this is more important. It's the birth of our country, Caitlin – there has to be blood!'

She shuddered slightly at the sentiment, but she did not question it. Padraig Pearse had said things like that. She liked it when he used her Irish name; it reminded her of her nurse, of childhood. She asked: 'Where are you staying?'

'That's not a thing for me to tell you now, is it?'

'Why not?'

'Your Inspector Kee might come back and ask some more questions. If you don't know, you can't tell him.'

She unwound his arm from her waist and stepped back. He might be a hero in the Volunteers, but she would not let him control her. 'Sean Brennan, do you think for one moment I'd tell the police a thing like that?'

He considered her, seriously weighing the question, and her genuine indignation. His face was shadowy in the growing dusk.

'No, *a ghra*, of course I don't. But I have to be as safe as I can, now I'm on the run. You wouldn't mean to tell them, but they have trick ways of putting the questions – you might be taken in.'

She thought for a moment, and then relaxed. He was right; it was his life that was at risk. 'I'm sorry, Sean.' She put her arms around his neck, and kissed him quickly on the lips. It was as she remembered. 'I only asked, because I want to be taken in by you. I want to be a soldier's girl.'

Surprised, he kissed her back, and she responded warmly. It was like the first time, outside her house. And she thought, this is what I need, this is what I want him for. The sense of touch, of contact with something real, outside my study and loneliness. But then he drew back.

'We can't do this here, Cathy. It's . . .'

'Madness. I know. We need somewhere to go.'

He shook his head, bemused. 'You shouldn't – women aren't supposed to talk like that, you know.'

If he had expected her to be ashamed, she was not. She was not accustomed to question her own desires. His embarrassment amused her. 'Really? I thought all girls spoke to you like that. I've been looking for you for three days, joy.'

'Look. Talk sense now. Are you hungry?'

She linked her arms around his waist, and pulled him close against her. 'Famished.'

'No, look. I didn't mean that.' There was another long, exploratory kiss before he could explain further. Sean felt things were getting out of control. Surely people must be watching; if there were any people foolish enough to be still out on this cold beach, on a dark December evening. 'I meant, hungry for food.'

'I'm hungry for everything.' She touched the tip of his nose with hers. 'Where shall we go?'

'There's a pie shop . . .'

'Mmmm.' She kissed him again, before he could finish. His resistance melted, and he gave himself up to the pleasure of it. After all, he thought, why wait? I may be dead tomorrow.

'Right then. Let's go.' It was going her way now. She broke out of his arms suddenly, and began to stride across the sand, tugging him after her by one hand.

'Hey.' He had not expected that, either. 'Wait a minute. Where are we going?'

'To the pie shop, lover. Aren't you hungry?'

As they sat in the pie shop, devouring pies at a battered wooden table next to a window running with condensation, a feeling of tenderness for Catherine overwhelmed him. Those fingers, those hands, that lively, delicate face, those lips which had clung to his and were now flecked with crumbs of pastry — they could have been shattered, ripped to bloody rags by the bomb he had thrown.

He reached out across the table, lifted her hand to his lips, and kissed each finger separately.

She smiled. 'Are you really so fond of me?'

'I am that.' He remembered when his little sister had been left in his charge, and had nearly been killed by a bull because of his own carelessness. He had felt a little like this then.

But Catherine was no little sister. The touch of her hands in his, the pressure of their knees jammed together under the little table, sent an electric charge through him in the way no child could ever do. Sean had the impression that the grubby seaside pie shop was a palace, alight with vibrant colours.

'Tell me. Did you really beard the Viceroy in his train?'

'I did.' She told him the story again and this time it seemed irresistibly funny to both of them. Her laughter was a thing of beauty in itself.

The shopkeeper interrupted sourly, picking up their plates and wiping the table with a cloth. 'If you two lovebirds would mind finishing. It's well gone six o'clock.' They looked round and saw they were alone. Catherine smiled and stood up. 'Yes, of course. Thank you so much. They were lovely pies.'

Outside, on the windy, dark promenade, they clung to each other for warmth. They were a similar height; it was easy to match their strides as they walked. Sean could feel her thigh pressing against his and held her closer.

She asked: 'Where shall we go?'

'I don't know.' The answer took a long time, because they turned to face each other, and then it seemed natural to kiss again. They formed an island of warmth together in the cold wind. Growing daring, he slipped his hands in under her unbuttoned coat, and rubbed her back through the thin woollen dress. She moaned, and pressed herself closer to him. Then a gust of wind snatched her hat and whirled it along the street.

'I'll get it.'

'No.' She laughed and held him back. 'It doesn't matter, Sean. I don't need it.'

'But – it's an expensive hat!' Never in his life had he imagined letting clothing blow away without caring.

'We'll get it later. Hold me like that again.'

And for a long time the hat was forgotten. On a winter night like this, the windswept promenade was one of the most private places they could have found. But at last a group of sailors came along, singing and whistling. Sean and Catherine broke apart, regretfully. She shivered, and buttoned her coat.

'Come on,' he said. 'We'll go to a pub for a drink.'

'All right.' She put her arm round his waist, and snuggled close against him. She knew her servants would expect her home, and would have cooked a meal, but she did not care. Her father had left on the afternoon boat for London, so she would have been alone anyway. She toyed with the idea of inviting Sean home. After all, why not? She was an adult now, she was her own mistress – if she wanted to invite a friend home, the butler Keneally and the other servants couldn't stop her! She imagined Sean in her drawing room, kissing her on the lemon-yellow ottoman, or on the green window seat, perhaps, looking down over Merrion Square ...

And her bedroom was just next door. *Don't think that, Catherine,* she thought, *that's one thing you can't possibly do.*

But the idea had an awful fascination. She wondered how it would be. She would take him up to her room, and they would sit and talk for a while, by the warm fire her maid would have lit – *God, it was cold out here!* – and they would kiss and then... She was hazy about how people got into bed. Her parents had had separate rooms with adjoining doors. But it was impossible to think of her parents making love. She would make an excuse and undress behind her screen and come to him in her long cream nightdress and – *he would have no nightclothes at all!* The beauty of the thought thrilled her so much that she sighed, and he turned and kissed her again as they walked along in the cold sea wind.

Sean would have no clothes at all! She had seen men half-naked in the fields, and been brought up to appreciate the beauty of the classical sculptures and paintings which filled her parents' houses. There was one in particular, a black shining one of a man and woman embracing, that had always fascinated her. But somehow, this was the first time she had thought of these things in relation to herself, and a real, living man! She would come out from behind her screen in her long cream nightdress and he would be there, quite smooth and naked in the lamplight, ready to crush her to him. His lips would press against hers as they had done just now and his hands roam her back and he would lift her and take her to the bed and *it was quite quite impossible.*

They went into a crowded pub and Sean left her sitting at a small table while he went to order drinks. She sat down weakly. Despite the sudden warmth and noise she was oblivious to her surroundings. Why was it impossible? She imagined herself going in through the front door with Sean and immediately she had to confront Keneally, the butler, who was older than her father. And then probably the cook-housekeeper as well and certainly Lucy, her maid. All of them would disapprove terribly of a lower-class person like Sean coming into the house at all, except through the tradesmen's entrance. But if she summoned enough courage she could face them all down because she was their employer and Sean was a student on her course. For heaven's sake, it was the twentieth century now and if a young independent woman wanted to invite a male friend into her house, she would! If anyone thought it was wrong, that was their problem. *Honi soit qui mal y pense.*

She sighed. That would all be fine, if she was just inviting Sean in to talk. It would be a fight worth fighting. She would enjoy the scandalized disapproval on the faces of Keneally and Lucy her maid as they brought in a tray of tea and toast, to find the mistress and the uncouth young man absorbed in the study of medical textbooks. Especially ones with pictures of bodies in. She could even imagine facing her father down, over the right to do that.

But I could only win a fight like that, Catherine realized, if I were really innocent and it was the other people who had the wicked thoughts. As it is, I want to take him to bed with me. And there's no way, no way at all, that I could face the servants if I did that in the house. They'd probably resign en masse, anyway.

For a while she toyed with the idea of sending all the servants to bed and then sneaking Sean up the back stairs; but the same objections remained. The servants had eyes and ears, they were not stupid. She would have to get Sean out, as well as in; and even if the servants didn't hear anything, she would never know that they hadn't. Every morning she would look in their eyes, and wonder if their respect for her had vanished.

Sean made his way carefully back to their table, bearing two foaming glasses of stout. He was pleased, she knew, that she chose to drink beer rather than something more ladylike such as sherry or wine. He had told her once that it was daring. Oh well, she thought, at least I can indulge my lesser desires.

Sean sat down facing her. They sipped the stout and smiled at each other, their eyes sparkling. The noise in the pub had lessened enough for them to talk.

'I never understood why you became like this,' he said.

'Like what?' Was he a mind-reader? Was her face so transparent that he could see what designs she had on him? If so, what did he think?

But Sean was on a different track. He waved his arm around the pub. 'I mean, why are you in a place like this, with a fellow like me, supping beer like a normal girl, almost? When you could be leading the life of O'Rahilly with Lord this and Viscount that, if you wanted.'

'Almost?' She teased him. 'What do you mean, like a normal girl, *almost*, Sean Brennan? Am I normal or am I not?'

He considered the question. 'In some ways yes, in others no.'

'Oh, wise philosopher.'

And is it normal to think of you in my bedroom, naked like a Greek statue? My mother would have said not, and father would too. I could slide my hands across his chest and – I wonder if his buttocks are smooth and hard like the man in that statue? I wonder what it would feel like when he came inside me?

She said: 'I think I'm a very normal girl. In all ways except wanting to earn my own living, and to see Ireland free.'

He pushed a stray lock of hair back from his forehead, and smiled. 'That's what I mean. It's not normal for girls of your class to want those things. Why do you?'

She stretched her hands out to the warm fire. He was right, it was an unusual path that had brought her here. Perhaps if she talked about it, she would stop thinking of where she wanted that path to lead, right now.

'All right,' she said. 'I'll tell you about a day in my childhood.'

It had been a rainswept, windy afternoon. She was thirteen then, and the war in France had just begun. Catherine had been riding alone along the clifftops near her home in Galway, watching the spray from the vast Atlantic rollers break over the headlands. There had been a storm far out at sea, and the spray burst in great fountains halfway up the cliff. Dark rainclouds were sweeping in from the southwest, and the occasional flash of pale sunlight lit the spray with an almost luminous glow. It fascinated her. Each wave hit the rocks with a shock like thunder, and

Catherine and her pony trembled as the pulse went through them. She felt awed and humble, as though the great god of the sea, Manaanan mac Lir, might appear at any moment before her.

Then the storm had reached the clifftop, and she had ridden away inland, hunched beneath the drenching sheets of rain. Instead of heading for home, she had let the storm blow her further east than her usual haunts, to an area of bog and pasture behind a mountain. Here, when the rain eased, she had come across a gathering outside a small cottage.

She had seen the place before – a small, thatched, untidy hovel, always with a skirl of dirty, barefoot children running around outside it, and a harassed woman in a headshawl. There was a small potato garden, a couple of poorly tended fields, a sick-looking cow. She had never liked the family much. Once she had tried to talk to them, but the man, a mean, scrawny individual, had cuffed the children and sent them inside, and then glared at her sullenly without speaking.

Since then, she had heard, the man had gone away to the war, one of the thousands who had answered John Redmond's call to fight for the Empire against the Hun.

But that day the woman and her children were all out on the road, in the rain. Around them was a heap of possessions – something that might have been a mattress, a table, three broken chairs, a spade, a rusty bucket. Half a dozen men were striding back and forth in the garden, carrying things, trampling heedlessly over the vegetables. As Catherine rode up, one of them dropped a pile of crockery on the road in front of the woman, with a crash. A plate had broken, and a chipped cup fallen in the mud.

'Whatever is happening?' she had asked. Ferguson, her father's agent, was directing the men. He had caught hold of her bridle. After all these years she still remembered the harshness of his rainswept face, the rough jerk of his hand on the reins.

'No business of yours, Miss Catherine. Be off with you now!'

'But what are you doing?'

'Never you mind! Clear off out of it, will you!' He had hit the pony a sharp clout on the rump with his stick, and to her shame she had gone away, letting the pony carry her down the muddy lane out of reach of the gang of rough, cruel men. She should have shouted back, she knew – no man on her father's estate had the right to speak to her like that. But she was only thirteen, and Ferguson ran the estate in her father's absence. Only when she was half a mile away had she stopped the pony to look back.

The men had been still there. They had erected a great tripod outside the house, made of three treetrunks about fifteen feet tall, chained together at the top. From a chain in the middle hung another treetrunk, shorter, thicker, parallel with the ground. This they were swinging against the walls of the little stone house, again and again. As she watched, a section of the stone wall fell in. The men heaved the battering ram a few yards to the left, where the wall was still standing, and began again.

Catherine had watched until the house was just a heap of stones. All the time two men kept guard over the woman and her children as they sat on their mattress, weeping and hopeless in the muddy lane. The drizzle fell gloomily on everyone. And Catherine trembled at each thud of the battering ram as she had trembled at the power of the sea. But while the power of the sea had filled her with awe, the power of her father's men filled her with shame and hatred.

She had complained to her mother, who was, by that time, beginning the illness that would lead to her death. Together they had asked Ferguson the reason. The man had been arrogant, condescending. Sir Jonathan O'Connell-Gort had left the business of the estate in his, Ferguson's, hands, he said, and he must do what he thought was best. The rent on the cottage had not been paid for months, and the husband had deserted his family. Besides, they had always been shiftless, and the land was needed for pasture.

'But he has gone to fight in the war!' Catherine's mother had said. 'For God's sake, he has gone to fight for the English, poor man – does he not get paid for that?'

Ferguson had shaken his head. 'He may have said that, my lady, but it was a lie. I've enquired, and no Irish regiment has any record of him. He's done a bunk, that's what it is – fled to some new fancy woman in the city, no doubt.'

'And does that mean you must throw his wife and children on the road?' Catherine had asked. 'Is it their fault that they have a shiftless father? Is that Christian mercy?'

'It's the law of the land, young lady. Rent must be paid, and this estate must be run at a profit. That's what your father appointed me to do, and it's in your interests not to interfere.' Catherine remembered how he had glanced from her to the fine oil paintings on the library wall. Paintings of her grandparents and great-grandparents — the people who had owned this house since Cromwell's days. She remembered the sneering look on his face. And where would you be, miss, without the likes of me? the look said. No fancy clothes, no fine house, no pony. Is that what you want?

But then the bubble of his arrogance had been burst. Lady O'Connell-Gort, Catherine's mother, had spoken, in a tone no one had heard from her for years. 'Where are the mother and children now?'

'How should I know, my lady? On the road to Galway, perhaps.'

'I want them found and brought back here.'

'But . . .'

'And you will rebuild their house, and restore them to their home. Do you understand?' Catherine's heart had sung. This was how she remembered her mother before her illness, and what she wanted her to be like again. A proud strong lady, ruling the estate in her own right, like a queen.

'I am sorry, my lady, but I answer to Sir Jonathan, not you.'

'That is my land. It is part of my inheritance. If you do not do what I say I shall have you dismissed.'

The row had gone on for some time, and had led to a bitter exchange of letters with Catherine's father. It was true that Sir Jonathan had said his wife was incapacitated by nervous illness; but he had not obtained a medical certificate to remove her legal partnership in the estate, and so, to Catherine's surprise and delight, her mother had won. Only, by that time, the poor family had disappeared, and Ferguson claimed they could not be found.

Sean was uncertain how he felt about the story. Part of him felt great anger at the plight of the poor Irish family. It might so easily have happened to him; it *had* happened to many of his ancestors, he knew. People who had starved in the great famine, or been crammed into the holds of the emigrant ships, which had left Ireland's ports every year until the start of the war.

Another part of him was intrigued at the thought of Catherine as a young girl, growing up privileged and wilful on the west coast of Galway. He had not consciously thought about her childhood before; somehow it increased his tenderness for her. She had not been the ordinary spoiled rich girl, surely.

'So what happened then?' he asked.

'I found them myself.' Her face in the firelight of the pub was flushed with the memory.

'And you a thirteen-year-old girl? How did you do that?'

'I got on my pony and rode to Galway. A priest helped, too.'

There it was. She had been difficult, determined, contrary even then. And I nearly killed her, he remembered.

'Where were they?'

'In the most filthy place I had ever seen. A line of rotten shacks in the back streets, with mud on the floor and an open sewer running between them. I picked a baby out of it; he was eating fishbones and potato peelings that his mother had thrown there.' She sipped her beer reflectively. 'The woman wasn't very pleased to see me, either. She spat at me and told me to go away. I started crying. But then I got the priest to make her see sense.'

'Did you take her back?'

Catherine nodded. 'Mother made Ferguson rebuild their house, and I tried to help take care of her. I felt I had a duty to, you see. Ferguson was right, in a way. Our family was only rich because of all that land we had taken from the people, long ago. So I began to want to put things right. I felt my eyes were opened, that day. That's when I began to be interested in Irish history, and medicine. I thought the one would help me understand, and the other, to do something. And I wanted to cure my mother, too, so that she could be a fine strong lady, as she used to be.'

She stopped. 'I'm sorry. Too much talk about me. It's because I'm lonely, and no one's interested. Except Father, who hates it all.'

The story had taken her mind into her past, away from her obsession with Sean. Now she looked at him and those feelings returned. He has such a nice face, she thought; clean, eager, idealistic. And that hair which he brushes so carefully yet is always flopping out of place. She felt a sudden urge to run her hands through it, hold his head to her breast while he — would a man kiss a woman's nipples, like a baby? She didn't know, but the idea fascinated her.

'I'm interested,' he said. 'That's what we're fighting for, after all. When we have the Republic, no one will be slung out of their homes by their landlords. But there'll still be poor people enough, even in Dublin. You should see where I'm lodging now.'

A thought struck him. Before, he had always felt ashamed of the idea of inviting her to his lodgings. She had been too obviously of a higher class, and he had been sure he would be embarrassed. Besides, at the grocer's, he and Martin had often had the fellows round. He wouldn't want to bring her into a room crowded with the boys. But now he had moved to a small room in a tenement, and if she meant what she said, why should he be ashamed? It was not what he had chosen, but only where he was forced to hide, to fight for the things she believed in.

'Would you like to see it?' he asked.

The thought, in slightly different form, had struck her too. She looked at her watch. It was just after seven. So long as she were home by ten, say, there need be no great scandal.

'Why not?' she said.

Sean had always known that lust was a sin but he had not known, until he met Catherine, that women could feel it. It had especially not entered his head that an apparently nice, well-brought-up young girl could act as if it were no sin at all.

Catherine excited and confused him. He had nearly killed her, but she showed no resentment. She had shown not the least concern about coming alone with him to one of the least salubrious, most overcrowded and unpleasant tenements in the city; and now when they were in his little, dirty back bedroom, she was radiant.

It was clear to him that she was not surprised by the social conditions. They had walked down dark, unlit cobbled back streets, past men and women in various stages of drunkenness; crossed an entrance yard where children were playing dispiritedly in the dark; and climbed a dank, peeling staircase to a small room at the back of the building; and all the time she had seemed in a state of abstraction, scarcely seeing where she was.

The room had a moderately clean bed, a desk, a chair, an oil lamp, a square of carpet on the floor, and a jug and basin. The window looked out across an alley on to a blank wall with a number of drainpipes running down it. She sat on the bed and he made a pile of sticks and coal for the fire.

'I doubt the British'll find me here,' he said. 'If the peelers did come, there'd be the most almighty row if they started to search the rooms downstairs, and there's a fire escape at the back, so I could get down there. Anyway, I hope I won't be here long. It's policy to move us around, when we're on the run.'

He thought how boastful that phrase '*on the run*' sounded, and wished he had not used it. But there was little else to be proud of, stuck alone in a hole like this. The only difference from prison, he thought, was that he could go in and out when he wanted. And have visitors.

He made the fire draw by holding a piece of newspaper in front of the grate. When it was roaring nicely he stood up and washed his hands in the basin. When he turned round she was kneeling on the carpet, holding out her hands to the blaze. She had pushed her short, bobbed hair behind her ears, and the fire sent ripples of warm light along the delicate lines of her neck.

He thought he had never seen anyone so beautiful.

He knelt down beside her and kissed the lobe of her ear.

I shouldn't do this, he thought. It is taking advantage and definitely a sin; but anyway she wants to and I want to and we are all alone here, no one need ever know.

The fire burned up brightly so he turned down the lamp; and the heat filled the whole of the tiny room. After a long, slow kiss, she turned her back towards him, bowed her head, and said: 'Sean, will you help me undo these buttons here, please.'

As he undid the first button he knew that this was it, it was going to happen to him tonight. So much worry and imagination, strict instructions from his father, solemn warnings from the priest, lewd talk at school, disturbing dreams alone in bed, and it came down to something as simple and solemn as this.

Her neck glowed warm and smooth in the firelight. He undid the second button and kissed her, just at the nape of the neck where there were a few soft hairs. She moaned gently, happily. He undid three more buttons.

She stood up, began to shrug her way out of the dress, then changed her mind. She kissed his lips.

'Turn your back, please. I want to surprise you.'

He turned away and closed his eyes, listening to the rustling, silken movements behind him. He felt an erection growing inside his trousers and was ashamed of it, not knowing what to do. Please God forgive me, I will not hurt her I swear. It is only love and I may die any day and never know it.

'All right. You can look now.'

He turned and she stood quite, quite naked in the

firelight. He had never seen a girl this way before. Her breasts were quite small and round and overwhelmingly beautiful, with little brown nipples that stuck out like buds. Her stomach was flat and her legs so long and soft and smooth – and there was hair there between her legs too, just a little wavy patch of it. Her eyes were shining, a little shy, afraid.

He reached out and crushed her in his arms.

And that was so strange and wonderful that he would never forget it. He was still wearing his boots, thick woollen trousers and flannel shirt. Her skin, everywhere, was soft as silk, delicate, defenceless as a baby's. He kissed her, and he felt like a great woolly bear holding a nymph, a goddess in his arms. As though she were Eve just stepped out of the garden. But she was human, hot in the fireglow.

His hands slipped down her back and felt her buttocks. She pressed herself to him and he felt his erection hard against her stomach. Then she stepped back.

'You're all itchy,' she said. 'You get undressed too.'

'All right.' He started to unbutton his shirt and then felt embarrassed. He did not think of himself as being beautiful like her. 'You turn your back then,' he said.

'I'll close my eyes.' She sat down in front of the fire, holding her knees up to her chin. He had seen a statue like that, once, in a park somewhere. A young girl watching the world, absorbed, innocent, curious, only half aware of her own beauty.

He scrambled out of his clothes.

Afterwards, as they lay in the narrow bed by the wall and watched the firelight flicker on the ceiling, she did cradle his head on her breast. She felt warm and maternal and . . . disappointed too. It had all happened so quickly. When he had entered her they had both seemed to lose control, there had been a sudden moment of pain and then he had thrust and thrust and she had cried out and wrapped her legs around him so that she could feel his smooth, hard buttocks under her heels and she had felt something wonderful rising and rising within her and then . . . then he had arched his back and shuddered and stopped.

She held his head to her breast and smoothed her hands through his hair and thought: It's over for him but not for me.

They lay entangled with each other and kissed and stroked each other's face. She ran a finger down his spine and said: 'You're beautiful, you are.'

'Me?' Sean was surprised. He didn't think men had beauty.

'Yes, of course you.' She raised herself on her elbow and drew back the blanket so that she could trace the line of his back and legs with her hand. 'Really beautiful. Muscular and smooth like a Greek god.'

It made him feel like an object, not himself at all. But her face smiling down at him was so warm and happy he could take no offence. Her small breasts rubbed his face and he kissed them drowsily, taking the small budlike nipples in his lips.

A coal fell down in the fire, lighting the room with a sudden burst of flames. Catherine's hand went on gently, insistently stroking his back and thighs.

A sadness that had begun to rise in him faded. He began to realize that it was not all over.

This time I must make it last, he thought. This may never happen to me again, I may be dead tomorrow. And she — she is not ashamed.

He pulled her down and began to kiss her quickly, eagerly: on her breasts, her neck, under her chin, her ears, her eyelids. 'I want to kiss you everywhere,' he said. 'It's not me that's beautiful, it's you — you're so lovely.'

She felt very tender all over and warm and moist down below. She ran her hands down his stomach and cupped her hands over his erection and thought: How did that ever get inside me? Then he came inside, slowly, much more slowly and for a moment they just lay there, trembling and looking into each other's eyes, using all their effort not to move.

She said: 'Oh, you, Sean.'

He said: 'Caitlin. I've got you now.'

She raised her legs, slowly, until they were crossed behind his back, his little hard buttocks under her heels, and she said: 'No, I've got you.'

Then she squeezed him gently, as if urging a horse to walk, and they began to move.

A long time later, they got dressed. The fire had died down to red embers. Sean peered at his watch. It was quarter to ten.

Catherine was glad he had not lit the lamp. She was afraid of what the light would do to the nestlike intimacy of the room. She was worried about her hair, though. There was no mirror in the room, but Sean lent her a comb, and she straightened herself up as best she could. She was glad she had had her hair cut short; the long tresses she had

had as a child would have been impossible to manage like this.

'Will you walk me home, my love?' she said.

He nodded, and thought for the first time of the neighbours they might meet on the stairs, the stories that would be told. He didn't want it to get out, he didn't want to face the nods and winks of the other Volunteers. He had thought a soldier should be like a priest, free of all ties, all weakness. It could so easily be made to seem sordid, what they had done.

He said: 'I'll try and find a better place if I can.'

'It's not the place, it's who's in it.' She kissed his lips softly, and rubbed her nose against his. 'Sean. You will love me, won't you?'

'Of course I will.' He suddenly felt hugely protective, the more so because he knew he was unable to offer her any real protection at all. He put his arm round her, and opened the door. 'Come on, little woman. I'll take you home.'

The journey through the night streets began quietly enough. Each room in the tenement grumbled and twitched with life, but they met no one on the stairs. There were people in the streets outside, but none that Sean recognized. He deliberately led them a circuitous route, turning back on themselves several times, and waiting in a doorway once, kissing, to see if anyone followed.

It was not until they were within half a mile of Merrion Square that the evening erupted. A lorry drew up at a crossroads in front of them. Four soldiers got out, their tin hats and rifles clearly silhouetted against a distant streetlight. Sean drew her quickly into an entry. 'It's all right, they're facing away from us,' he said. 'But we'll go back and round the other way.'

She whispered: 'All right. But what are they going to do?'

He didn't need to answer. As the line of soldiers waited, blocking off the nearer end of the street, two lorries roared into it from the other end, headlights blazing. They stopped halfway along, orders were shouted, and armed men poured out of it. They hammered on a doorway, and, as soon as it opened, rushed inside.

Sean said: 'They're looking for people like me – and even you, perhaps. Anyone who can give them information about Sinn Fein. I don't think they'll find much, though. Just drag some more poor people out of their beds, and gain us more support.'

People threw open their windows to see what was happening, and jeered at the soldiers. A man was dragged, struggling, out of the house, stood up against the railings and searched. When he protested, he was punched, kicked and bundled into the back of the lorry. A woman, perhaps his wife, came out in her nightdress, screaming. Three Tommies took her arms and hauled her back inside.

'It's monstrous!' said Catherine. 'What right have they to do that, in our city?'

'You ask your father,' Sean murmured quietly.

The cold anger in his voice made her shiver. She held his waist tightly, and hoped he was unarmed.

He watched for a moment longer, then turned his back on the scene. 'Come on. We'll go up this way. Walk slowly, and remember to look like we're lovers.'

That part was not so hard. On the way they met two

policemen, hurrying towards the noise. Sean bent his head towards Catherine, and they gave him hardly a glance. But the joy had gone from it. She thought he was annoyed, embarrassed by her presence.

At the corner of Merrion Square, they stopped. All the lights were on, downstairs, in the O'Connell-Gort house. Catherine straightened her back. They could not part in silence.

'This is it, then,' she said. 'Young lady Catherine goes in to face an irate butler, and a maid and housekeeper driven wild with worry. Wish me luck, Sean.'

He grinned. 'I do that. You'll face them down, surely.'

'I'll have to. After all, I'm my own mistress, and I've done nothing wrong, have I? Have we?'

Don't reject me now, Sean, she thought.

He didn't. Instead, he drew her, straight-backed and indignant, into his arms, and kissed her hungrily. She thought: There's a streetlamp over there. Anyone who looks out will see me being kissed by a common, cloth-capped Mick.

Then she forgot all about it.

When they paused for breath, she said: 'When will I see you again?'

'Not tomorrow. I'll be with the Volunteers all evening, and it's no good in the day. Tuesday night, at the Keating Branch.'

'All right.' Two days. It seemed so long. 'Sean?'

'Yes?'

'Take care of yourself. And...' The vision of her normal, respectable life returned to her. It seemed quaint. 'Her ladyship thanks you for a wonderful evening.'

He seemed nonplussed. Then he touched his cap and grinned. 'To be sure, ma'am. My pleasure.'

He turned and strode quickly away, while Catherine squared her shoulders and walked towards the bright lights and imposing pillars of her Georgian home.

6

'So THERE YOU have it, gentlemen.' The Prime Minister passed the buff manila envelope across his desk to Harrison. 'The decision of the Cabinet as I have explained it to you.' David Lloyd George, a short, mercurial Welshman with twinkling eyes and a drooping moustache, leaned back in his chair and steepled his hands under his chin. 'How do you think Lord French will take it?'

Sir Jonathan sat very straight in his chair. On the long

journey over from Dublin with Harrison he had thought a great deal about government policy in Ireland. He had arrived in Westminster in time to see Lloyd George present his revised Home Rule Bill, which would give a partial self-government to a divided Ireland; at once too much and too little, Sir Jonathan thought, and far, far too late: without doubt it would be derided and exploited by the Sinn Feiners, and gain the government nothing. What was needed was a consistent policy, real interest instead of neglect from the politicians, and firm, unyielding military control.

Now he was here in the Prime Minister's study to brief him on the military situation. 'Lord French would have preferred a clear declaration of martial law, Prime Minister,' he said.

Lloyd George sighed. 'I have already explained why that is not possible. It is essentially a police matter. But the army already has extensive powers under the Defence of the Realm Act. If you use those, and arrest the leaders, it will have the same effect.'

If we could find the leaders, Sir Jonathan thought, and then trust you politicians not to do a deal with them once they are caught. He said: 'In Dublin at least, Prime Minister, the effective police force is at a very low ebb.'

'So you have told me,' Lloyd George snapped. 'It is your job, Colonel, to give them support and stiffen them up.'

So easily said, Sir Jonathan thought. This is getting us nowhere. The man lives in another world. Another country.

Harrison gave a small, apologetic cough. The two men's eyes turned to him. His large, goldfish eyes peered through his spectacles at Lloyd George. 'And ... er ... the other matter we discussed, Prime Minister?'

Sir Jonathan stiffened. All the way across the Irish Sea, Harrison had been urging on him the merits of this other policy, which he had first broached in the Viceregal Lodge a few days ago. Despite the firm line he had taken with the two policemen, Sir Jonathan had qualms about it. The sincerity of that Inspector – what was his name, Kee? – had impressed Sir Jonathan despite himself. Of course the army should not normally resort to secret murder. But then, how would the man have felt if his own daughter had come within an ace of being torn to mangled shreds by a terrorist's bomb? And if the politicians would not give them open, consistent support, what else was there? The other policeman, Radford, had looked as though he might understand that. As Harrison clearly did.

Lloyd George did not answer Harrison's question at once. He pushed his chair back, stood up, strolled to the window, and looked out. It was already dusk, and the garden of 10 Downing Street was grey, indistinct. He clasped his hands behind his back, fiddling with them under the tails of his frock coat. His voice, when he spoke, was measured, cautious, resonant.

'I understand your difficulties, gentlemen. This is not an ideal world, and when we are dealing with cutthroats and murderers it is necessary to consider methods which in public we should abhor. So if you were able to find a man brave enough to venture into danger to do this work, he would, of course, deserve our full support. Terrorism must be put down, and the rule of the law upheld, by each and every means open to us.'

He turned to face them, stroking his moustache thoughtfully. 'Does that answer your question, Mr Harrison?'

Harrison slipped the manila envelope into his briefcase, and stood up. 'I think so, yes, Prime Minister,' he said.

The devil it does, Sir Jonathan thought.

The room had a beautiful view. The nursing home was on the cliffs outside Bournemouth, and Sarah Maidment was propped up on pillows in her bed so that she could see out, over the clifftop gardens, to the sea. It was an afternoon of sun and showers, and the sea reflected the different moods of the sky above it: deep indigo under rainclouds to the west, sparkling blue close inshore, a hazy, luminescent grey far out on the horizon. But Sir Jonathan, as he stood in the doorway of the private room clutching his bouquet of flowers, doubted whether Sarah could see much of it.

She had changed drastically in the month since he had been here last. The once jolly, round face was pale and sunken now, the bones clearly visible through the skin. The sinews in the neck and hands stood out quite starkly too, and her hair was completely white. She turned her head slowly to face him, and he saw that her lips were cracked. Only the eyes – bigger now, cornflower blue like the sea – retained something of the woman he had once loved.

'Johnny?' she whispered. She didn't smile. Perhaps it hurt.

He held out the flowers. The nurse, coming in behind him, took them officiously and arranged them in a vase beside the others. She adjusted the pillows behind Sarah's head, said: 'Just ten minutes now. She's very tired,' and walked smartly out.

Ten minutes. Sir Jonathan sat down beside Sarah and took her hand. She had never been a great beauty; but she had given him comfort and laughter where his wife, like Catherine, had given him intensity, drama, strain.

He asked: 'How are you, my dear?' He felt foolish as soon as he had said it, but what else was there to say?

The answer came in a whisper, so that he had to bend his ear to catch it. 'Very ... poorly, Johnny.' She flapped her hand urgently towards a glass of water, and he raised it to her lips to help her drink. He realized it was cruel to make her speak.

To fill the silence, he began to talk himself. Awkwardly at first, telling her where he had been, something of his business in London over the past two days. Her big blue eyes watched him vaguely, travelling over his face, his hands, his clothes. It was borne in on him that this was the last time they would ever see each other; the nurse had made that clear, outside the room. He began to talk instead of the good times they had had together, what they had done. He could not speak of love, he was no good at that. But he managed to remember a play they had laughed at, a party when everything had gone wrong, a time they had got lost together in a cart in the country, a day they had made love in a bathing hut. Her eyes shone; the skeletal face creased in what was meant for a smile; he raised the glass to her lips again and heard the nurse tap softly on the door behind him.

He kissed Sarah gently on the forehead, on the eyelids. The skin was thin, like waxed paper.

'Goodbye, old girl,' he said gruffly. 'Goodbye now. God bless.'

Outside he could not see very well and he sat down on a metal chair in the echoing, disinfected corridor to blow his nose hard and dab at his eyes. He had seen more death in his life than he had ever wanted but each time it was worse.

Later, sitting in the train on the long journey back to Holyhead, he remembered the pictures of her two sons and grandchildren on her bedside table, and the things he had not said. He had come with the idea that perhaps he could abandon everything in Ireland, leave it all to her sons, forget the hopeless struggle. But without Sarah it would not work. However much he respected her two sons they were not his own. He did not ever want to see them again, except at the funeral.

There was only one person left in the world who really mattered to him now, and that was his own daughter Catherine. And for her, he would fight to keep his inheritance, and pass it on intact.

Next morning, Sir Jonathan sat opposite Harrison in the first-class dining room of the ferry. They were only half an hour out from Anglesey, but already the windows were streaked with spray and it was clear it was going to be a rough crossing. Harrison, to Sir Jonathan's surprise, seemed in good spirits, quite indifferent to the ominous rolling and pitching beneath them. He sliced the top off an egg, and peered briefly into it before starting to eat.

'Well, we've got what we wanted, Colonel,' he said.

'How do you mean?' Sir Jonathan was not sure that

food was a good idea, and his physical misery was compounded by the memory of Sarah, alone in her room in Bournemouth, fading away without him.

'We've got permission to hire our assassin.'

The words, baldly stated by the little round bespectacled civil servant, sounded vaguely indecent, like a schoolchild speaking brightly of a world it does not yet understand.

Sir Jonathan frowned. 'Is that what you understood Lloyd George to mean?'

'Certainly. No politician could have expressed himself plainer.' Harrison sliced a finger of bread and butter and dunked it in the egg. 'Our only problem now is for you to find the man. Shouldn't be too difficult, I suppose?'

There were several reasons why Sir Jonathan did not answer at once. In the first place, he was not nearly as sure of the Prime Minister's unqualified support as Harrison appeared to be. Lloyd George's meaning, Sir Jonathan thought, was as easy to pick up as quicksilver. Secondly, he was far from confident that any one man *could* find Michael Collins. Especially if he was to come back alive. In any case, he was in no mood to talk about death and murder that morning. Perhaps because the memory of Sarah was still too close to him, perhaps because the motion of the ship was making any form of coherent thought increasingly difficult. He had come to his decision the night before, but he still found it distasteful. He decided that the sight of Harrison cleaning out the inside of his egg was too much to bear, and stood up abruptly.

'Not difficult at all,' he said. 'I know the very man.'

Then he strode smartly towards the promenade deck, and the fresh air he so desperately needed.

7

THE DAWN WIND whispered through the reeds, and somewhere on the lake a moorhen croaked sharply. Andrew Butler could just make out the tips of the reeds in front of him. They rustled together restlessly, like the points of bayonets, he thought, waiting to go over the top. In the east, the faint grey light along the horizon deepened to a glow of pale lemon. The first finger of sunlight pierced the clouds like a searchlight.

And it was quite, quite silent.

He cocked the double barrels of his shotgun, and waited.

The moorhen croaked again. A coot paddled on to the black waters of the lake, the white mark on its bill faintly visible in the growing light. It jerked its head sharply from side to side, gave a sharp 'Pip-pip!' and then dived suddenly under the water.

A stockdove cooed in the forest behind him, and a cock pheasant crowed. The dog crouched at Andrew's knee whined and stood up, its nose pointing, its feathered tail straight out behind it, trembling with excitement. Andrew put his hand on its neck to calm it, and hissed at it through his teeth.

'Ssssst, boy.' But it was a young dog, and did not immediately obey. Andrew growled at it in his throat and forced it down with his hand.

Then the duck came.

The first pair came from the southwest, over a stand of trees to his right. He heard them before he saw them, the quick *sing-sing-sing* of their wings out of the semidarkness. They circled, once, high overhead, turning to land into the wind. He tracked them all the way, the two barrels of the shotgun slightly ahead and below to allow for the deflection. Their bodies glowed with the pale lemon colour of the rising sun; their wings fanned the air busily and then spread into a wide, forward-facing curve as they planed in towards the surface of the lake, webbed feet braced to meet the shock.

The two ducks skidded along the black surface of the water, sending white spray up to sparkle briefly in the sunlight. Then they stopped, shook themselves to clear the water from their backs, and paddled towards the reeds.

Andrew lowered the gun. It had been too easy, he told himself. There had even been a moment when they had been so close he could have got them both in the same cone of shot. To test himself he needed a harder shot, further away, moving faster.

But it was not only that. He thought of himself as hard, unsentimental, professional; but he nearly always found an excuse not to shoot the first ones, now. In memory of the German machine gunners, at Hill 60 outside St Julien, who had found an excuse not to shoot him when he led the first wave across at dawn. He had run so damned hard, his heart nearly bursting with the effort of carrying sixty pounds of kit and lifting his feet out of the stinking bog that the artillery had churned into quicksand, and he had *known* all along that the machine-gunners had him in their sights. How could they fail, with the early-morning sun behind them and three days of artillery pounding to warn them? Yet they had held their fire and let him get through the only gap in the wire, and he had run on and on like a demented maniac, fifteen, twenty yards ahead of the men he was supposed to be commanding, until he could see the line of little pointed metal helmets sticking up above the German trench, and the dark eyes in the mud-covered faces staring at him. A man running to his own death.

Then the machine gun had opened up, not at Andrew, but at the line of his troops behind, as they struggled to follow him through the wire. Andrew had dived into a shell hole, and in that first half-minute, twenty-six of the company behind him had died. Why the machine-gunners had not fired at him he would never know. But it was too late then, they could not see him, and it was the biggest mistake that that group of Bavarians ever made. In a shell hole only ten yards from the German trench, Andrew lined up six grenades in front of him. With the first, he scored a direct hit on the machine-gunners who had spared his life; the other five he lobbed at five-yard intervals into the trench itself. Then he jumped into the trench after them.

In one hand he had a revolver, in the other a long, slim bayonet which he had spent hours polishing and honing to a razor edge. The trench was a shambles of twitching bodies. One of the bodies grabbed his leg. Andrew stuck the bayonet into the man's neck behind his ear, and ripped his throat out. To his right there was no movement, to his left three soldiers in greatcoats and pointed helmets lunged down from the firing step towards him. Andrew shot the first two before they could turn their long, unwieldy bayoneted rifles to face him. The third was quicker. His jagged, sawtoothed bayonet laid open Andrew's cheek from jaw to scalp, grinding against bone so that the flesh was all gone and the teeth showed. Andrew jerked aside, but as he fell he shot the man in the stomach and then again in the head and then he dragged himself to his feet and stabbed him through the eye. Then he clapped a field dressing over the bloody remains of his face and lurched along the rest of the trench looking into all the dugouts and sticking his bayonet into any of the wounded who still moved.

When his sergeant and six survivors reached him three minutes later, Andrew was the only person in the trench still alive.

They held that section of trench for six hours, and were then ordered to retreat. Andrew was awarded the Military Cross.

Before he left, his head cocooned in bandages, Andrew had looked at the corpses of the German machine-gun crew. They were very young, hardly out of school. One had tried to grow a moustache but the hair was as soft as a baby's. His face was frozen in a grimace of utter terror.

He remembered that face now, as he stroked the quivering dog and watched the coot pop up on the black lake, and paddle in little zigzags across the surface. The machine-gunner had not spared him out of mercy, then, but only out of fear: a paralysing fear which had frozen his finger on the trigger. It was not a weakness which Andrew would ever allow himself.

He who strikes first, he thought, lives to strike again.

If he had struck a little faster, he would still have a decent face.

A second flight of ducks flew towards him out of the east. Four of them, high up. As they came in sight of the lake their wings stopped beating and they began to plane round in a wide circle, as though still not quite certain whether or not to land. They divided – two continued to plane down lower, the other two flew round again in another circle. Andrew tracked the higher two, the harder shot. As they reached the trees to his right, he fired. One barrel – two; and both birds fluttered down, in a scattering of feathers, one bouncing off the high branches of a pine tree.

At the sound of the shots the other two ducks ended their dive and began to fly away from the lake, their necks stretched upwards, their wings whirring in panic. Andrew put down his shotgun and picked up a second, which was lying loaded on a bank beside him. One duck was flying to his left, the other straight towards him. He hit the duck going left first, and then raised the gun sharply overhead to try the second barrel. But he was too late. The duck was past him and skimming the treetops. Though he pivoted swiftly he could not get a line on it before it was gone. He lowered the shotgun ruefully.

'Three out of four,' he murmured. 'Getting slow.'

He had perfected the trick of hitting four in a row in the year before the war, when they had still had shooting parties at Ardmore, and his parents had been alive. It had brought him loud applause, and several guineas in bets, as others tried to emulate it and failed. Now his parents were dead, and he would have to organize any shooting party himself. But he had little desire for company, and anyway, all the friends he valued were dead.

The dog, which had leapt up at the first two shots, had turned in confusion at the third. It was a young dog, it didn't mind about his face. As far as the dog knew, he had always looked like that. It stared at him expectantly, quivering with excitement. He pointed to the nearest duck, which had fallen in the lake. 'Go on, boy! Fetch!'

As the swimming dog's head cut an arrowhead across the dark waters of the lake, Andrew saw how the sun had now fully risen into the morning sky.

The day had begun well enough, but now the rest of it stretched in front of him, empty. Like the house itself, Ardmore, which he had come home to, after the war.

He wondered how he was going to fill it.

When he came in sight of the house he paused, as he always did. Ardmore, the house was called – the Big Hill – but in fact the hill itself was behind it. Andrew stood on the hill now, looking down at the back of the house in which he had been born. From up here it did not look so beautiful – a square, solid block of a building, three stories high, with dozens of chimneys grouped in four great stacks, and a jumble of yards and stables behind it. The real beauty of the house could only be appreciated from the front, where the twin columns of the entrance looked across lawns towards the sea. All visitors approached the mansion that way.

To his surprise, Andrew saw that some visitors were approaching now. A small black model-T Ford was inching its way through the tall wrought-iron gates, three-quarters of a mile away. He watched them through his field glasses. One of the passengers, a young man in a long coat and cap, was holding the gates open. When the car was through, he climbed on to the running board and got in, without bothering to close the gates behind him.

Andrew was surprised. Hardly anyone came to see him, these days; and no one came unannounced, so early in the morning.

When he reached the house, the three were already in the hall, talking to Henessy, his father's old butler. Henessy looked unusually flustered, Andrew thought; the red veins on his bibulous old nose stood out more than ever, and he was taking anxious little steps backwards and forwards in front of the visitors, as though he did not know which one to speak to first.

They, for their part, were taking scarcely any notice of him. One, a large, heavily built young man in a thick tweed jacket and flat cap, had picked up a delicate statuette of Venus from a side table. He was holding it in hands as big as a butcher's and examining it with distaste. Another, slimmer but still tall and heavily built, was walking up and down with his hands in the pocket of his trenchcoat, gazing at the family portraits in the hall, and trying to peer into the rooms that led off it. The third, a short fellow with horn-rimmed glasses perched on an unusually short snub nose, was pacing up and down in front of Henessy looking at his watch.

It was immediately clear to Andrew that these were not the class of person who ought to be in the main hall at all. But for some reason, his servants were unable to deal with them.

'Good morning, gentlemen,' he said in a clear, hard voice, that cut through the querulous protests Henessy was trying to make. 'Have you come to see me or my housekeeper?'

A second glance had shown him that Mrs Macardle, his usually forceful cook and housekeeper, was watching from the passageway at the end of the hall, which led into the kitchen.

The three young men turned to stare at him. There was a studied, deliberate insolence in their manner, something he had met once or twice in Flanders, amongst men from regiments who were near mutiny. It had been a shock then, he remembered; the sudden sick realization of how few the officers were, and how the men could turn the whole structure of the organized world on its head, if they chose.

The fellow with glasses spoke first. ''Tis yourself we're here to see, Mr Butler.'

Andrew waited, deliberately staring them out. With his two shotguns broken open over his left arm, the string of ducks stuffed into the game bag, and the setter gazing up at him, he was faintly aware of his resemblance to the twelve-foot portrait of his grandfather on the wall behind the man in the trenchcoat. Except that his grandfather had not had a jagged, seven-inch bayonet scar down the left side of his face. He stared at each man coldly, letting the fact sink in that this was his house, and they had no obvious reason to be in it.

But they did not seem as cowed as they ought to.

'It's about money,' said the biggest man suddenly, the statuette still in his hands.

'I see.' Having established a sort of dominance by silence, Andrew moved on swiftly. He strode into the hall, unslinging his game bag and handing it to Henessy. 'Well, we cannot discuss that here. Show these men into the library, will you, Henessy. I'll join them in a moment. And . . .' He put his guns on the floor and took the statuette gently from the big man's grip. 'I think we'll put that back, if you don't mind. It's rather valuable and very fragile. The library is over there.'

He watched them go, picked up his guns, and strode out of the back of the hall towards the gun room. Mrs Macardle followed him.

'Who are they, Mary?' he asked. 'Have you seen them before?'

'Sure I know two of the beggars,' she said. 'That's Michael Rafferty from the butcher's shop in Youghal, and Frank Davitt, a saddler's apprentice in the next street. But the little fellow with the snub nose is a mystery to me. It's likely they've sent him down from Cork or Dublin to take charge of the others.'

'Take charge? But what would they be wanting with me?' He unlocked the door of the gun room, and put the two guns in their racks. Mrs Macardle stood in the doorway.

'They're our local Volunteers, Mr Andrew. The Sinn Feiners.'

'Ah.' It fell into place. 'So that's why Henessy was so flustered.' He smiled, picked up his service revolver, and slipped it into the pocket of his hunting jacket. 'Well, Mary, I'd better not keep them waiting then, had I?'

The library at Ardmore had been Andrew's father's great pride. A scholar as well as soldier, he had collected well over five thousand books himself, to add to those already there. It was a long room, with a view out over the park towards the gatehouse and the sea. It was a place for work and relaxation, with two fine carved desks at either end, and a set of comfortable leather armchairs cluttered around the fireplace in the middle.

Although he himself had never cared much for the room, it annoyed Andrew intensely to see his three visitors seated, still with their coats on, in his father's favourite armchairs.

He strode across the room and stood in front of them, his back to the fireplace. A housemaid had hurriedly laid a fire which was beginning to smoke, but gave no warmth. He felt the room had a cold, uncared-for, unwelcoming air to it this winter morning.

'So. You've come about a question of money, have you?'

He looked at them each in turn. It seemed that the smaller young man, the outsider with the glasses and snub nose, was their leader in this. Presumably the butcher's boy and the saddler's apprentice were bodyguards to his lordship.

'Well, this is how it is, Mr Butler.' The young man ventured a smile, but he had not the charm of it. Perhaps it was shock at the way the weak morning sunlight picked out the horror of the white jagged line down Andrew's face. 'As you will surely know, the people of Ireland have voted for a republic.'

Andrew raised his good eyebrow, but said nothing.

The young man ploughed on. 'And as representatives of that republican government, it is our duty to raise money to finance the actions of the said government during the period of enemy occupation. We do this by selling government bonds, which can be redeemed in five years. And since you are without doubt a wealthy man, I have come to invite you to purchase an appropriate number of these bonds. Think of it as an investment if you like, to safeguard your future as a citizen of the republic.'

Andrew regarded them coldly. Then he said: 'An appropriate amount. Do you have any idea, Mr, er . . .'

'Slaney, Mr Butler. Brian Slaney.'

'Do you have any idea what an *appropriate amount* might be?'

'For a man in your position, Mr Butler, I would suggest somewhere in the region of a thousand pounds.'

'I see.' A little devil began to laugh in Andrew's mind, betraying itself in a thin, mocking smile on his lips. 'And would you have any of these bonds with you, by any chance?'

The young man pulled a folder from inside his jacket. 'The government hasn't actually printed the bonds themselves yet, Mr Butler, but I am authorized to sign a receipt.'

He gave Andrew a sheet of paper. It was thick, beautifully embossed in gold, green and black lettering, with the name of *Dáil Eireann* at the top. 'It's issued by the Finance Minister, Michael Collins.'

Andrew fingered the paper thoughtfully. 'And if I make this investment of a thousand pounds, what benefits do I get?'

The young man was becoming enthusiastic. 'Well, it's like any other bond, Mr Butler. The government would expect to redeem it at a fair rate of interest. I can't say how much at present, but...'

'What about protection?'

'I beg your pardon, sir?'

'Protection.' Andrew glanced at the two bigger men, watching stolidly from the two leather armchairs. There was, he noticed, a heavy bulge in the saddler's trenchcoat pocket. 'Any genuine government grants its citizens protection, with a police force and so on. Does your government do that?'

'It's your government too, Mr Butler. Yes, of course it provides protection. There are the Volunteers, the Republican courts, the...'

'Does it provide protection against blackmail?'

'I beg your pardon, Mr Butler?'

Andrew took a deep breath. These men were dangerous, he knew; but the little vengeful devil in his mind was laughing now, stoking a fire of rage that would overcome all caution. 'I mean, does the government of this republic of yours provide protection for the citizens of Ireland against armed criminals who go around the country demanding money in return for worthless pieces of paper like this?' He crumpled the embossed receipt up, threw it into the smoky fireplace behind him, and took his service revolver out of his pocket. 'Because if it doesn't, Mr Slaney, I'll just have to rely on this, won't I? Unless of course I trust His Majesty's Royal Irish Constabulary. Which I do.'

The sight of the revolver had brought the other two to their feet. Andrew smiled, watching them carefully. 'Which regiment did you gentlemen fight in during the war, may I ask?'

The butcher's assistant, Rafferty, blurted out: 'We're Sinn Feiners, Irish Volunteers, we didn't join up to die for no damned British Empire!'

'I see,' said Andrew pleasantly. 'Cowards, too, then. Your decoration is the white feather, is it not? I think you gentlemen had better leave, quickly. *Now!*'

The shock of the shouted last word made them jump, and they moved towards the door. As they reached it, Slaney turned round, pointing to the fireplace, where the receipt was blazing merrily.

'We came decently to make you a fair offer, Mr Butler, and your answer was the flame. You remember that, when you sleep at night – you in your great house that you robbed from us all!'

Now there's a fine threat, Andrew thought, as he watched them go down the steps and scramble into their tiny Ford.

You should have shot them while you had the chance, said the vindictive little devil in his mind.

But this is peacetime, he told it.

At the beginning of the war Andrew had had some sympathy for the Germans because he had a German mother. He had been to Germany several times as a schoolboy, and spoke the language fluently. In 1914 he had been twenty-two, still studying at Trinity. But then his elder brother, Peter, had been killed at the first battle of the Marne.

Andrew had been distraught, and the desire for revenge hatched like a dragon in his heart. He joined up, and his mother — a vivacious woman whom both boys idolized — spoke bravely of duty and loyalty to her adopted empire, and kissed him when he left.

By January 1915 he was at the front, by the end of the year he was a prisoner in a vast muddy compound in Hesse. In the spring of 1916 a letter from his father told him that his mother had been shot dead in the Easter Rising, by a bullet from a rebel outpost near Bachelor's Walk. By Sinn Fein Volunteers, Andrew thought, with guns which had been sold to them by the Germans in 1914.

It was soon after that that he escaped. He climbed over the wire, killed one of the guards with his own bayonet, took his clothes, and disappeared into the German countryside. He headed south, travelling mostly by night, using the bayonet to steal when he had to. Three times he was nearly captured: each time he left dead men behind him. The way the bayonet slid into throat or stomach so smoothly, the grind against bone or cartilage as it came out, fascinated him. This killing was unlike that of the trenches; here, he looked into a man's eyes first, and saw the recognition and the fear. Afterwards, there was a feeling of great, sensual pleasure, of enormous power, triumph and release unlike anything he had ever experienced. Later he would clean the weapon for hours, obsessively, half-exultant, half-ashamed, listening to the little devil whisper to his mind of revenge.

He headed south, towards the Schwarzwald – the Black Forest. Here, he hoped, there would be fewer people. He would be able to hide, perhaps hunt, and travel on to the Swiss border.

When he reached the fringes of the forest he was exhausted. He had been travelling for ten days and had eaten on only five. He needed food, rest, and shelter soon, or he would collapse. But each time he stole or killed, the hunt came closer behind him.

In the end he decided to approach a small isolated cottage at the mountainous end of a valley. It was surrounded by pine woods, there was no other house in sight, and he had watched it all day without seeing anyone come out except a single young woman.

He tried to clean himself up but all he could really do was pick the twigs out of his hair and brush some of the mud off his clothes. His face was still dirty, unshaven, and skeleton thin, his clothes old, ill-fitting and torn. When he walked into the kitchen and tried to speak to the young woman, she screamed. He used his best German, and smiled, but it only made matters worse. She threw a pan of warm water at him and ran out of the door.

He had to follow. She was running down the valley, towards the next farm, which was two or three miles away. When she got there she would call out a search party and Andrew would be recaptured or shot. He thought of stealing food and hiding in the forest but he did not think he could survive many more nights in the open. So he summoned up his last reserves of energy and sprinted after her.

Sprinted was hardly the word for it. After the first few

yards his legs were shaking and he could feel his heart pounding as though his whole body were just a transparent skin covering it. But the girl did not run fast either. After the first quarter of a mile she looked back, saw that he was gaining slightly, leapt over the ditch at the side of the road, and ran into the forest.

She probably thought she could lose him in there. He caught a few glimpses of her brown dress and white apron ahead of him in the trees, and then she vanished. He stopped, his breath coming in great gasps, and looked around him frantically. Then he heard the snap of a twig behind him, turned, and saw her running downhill towards the track again. He ran to cut her off, she tripped and fell, and he was on her before she could get up.

He was too weak and exhausted to do anything but lie on top of her and try to pin her down. He thought of the bayonet but he had never used it on a woman. She rolled on her stomach and struggled free, but he managed to grab her ankles and pull her down again before she had gone a yard. She turned over, sat up, and hit him on the shoulder with a dead pine branch. He snatched it out of her hand, threw it away, and lay down flat on top of her with one hand holding each wrist. For several minutes she writhed and fought but he was just too heavy for her to get him off.

After a while the nature of the struggle under him changed. She closed her eyes and tried to push him off mainly with her hips. He rubbed his face against the side of her neck, and she turned her head and kissed him hungrily on the lips.

He had been too surprised and exhausted to do anything except hold on and kiss her back in case it was a trick, but she had kissed him so passionately and rubbed her pelvis so hard against his that he became hard and the more she writhed the harder he pressed her down until they had both climaxed almost together, he inside his trousers and she with great gasps and cries of 'Ah! Ah! Aaaah!' which he was terrified would bring someone down on them from the track.

But there was no one there and a little while later she kissed the lobe of his ear. He lifted his head and looked down at her. Her eyes were open. They were a bright cornflower blue in a broad face with a wide, generous mouth and flushed cheeks. Her hair flopped on the pine needles beneath her in two flaxen plaits, and her arms were still pinned above her head by the grip he had on her wrists.

They gazed at each other in fear and wonder.

He said, in his best German: 'I don't want to hurt you. I need food and shelter.'

She said: 'You are Hans.'

'My name isn't Hans,' he began, but she interrupted: 'Yes. Yes, it is. You are my Hans come back.' And she held up her mouth so appealingly that he kissed her again.

Then he had said: 'If I get off you, will you come back to the cottage quietly?'

She had nodded, and they had walked back slowly side by side, he a little behind her and ready to grab her arm at once if she should change her mind.

Once inside the cottage her attitude had begun to change again. She gave him some food and sat at the table watching him eat, and her face began to cloud over with suspicion. Then he made some mistake in German and she said: 'You are a foreigner.'

'Yes,' he said. 'I am a Prussian. I have run away from the army because I can't stand it any more. If they find me they will shoot me.'

She looked slightly mollified about that but he wasn't sure if she believed it. Prussia was about as far away from the Black Forest as you could get, and that was where he had learnt his German, so it was possible. He asked her about Hans. For answer, she took a photograph and a letter from a jar on the top of the dresser. The photograph was of a young man with a moustache and face not unlike Andrew's, in a spiked German army helmet. The letter was from his colonel, telling his wife that he was dead.

'But I know he is not dead,' she said defiantly. 'Every evening I hear his voice in the woods. One day he will come back.'

Andrew looked at her sadly and decided she was mad.

Then an idea struck her. 'I have a widow's pension from the government. Perhaps my Hans pretended to be dead so I would get the pension, and then ran away like you. Perhaps he is walking here now.'

'Perhaps,' Andrew said. If the German army was anything like the British, deserters were shot, publicly, to encourage the others.

But the idea had its possibilities. 'If he is running from the army like me, your Hans will need a woman to give him food and shelter, too,' he said.

She looked at him, and nodded slowly.

He stayed there for two months. By the end of the first evening he had decided she was simple, and unhinged by the loss of her husband. He was terrified that she would run and fetch someone while he was asleep so he made her sleep with her hands tied to the head of the bed. Also he told her that if anyone arrested him, he would inform them about Hans.

By the end of the first week he had realized just how much young Hans was missing. In the evening Elsie walked up into the woods, collecting wood and listening for Hans's voice, and Andrew followed her because he was afraid to let her out of his sight. Then she looked over her shoulder and began to run, he chased her, and there was a repeat performance of their first meeting. This happened nearly every day. It became a game they began to elaborate on. He said that she could only go out into the woods without her shoes, then without her skirt, then without any clothes at all. Still she ran. Always he caught her, always she pulled him down onto her, into her. Andrew had never known any game could be so exciting.

At night, when he tied her wrists to the bed, she writhed and looked up at him as she did in the forest. He took off her clothes and looked at her, and she moaned and shifted her hips. Then he discovered, by experiment, how a woman could be brought to her climax with his hand, or his tongue, and that it was as much a pleasure to do that and watch her, as it was to have an orgasm himself.

After a week he had known he was in love with her. The horror of the war in France, the fear of arrest and return to the squalor of the prison camp, were always in his mind as a threat and a contrast which made their lovemaking more desperate and urgent. They made little conversation; she was not talkative and had no knowledge of the world beyond her valley. After a while he came to trust her, too.

An old man and woman came up from the village. She talked to them while he hid in the house, but she did not give him away. But the escape games continued, for their own sake.

He might have stayed for ever but one day in October the old couple told her that a detachment of recruits had been billeted in the town at the foot of the valley, and the next day a platoon marched up to the house behind a mounted officer with a map, reconnoitring. Andrew hid in a cupboard until they had gone. That evening he had tried to persuade her to leave with him, but she refused. Hans would come back, she said, she had to wait for him.

Andrew left the next morning, before dawn, walking south towards Switzerland. He never saw her again.

Andrew escaped from Germany to a world where his father was dying, his mother had been killed by rebels, and the Empire faced defeat. He returned to the trenches, embittered, not caring whether he lived or died. For two more years he fought in the mud, expecting death every day, sometimes seeking it, and gaining a reputation for cold, detached ferocity. But death only mocked him, dragging a cruel finger down his face and giving him medals. So when the war ended he had come back to Ireland as an unwanted war hero, a landlord, and a recluse. He had gained the habit of warfare, and lost his hopes of love.

New Year's Night came a fortnight after the visit of the Sinn Feiners. Henessy, the butler, had worked for fifteen years in Scotland, and grown attached to the Scottish custom of Hogmanay. Andrew's father had indulged him, and Henessy had introduced various inventions of his own, including a midnight game of football with a burning whiskey barrel, so that before the war the New Year's festivities at Ardmore had become something of a local tradition – not least because of the obvious need to consume the contents of the whiskey barrel before burning it.

Despite his age, Henessy had asked permission to welcome in the year 1920 in the traditional way. So for an hour or two Andrew had sat in the great kitchen, listening to the stories and songs of his servants and the villagers and friends they had invited. But he was not in convivial mood, and soon after midnight he went to bed, knowing that he was lifting a pall of respectability from the proceedings, which could now take life without him.

He lay in bed and fingered the long raised line of his scar. It was the main reason he gave himself for avoiding human company. When he had visited the girls in brothels in London and Paris they had gawped at it in pity or disgust, and he had caught the same look in the eyes of the serving maids here. And yet the right-hand side of his face was handsome enough; he could speak clearly, see, had good lungs, all his limbs intact; more than dozens of poor fellows he had known.

He wanted Ardmore to be a great house again but he hated company. He had begun to buy in horses, with the idea of starting a stud, breeding perhaps for the turf. But it was a slow business, needing a stock of patience which he lacked. Some days he could be charming, on others he sank into a black mood, brooding. The little devil in his mind whispered to him of the pleasure they had had in Germany, on the run; and he told himself there was no place for that in peacetime, at Ardmore. He wanted the place to be the haven, the paradise it had seemed in his childhood. But for that he would need a wife and children. And a wife would have to be as dashing and handsome as his mother, as thrilling as Elsie. He fingered the ridge of his scar, and remembered the way the new housemaid had winced in distaste at the sight of it this evening.

If she thinks you're so horrible, the devil inside him whispered, why don't you strip the clothes from her and lash her little pert buttocks with a riding crop until they look the same? He smiled to himself, knowing it could never happen. Ardmore was a peaceful, civilized place now. In time, perhaps, it would grow into something he could be content with. He fell asleep, listening to the distant sounds of revelry and laughter downstairs.

Four years of war had made him able to sleep through any noise, so the whoops and shouts did not disturb him. Not until five o'clock did he wake, and realize that something was wrong.

It was still dark, and the noise downstairs was as loud as before. He sighed, and pulled the pillow over his head.

Then he heard a scream, and smelt the smoke.

He leapt out of bed, and dragged back the curtains. Light flickered over the lawns – huge tongues of red light and shadows, dancing across the grass. He saw figures running. One, who looked like a housemaid, was lugging a bucket of water from a pond.

He flung the door open and ran out into the corridor. But he could see nothing; great clouds of smoke billowed round him and there was a draught, like a gale, blowing past him up the stairs. He couldn't breathe. His throat was like sandpaper and he began to cough continually. Using his hands to feel the way, he floundered back to his room and slammed the door.

He pulled off his nightshirt, dunked it in the ewer, and put it over his head, like a gas mask. It might do. He pulled on a pair of trousers, opened the door, and hurried along the corridor.

He remembered burning buildings in Flanders. Keep low, he told himself. Go below the smoke. As he reached the head of the staircase, he saw flames rushing up it like a chimney — ten, twenty feet high. What could it be, in the stone hall? Ah, God — as he watched, blisters burrowed like moles across the surface of the oil painting of his grandfather, and then the portrait exploded into flame.

There was no way down there. He struggled back along the corridor to the servants' staircase. But there was a solid wall of black smoke pouring up there too. If he did not get air in a moment he would drown in all this smoke. He reached up and pushed open the door of the nearest bedroom. It was the one his mother had used, before her death. The smoke poured in, but he slammed the door shut behind him and for a few precious moments he was able to breathe.

He stood there, his bare chest heaving, gasping in the clean air. The light of the flames from outside the window flickered luridly over the soft shell-pink of the armchairs his mother had so liked, the damask bed-hangings, the mirrors of the walnut dressing table. That would all be burning beautifully soon. Already the floorboards were hot under his feet.

He hurried to the window and opened it. Outside there was a windowsill, then nothing – a twenty-foot drop to a gravel drive. Too far. He ran to his mother's bed, ripped the counterpane off, smashed a small pane of glass beside the stone upright in the window frame, and tied the counterpane to it. It was thick, heavy, difficult to tie. As he did it he had a sudden vivid memory of hiding under this counterpane as a child, pretending to fight the lions and embroidered Chinese dragons, while his mother laughed indulgently. Never again. The flames were licking under the door. He tugged hard on the sheet. It would hold. He climbed out of the window and walked backwards down the wall with the counterpane in his hands, his bare feet pressing against the stone.

Some eight feet down he reached the end of the counterpane. Below him he could see the curtains in the library window blazing like a blast furnace. He swung out from the wall, let go, and dropped.

He hit the gravel, rolled over, and stood up. Stones had embedded themselves in his skin, and he brushed them off. Then the library window burst and he stepped back, shielding his face against the sudden blast of heat.

Flames were blazing out of every window on the ground floor, and great gouts of black smoke were pouring out of the chimneys and windows upstairs. As he watched, there was a crack as something important fell in, and a tongue of flame roared through the smoke over the roof.

'Dear God.' He ran round the side of the building to the stable block and heard the screaming of terrified horses. The stables themselves weren't ablaze yet but a hayloft was beginning to burn. Inside it was bedlam: three horses rearing and screaming and old Henessy struggling with a bolt on a stable door as though it were as hard to open as a bank vault.

He pulled Henessy aside and set the horses free. But it was a mistake. They clattered out nervously, saw the blazing straw, and bolted back inside. They were shuddering and kicking at shadows. Andrew managed to lead one free and tie him to a tree. As he ran back he saw Henessy staggering towards him with the second. But the stable roof was alight now and before Andrew could get near the third it collapsed, trapping the terrified animal inside.

Andrew stood, watching, until the screams ended. Then he walked to the pump behind the house where he found Mrs Macardle.

'What happened? How did it start?'

'I don't know, sir, truly I don't. We were all singing, and then some more fellows came from Youghal and they was playing the game with the whiskey barrel, and I went to bed. And then this!'

'Who were the other ones who came?'

'I don't know, sir. But it was the whiskey barrel...'

'Never. One fire in a whiskey barrel couldn't cause the whole house to go up like this, all at once, without any warning. This was deliberate. And I know who did it.'

He walked away, round to the front of the house again. The upper floors were ablaze now, and the roof was caving in. He stood in the middle of the lawn and watched. Shortly before dawn, the main chimney stack collapsed, bringing down the rest of the roof and smashing through the two upper floors. When daylight came, there was nothing left but four blackened walls, and the ashes blazing merrily within.

8

THE WIND SWEPT in from the northeast, howling round the corners of the tenements, picking up leaves and rubbish and whirling them along the streets. Somewhere a tin bucket rolled to and fro, clanging against railings. The wind brought rain with it too, stinging cold sleety rain that lashed the faces of the few pedestrians foolish enough to be out, making them hurry to their destination, their hands thrust into their pockets, their chins tucked deep into the upturned collars of their coats.

Catherine and Sean clung to each other, struggling with the small blue umbrella she had brought. A few minutes ago they had been in the little tenement room, the heat of the fire glowing on their naked bodies; Catherine gasped with shock at the icy, stinging contrast of the sleet lashing her face. Inside her coat her body was still warm, languorous; and as she struggled along the street into the storm she could feel the pressure of his hips against hers and imagine every line of his body moving beside her.

Because of the rain they took a less roundabout route than usual, but still they stopped once or twice, shivering and kissing in doorways while they glanced up and down the street for anyone following. Once Catherine thought she saw the same tall young man for the second time, but before she could point him out to Sean he was gone, and they did not see him again.

Catherine insisted on leaving him while they were still out of sight of her house in Merrion Square. 'It's too much of a risk, Sean,' she said. 'Father will be back tonight, and it would spoil everything if anyone saw us together.'

'He'll have had a rough trip, in a storm like this,' said Sean. 'Even the sea hates Ireland's enemies.'

'Don't speak of him like that, my lover.' She kissed the freezing rain from his lips, and licked a drop from the tip of his nose with her tongue. 'He only does what he sees as his duty. And I have to live with him, after all.'

She thought, for an instant, that he would say: 'No, you don't have to live with him, you can leave home and marry me.' But he didn't; and anyway it would be far more complicated than that. If she left home she would lose her inheritance, and the power and freedom which that would give her. She could use her parents' wealth to build hospitals, and benefit the poor from whom it had been taken. But to do that she had to get control of the wealth in the first place.

She had never discussed this with Sean. She was not quite sure he would understand. *I will defy my father if I choose but that doesn't give my lover or anyone else the right to mock him.*

Sean said: 'Yes. I forget sometimes. You're a fine lady and I'm just the gardener's boy.'

'Sean! Not exactly . . .'

'I know.' He stopped her mouth with a kiss, long and casual and masterful, so that she forgot the protest she might have made. Then he stood back and said: 'Home you go now, my lady. Daddy's waiting with cocoa and the Union flag.'

It was not enough to quarrel about, but she resented it nonetheless. The words were like a pat on the rump, they demeaned her. But it was probably just because he hated to see her return to a home so utterly different from his own.

As she handed her dripping coat and umbrella to Keneally in the hall, she saw her father through the open door of the drawing room. He was sitting by a blazing fire, reading the *Irish Times*, with a glass of whiskey on the table beside his armchair. He looked up as she walked in.

'Out to your Irish classes again? I should scarcely have thought it was worth it, on a filthy night like this.'

She answered in Gaelic: '*A little rain never scared a true Irishwoman yet.*'

Sir Jonathan scowled. If he understood he would not admit it. 'Don't swear at me, girl. Why the devil don't you learn more Latin, if you want to do something useful? That's what all the medicos speak, isn't it?'

'That's only to confuse the patients.' She didn't want to quarrel; she felt too relaxed and indolent for that. She stood in front of the fire, warming herself, and thought: Father looks tired and — shrunken in on himself, somehow. Why is that? 'Did you have a bad crossing?'

'Foul.' He sipped the whiskey, grimaced and said: 'This is the only thing I've kept in my stomach all day.'

'If you weren't so important, you wouldn't have to go.'

'No.' He stared at her, thinking it was a strangely unaggressive way for her to refer to his work. She looked radiant, somehow, her cheeks glowing, her wide dark eyes sparkling in the firelight. She sat on an embroidered stool in front of the fire and flicked her short dark hair from side to side, combing it with her fingers to dry it in front of the flames. He might be wrong, but she seemed unusually happy. He was glad of it; she was all he had left. Abruptly, he decided to confide in her.

'I saw Sarah Maidment in Bournemouth.'

'Oh?' A slight shiver went through her. She thought: This is it, then. He has decided to disinherit me and leave Killrath to one of her sons. If he does that I shall be free to leave home and live with Sean. In love and squalor. She asked: 'How was she?'

'Dying.' Sir Jonathan looked away from his daughter, into the fire. 'We said our goodbyes. I shan't see her again.'

'As bad as that?'

'Yes. You'll see plenty of death, if you persist with this career of yours. It's not pleasant.' He sipped his whiskey and gazed at the glass in his hand, reflectively. 'Anyway, you never liked her, I understand that. I suppose it shows loyalty, in a way.' He paused, and looked up at her. 'She was a good woman, though, whatever you think. If she'd been born with a silver spoon in her mouth, like you, she could have been as fine a duchess as any in the land.'

Catherine thought of the little dumpy woman she had met in this house during the war; charlady taking over her mother's place. In principle she agreed with what her father said; but in practice ... it was a quarrel she did not want to repeat, not now. She wondered if her father had ever thought he would take such a mistress when her mother was young and beautiful, the toast of Galway. If he had loved her and been faithful, so much would have been different. I might even have become the daughter he wanted.

There was a silence. The fire crackled and the flames cast long dancing shadows on the walls. Catherine said, slowly: 'I suppose we're all born to a certain fate, and we can't escape it completely, however hard we try.'

'Very philosophical of you, my dear.' Her father drained his whiskey glass. 'And your fate is to keep our agreement, and inherit this house and Killrath. I wish you much joy of it.'

Catherine sat on the edge of the comfortable armchair, holding out her hands to the blaze. She thought of Sean trudging back alone through the wind and sleet. 'I don't know if I *can* keep the deal, Father. Anyway, my fate may be to change things.'

'That's what you think now. But it's my fate and duty to pass on our heritage to you intact. Just as it's my duty as a father to lead you down the aisle and hand you over to a decent young man. I look forward to that day, you know.'

She looked across at him, smiling sadly. 'You may have to wait a long time, Father, I'm afraid.'

Kee put down his pen gratefully as Radford came into his office. He hated writing reports. The point of the job was to be out on the streets, observing, talking to people, making arrests. Not pushing paper around.

Radford flung an envelope on the desk and said: 'That's it, your copy of the postmortem on Savage's body. Nothing in it that you couldn't have deduced in the first two minutes. The body's being collected by relatives this afternoon and they've arranged a funeral for tomorrow.'

'With a eulogy by the priest and a massive parade of Sinn Feiners, no doubt.'

'Probably. It's in the Pro-Cathedral.' Radford hesitated. 'There's been no request for police to marshal the funeral.'

'There wouldn't be.' Kee met his colleague's eyes, and saw that the same idea had struck them both. 'No doubt young Brennan will be there.'

Radford nodded. 'Not just him, either. Chances are they'll all want to pay their respects.'

'And us without a hope in hell of getting anywhere near and coming out alive. Not without an army escort, of course.'

'I've already canvassed that idea. The military view is that it would be impossible to make arrests without endangering the public. The Volunteers will be armed, and the soldiers wouldn't know who to shoot at and who to miss. There'd be a massacre.'

'Hm.' Kee rubbed the skin behind his ear. 'That's why detectives wear plain clothes.'

'We can't just join the crowd, Tom. It'd take more than you and me to make an arrest in a place like that, and the Shinners know all the other G men by sight.'

'At least we can keep an eye on things, can't we? See who comes in and goes out? Follow young Brennan home, perhaps?'

Radford nodded. 'We can do that, Tom, at least. The funeral's at two-thirty tomorrow. I'll organize it.'

The river Blackwater swirled under the single arch of the stone bridge. The river was full, and the water had overflowed the bank in some places. The solitary fisherman had been there for most of the short winter afternoon.

He never went more than a few yards from the bridge, although there were much better stretches of the river upstream. There was nothing in his keepnet. But Andrew Butler didn't mind. For him, the excitement of the afternoon had nothing to do with fish.

During the four hours he had been there only three cars had passed him. One, as Mary Macardle had predicted, had been the black model-T Ford. Andrew had recognized the two young men in the front seat, and there had been another in the back. He was almost certain they had not recognized him.

Behind him a wood came within ten yards of the riverbank, and there was a pile of cut logs waiting to be carried away. On the opposite side of the stream, the peat bog stretched endlessly. Little white heads of cotton grass nodded in the wind, and above them, dark-grey clouds swirled from the west, carrying the threat of rain.

Andrew could see any car approaching the bridge for miles, but there was less than an hour of daylight left. After that he would have to give up, or risk ambushing the wrong car.

He had moved two of the logs from the pile by the forest to the edge of the bridge. There were two shorter lengths of wood as well, quite thick, about three feet long.

All his guns had been lost in the fire, but he had a hunting knife on his belt, in the small of his back. It was very similar to the bayonet he had used in Germany. Surprise, he knew, would be his biggest advantage. That, and the lust for revenge.

He had tried to make something of Ardmore, he thought. He had bought the horses, cherished the shrine of his mother's room, tried to settle down and ignore the devil in his mind. And now they had done this to him.

There was a movement far away, across the bog. A car, crawling towards him through the twists and winds of the road, like a little black beetle casting here and there. But there was only one way a car could go, in the end.

He focused his field glasses on it.

It was a model-T Ford.

He dragged the two logs into position across the bridge. Each log was about eighteen inches in diameter. The first one was a couple of yards below the hump on the side away from the car, the second a yard beyond that. The driver would not be able to see them until he had driven over the hump of the bridge. Each log had a large stone behind it at either end, to stop the car pushing it back. When the car came over the bridge it would hit the logs, and if the first log didn't stop it, the second would. He hoped it would be going fast. That way the passengers would be stunned and probably injured by the accident. Then he would just have to finish them off. When they were dead, he could make it look as though the car had smashed into the low wall of the bridge, and tipped into the river.

When he had finished, the car was about three-quarters of a mile away. Andrew picked up his fishing rod and stood quietly beside the bridge, watching.

It was getting darker, and when the car was about five hundred yards away rain began to fall. Great heavy drops at first, then hard lines of sleet, driven by a southwest wind.

Andrew picked up his field glasses again. He could see two men in the front, but rain blurred the lens and he could not make out their faces.

Ten yards from the bridge, the car stopped.

A man got out and fiddled with the windscreen wipers. He shouted something to the man inside but the wipers still didn't seem to work. Then he lifted the bonnet.

A second man got out and strolled down to the water. It was the butcher's assistant, Rafferty. Andrew turned his collar up, pulled his cap down low over his eyes.

Rafferty called across the stream: 'Have you caught much?'

Andrew shook his head, but didn't answer. The sleet came down even harder. Rafferty hunched his shoulders against it.

'You're mad to stay out here!' he yelled. 'Touched, man! Will we give you a lift?'

Andrew shook his head again. Rafferty shrugged and plodded back to the car.

The first man stood up and closed the bonnet. He was much shorter than Rafferty. He took off his glasses to wipe them, and Andrew could see the broad nostrils of his short snub nose, almost like a pig's snout.

The windscreen wipers were working. The two men got in, the car headlights came on, and the car drove up on to the bridge.

Andrew put down his fishing rod. The car drove over the hump of the bridge, hit the first log with a bang, and stopped.

Andrew picked up one of the three-foot lengths of wood, walked up on to the bridge, and smashed the windscreen with it. Then he swung it back again and thumped it as hard as he could into Rafferty's face.

The little man with the snub nose, Slaney, screamed and got out of the car on the far side. Andrew swung at him with the club and hit him on the arm. Then he looked to his right and saw a third man getting out of the back seat. Hardly a man, really – just a boy with a white, shocked face. He had a revolver in his hand.

There was no room to swing the club in the narrow space between the car and side of the bridge. Andrew pulled it back and jabbed it into the boy's stomach. As he doubled forwards, Andrew raised his knee into the boy's face. The revolver dropped from his fingers. Andrew pushed him backwards into the car door, bent down and picked the revolver up. He thought: Who the hell are you? And where's Davitt?

Slaney was screaming at him from the front of the car. Andrew turned and saw that he, too, had dragged a revolver out of his coat pocket. He was having trouble with it because his right arm wouldn't work and he had to hold it in his left. It was wavering, but pointing directly at Andrew.

Slaney shouted: 'Drop that now, or —'

Andrew shot him in the stomach.

It's too late now, he thought. I can't disguise this as an accident. Then he felt hands on his sleeve. The mountain of Rafferty was lurching out of the car, moaning, his face covered with blood from all the cuts of the broken windscreen. His great butcher's hands seized Andrew's right arm at the wrist and elbow, bending it back against the joint so that it would break.

Andrew screamed, dropped the revolver, and pushed against Rafferty, knocking him off balance, back into the car. As they fell, with Andrew on top, the butcher's grip loosened slightly. Andrew felt behind his back with his left hand, and pulled out the hunting knife. Pushing down with his imprisoned right hand, he arched his back and stabbed upwards with his left. The knife went up into Rafferty's throat.

Andrew jerked himself free as the fountain of arterial blood sprayed up everywhere. It spattered on the car roof, and pumped through the broken windscreen, on to the bonnet. Finish this now, he thought. The boy was struggling on his hands and knees beside the car. He looked up at Andrew and said? 'No! Please don't!' Andrew picked up the club and hit him with it, hard, at the base of the skull. Then he went to the front of the car and did the same to Slaney.

The sleet was still pouring down. He noticed it for the first time. The car was a shambles. Rafferty was still twitching and writhing in the front seat as the last of his blood sprayed out of him.

Andrew leaned over the parapet of the bridge, breathing heavily. For a moment he thought he might be sick but he was not. He spat into the water and turned round.

He had to decide what to do. The bullet and the knife wound complicated things. If they had driven hard into the logs, and he'd finished them off with the club alone, it might have looked like an accident, but not now. Nevertheless, he had to gain time, so that he was far away before the bodies were found.

He lugged Slaney and the boy back into the car. He took off the handbrake and rolled the car back down the slope to the foot of the bridge. Then he turned the steering wheel, and pushed the car hard down the bank towards the river. It was deep this side of the bridge, he knew, and the current was flowing strongly.

The car tipped one front wheel in, rolled on its side, and slipped slowly under the brown, muddy water. To Andrew's intense relief, it disappeared completely from view.

He hurried back across the bridge, and put the logs back on their pile. Then he picked up the fallen revolvers and looked at the road.

It was covered with blood.

He had a water bottle in his fishing bag, and he spent the next ten minutes carrying river water up and pouring it over the road. At the end of ten minutes the stains were less obvious. The sleet had stopped, but a steady drizzle continued to wash it away.

It was nearly dark now.

As he tried to dismantle his fishing rod, he found his hands were shaking. Carefully, he folded his arms and breathed deeply. After a few minutes, the shaking had lessened. He folded the rod, emptied his keepnet, and slung his bag over his shoulder.

When he turned round, he saw a man watching him from a car.

'Any luck?' the man asked. 'Rotten day for it, I should think.'

'Yes,' Andrew heard himself saying. 'It was fine earlier, though. I got a few.'

'Jolly good show. I say, do you want a lift?'

'No. Thanks all the same. I like the walk. It's not far.'

'Suit yourself.' The man put his head back inside his car and drove away over the bridge. Andrew watched as he disappeared into the darkness across the bog.

'Drive carefully, old chap,' he whispered to himself. 'A fellow could easily have an accident in weather like this.'

He fingered the scar on his face, wondering if the man had seen it. Then he walked quickly down the road into the forest, to the place where he had hidden his car.

9

IT WAS VERY peaceful in the church. Sean fancied he could still hear the echo of the funeral hymns murmuring to each other in the stone galleries high above his head. There was the scent of incense and candle wax, the resonance of distant footsteps, the quick mutter of prayers from the side chapels, where people knelt in the pews, clicking their rosary beads.

Martin's parents had left a few minutes ago, after the last wreath had been laid on the grave. They were ordinary farming folk from the Country Mayo: the father big, red-faced, with a wide leather belt and a suit that had seen better days; and his wife, a solid, decent woman, white-faced under her black shawl. Both had looked confused, uncomfortable at a ceremony at which they knew so few of the mourners. Michael Collins himself had helped to carry the coffin; Paddy Daly had been there too. It was risky to gather together so openly, but it would have been a dishonour to have skulked away, and sent him to his grave alone. Volunteers and kilted boys of the Fianna had kept watch outside. There was no danger in staying behind; as far as Sean could see, no known G man could have got within a half mile of the place unseen, and a detective would have needed a company of armed troops to have broken into the church itself.

They had fired a volley of shots over the grave, but there had been no speeches. As Collins had said two years ago over the grave of Thomas Ashe, the gunfire itself said everything that needed to be said.

Sean had spoken a word or two to Martin's parents, but they seemed dazed, unable to distinguish him from the crowds of other unknown friends their son had acquired. They reminded him of his own parents – solid honest country folk, anxious for their son to get on, bewildered by the discovery that he was so deeply involved with a movement of which they knew so little.

Sean had never told his parents he was a Volunteer. His father, a prosperous dairyman in the Country of Wexford, had sent his son to the Jesuits of Belvedere College in Dublin, the best school he could afford, and had been delighted beyond measure when Sean had got his place at UCD. No one else in the family had ever shown signs of joining one of the professions. His elder brother, Liam, was to inherit the business, and his three sisters seemed destined to marry farmers or tradesmen as their mother had done, and raise large families of their own. Sean had been the child prodigy – but it was because he had been at Belvedere in 1916, visiting a schoolfriend for the holidays, that he had seen the heroism and black tragedy of Pearce's Rising at first hand. The boys had slipped out, watching as much as they could, once or twice running errands, on one famous occasion smuggling two old rifles into Boland's Mill; and from then on Sean had been convinced that the cause of the Volunteers was one for him. But he had never told his family. Although the old Fenian songs could bring tears to his father's eye, it would have been a mortal shock to the old man had he learnt his brilliant son was one of them.

A shock not dissimilar to that which Martin's parents were suffering now.

Sean felt the need to confess more urgently than ever before. The guilt of Martin's death weighed him down; only a priest could absolve him of it. But it was important that, if he were to bare his soul, he should receive comfort and understanding, rather than condemnation. When he saw that Father Desmond was due to receive confession after the service, he decided to take advantage of it.

A middle-aged woman came out of the confessional box. Sean got up and stepped inside. He bowed his head close to the grill, his cap in his hand.

'Forgive me, Father, for I have sinned.'

'*Dominus sit in corde tuo.* The Lord is always ready to forgive.' The familiar comforting phrases took him back to the church at home, the fine new suit he had worn for his confirmation. 'Do your sins lie heavy on you, my son?'

'Very heavy, Father.'

'And how long is it since you have been to confession?'

'A month, Father. Maybe more.'

'That is a long time, my son. What are the sins that oppress you, which you would like to lay on the shoulders of our Lord?'

Sean took a deep breath. 'I – have sought the life of another man, Father.'

The response from the other side of the grill became less automatic. 'I see. When was that, my son?'

'I was with Martin Savage, Father. I was his friend.'

'You were one of those who sought the life of Lord French?'

'I was, Father.'

There was a pause. Sean had the impression that the priest glanced up towards the grill. But it was impossible to see a face clearly through it, even if he had wished to.

The priest asked: 'Did you do this out of hatred?'

Sean thought for a moment. 'Not out of hatred for the man, no, Father. Hatred for the things he stands for. Hatred for the oppression of our people. It was an act of war. I did it as a soldier of Ireland!'

There was a silence.

'And there is another sin, Father, greater than the first. I . . . you see, it was because of me that Martin died.' His voice cracked slightly. Although he had confessed it before, to Catherine, and to Paddy, there was an importance in telling the priest that brought the tears more easily.

The voice from the other side of the box was gentle, sympathetic. 'Take your time, my son. Tell me about it.'

So he went through it, slowly: the wait outside the station, the trouble they had had with the cart, the bomb that came too early and alerted the policeman, and then his – Sean's – shout to Martin: 'We've got to be sure of French. Can you not get closer and put a bomb right inside it?' A few seconds after those words, Martin had died.

'Were you his officer, to order him to do that?'

'No, Father. I was just his friend. We were in it together. But he died and I lived.'

As he finished Sean heard the clock chime outside, and the murmur of voices, raised, somewhere in the nave.

'My son, it was not you that killed Martin. That was done by a bullet from a British Army rifle. And it was not you that made him risk his life and run out into the road. That was a thing he chose to do. You ran into the road with him, as I understand it?'

'I did that, Father. But only afterwards. I had no bombs left, you see.'

'But it was a risk you took as well as him. You all shared it together. It has pleased God to take Martin to Himself now, and to spare you for other things. That is His way, and it is not for us to question the wisdom of the Almighty. But I am sure He did not mean you to bear a cross of blame for your friend's death. That was a matter outside your control entirely. I absolve you of it freely. Let us say a prayer together for your friend's soul, and let the burden be lifted from you.'

And it did feel like that, quite literally. As he prayed, following the priest with the ritual, healing phrases, Sean felt as though his shoulders were somehow lighter. He sat up, after the prayer, straighter than before.

'As for the motive for your action, the military ambush upon Field Marshal Lord French...' Father Desmond paused, as though seeking precisely the right words. The argument outside had not ceased. It penetrated Sean's mind dimly, as something vaguely improper in a church. The priest resumed: 'Many things are done by soldiers in war, which involve men in a burden of most grievous sin. The deliberate seeking-out of a human life is always one of them. But as in all human actions, the underlying motive in our hearts is the key which must guide us. If a man kills another in warfare or hatred or a desire for gain, that would indeed endanger his immortal soul. As his soul would be endangered if he killed with cruelty, or deliberately slaughtered noncombatants, like women and children and ordinary civilians - that would be a foul and cowardly business surely. But you have done nothing as low as that, my son. It is for you to look into your heart and be sure of two things. Firstly, that your motive for this action was pure; and secondly, that the action itself was one which you will be able to lay before the Lord God Almighty, on the final Day of Judgement. If you can do that, then the sin was a mortal one. Let us pray that it was so.'

After they had prayed together again, the priest laid a penance on Sean of twenty Hail Marys to be said every night. Then he said: 'Are there any other sins I should know about, my son?'

Sean answered: 'Oh. Well, there is one.' He had not, truly, thought of mentioning this before, but the relief the priest had given to him was so unexpectedly great, that he thought the man might understand everything. If he could confess it all, he would be able to walk out of here truly cleansed and innocent, begin his life anew as the church intended.

He said: 'I have lain with a woman.'

The priest sighed. It was a small sigh, quickly covered up, but it pained Sean greatly. The sigh implied that the sin was an ordinary one, the sort the priest had heard many times before. Sean was not sure, but it also sounded as though this sin might not be so easily forgiven as those which had gone before.

'Tell me about it, my son.'

That was not easy either. Sean felt his face grow hot. 'Oh, it . . . that's not really necessary, is it, Father?'

'If you wish to be absolved of the sin, first you must confess it, and lay it before the Lord. Tell me.'

'Well, I . . . we went to my room and, we lay together, Father.'

'You say that you lay together. Did you perform the carnal act of lust?'

'I . . . well, yes, Father, we did.'

'How many times?'

Sean's blush had gone, and his face was now quite drained of blood, white. This was awful. He felt like a Judas, whispering secrets to some spy outside the door. But all through his childhood he had been taught that the rite of confession was sacred. He whispered: 'Four times, Father. Four separate days.'

'And the girl. Was she a street girl that you paid?'

'*No!*' His denial was so vehement that he wondered if it had been heard outside. He could not stand this. He thought he would get up and leave now. But somehow he could not. The weight of everything he had learnt in childhood kept him there.

'So. Did she go with you willingly, or did you force yourself upon her?'

'Oh, Father! Willingly, of course willingly! It was an act of love, for God's sake! I should never have told you of it — it was between her and me!'

'My son! My son! Don't you understand? God was there in the bedroom with you, just as He is everywhere. Such an act of lust as you describe was a sin, not only for you, but for the girl also.'

'I'm sorry, Father, I don't want to talk about it.' Quite suddenly, Sean pulled back the curtain, and stepped out of the box. He was shaking, furious. Everything he had ever learnt told him the priest was right and yet it was not so. What did he know about it after all, the shrivelled old fool? Probably knows nothing about women except what he hears in that box.

Sean felt more than ever like a Judas. He had betrayed Cathy to the Pharisees. Still white-faced, he stalked towards the door.

A hand gripped his arm.

He brushed it off angrily. 'Leave me alone, you old eejit!' Then he saw it was not the priest at all, but a big man in a thick coat and hat. Square, determined face, short thick moustache — what the devil did he want?

Two black-robed canons were tugging at the man's coat, remonstrating with him. One said: 'Really, Inspector Kee, you cannot ... this is a holy place of sanctuary ... in the name of God, I implore you!'

Then Sean understood. He remembered the voices he had heard arguing when he had been in the confessional. The police must have come in after the service, looking for anyone who had stayed behind. The detective snatched at Sean's arm again but Sean jerked back, nearly falling over his own feet. He ran towards the door. The detective was held back for a few precious seconds by the fluttering canons, then he brushed them aside and sprinted after Sean. Sean was almost at the door when another man, big, in a thick coat like the first, stepped through it. There was a large uniformed constable behind him.

'Lord save us!' Sean turned to the right, and sprinted

back into the church, up the nave towards the altar. He heard shouts, and the clatter of shoes on the polished floor behind him. They were chasing him towards the altar, for heaven's sake! For a moment he thought of running up to it and seizing the altar table itself, claiming sanctuary indeed. But would they respect it? And where would he go then, anyway? They could just besiege the church until they got him out. He had a gun in his pocket but he couldn't use it, not here, in a holy place like this.

I will if I have to, Sean thought.

There was a door in the south transept, too, but as he ran towards it two other detectives came through it. They crouched, and held out their arms wide, like rugby fullbacks ready to bring him down. No way there.

He spun round, looking wildly to left and right. The first detective was only ten yards away, dashing up the nave. Sean tugged at the pistol in his pocket. The detective slowed. But Sean's pistol was snagged in a fold in his pocket. As he tugged at it, the detective estimated the distance and nerved himself for a final dash.

Two choirboys came out of the vestry, to Sean's right, singing sweetly. A priest in red robes, with a tall golden cross, came after them.

The vestry door! Sean slipped to his right, avoiding the detective's outstretched arms like a scrum-half, and plunged into the procession. In the narrow door itself he collided with another priest carrying a censer. He swung the man round, shoving him and the now flailing censer towards the detective, and crashed into a gaggle of choirboys. Then he was past them and into a tiny changing room littered with boys' coats. It had two doors.

Which?

He opened the first and it was a cupboard. A selection of coats and priestly robes confronted him. A mitre fell off a shelf on to the floor.

Sweet Christ! He turned and the detective was floundering towards him through the chaos of choirboys. The other door was three yards away, *towards* the detective. Sean put his hand in his pocket and this time the revolver came out without snagging.

The detective tripped, clutched a choirboy, and stood still. 'Don't shoot the boys,' he said.

Sean said: 'You stay there and I won't.' He cocked the pistol and stepped warily those three long yards across the room. Halfway there he stumbled on a satchel on the floor, and the detective crouched, ready to spring. But Sean didn't fall and the detective had a choirboy in front of him, either as a shield or by accident.

Sean reached the door. It had a key in it. He had an idea.

'Get back!' he yelled. 'Right back behind these boys! Or I'll shoot!'

The detective stepped back. When he was four yards away Sean took the key, opened the door, and stepped outside.

It was harder than he expected to fit the key in the lock on the outside. He was doing it left-handed, and he fumbled. One second gone, two – *Is there a bird's nest in this keyhole, or what?* Then the key fitted and turned.

A second later a fist smashed against the inside.

Sean looked round the churchyard. He was on the opposite side of the church from the other two entrances, and there was no policeman in sight. Twenty yards away, there was a maze of narrow streets.

He sprinted through the graveyard towards them.

Kee had laid his plans carefully. He and Radford had watched the funeral without being seen; they had identified Brennan from his photograph as he went in, and had been certain he had not come out. He had set a guard on all the main entrances to the church, and they had made their way in without being challenged by any of the Volunteers or Fianna who had marshalled the service. He had been sure the operation would restore the prestige of G Division.

Now, inside the vestry, he gave the door a kick that shook it on its hinges. Then he turned to face the gaggle of terrified choirboys and shocked priests.

'God damn it!' he shouted. 'God damn it all to bloody hell!'

The dissecting room was like a temple in hell, Catherine thought. A temple of a dozen altars, and on every altar a body, and round that body priests in white coats with knives. But it was not hell because it was too cold in here, and the bodies felt no fear.

She tested the edge of her knife with her thumb. It was sharp, like a razor – it did not rasp across her skin as she had expected, but lifted a wafer of it instead. A pearl of blood squeezed out. She wiped it absently on her white coat, and looked down.

The body of an old woman lay on the grey slate table in front of her. Human, but invulnerable. The skin pale,

waxen, rigid. The old wrinkled breasts sagged sideways;
the stomach hung in loose folds, obscene. The eyes were
closed, but the mouth – by some error the mouth was open
and the teeth gleamed, in a parody of a smile. As though
the woman had died in ecstasy, eyes closed, mouth open
and apart, head tilted slightly back, waiting . . .

For whatever was to come hereafter.

Do I look like that? Catherine wondered. Is that how
Sean sees me? How he will see me in thirty years' time?

She even looked down to see if the legs were open, knees
raised, but of course they were not. It is an obscenity to think
like this, she thought, but then everything here is obscene, all
of it, and it is not. It is how we are. The final reality.

She met the eyes of the two other girls – eyes wide and
fascinated as her own. The light in the vast dissecting room
was pale, cold, clear from the windows high in the roof; the
sound at once hushed and reverberant, as in a church or a
tomb. Most of the other groups had already begun; there
was a soft murmur of voices, a hushed intake of breath
from the tables a few yards away. But here all waited on
Catherine. She had been chosen, they had given her the
knife.

She placed it at the point of incision, in the middle of the
chest, where the ribs met, and pressed. Gently. It did not
need much pressure. The skin parted easily, like an oilskin
jacket but in silence. No sound at all of the tear that was
leaving a long red wound all the way from the solar plexus
to the navel, and beyond, below. All the way down and the
skin peeled back as though the body were that of a rabbit
or a frog, only it was not, *this is real this is a human this is
what I will be like in thirty years this is what we all are . . .*

There was a foul gurgling sound as one of the girls opposite turned away to be sick in one of the bowls provided, and a corresponding snigger from one of the boys' tables nearby. This was what the male students had expected, what one of them had already succumbed to himself. But it did not affect Catherine. She continued the incision, fascinated at the layers of fat revealed beneath the skin, the organs all more or less where the textbook had said they would be, but different sizes somehow.

And there was no blood.

Despite her care she had cut an artery. If this were a living body there would be blood everywhere, she thought, spurting up into my face and all over the floor – I would be red to the armpits. But although there was blood on her fingers and palms, there was remarkably little elsewhere. The organs, as she put the knife down and began to touch and feel and identify, were cold and slippery like meat. It was already easy to forget they were human.

Until she turned and looked at the face. Unchanged, smiling, ecstatic. Like the image of Jesus with his side transfixed by the spear, and his eyes turned up to heaven, visionary. This old woman gave her life for us, too, Catherine thought, so that people like me could study, and learn to cure others. I should not be afraid or disgusted, her body is beautiful in its way. We all are, every one of us. It is a privilege to do this, it is what I wanted to learn, I must not be squeamish now.

So all morning, white-faced, reverent and solemn, she and the other girls completed the first stage of their dissection, identifying the organs they had studied only in books, finding the fatty build-up in the heart that had led to the old woman's end, noting the impurities in her liver. There was some hilarity and attempts at horseplay from one or two of the other tables, a reaction to nerves, but Professor Connor stamped on it quickly. He too, Catherine thought, saw this place as a temple of learning, not a meat shop.

And then it was done and the old lady, whom they would come to know well over the coming weeks, was packed away in ice, her face still blind and ecstatic.

Catherine washed her hands, changed her coat, and walked out on to the front steps of UCD. Trams, bicycles, and pedestrians bustled everywhere in front of her, busy, ignorant of death. After the hushed clinical horror of the dissecting room, the winter sunshine was intoxicating. Impulsively, she ran down the steps, sending up a burst of pigeons from around her skirts, and set off towards the river.

If only Sean had been there in the morning. He had said he might have to drop out of the course for a while, but this was the first time it had come home to her. No one could qualify without completing their dissection. She had looked carefully round the room but he had not been there, not answered the roll.

She would have liked to talk about it with him. She had not been in the presence of death since her mother died, and that had been quite different. Shattering. That once proud beautiful woman frozen in her bed like a waxwork. Although she had expected it for so long, it had seemed to Catherine unbelievable, impossible. And there had been such a welter of feelings; anger, relief, and, above all, a growing resolution that *it would happen to her*. Whatever hardships come my way, Catherine had told herself, I will never turn in on myself like that, never be beaten by either men or disease. I will find out what went wrong, and take control of it.

This morning had been a small step in that direction. Death had become a little more banal, a little more approachable. She had taken the knife, she had opened the body, she had looked inside and seen how it worked and what went wrong. She knew more than before.

More than Sean, too, she thought, about that. I am a step nearer being a doctor than he is. She stood on O'Connell Bridge, feeling the winter wind cold on her face in the sunlight, and looked at the people around her. There was a mother pushing a pram, with two toddlers clinging to her skirts; some young men in flat caps leaning on the parapet; an old woman making her way slowly, carefully, across the road.

Catherine watched them all with a strange fascination. They were at once closer to her and more distant than before. The old woman had arthritis, she thought, and the bandy legs showed she had suffered from rickets in her youth. She was probably short of breath because the spinal curvature did not give her lungs enough room in the chest to breathe. Probably the liver would have those white spots on it that I saw today. I understand all that better now than I did, because I have been inside and touched it. Nothing these people think or believe matters at all, because a clogged artery or rotting liver can bring it all to an end in a moment.

But that's just why it does matter, she realized suddenly.

Any one of these people could die here on the street at any moment and not come back, not now, not ever. They would be just wax and bones and meat, like my mother and two brothers and all those millions who died in the war in France and Belgium and the old lady on the table. Each one of them had hope and love and ideas, until their bodies failed and it was all gone. That's what I want to learn, to hold death back and give them time. That's why I want to be a doctor.

She wished Sean was there to talk about it with her. Then she thought of him on the road at Ashtown and the way he had spoken of his friend Martin dying there. Death could come to Sean at any moment and *he is learning to bring it to others*. She had a sudden vision of the city as a living creature like the human body, afflicted with the disease of war. The streets were infected with British troops and police, eating up the alien bacteria so that the city's blood could be pure.

But each white blood cell only lives a short time, she thought. *Oh, God, I don't want Sean to die*. I support the revolution but I wish he were not part of it. I don't want him killed and I don't want him to do the killing either. It's too final, it's too much of a sacrilege. I couldn't bear to see Sean on the slab like that old woman this morning.

Or to see someone he'd put there.

She walked slowly along the quays by the river, thinking. Ahead of her, a young couple sat comfortably on a low wall, their arms around each other, throwing crumbs to a couple of swans. As Catherine passed, the girl threw back her head and laughed, and the boy hugged her and kissed her under the ear.

Catherine smiled, caught the girl's eye, and looked away, shivering suddenly with loneliness.

Tomorrow night, she thought eagerly. At the Gaelic League in Parnell Square. He promised to be there.

If he's still alive.

10

THE SERGEANT KNOCKED at a heavy, oak-panelled door, and ushered Andrew in. 'Mr Butler, gentlemen,' he said respectfully.

'Thank you, Sergeant. That will be all.'

It was a comfortable, medium-sized office, with a large desk facing the door. Light streamed into the room from a window behind the desk. But there was no one sitting at the desk. Three men were rising to their feet from a group of armchairs which were clustered around a cheerful fire blazing in a grate to the right. One of them came forward and held out his hand.

'Welcome, Andrew. Good of you to come.'

Two days ago Andrew had received a letter from his old commanding officer, Sir Jonathan O'Connell-Gort, asking him to come here to Dublin Castle. And since the letter had hinted at the possibility of employment, and Andrew desperately needed money to rebuild Ardmore, he had come.

Sir Jonathan indicated the other two men. 'Commissioner Radford of the Dublin Metropolitan Police. And Mr David Harrison.'

Andrew shook hands with them both. Radford was a fit, broad-shouldered man in civilian clothes, his hair parted in the middle and plastered neatly back over his head. A former athlete, Andrew thought, a rugby full-back, perhaps. Beside him, Harrison seemed small, drab, self-effacing – subfusc was the word that came into Andrew's head. He bobbed his head, proffered a limp, soft hand, and shrank back immediately into his armchair, where he crouched like a small mouse, furiously polishing his spectacles, as though the effort of getting up had caused them to mist over. Without them, his face seemed naked and defenceless; when he put them back on, Andrew was alarmed to see how his eyes appeared to grow suddenly bigger, like eggs dropped into a glass jar.

'Sit down, my boy, sit down,' said Sir Jonathan. He turned to a table where there were a number of bottles and decanters, and poured a drink. 'Cigarette?' The room was already hazy with smoke, as most of the men's clubs and offices were.

'Thank you, no.' Andrew took the drink in the elegant cut-glass tumbler, and sat quietly on the edge of his chair, waiting. He made no attempt to speak.

Sir Jonathan sat down. 'I was so sorry to hear about Ardmore,' he said. 'It was a terrible thing, a wicked crime. It must have come as a great shock to you.'

Andrew's face set grim and hard, as though he were facing the cold wind outside. 'It was a surprise, certainly. I try not to let anything shock me, any more.'

'Will you be able to build it up again?'

'I don't have the money.'

'But you will not sell up and leave. I hope? That would be a foolish thing to do now; you will get nothing for the land, in these times.'

'Oh no. I shall never leave Ardmore. That is my land, my country. I shall rebuild it one day, when I can.'

The Ulsterman, Radford, watching Andrew closely, saw something in the rock-hard utter certainty of the young man's scarred face that he could recognize. 'And the arsonists?' he asked. 'Have they been caught?'

Andrew's eyes, when he looked at the policeman, were quite cold and hard. There was no hint of amusement or irony in them. But Radford, who had been shown a newspaper report about the three young men who had drowned in the Blackwater River, felt a tinge of fear at the precision of the response.

'The police have not caught them, no. But there are many mysteries in our country which the police cannot solve.'

There was a silence. Andrew was aware that all three men were watching him intently. He looked back at each of them in turn, quite coolly, unmoved, unembarrassed. He did not venture to speak.

The silence lengthened. No one broke it. A door banged somewhere, far away down a corridor. The fire crackled, and a log fell on to the grate near Harrison's foot. The little man muttered something, turned his pebble eyes away from Andrew, and fumbled with the tongs to put the log back.

'Well, we in Dublin have had our troubles, too,' said Sir Jonathan at last. 'You read of the attempt on the Viceroy's life?'

'Yes, of course. And you have caught none of them?'

'None; except Savage, the man who was shot. The devils melt back into the slums. No one knows anything. Or if they do, they regard us as the enemy. Even Commissioner Radford's police can only venture out in armed groups.'

'I see,' Andrew said again. He thought with amusement of his solitary walk through the city this morning, and remembered how dreary and peaceful it had all seemed. 'You speak of it as though it were a war.'

'It *is* a war, Mr Butler,' said the small man, Harrison, speaking suddenly for the first time. 'I would have thought you would appreciate that, after the loss of your home.' His precise, English voice and intense pebble eyes made him seem more than ever like a mouse; or a brain perhaps, equipped only with a rudimentary body. Andrew imagined him haunting books and codes in a library somewhere, scurrying in and out among the shelves, sleeping in a lair behind the wainscot. As if to prove it, the man pulled a crumpled paper out of his pocket, and began to read:

' "*We solemnly declare a foreign government in Ireland to be an invasion of our national right which we will never tolerate, and we demand the evacuation of our country by the English Garrison.*" That is a declaration of the rebel MPs meeting in the Mansion House, and they claim that this gang of street assassins is their national army carrying out a war against the British invader. They have murdered eighteen policemen since they wrote that, and now they have come within a breath of Viscount French.'

'Eighteen policemen,' Andrew murmured. He thought of Passchendaele – 40,000 dead in a morning, for nothing. The best part of his three companies dead in twenty minutes, when they had gone over the top after the barrage. And now, all this fuss about eighteen policemen in a year. Ardmore was worth more than that.

The little man misinterpreted him. 'Yes, indeed,' he said. 'And many more to follow, no doubt. It is a real war, a shooting war, whatever is pretended in public. But our side are bound by the rule of law. We cannot fight back as we would wish. As you know.'

There was a pause. Andrew waited, but none of the three men seemed willing to break the silence, and come to the point of the interview. 'Do you not know the names of the killers?' he ventured, helpfully.

'Some of them, yes,' said Radford quietly. 'Dan Breen, Sean Treacy, Sean Brennan. There will be rewards out for them soon, and my men are looking for them every day. But they are not ... not really at the centre of it, for all their bravado. They are not the brains behind this business. I want to get at the man who sends them out to strike.'

'And that is?'

'Michael Collins.' Oddly, all three men spoke at once, but Andrew only heard the sibilant whisper of Harrison. The mousy little man hissed the name as though it were that of a snake, and the cold pebbly eyes seemed to swell with hatred. 'Collins,' he went on. 'He has eyes even in this castle, Major Butler. He knows what we are doing; he sends his men everywhere. He picks off our best detectives, chooses their most unguarded moment to send his assassins in to kill them. He may be waiting for a moment to kill all of us here. And he is their commissar, too, their paymaster. He is collecting a loan, by force and trickery, no doubt, to finance this gang of his; and he is very efficient indeed. I would not be surprised to learn that he has collected as much in the past few months as the Inland Revenue itself. And with it he can buy more guns, more bombs. We know these things are coming into the country, even if we cannot stop them. It is my job to watch this business, Major Butler, and I can assure you that in a few months it will not be just assassination we are dealing with. This man is collecting enough money to finance a major war throughout Ireland.'

'And unfortunately, he has the brains to know how to organize such a war, too,' said Sir Jonathan slowly. 'So that, Andrew, is why we want him dead.'

Another pause. The grey finality of the last word sounded out of place, shocking, in the respectable book-lined room. Andrew sat very still, feeling the pulse of adrenalin flood through his veins.

'And that is why you sent for me?'

'That is why we sent for you.'

Andrew looked at each of the three curiously. Despite Sir Jonathan's bluff, decisive manner, there was a definite air of anxiety in the room. Naturally: Andrew realized that he held the reputations of a senior army officer, a police commissioner and a senior — whatever Harrison was — between his fingers. They were proposing murder. If he refused, and told this story to the press, their reputations would shatter as easily and irreparably as if he dropped his cut-glass tumbler on to the stone grate.

He smiled, and sipped his watered whiskey. 'Why me?'

Sir Jonathan chose his words carefully. The night before had been a sleepless one for him, and he had thought about what he would say then. 'First, because you are one of the best marksmen and bravest fighting soldiers I know. I have read every one of your medal citations, and I know they speak no more than the truth. You are the equal of ten other men in battle. And secondly, because you are an Irishman who believes in the Union and the Empire, and who would lose everything if these men came to power. As you have already lost your house.'

Andrew thought for a moment. 'And also, perhaps, because you believe that the men who drowned in the Blackwater last week were not killed simply for money?' he asked softly.

'That too, perhaps. We don't know who killed them.'

'No.' Andrew held the glass between his fingers, over the edge of the grate. 'Can you not just arrest this man Collins?'

'The police are trying to do that all the time,' said Radford irritably. 'And they will continue to do so.'

'But they don't succeed,' said Sir Jonathan. 'And even if we did arrest him, we have nothing to charge him with. No witness has ever seen him carrying a gun – no witness has ever seen him at all! We could only intern him, and in a few months the government would change its mind and set him free. If he didn't charm the prison warders to do it first.'

'So you want me to murder him?' said Andrew, conversationally. He held his tumbler very gently between his fingertips; looked at it, then put it down carefully on a table.

'First you would have to find him,' said Commissioner Radford hurriedly. 'And then, officially, of course, we would like you to arrest him. But in practice that would be very difficult for one man on his own. Collins is a big man, he is likely to be armed, and certain to resist arrest. If you could get near enough to arrest him, and he were to show fight, we would not want him to escape. There would be no danger of your being prosecuted for murder, if you were to shoot an armed gunman resisting arrest.'

Andrew stared at him coldly. 'I am glad to hear it,' he said. 'I was not offering myself for prosecution. But neither, if, as you say, I am to operate alone, do I intend to give any man the opportunity to shoot at me first, in order to justify my actions. It will be murder and you know it, just as much as it is murder for the Sinn Feiners to shoot a policeman.'

Sir Jonathan rose to his feet. 'If that is how you feel about it, Andrew, then I am sorry we have troubled you. Of course we had no right to ask you such a thing. When you leave here I would be grateful if you would forget everything you have heard –'

'No, wait.' Andrew held up his hand to check the flow. 'I didn't say I would not do it, only that we must get our terms straight. You are asking me to murder a man, and promising to lie about it afterwards. I will kill him, and you will say I did it in self-defence. Is that right?'

Both Radford's and Sir Jonathan's faces were flushed, either with indignation or guilt; Andrew could not tell which. But the little mouselike figure in the corner spoke first.

'Yes, Major Butler. That is quite right.' A ghost of a grey smile flashed under the cold, pebblelike eyes, and was gone. 'Of course these gentlemen will lie for you. That would be the least you could expect. In the strict eyes of the law it would be murder, of course, but in fact you would have done a brave, daring deed for your country. Think of it as an act of war. For there is a war, whatever the strict legal position may be. The IRA have declared war upon us. They have tried to kill our most famous general. In justice they can hardly complain if you do the same to them. You would deserve the gratitude of us all.'

'I see.' Andrew looked at them each in turn, in silence. For a while no one spoke. 'And apart from gratitude, what else?'

'Two things,' said Sir Jonathan. 'You would be paid, of course – at the full rate of a major in the Intelligence Service, with six months' seniority restored. But I scarcely think you would do it just for that.'

'No,' Andrew agreed.

'And then there is a reward, of £10,000. For information leading to the arrest of Michael Collins, dead or alive. It will not be publicized, because the man is not charged with any offence. But it will be paid. You have my word as a gentleman on that. And I will give it to you in writing, too, if you wish.'

'Yes,' said Andrew slowly. 'I would like that. That would help to rebuild Ardmore.'

'So you agree? Or do you need more time?'

'Oh no,' Andrew shook his head mockingly. 'I agree. If I can have your signature on the document about the reward. And you promise to lie for me, as this man says.'

Sir Jonathan stiffened. He had hoped to avoid this, but he had meant what he said. He got up and walked to the desk. 'I have it typed here, with a copy for each of us. One will be kept here in Mr Harrison's safe. The other is for you. I need hardly stress to you that it is to be kept most secret. Its propaganda use to the enemy would be enormous.'

He took out his pen and signed two sheets of paper. Rafford and Harrison watched. Andrew took one and put it in his pocket.

Sir Jonathan held out his hand. 'Capital, my dear fellow! I knew we could count on you! And you have my word on it, there will be no repercussions. None.'

Commissioner Radford held out his hand too. 'We'll need to keep in touch, so that we can give what help we can. My department can offer some cooperation, so long as we keep your main purpose secret. You can come down to my office this minute, if you choose. We do not have much on Collins, but I can show you the files.'

'I would not dream of it.'

'What, man?'

'I said I wouldn't dream of it. Let me ask you one

question, gentlemen. Who knows of this plan, outside this room?'

The three men looked uncomfortable. 'No one,' said Sir Jonathan, awkwardly.

'No one?'

'The idea has – er – has been discussed in very general terms at the highest government level. Only along the lines that such an action would be a blessing to the country. No more than that.'

The highest government level. That could only be the Cabinet itself. Churchill, Fisher – Lloyd George, even. Andrew considered. This meant he could count on full support from everyone who mattered. Insofar as anyone could ever rely on politicians. These three men were asking him to do the government's will.

On the other hand, politicians were notoriously bad at keeping secrets. He looked at Sir Jonathan carefully.

'My name has not been mentioned?'

'My dear chap, no! Of course not!'

'So the details of this plot have been thought up by you three gentlemen on your own?'

'If you choose to put it like that, yes.'

'Good. That is how it must remain. I shall not come to police headquarters, Commissioner Radford – not now, nor at any time. As you say, you have already lost most of your best officers. That can only mean that someone in your force is feeding information to Collins. If he hears about me, I shall be dead on the street in a day. I do not want my name to be mentioned by you to any person at any time. Is that clear?'

Radford flushed. 'Of course. But surely you don't mean

to proceed without any help from us at all? My men are not all traitors and fools, you know!'

'I hope not, for your sake. But I cannot run the risk. I'm no good at disguises and I don't intend to use them. Indeed, with a face like mine I could not. What I can do, though, is cooperate with you personally. Any equipment or information which I need, you can bring to me at an address which I will give you.'

Reluctantly, Commissioner Radford agreed. He took a small, creased photograph out of his pocket and gave it to Andrew.

'That,' he said, 'is all most of my officers have to go on. It is the only photograph that we have of Michael Collins. If you can identify him from that, you're a better detective than I am.'

Andrew looked at it. It was a blurred, overexposed picture of a man with black hair brushed sideways across his forehead, a round, rather heavy face, with a strong chin and dark, shadowed eyes. The face was staring at the camera, rather vacant, lost – like a young man leaving home, Andrew thought, off to the war or a job in a distant city.

'It was taken in 1916, after the rebellion. He was being sent away to prison in England with the rest. They spent the next six months in a camp at Frongoch, in North Wales.'

Living off the fat of the land, after they had tried to shoot us in the back, Andrew thought. While I was stuck in Flanders, knee-deep in mud and bones.

The young man in the photograph looked awkward, vulnerable; but Andrew did not feel sorry for him at all.

11

WHEN ANDREW'S GERMAN grandparents had first visited Dublin, in the 1880s, they had bought a three-storey terraced house in Nelson Street. It was not very grand, for the parents were not that rich, but it was in a decent enough street, which at the time looked as though it might become fashionable. It had not done so, but that was not his parents' fault. His mother had loved the house, and Andrew, in turn, had lived in it as a student. Now it was the only house he owned; a private, lonely place full of mould and damp and memories, where he could brood without interruption. A place, too, where no hotel porter or waiter working for Sinn Fein could report on him as a visiting British officer. He had not realized how important that was, until he had met Sir Jonathan in the Castle.

After the meeting he sat alone in his living room, smoking. The smoke curled in lazy circles above him, obscuring the ceiling. He considered the possibilities.

Killing Collins would be easy enough. He could do it with a gun, a knife, a bomb, with his bare hands if necessary. Andrew had killed enough men to know that all he needed was surprise and utter determination. The problem was how to find the man. The more he thought about that, the more impossible it seemed.

Collins was able to move freely around Dublin because half of the city supported him, and the other half was afraid or didn't want to become involved. Andrew had no doubt that any phone call he made, any letter he sent to the police or the army, could be intercepted by Sinn Fein workers in the Post Office. Hotel staff, delivery boys, news vendors, hospital nurses, doctors, shop assistants — any of these might be Sinn Fein supporters, ready to pass along information they thought suspicious, not to the police, but to the IRA. This was what the government's clumsy policy of coercion, delay, and deceit had led to: exactly the opposite of the normal situation, in which the public supported the police.

But the politics of it were not Andrew's concern. The Republicans had burnt his home, they had conspired with Germany during the war and killed his mother; that was enough for him. But how would he go about finding the man?

He imagined himself wandering the pubs and hotel bars in the city, striking up conversations with strangers, asking if they had seen Mr Collins lately. Perhaps he could pull the photo out of his pocket to jog their memories, offer them a small reward? The idea was absurd; the Shinners would be on to him as soon as he opened his mouth. And once seen, his face was against him: he was so much easier to recognize than other men.

Perhaps he could offer to join the Volunteers, saying he

had fought in the war and seen the light? Not impossible, but highly unlikely. They would be suspicious, check up on him. If they found out he was a landlord, they would never believe him; so he would have to invent a whole new identity. And even then it was highly unlikely he would get to see Collins: he would be a new recruit, given simple duties at first, watched to see how well he did.

So how *could* he get near the man? Collins was Finance Minister as well as being in charge of Intelligence operations and assassinations of the police. Andrew wondered about the embossed receipt Slaney had tried to sell him at Ardmore. A receipt printed with the signature of Michael Collins. What would Slaney have done with the money once he had collected it? Brought it up to Dublin, probably, delivered it to the Finance Minister in person. What if Andrew took his place? He could turn up with a bag of notes, and shoot the man while he counted them.

Fine. But how would he know where to take the money? Only by catching someone like Slaney, and forcing the information out of him. The man would not only have to be tortured to get the information, he would have to be kept out of circulation so he couldn't warn Collins afterwards. There might be passwords, well-known meeting places, couriers to collect the money at the station. Couriers who knew who normally brought them the money.

Too complicated, Andrew thought. Another bad idea.

He stubbed out his cigarette, and pulled the blurred photograph of Michael Collins out of his pocket. This was the only picture they had, of a wanted man who was a Member of Parliament and holder of four posts in a rebel government – one three-year-old cutting from a group photograph.

He stared at it for a long time, but it told him nothing. I have to get into that man's mind, he thought. If I am going to catch this beast, I must learn to think like him. I need something that will take me straight into his presence, without anyone being suspicious about my face or my background. But what?

Abruptly, he stood up, put the photograph away, unlocked his door, and strode downstairs into the street.

He crossed the river and strolled across St Stephen's Green, looking at the ducks and mothers pushing prams. In one corner toddlers were playing hide-and-seek in some irregular, grassy ditches – the remains of the trenches that the Citizen Army had dug on the first, heady morning of the Rising in 1916. Andrew smiled contemptuously. What utter amateurs, to dig trenches in the middle of a city square, overlooked by tall buildings! Most of the British Army has spent four years trying to get out of the foul deathtrap of the trenches, and fight a war in the open – these play actors couldn't wait to dig them in the middle of a city park. They had even laid out a picnic in a summer-house, he had heard. But the moment they had fired on the Shelbourne Hotel, they had scampered away to the College of Surgeons, leaving their cucumber sandwiches and soft drinks behind.

Collins had brought the IRA a long way since then. They no longer stood up like statues waiting to be shot at, they disappeared into the sea of people. But they were not strong enough to take on the British Army, whatever they pretended. They'd need whole shiploads of German guns for that, not just the single one which had scuttled itself off Cork in 1916. But the war is over, it's too late to ask Kaiser Bill for help now.

Isn't it?

Andrew checked in his stride, nearly running over a small child who was chasing a hoop. The germ of an idea began to hatch in his mind. He lit a cigarette, his fingers trembling slightly with excitement. Perhaps. It wasn't all clear yet, but he could see no immediate objection. He smiled, and began to walk back past Trinity College, waiting for the details to emerge in his mind.

If I were Michael Collins, he thought, I might just be interested in that.

'Lord save us!' Michael Collins's voice boomed across the little room. Paddy Daly looked up curiously.

'Whatever is it now, Mick?'

Collins waved a big hand impatiently. 'Wait till I've finished. Then you'll see all right!' He laughed, drummed his fingers on his desk, and gave a whistle of pure amazement.

Sean watched, bemused. It was an impromptu meeting of the Dublin division of the IRA. He himself had brought in the letters, one of which Collins was now reading. The others in the little upstairs room in Bachelor's Walk – Paddy Daly, Liam Tobin, Mick McConnell – sat around smoking or waiting patiently. Richard Mulcahy, the IRA Chief of Staff, was also there, as was Cathal Brugha, the Dáil's Minister of Defence.

Collins was always like this – restless, ebullient, so bursting with his own energy that no one could survive five minutes with him without being overwhelmed by the force of his personality. He worked twice as hard as other men, twice as fast; and with so much noise that no one else could do anything without being interrupted once a minute.

Now, as he sat at the desk reading a letter, a smile of pure delight shone out of his face like the sun; and was then chased away by a frown of deepest suspicion, equally theatrical. He finished the letter, and drummed his fingers again noisily on the table, deep in thought. Then he suddenly laughed, and threw himself back on his chair, so that he banged against the wall, resting on its two back legs. Collins was a very big man, fifteen stone at least, and the flimsy chair creaked ominously under the treatment. He pushed his thick black hair away from his forehead, and beamed at the others.

'Now listen to this, you lot!'

As if they could do anything else.

He flourished the letter dramatically, and began to read.

> *Lambert's Hotel*
> *Dublin*
> *12 January 1920*

Mr Michael Collins
Minister of Finance
The Mansion House
Dublin

Dear Mr Collins
I write to you in the strictest confidence, and you will treat this letter accordingly, I trust.

I had the honour, until November 1918, in the army

of His Majesty Kaiser Wilhelm II, to be an officer. During the time of the war, I was to the General Staff attached, and met several times with your esteemed countryman Sir Roger Casement, he who later so tragically in London was hanged. As you know, Mr Casement was in Germany hopeful of recruiting Irish prisoners of war to fight in Ireland against the British; and also he wanted to buy many guns for you and your country in your war of national independence to use. Despite the needs of our own soldiers, we were able to provide 20,000 rifles which we from Russian prisoners had taken, together with 4 million cartridges, and 10 machine guns. Most unfortunately, these weapons did not reach you, because our Captain Spindler was forced to sink his ship, the Aud, near Cork to avoid capture by the British Navy.

I think perhaps you will share with me my belief, Mr Collins, that had these weapons reached you, the course of the war, and of your country's history, might well changed have been. I say this as one who knows it well that you yourself fought against the British Imperialists in Dublin that Easter of 1916.

'It's a rum sort of English he writes,' said Paddy. 'All the words in the wrong places, somehow.'

'Probably because the man's a German,' said Collins. 'Or if he isn't he wants us to think he is.'

I write to you now because, at the end of the war, into my possession there fell some 20 Maxim water-cooled machine guns, and one million cartridges. I do not have to tell you, perhaps, that these guns by far the most effective small-arms weapon were on either side during the entire war; on one occasion I myself witnessed two of them destroy a Scottish battalion in ten minutes.

Also, I have nearly one hundred Mauser Selbstlade-pistole C-96, and some Parabellum Artillery pistols, which I can sell to you. You will understand, I suppose, that so far all in my power has been done these weapons out of the hands of the British and French armies to keep. However, I myself do not need them; whereas it occurs to me that perhaps you do. I, on the other hand, need money. As you are the Finance Minister in your government, it may be possible that we can do business.

For such a deal, I must meet you personally. I am resident in this hotel for the next week. If this idea interests you, please make contact. If not, you will destroy this letter, I trust.

Your most sincere and humble servant,
Count Manfred von Hessel.

'There you are!' Abruptly Collins slammed his chair forwards, stood up, and began to pace up and down, his hands in the trouser pockets of his thick suit. 'Well, boys, what do you think?'

'We could surely do with them,' said Richard Mulcahy. A lean, fit, intense young man, he had led by far the most effective action outside Dublin in 1916. Unlike every one inside the city at that time, Mulcahy had believed in a war of speed and movement. His brigade had attacked the British, engaged them in small, destructive actions, and then got away – as the Boers had done in South Africa. It was a strategy he and Collins favoured for all units now. There were to be no more grand symbolic martydoms.

Cathal Brugha looked at him sarcastically. A man of undoubted bravery, Brugha found it hard to maintain friendly relations with his more energetic colleagues. 'The pistols, maybe,' he said. 'But not Maxim guns, surely? Have you seen the size of those things? Where are you going to fire them – down O'Connell Street?'

'I was thinking more of the country,' said Mulcahy patiently. 'With a weapon like that, our lads in west Cork and Wexford could take on a whole company of British troops and hope to beat them.'

'Sure, and then they'd send over four more regiments,' Brugha snapped back. 'I've told you before, what we need is to send someone over the water to kill Lloyd George and the British Chief of Staff. That'll bring it home to them. And we won't do that with a heavy machine gun.'

'But we could have done with one at Ashtown!' Collins burst in irritably. 'By God, if we'd had one of these things there, young Martin would still be with us, and Johnny French would not!'

'We could that,' Paddy Daly agreed, glancing at Sean. The young man should not really be in on this discussion, he thought. But I'd trust him with my life; it cannot do much harm. 'What troubles me,' he went on thoughtfully, 'is two things. First, how much does the fellow want for them?'

'A lot, I should think!' said Collins. 'That's why he wants to talk to me. Minister of Finance, do you not see it here, at the top of the letter? The man thinks he's writing to a Rockefeller!'

'Well, that's right. We've not collected all the poor folk's savings just to hand them to some German count. But there's another thing, now, Michael. Is this fellow genuine at all?'

'And how does it matter if he's not? Do you think I'll be signing him a cheque just for a pretty picture in a catalogue? No guns, no pay, it'll be, Paddy!'

'I know that, Michael. But does it not strike you too that his is just the sort of pretty fly the British might float on the water to see if we bite? Twenty big Maxim guns would take a deal of carrying. If this man is not all he seems, we'll be leading our lads into one hell of a fine ambush when we take delivery.'

'That's for us to arrange when we're convinced he's got them,' Collins said. 'But first you're right; we need to know if the fellow's genuine. What do you make of the letter?'

He passed it round.

'It's proper hotel paper,' said Mulcahy. 'And the English is funny, as Paddy said. That could mean he's German.'

'Or it could mean he just wants us to think he is.'

'Why Lambert's Hotel, of all places?' said Brugha suddenly. 'That's a favourite with old lady dowagers from the colonies, isn't it? If he speaks English as badly as he writes it, he'll stick out like a sore thumb in a place like that.'

'That's true.' Collins sat on the edge of his desk, rubbing his face thoughtfully with the palm of his hand. 'But I don't have to meet him there. Look, this is what we'll do. I'll write to the fellow and agree to a meeting in a couple of days. Paddy, you go to see him, and if you think he's the genuine article, fix up a time and place. You can take young Sean here and keep watch on him. Find out where he goes, what he looks like, who he meets. That shouldn't be too hard, even in Lambert's. Do you think you can find time in your love life for that, young Sean?'

As always when Michael Collins smiled at him, Sean felt warmed by an inner fire. Despite the man's overbearing ebullience and rowdiness, there was a blaze of energy within him that drew all the Volunteers towards him like moths round a flame. He knew all their names, what they had done, where they came from. His mastery of detail incorporated not only his financial work, his intelligence service, and the administration of the Dublin Volunteers, but also the humanity of the young men and women who worked for him. Those whom he valued he would work into the ground; but they always knew that Collins himself was working harder. If one man can ever gain Ireland's freedom, Sean thought, he can.

He was a little embarrassed that Collins knew of his affection for Catherine. Collins had met her at the Gaelic League, even given her a great big hug when he heard how well she spoke the language. But then Collins did not know, of course, that she had visited him in his new room; and for all his bluff physical heartiness Sean was not sure how Collins would take that. After his experience with the priest, he didn't want to find out.

So he blushed, grinned back boldly, said: 'A few minutes, Michael, maybe. I'll fit it in while the lady's doing her hair.'

Collins growled at him and gave him a mock punch in the chest. 'It's more like a few days this is going to be,

Seaneen! You joined up to be a soldier, not a love-sick poet, you know! I want you to find that German and watch him just like he was the Countess Cathleen herself – or Mata Hari, if that's what you young fellows prefer. If your young lady's lonely the while, send her to Uncle Michael – I could do with some lessons in the Gaelic. Now clear off out of it – we've serious business to discuss!'

12

As MICHAEL COLLINS had said, Lambert's Hotel was not the sort of place where Sinn Fein supporters often stayed. Neither was it a place well known to officers of the British Army – people who might know Andrew and be surprised to see him addressed as Manfred von Hessel. The hotel was, in fact, a moderately genteel establishment favoured by the elderly. There were several permanent residents, old ladies and gentlemen who tottered in and out amongst the potted palms and giant aspidistras that were a feature of the place. They had their own set routine: coffee each morning in the heated conservatory, where the proprietor's pet canaries were allowed to flutter freely in the luxuriant foliage overhead, bringing back reminiscences, for some, of younger days in Malaya and Burma; their own tables in the dining room, with the best views of cold winter streets outside; and evenings for bridge and whist each Tuesday, Thursday, and Saturday.

The owners of the hotel, in their sixties themselves, cherished these ancient residents just as they cherished the plants, the antique, polished furniture and the exquisite arrangements of dried flowers and stuffed birds that were everywhere under bell jars, to keep them free of dust. Their other clientele – middle-aged commercial travellers, and foreigners visiting the city for the races, perhaps, or the theatre – were treated with a detached, gentle courtesy that made it clear to them that they were guests in a unique establishment with unchanging traditions and a quiet, restful charm all of its own.

After a day or so, most guests either decided that they liked it, or left, shaking their heads in despair.

Andrew – as Manfred von Hessel – liked it very much.

He liked it for several reasons. First, no one who knew him as Andrew Butler would ever come to a place like this. Second, it was highly improbable that there were any active Sinn Feiners on the hotel staff. The staff were mostly too old, and lost in a dreamy backwater, to care about such matters. So his room was unlikely to be searched, or his movements spied on. And third, he hoped the hotel would appear to Collins as a plausible, if slightly eccentric, choice for a foreigner who wished to avoid the unwelcome attention of the authorities. Hotels used by Sinn Feiners might at any time be searched by the police or army, and Manfred von Hessel would naturally want to avoid any risk of that.

But the fourth reason was that it was only five minutes' walk from his own town house, in Nelson Street.

Apart from an elderly housekeeper, Mrs Sanderson, who came in once a week, the house was empty. The solitude pleased him. In the evenings, he sat alone by his fire, brooding, and listened to the occasional shout or clatter of sound from the street. He felt a little like a ghost, and relished the thought.

He had had a second key made, for Radford.

Andrew hated the idea of cooperating with Radford at all. But if it had to be done, they would have to meet face to face — telephones or letters were impossible. And so the house in Nelson Street was a godsend.

He had met Radford there twice in the past week — once to explain his plan, once to take delivery of a leather bag with two oilskin packages in it. The second time he had shown Radford his letter to Collins before it was sent. They had agreed to meet tonight at eight o'clock, to discuss the response, if any. Andrew hoped someone would have got in touch with him before then.

The first approach came at four o'clock. He was sitting in the conservatory of the Lambert Hotel, sipping tea. There was an animated discussion at the table opposite him, about the relative merits of Raffles Hotel in Singapore, and the Imperial in Colombo. Andrew listened with amusement. The canaries flitted to and fro in the shrubbery, and he wondered what would happen if they dropped something unpleasant in the old people's tea.

An elderly waiter pushed aside a swathe of dangling greenery. 'Mr von Hessel? I'm sorry to trouble you, sir, but there is a gentleman to see you.'

'So? Send him through, please.'

In a few moments the greenery was moved aside again, this time by a large, healthy-looking Irishman in a thick coat and flat cap. He looked suspicious and ill at ease in these surroundings, as Andrew had expected he would.

'Mr von Hessel?'

'Yes.' Andrew smiled, stood up, clicked his heels together with a small bow, and held out his hand, in the way that his mother's German relations did. The Irishman shook hands, frowning.

Andrew said: 'And you?'

'Er – Daly. Patrick Daly.'

'Will you sit down? Some tea, perhaps?'

'No, thank you.' Paddy Daly glanced irritably at the ancient residents, who were scrutinizing him avidly from their table behind two potted palms. 'Look, is there somewhere else we could talk? It's a private – a business matter.'

'As you wish.' Andrew turned, and bowed politely to the old people. 'You will excuse us, I hope. Some day I must speak to you of the delights of the Hotel Otto von Bismarck in Dar es Salaam. This way, please, Mr Daly.'

He led the way to his rooms on the third floor. He had a

sitting room and a bedroom, both facing out on to the street. Andrew lit the oil lamp and indicated an armchair, but before he sat down, Daly walked to the window and stood there, gazing out.

'A fine view you have, Mr Hessel,' he said.

'It is a beautiful city, in the daytime,' Andrew agreed. But now, at four o'clock, it's getting dark, he thought. And no doubt you make a fine silhouette there in the lamplight, for whoever is watching from the street outside. So now your friends know which room I'm in. It's as good a way of signalling as any.

'I have a letter for you.' Daly held it out.

Andrew broke the seal and read.

> *Dáil Eireann*
> *c/o The Mansion House*
> *Dublin*
>
> *14 January 1920*
> *Count Manfred von Hessel*
> *Lambert Hotel*
>
> *Dear Count von Hessel,*
> *I have received your proposal which is, on face value, very interesting to me. I will meet you within the next few days. The arrangements will be made by the bearer of this, whom you may trust absolutely.*
> *Michael Collins*
> *Minister of Finance.*

Andrew refolded the letter, slipped it back into its envelope, and tapped it on his knee reflectively.

'So, Mr Daly,' he said. 'You are a colleague of Mr Collins. Shall we say a soldier of the Irish Republic?'

'You can say that,' Daly agreed. *And who the hell are you?* he thought, as he studied the face before him. The left cheek was horrifically scarred; the white ridge of the scar zigzagging across it like the track of some drunken, sharp-toothed snail; but the rest of the face was sharp, cold, intelligent. Daly had not met any Germans before. He only knew of the propaganda stereotype: square head, bulging eyes, broken, snarling teeth. This man was nothing like that; but then of course he wouldn't be. That was all lies put about by the British. This man seemed suave, confident, with the arrogance of an English landlord. Yet he had those funny foreign mannerisms, and the accent seemed genuine enough.

Nonethless, Daly was suspicious. Bluntly, he said: 'You say you've got some machine guns to sell. Where are they?'

Andrew raised an eyebrow. He took out a cigarette case, offered one to Daly, and, when the Irishman refused, tapped his own reflectively against the hard metal of the case before lighting it. His voice, when he spoke, was deliberately sharp.

'I had asked for my proposal to be kept in strictest confidence, but I see you know everything. How many others, then?'

Daly was impressed by his tone. 'Not many. Only the inner council. I'm the officer in charge of the Dublin Squad. I have to know. Where are these Maxim guns?'

'In Germany.' Andrew took a drag of his cigarette and waved his hand contemptuously around the hotel room.

The gesture asked: You think I could hide them here? He gazed at Daly calmly, assessing his strength. No fool, he thought; no weakling either. He doesn't trust me, and if he decides his opinion is right, he'll kill me without a thought.

Andrew decided to humour him. 'I have the pistols here, of course. You will like to see them, perhaps?'

He got up and fetched a folding leather bag from a wardrobe. He lifted out an oilskin bundle, unwrapped it carefully, and held out an automatic pistol. It was heavy, clean, well-greased.

Daly looked mildly interested. 'I've used them. Nine-mm Parabellum. But it's got a longer barrel than ours.'

'Correct,' Andrew said. The weapon was nearly a foot long. 'This is the artillery model. Much more accurate than the small one, and the sight – is that how you say? – this aiming part, is good for 800 metres. Also, it is possible to fit with this – what we call snail magazine – to hold thirty-two cartridges instead of eight.'

Andrew passed over the pistol and magazine. Both were empty; there was no sense in taking unnecessary risks. Daly played with them curiously for a few moments.

'Interesting,' he said. 'But it's a big thing to carry round in your pocket. Have you not got any of the smaller ones?'

'Unfortunately not. Most officers at the front required the best possible aiming power. I have also this.' Andrew unwrapped a second oilskin bundle, to reveal an equally large pistol with a magazine in front of the trigger guard, and a large red number 9 stamped on the butt. 'Mauser *Selbstladepistole* C-96. Also fires 9-mm Parabellum cartridge.'

Daly examined that too, clearly impressed with the weight and quality of the weapons. 'All right,' he said. 'Still, it's a pity you didn't bring the Maxims.'

Andrew reached inside his jacket pocket, took a photograph out of his wallet, and passed it across. 'You have not seen a Maxim, perhaps. Here. I have twenty like this.'

Daly looked at the photograph. Despite his suspicion, he was fascinated. The gun was short: about two and a half feet long, perhaps. It was mounted on a low four-legged stand slightly longer than itself. There was a periscope sight at the rear end, and the gunner presumably gripped the gun and fired by looking through this and holding on to two handgrips just below it. There were pads on the rear two legs of the stand, for him to rest his elbows on. There was no stock, so he imagined the stand absorbed most of the recoil. The bullets were fed in by a belt from the side, and a curious long rubber hose trailed from the covered muzzle, ending in what looked like a squashy foot-bellows.

'What's this?' he asked, pointing.

Andrew smiled. 'The gun is water-cooled, you understand? When the barrel is hot, the water becomes steam. But we do not want the enemy to see steam rising from our firing positions, and also it wastes water. So the steam goes down this tube, into the bag, and it ... how do you say? It cools and is water again.'

'It condenses,' Daly said. It looked a highly effective piece of precision engineering, almost like a telescope, rather than a gun. The bottom of the stand had a number of solid-looking screw callipers around it, no doubt to enable the gunners to aim it precisely at a pre-set target.

Andrew was gratified by the Irishman's obvious interest. Elaborating his role as arms salesman, he said: 'That is the most efficient weapon of its kind in the world. I myself have seen two of them destroy a battalion in five minutes.'

It was nearly a true story. Andrew himself was one of the four who had survived. He felt a sudden rush of pain and anger at the memory, and stilled it by biting the inside of his lip.

'A beautiful piece of German engineering.'

'Thank you.' Andrew remembered how quiet the water-cooled Maxims had been, after the bludgeoning artillery. Tick, tick, tick – like a distant woodpecker. And we all fall down.

Daly handed the photograph back, and met his eyes. 'It looks too heavy for us to use in the city, of course, but out in the country – it'd be pure bloody murder.'

'As you say.' Andrew took a soothing drag on his cigarette, and watched Daly calmly. You're hooked now, Paddy, he thought.

'So how did you get them, Mr Hessel?'

'I was an officer in the General Staff, with responsibility for – what is it you say? – supply. I control the trains from the factory to the front. When the armistice comes . . .' He shrugged and blew a smoke ring. 'The railway runs close to my father's *Schloss*. Underneath it are many cellars.'

'So how will you get them to us?'

'That is my problem. First, we must make an agreement about the money. And for that I need Mr Collins.'

'This country isn't rich, you know,' said Daly.

Andrew stubbed out the cigarette decisively. Humouring Daly had gone far enough, he decided. 'Perhaps not. But I don't negotiate with you. I make my business with Michael Collins only, understand? Him and me alone together.'

Daly scowled. 'Oh no, you won't be alone. Mr Collins is a bit too important to us for that. The most important man in Ireland, probably. I'm his bodyguard.'

That's pity, Andrew thought. But he waved his hand again, dismissively. 'All right, guards, I do not mean guards. I mean, the business of the guns must be made between him and me alone, you understand? I will not negotiate with any underofficers.'

Daly nodded. 'That's clear enough,' he said. 'He's the boss. But it won't be for a day or two. Mr Collins is a busy man.'

'I too am busy. I leave Dublin on Friday. If you do not want the guns, say so. Otherwise, I must know where and when to meet.'

Oh no you don't, Paddy thought. No appointments booked days ahead, so that you can have a regiment of tanks waiting outside when we get there. He said: 'You'll find that out when I come and get you. Not before.'

Andrew thought carefully. This was what he had feared. Radford had insisted that the police must be involved; but conditions like this were going to make it impossible. If so, Radford would just have to accept it.

He said: 'You do not trust me with an address?'

No, I don't, Paddy thought. But on the other hand, it'll be a test. And we've got young Sean outside to follow it through. He said: 'Do you know Brendan Road?'

As he spoke, he watched Andrew's eyes carefully. Was there a flicker there, a slight involuntary acknowledgement that he had given away a vital piece of information? Paddy wasn't sure. The cold, hard nature of the man had begun to impress itself upon him. Perhaps the German was genuine. Certainly he could have been a soldier – a tough one at that. He knew what he wanted, too; and the story of the guns was plausible enough.

Andrew said: 'No. But I can hire a cab, if you tell me the number.'

Daly said: 'Forget it. It's better for me to meet you here. I'll come tomorrow – either between ten and half past in the morning, or between four and five in the afternoon. Will that do?'

Andrew could think of no reasonable objection, so he agreed. Daly stood up to go. Before he left, he strolled casually to the window again, where anyone in the street outside could see him.

When he had gone, Andrew slipped through to his bedroom, where the lamp was not lit. He stood as far back in the room as he could, so that no light would shine on him from outside.

He saw Daly cross the street quickly. There was a young man in a flat cap, lounging in the doorway opposite, who made the mistake of watching Daly all the time as he crossed the road. Daly did not stop or turn his head as he walked past the young man, but Andrew thought some words passed between them, nonetheless.

He smiled, stood still, and watched his watcher watching him.

It was cold in the street, and shortly after Paddy Daly came out, it began to rain. Sean turned up his collar and shrank back as far as he could into the doorway. Even so, he felt conspicuous. It was clear he had no business in the building, and he had been there an hour already. Then a man came out of the door, unexpectedly, and Sean moved away with a hurried apology.

He took to pacing up and down the street, looking as though he were going somewhere, but never allowing himself to get quite out of sight of the hotel entrance. The rain settled into a steady downpour, and began to soak through the shoulders of his coat and drip from the peak of his cap.

He still hadn't even seen the German. Paddy Daly hadn't stopped to speak to Sean in the street, but he had sent a complete description to him, via Frank Brophy, the lad who was watching the back. 'He's a tall fellow,' Frank said. 'Twenty-five to thirty years old. Left cheek all scarred to hell. Quite fit, strong-looking, like an army officer. Black hair, little pencil moustache. Very cool-looking customer, Paddy says. Not likely to be any others like him in that hotel.'

I hope not, Sean thought. In some hotels there are dozens of men like that. Even with a few scars, missing eyes, faces half blown away. But very few came and went into Lambert's; and certainly most of the customers here were old.

The street became busier after six o'clock, and Sean stationed himself directly outside the main entrance, a damp newspaper in his hands. The oil lamp in the German's room was still on, he noticed. The smell of cooking drifted out towards him, and an ancient couple paid off their horse-drawn cab and stepped into the foyer. Sean imagined the German officer marching smartly downstairs, bowing stiffly to all the waiters, and settling down with a sigh of satisfaction in front of fresh warm rolls, butter, and a piping hot bowl of soup.

He began to think of Catherine.

They were due to meet later that evening, at the Gaelic League. It looked as though he was going to disappoint her. He had left a note there earlier, for her to find. The note apologized but didn't explain why. She would have to realize, if he was on active service, he couldn't always be clinging to her skirts.

Active service, indeed! The rain had begun to trickle into his socks now. A sudden, painful vision came to him of Catherine in his room by the hot, blazing fire, with no skirts on at all . . . It was so overwhelming he nearly walked away that very moment.

When he had met her, he had never believed such a fine thing could happen to him. He had not even been able to imagine it. The girls he had known, his sisters, the girls of his village, had been ordinary, bumptious creatures, with their share of snub noses, gawkiness, giggles, silly secrets, bossiness, generosity, and love of children. There had been no mystery to them; no sense that eventual marriage would be anything more than a further round of the same, with a wife becoming rounder and more distant and harassed as her children multiplied around her. To the young Sean, women provided cooking and comfort and children and control. They were something a young man would want to escape from as long as he could; his own father, like most men in the village, had not married until he was nearly forty.

Catherine had awakened something in him which he had not known existed. From the moment he had seen her he had not been able to get her out of his mind. He had wanted to talk to her just so he could watch the way she spoke, admire the perfection of her hands so close to his on the book. Images of her had filled his dreams at night. The graceful way she walked obsessed him; he imagined her swinging into the saddle of a great brown hunter, leaping hedges, cantering along country roads. She was very fit, yet so slender. He was fascinated with the way her body contrasted with those male ones he had wrestled and struggled against on the school sports field, and was overcome with tenderness, a desire to hold and touch . . .

As he had now done. He had not slept for hours after she had left him the other night. The vision of her had stayed with him so clearly he had thought he might be arrested in the street for following a naked ghost. And the day after he had found it so hard to think about what Paddy Daly was saying that his orders had to be repeated three times.

He knew it was a sin, but he did not want to see it as the priest had. Once or twice when he was alone he felt shame, but that was for the squalor of his room, for the fact that he could offer her no home, no future. But that seemed so far away when he saw her; it did not matter.

The other reason for shame was that she was taking him away from his duties. The future of the Republic might depend on his surveillance of this German officer, and here he was, remembering the touch of her thighs ...

A man came down the steps of the hotel, briskly, and set off across the street, dodging between the traffic. He had his back to Sean, his coat collar turned up against the rain, and a soft hat pulled down over his eyes.

Is that him? But I didn't see his face, Sean thought, I can't tell.

The man was moving so quickly along the far side of the street that in a moment he would reach the crossroads and be gone. Sean glanced inside the foyer, then set off hurriedly after him.

At the crossroads the man turned left. Sean was on the wrong side of the road. A motor lorry was coming towards him on one side, and an ancient hansom cab clattering along on the other.

Sean dashed out between them.

When he reached the crossroads, the man was gone.

There were a group of men staggering out of a pub, and beyond them, no one at all.

He sprinted down the side street towards the next junction, nearly forty yards away. When he got there, there was no sign of the man in either direction. Only then did he think to look back.

I've lost him, he thought. I've lost the bugger in ten seconds flat!

It had been even easier than Andrew had hoped. Before he

had left the hotel, he had checked from his window that O'Shaughnessy's Bar on the corner had, as he remembered, an entrance in the main street as well as another round the corner. He had gone round the corner, stepped in at one entrance, glanced through the windows to see Sean sprint past, and calmly walked out of the other. Now he strode briskly past the Lambert Hotel in the opposite direction.

It was twenty past eight. Probably Radford would reach the house in Nelson Street before him. It didn't matter, Andrew had given him a key.

He took a deliberately circuitous route, doubling back on himself several times, until he was quite sure no one at all was following.

Radford felt distinctly uncomfortable in the empty house. He had let himself in at the back with his key, but despite his caution he had bumped into a dustbin and set a cat yowling, which was hardly the way a professional burglar would have made his entry. The last thing I need, he thought, is for some honest citizen to get suspicious, and call the police.

Well, almost the last thing. There were other people the neighbours might call. Twice in the past week Radford had been followed in the street by burly men in cloth caps, who watched him intently, and kept their hands in the pockets of their coats. Even in the spy campaign in Belfast during the war, that had never happened. He had taken to wearing a bullet-proof waistcoat, and, even so, had to nerve himself each time he went out alone.

He wished he could have brought Kee with him, but Kee would never have approved of this. That was the trouble with old Tom, he could not see when rules had to be broken. *If we play it by the book in this city, we won't survive.* But even if he could have persuaded Kee, the man Butler had insisted that no one else in the DMP should be involved. He could not fault Butler's reasoning. Undoubtedly there were people in the Dublin force sympathetic to Collins, and since Butler had no idea who they were, he preferred to trust no one. *I would do the same in his place,* Radford thought. *Especially if I were risking my neck as he is.*

On his other visits Butler had been here before him. This time he explored the house quietly, shining a torch around each room to try to get some idea of the character of the man he was dealing with. But the chief impression was of emptiness; of a house untenanted, bereft of its soul. The walls had pictures of horses hunting and racing, sketches of a large country house, pictures of sailing ships. Most of the furniture was solid, heavy, old-fashioned, though the bedding and curtains were a blend of light pink and lemon colours in one bedroom – a woman's, he supposed. To his surprise he found a number of German books and magazines in here, too, beginning to yellow with age. Then he remembered – Sir Jonathan had said something about Butler's mother being a German. That must be where the son had learnt the language so well. Well enough to fool the Sinn Feiners, anyway, he hoped.

The room he settled down in was a sort of living room and library combined. There were books on three of the walls, comfortable leather armchairs, and yesterday's ashes in the grate. There was a bottle of whiskey on the table too, an unwashed glass and some biscuit crumbs. Presumably this was the room Butler used, when he came here and sat, alone.

The thick curtains were closed. Radford lit the oil lamp, poured himself a glass of whiskey, and sat down to wait.

This is an odd man, Butler, he thought. Cold, hard, sharp as a whiplash when he speaks, and apparently in love with danger. Yet he's been out there in the carnage with the rest of them – got a row of medals to prove it. Most of the men Radford had known who had come back from the western front were shadows of themselves; they wandered around as though something inside them were missing, or sat listening and staring at God knew what awful memory. Many of them trembled, or shook and started for no apparent reason; and they could get angry quite suddenly, and walk out of rooms. Radford supposed that the everyday world seemed strange to them, meaningless perhaps after what they had been through. The thing that seemed to comfort them the most was to find someone who had lived through the same battle that they themselves had been in. They would relive it in every detail, for hours on end, as though those had been the finest days of their lives. And yet most of them said they never wanted to see a gun again.

Not a lot of this seemed to fit Andrew Butler, Radford thought. Despite the horrific wound on his face, there was nothing dazed, shaky, or gun-shy about the man at all. He had been through the worst of it like the others, yet Radford could not imagine him reminiscing nostalgically with his comrades. He wondered if the man had any comrades – indeed, if he had anyone he could talk to. This house bore no witness of it, and Butler's country home had been burnt down. Surely every man needs some companionship, to get the war out of his system, he thought – yet here he is, all alone, volunteering for one of the most dangerous jobs he can find.

He heard a quiet, scratching, scrabbling sound. Rats, perhaps, or was it a key in the lock? Radford got up and stepped softly across the room, to stand in shadow by a curtain. He was away from the oil lamp here, and could see the door. He rested his hand on the revolver in his pocket and waited. No sense in trusting what you can't see.

Footsteps in the corridor, a tall figure dimly lit in the doorway. Sharp, intense face, scar, shadowed eyes, narrow moustache. It was him.

'Radford?'

'Here.' He moved slightly. The figure turned swiftly to confront him, then they both relaxed.

'All right.' Andrew stepped into the pool of light, surveying the room briefly. 'You're alone? Good. And made yourself at home, I see.'

He took another glass from a cupboard on the wall, poured himself a glass of whiskey, and sat on the arm of a chair.

'It's tomorrow,' he said. 'In Brendan Road.'

Radford felt a surge of excitement. 'Where? What number?'

'I don't know. Or what time. They're coming to collect me at the hotel, either late morning or late afternoon. That's it.'

Radford thought. 'I don't know where it is either. But I can find it on the map, and keep it watched . . .'

'Listen.' Andrew leaned forward, staring at Radford and emphasizing each point with a stabbing finger. 'I don't want a single policeman seen on that street until I'm inside. Nor anywhere near. This whole show depends on them trusting me. If you can't keep out of sight, don't come at all.'

'Sure,' Radford said. 'But you'll need us afterwards. You don't know how many guards he'll have with him. If they're too many for you, I can still flood the place and take him alive.'

Andrew shook his head. 'There won't be too many for me.'

'How do you know? What if they search you before you go in?'

'Leave that to me.'

Radford sighed. It seemed to him the man was mad. Perhaps this was the way the war had damaged him: he had a desire to die in a blaze of glory.

'At least we'll be there to get you out. With luck we'll arrest quite a number of them.'

'Listen.' Andrew leaned foward again. 'I've told you the name of the street, but I want your word that it won't go any further – no one else is to know – until you see me go down the street. You can have your men in the general area, but they don't know – none of them – what the target is, until you call them up. Understood?'

'If that's what you want.'

'I do.'

'So we wait until you come out? How long? I can't keep a street like that sealed off for any length of time without someone noticing.'

'Give me half an hour. If anyone comes out after I've gone in, you can pick them up, but only when they're out of sight of the house. If I don't come out in half an hour, you can knock on the door and put me in a box.'

'And if someone sees us before then? It's difficult to keep a large number of men outside a place like that without being noticed. Look.' Radford spread out his big hands, trying to explain. 'You're leading us to him, there's no question about that. But it may be a lot better politically if we just arrest Collins. It'll restore belief in the police, and show the government can be strong without . . .'

'And in two weeks he'll be free. How many people has that man sprung out of prison already? How many prison officers work for him? Anyway, do you think this government's got the guts to hold a man like that for long? They'll do a deal with him, you know that. No, Mr Radford, tomorrow I'm going to try to kill him. That's what we agreed on that contract Sir Jonathan signed. That's what I'm going to do. You can come in and clean up the mess afterward, if you like. If I've failed, you can charge him with murder.'

Radford sighed again. He wished he had not agreed to this. Kee would say it was a crime and strictly he would be right. This wasn't what he had joined the police to do. But then ordinary criminals didn't carry guns and declare war. Ordinary criminals didn't set out to decimate the police force. If he played it strictly by the book, Radford thought, there soon wouldn't be any detectives left alive in G Division for him to command. And Sir Jonathan and Harrison had convinced him that Butler's mission had prime-ministerial backing. That was why he was here, to keep them in touch with the details of their plan.

'All right. We'll do it your way.' He raised his glass. 'You're a brave man, Major Butler. I wish you luck.'

13

IT WAS NOT easy to arrange meetings in the little back room in the tenement, but Sean and Catherine managed it three more times in the weeks after Ashtown. They met in the evenings, once after, and twice instead of, the Irish classes at Parnell Square. 'You'll be losing the language,' Catherine said to him the second time, and for the next half-hour she spoke only Gaelic, whispering soft endearments as they kissed and wrestled languorously on the narrow bed by the blazing fire. It was an odd feeling: the words she knew were the sort a nurse would say to a young child; she had not learnt the words you would use to a young man who lay naked and sweating above you. So the baby words seemed naughty and thrilling and exciting in themselves. As though they were two children who had escaped the adult world, and were doing something deliberately wicked in a secret hiding place of their own.

The next time, by way of reply, he read to her from a book of Irish love poetry he had found. He sat on the bed, while she knelt before him, warming her naked body in front of the blazing fire. He stumbled over the unfamiliar words, and she tried to correct him, dreamily, watching the dancing patterns of the flames. When he had finished she leaned her head back against his hips, and ran her fingertips teasingly along the inside of his thigh. She giggled as she saw the obvious result.

'I have a poem too,' she said in English. 'I was reading it today, and thinking of you. Listen: I'll tell you what I remember. My lover is handsome and strong; he is one in ten thousand. His face is bronzed and smooth — well, yours is smooth, anyway — his hair is wavy, black as a raven. His eyes — were like doves, I think, doves washed in milk, whatever they look like. He is majestic, like the mountains of Lebanon, with their towering cedars. His mouth is sweet to kiss; everything about him enchants me. That is what my lover is like.' She looked up at him, her dark eyes under the short bobbed hair twinkling in the firelight, her face small and mischievous. 'There — don't you like it?'

'Sure, it's beautiful,' he said. But he was a little hesitant.

He was still disconcerted by the frank delight she took in his body, paralleling, even surpassing, his delight in hers. 'Where did it come from?'

'The Bible, of course. It's the Song of Songs.'

'The Bible? Oh, come on now.'

'It's true. It's the song between Solomon and the Queen of Sheba. Have you never read it? They must have been lovers like us – except they had a palace, of course.'

'Yes, well, that's not my fault.' He remembered the priest, uneasily. The smells on the staircase and the noise from the other rooms had begun to irritate him tonight as well, besmirching the little cocoon they were trying to make together.

'No one said it was, silly.' She bit his buttock with her sharp little teeth, provoking a wrestling match which ended with him sitting astride her on the bed, her wrists pinned down on the pillow by his hands. He watched her breasts rise and fall with the exertion of the fight, and gripped her hips tightly with his thighs to stop her wriggling and throwing him off. She lifted her head and looked down between her breasts at his erection.

'So you *are* like a cedar of Lebanon,' she said. 'I thought I'd taken care of that already.'

'Not quite.'

And then for a while there was no sound in the room but their breathing, the creaking of the little, unstable bed, and the wild sharp cry that she gave at her climax.

Then someone started hammering on the floor from the room below. It impinged on Catherine's consciousness gradually. At first she thought it was just the coursing of blood in her ears.

'What's that?' she asked.

'Ignore it.' Sean lay exhausted, his face half muffled in the pillow beside her. 'They'll give up in a minute.'

He was right. The sound stopped, with an indistinct curse from downstairs. They lay quietly, listening to the crackle of the fire. For the first time Catherine thought of the half-dozen families around them, huddled in their tiny rooms, who had probably listened to the sound of the bed creaking and her cries.

Somehow the beauty of it had gone for both of them. Sean was tired; the failure outside the Lambert Hotel earlier in the evening had made him feel a fool, and now this interference of the neighbours made him feel trapped, hemmed in by pointing fingers who would one day drag him out to prison, or a police bullet in the head.

He got out of bed abruptly, and began to put his clothes on.

'What are you doing?' she asked.

'It's past ten o'clock. God knows what they'll be thinking in that posh house of yours. Anyway, I want to get out of this place. I can't stand it. I'm going to ask Paddy for a move tomorrow.'

'Where to? Will you find another room where we can meet?'

'God knows. I want somewhere cleaner. You've no idea what this place is like to wake up to in the mornings. The filth, the smells, the queues for the privy. I hate it.'

'But you'll find somewhere where we can meet, Sean?'

'Sure, I hope so. Most of them have got landladies, though. It might be hard.'

Catherine was astonished. She sat up in bed, her breasts rosy in the firelight. She made no effort to get dressed. Sean pulled on his socks irritably.

She said: 'What do you mean, Sean? We've got to have somewhere to meet.'

A bootlace snapped, and suddenly all Sean's fears and doubts surfaced at once. 'Why have we? Look, Cathy, you may not have thought about this, but I have. It's a fine thing, but look at it straight. What's a fellow like me got to give you? Just a grubby room in a tenement, and the chance of being shot any day by the police or army. That's no good for a girl like you.'

'Sean . . .'

'It's got to end some time, hasn't it? Look what happened to me today. I was supposed to keep watch on a man in a hotel, a really important one, and I spent so much time thinking about you that he just walked away from me in the street. No one knows where he is now. The fellows are starting to talk. They all know I've got a girl but if they knew what we really do I think – I don't think they'd let me stay in the Volunteers.'

Her shock at the outburst robbed her of speech for a while, but anger was not far behind. Anger, and a horrible growing sense of disgust; of a trust that had been betrayed. She had not seen their love as a hindrance to his career, or a subject for discussion with the boys.

'Why couldn't you stay?' she said. 'Surely they know I support the Republic – isn't that enough?'

'It's not that, Cathy. If I'm to be a soldier, I shouldn't have a thought for anything else. I shouldn't really have

come tonight, perhaps – I should be out tracking that man.
It's a sort of sin to the movement, to be thinking all the time
of a woman; not a sin like the priest said, exactly, but . . .'

'What do you mean? What priest?'

'Father Desmond. I went to confession.'

'And you told him about me?'

'Not in so many words. I just said I'd been with a
woman.'

'Oh. Been with a woman! And what did he say?'

'What do you think, Cathy? That it was a sin. But don't
worry, I walked out of the confessional.' For a moment
Sean's irritation was past. He grinned, not realizing the
damage he had done.

She said: 'Well, that's fine then, isn't it? You bring me
here in the night, and in the daytime you go to a priest and
tell him all about it. And I suppose he told you I was the
scarlet whore.'

Sean had finished dressing. He sat down in the only
armchair, and glanced across at her. The intensity of her
gaze scared him. For the first time ever he thought of her as
a burden. That slim, naked figure in his bed; he might
never be rid of her.

'No, Cathy, he didn't say that exactly. But the man had a
point, you know. It's a sin for you too. I mean, have you
thought what will come of all this? We could never marry,
could we? What if there was a child?'

'What if – you ask *me* that? Sean. You ask me that
now?'

'I should have asked it before, I suppose, but . . .'

'But what?'

'But you didn't seem to worry, so why should I?'

'And you a student of medicine. So-called. Have you read Knowlton?'

'Who?'

'Charles Knowlton. *The Fruits of Philosophy, or the Private Companion of Young Married People.* It's a book about how to avoid babies.'

For the first time in the conversation Sean was speechless. He simply gaped at her. It reminded her of his reaction to some of the medical lectures, but now she felt contempt, not compassion.

'I see you haven't. Well, I have. And I've been making use of the advice in it. Just as well, isn't it?'

He found his voice. 'What do you do?'

'I stick a sponge up myself.'

'My God. Is that – why you didn't bleed, the first time?'

A faint trace of a smile crossed her face. It was very faint; there was no warmth in it. 'No. That was an accident on a horse, when I was fifteen. Lucky for you, wasn't it?'

The whole conversation offended him. It brought them together in a way he didn't want, not at all. He said: 'But that – that's killing life. That's a sin against God, for sure.'

There was a silence. It went on for some time. Sean's words hung heavily in the air between them. Then Catherine got out of bed and began to get dressed in front of him. There was nothing provocative about the way she did it. Her nakedness seemed an insult, almost. She was careless about the way she put on her clothes, brisk, matter-of-fact. She ignored him, as though he had been a chair or a stuffed baboon.

When she was dressed she took a comb from her bag and

began to push her hair behind her ears with swift smart strokes. Her eyes sparkled in the firelight, but no tears fell. She said: 'I suppose you, then, have been making love to me all this time in the belief that I would probably get pregnant, and that then you could disown me.'

Certainly he felt shame now. But also a sullen, deep resentment at the way he had been used. No women did that. No women he knew. He had never even heard of a woman doing it.

In a sort of harsh whisper, he said: 'I never thought of it.'

She turned then and faced him. She had the comb between her teeth, and she was fastening her hair back with a pin. When she had done that, she took the comb out, and said sadly: 'Sean. Sean, I knew most men were stupid, but truly I never thought it of you.'

For the first time he saw she was crying. He stood up and held out his arms to embrace her. For a moment she let him hold her, but she stood quite still and cold in his arms, shutting him out. Then she brushed him away.

'Come on. I want to go home.'

For most of the walk home they didn't speak. It was not a conversation either could have carried on in front of men singing outside pubs, or army lorries cruising the streets. Sean was tired and furious. But near Merrion Square he began again.

'I suppose you have done this with other men.'

They had been walking side by side, without touching. He had stopped as he spoke, but she walked on briskly, looking straight ahead.

'Why should you suppose that?'

'Why else would you have read about it?'

She stopped then, suddenly, so that he almost ran into her.

'To avoid having babies, that's why! So that when I did meet the man I wanted, I could really love him, as I have loved you, Sean, without being afraid or worried about what would happen. That's what I thought. I thought it would be beautiful and it was, Sean, it really was, until tonight. You don't really love me, though, do you?'

'It's not that. I – I'm not sure I should be thinking about that, now with the war on. I've got to concentrate on one thing. Anyway, you shouldn't have done that – what you did. It's wrong.'

She stared at him with her heart breaking. She thought how she had kissed – almost every part of him. I thought a woman could be free like a man, she thought, but it isn't so. Not if the man won't let you.

She said: 'Sean Brennan, you don't really like me at all, do you? You just like killing, for your wretched idea of a new Ireland. You didn't even think about me.'

She waited for an answer, but there was none. So she turned on her heel, and walked away from him alone, into Merrion Square, where the lights of her father's house were burning brightly.

When Catherine got home she went straight to her bedroom and wept, pressing her face into her pillow to muffle the sound. I was so sure, she thought; sure that he loved me as I did him. Sure that a boy who was fighting for the freedom and future of the country would see how girls can love equally and freely without guilt or shame, just for the beauty of the act itself. And all the time I was nothing for him but a passing pleasure that got out of hand, a distraction from the serious business of killing. He thinks it's a sin because I made sure we could have no child . . .

So where the hell is your sin then, Sean? a voice screamed inside her head. She snatched her pillow and flung it across the room. It knocked a china figurine of a horse off the mantelpiece. Oh no, she thought. She groaned, got up and tried to pick up the pieces; but it was smashed beyond repair. It was a statuette she had had since she was eight; her father had given it to her when Blaze, her first pony, died of the colic. She had cried all night then, too, for many nights; it was then she had learnt the trick of smothering the sound in the pillow, when her parents could bear her grief no longer. Her father had seen the statuette in a shop, and bought her it because it had almost exactly the same markings as Blaze. She had put a wreath round its neck, and promised to keep it always.

Those were the days when her parents still lived together and seemed to love each other, and she and her brothers talked and laughed together at the same table, and rambled endlessly along the cliffs. Those days were long gone now. If they had continued, perhaps she would never have felt the need to break away, to defy her father, make her own career, and choose a lover from the slums. She could have turned to her parents for love and advice instead of facing betrayal and failure like this on her own.

She swept up the fragments of the broken horse into a small pile by the side of the hearth, crawled back into bed, and turned her face to the wall.

Towards dawn sleep came – the sleep of exhaustion. She dreamed that she was riding her pony across the beach. It was the big wide beach near her home, a beach of white sand five miles long at low tide. The sea was far out, little white breakers curling gently on her right. Flocks of seagulls were paddling around near the sea's edge. She trotted towards them and they lifted away as they always did, screaming raucously and circling behind her. She kicked the pony to a canter through the shallows, and they went on madly, splashing through the clear inch-high waves that rushed in over the flat hard sand. Far away in the hazy distance was a fisherman, a tiny figure pulling a coracle out of the sea. As she galloped towards him, the warm summer wind blew on her and her clothes flew off, piece by piece, into the air behind where the seagulls snatched them. But although the sun shone on her and in front of her, she was sure there was thunder behind. When she reached the man he turned and looked up at her with Sean's face, and spat. And then she was past and galloping on in the cold wind, with the sun gone somewhere behind a cloud, and there was a horse behind her. She could hear its hooves drumming and drumming on the sand but she dared not look back. Her pony was tired and beginning to stumble. Each time he stumbled, a leg fell off.

She woke, sweating and unrefreshed. More from habit than anything else, she washed, dressed and went down to breakfast. To her dismay her father was there, eating a plate of mushrooms and kidneys. He looked depressingly cheerful, and unusually pleased to see her. Before she could escape, he stood up and pulled out a chair for her. She sat, meek, dutiful, depressed.

'Now, my dear, what can I pass you? Same as me, perhaps? Kidneys? Eggs are pretty fresh, I had one of those.'

'Just tea, please.'

He poured her some. She cupped her hands around it and sipped. It was hot at least. Stewed as well but she didn't care.

'You came in late last night. More of the Gaelic, eh?'

She nodded. Once the Irish classes had been a focus of conflict between them; now they were a welcome excuse.

To her surprise he made no disparaging comment. She couldn't help noticing that he ate with unusual gusto; his whole manner radiated energy and what passed with him for good humour. In a way it was a tiny comfort; a distraction from the bleak wasteland of her own thoughts. She gazed at him balefully over the tea. This is my own father, she thought: he betrayed Mother and sent her mad; his mistress is dying of cancer; both his sons have been killed in the war; he's threatened to disinherit me unless I marry – and he's happy. Maybe men are a different species.

He finished the kidneys, wiped his moustache with a napkin, and sat back to look at her. His good humour faded a little.

'You look like death, girl. What's the matter with you?'

She felt the tears prick in the corner of her eyes and thought: If I start to cry now I'll never stop for hours and that would be too, too messy and humiliating altogether. So she tried to smile, failed, and said: 'Just a bad night, that's all. Too much study, I suppose.'

'Hm.' He considered her answer. 'You work too hard, girl. You should get out and enjoy yourself more – ride, go to balls, the races, something like that.'

'What? We haven't got any horses here, Father.'

'Could have. Still got the mews – could clean that out.'

She sighed. 'I don't want to ride, Father – not in midwinter in the middle of Dublin. Anyway, I'm too busy: I've got my studies, and this house to run.'

'Yes, all right, all right. Just thought it would put some more colour in your cheeks, that's all.' He pulled a bell rope to call Keneally and order a fresh pot of tea.

When the butler had gone, Sir Jonathan leaned forward confidentially. 'Now there's a thing I've meant to say to you, Cathy. This house – your side of the bargain. You've done a damn good job, I reckon. Decorations good, servants respect you – pretty fine achievement for a girl your age. Struck me last week when I came back from London. Place is a real home, in its way.'

The servants respect me? Heavens, she thought, do they really? Certainly she had been sharp as a whiplash when she came in the first night she had made love with Sean. She had issued two orders to Keneally on the doorstep when he had met her, before the man had had a chance to voice any concern. It was the only way, she thought – always be ahead so there is no chance for questions. But she had been living on a tightrope. Has it really worked, she wondered, or is Father just blind, as he is to so much else?

She sipped her tea, and said: 'Well, thank you.'

Keneally brought in the fresh pot, and poured. Sir Jonathan said: 'I just wanted to say it. Give credit where it's due. But there are other parts to our deal, as you know.'

Here it comes, she thought.

'You need to be brought out into society more, meet the right sort of young men. So now that we've got the place into good order, I think we should start entertaining.'

She put down her cup with a clatter, slopping tea into the saucer. 'Oh no, Father – I can't do that.'

'Why not? Just a few guests for dinner once in a while – I'm not thinking of throwing the place open to a grand ball, of course not. Never manage that these days, more's the pity. But you could order a meal, couldn't you – tell cook what to make, that sort of thing? I'll take care of the guests. Nothing to it.'

'Father, please. Not just now.'

'But it'll take you out of yourself, you silly girl, bring you to life, away from your miserable books and student politics. Launch you, too, the best way we can. Bring a few young fellows here, see how you like 'em. Remember the other part of our deal.'

She shut her eyes. He thinks I'm a mare on heat, she thought; he'll open the door and all the young officers will come sniffing round like stallions. The thought was too absurd for words.

'Anyway, I thought we'd start next Saturday. I'm going to the races with Colonel Roberts and his wife – he's got a part share in two runners, he says. So I asked them back here afterwards for dinner. MacQuarry might come too, with his lady, so that'll make six; and then I can hunt up a couple of young officers for you, to make up the younger party. We should manage it, wouldn't you say?'

'You mean you've already arranged this?'

'Partly.' He sipped his tea and smoothed his moustache with his finger. 'Got to try to keep things going, even in the midst of these blasted outrages, after all. Look.' He leaned forward again and, to Catherine's great surprise, took her hand in his. 'We've been through some pretty bad times in the past few years, Cathy my girl, and I've no doubt you've thought pretty harshly of me once or twice. Wouldn't be normal if you hadn't. But we've made a deal and so far as I can see you're sticking to your side of it, and I want to stick to mine. Then we'll make a new start in the family, if we can. Play our part in bringing the country back to its senses. What do you say?'

You're mad as a hatter, she thought. You're completely out of touch. I've been making love to a revolutionary in the slums, and now you want me to arrange a dinner party for British officers.

Her lower lip trembled, and she felt a horrible urge to burst into hysterical laughter. To subdue it, she passed her cup for some more tea, and concentrated grimly on the way the tea flowed out of the spout into the cup, as though her life depended on it.

Then she said: 'All right, Father. I'll arrange the dinner for you.'

Kee said: 'I don't believe it!'

'It's true, sir. I'm quite sure it was her.'

The young detective flushed. He had only recently been promoted from the uniformed branch, and he was anxious to do well. But he was not immune to the resentment felt by many of his colleagues for the two blunt Ulstermen who had been brought in over the heads of southern Irish officers to run G Division. The detective, Allan Foster, was a tall, well-built young man, and now he had to stand to attention and look down at Kee, who was apparently calling him a liar.

'Listen, Foster. You know who this young woman is? Her father's on the General Staff in Dublin Castle. He owns a house in Merrion Square, and half of west Galway as well. The man's a bosom friend of Lord French himself. You know that, don't you?'

'I knew most of it, sir, yes.'

'And you mean to tell me that his one and only daughter spent most of last night somewhere in a godforsaken rat-infested tenement in one of the worst slums in this city? With someone who might have been a Sinn Feiner?'

'Yes, sir.' Foster stood rigidly to attention, staring into the air somewhere over Kee's head. Kee looked at him, sensing his hostility. Then he sat down behind his desk and waved his arm at a chair. 'Sit down, for God's sake, and relax. Let's go through it again, shall we? You followed her from Merrion Square, you say. And you're quite sure it was Miss Catherine? Not a maid, for instance, taking money to her relatives?'

Foster looked pained. 'I've been watching her for a week now, sir. I know what she looks like.'

So do I, Kee thought. It's a memorable face, too. Those clear, innocent-looking eyes; a general air of fragile delicacy as though butter wouldn't melt in her mouth. 'Go on.'

'Well, she's been out three times alone in the past couple of weeks. I've already reported that, sir.'

'Yes. To the Gaelic League in Parnell Square. To learn bog Irish, as far as we can make out.'

'Sir. And I've seen her with the same young man there. I think he fits the photo you gave me, but it's hard to be sure.'

Kee nodded. Sean Brennan. It made sense. 'So. Tell me about last night. She came out of the house on her own, did she?'

'She did that, sir. At first I thought she was off to Parnell Square again but when she got over the river she turned right, up Amiens Street towards the North Circular.'

'I know it.' Kee nodded. It was not so far from North Strand, where the dead boy Savage had had his rooms.

'Well, I kept her in sight, sir, all the way, and she met the young fellow at the junction with Portland Row. They had a brief discussion, then they went to a pub for a drink. I thought I'd lost them, there, because it wasn't the sort of place I could be in myself alone for long without exciting comment. So I hung about outside, going up and down the street every five minutes and hoping for the best. But I was lucky. They were only in there for about twenty minutes. Then I followed them to the tenement.'

'Stop there a second, now. You're sure it was the same couple who came out?'

'No doubt at all, sir. For one thing, she had a blue coat with a fur collar, like a stole – you don't see many of those around that area. And anyway, they were walking towards me. I had to go straight past them, near as I am to you now. I saw her as they came past – she looked right at me.'

'If you were that close, you must have seen the boy's face, too. Was it Brennan or was it not?'

Foster looked embarrassed. 'Well, like I say, I think it was, sir. But it was the girl I was following, not him; and with her looking me in the face like that, I was petrified she'd recognize me, too. I hadn't time to think of him.'

Kee sighed. 'It may have escaped your notice, Detective Foster, but the reason you were following this young woman is not because I'm interested in her behaviour, scandalous though it is; it's because I hope she's going to lead us to Brennan.'

'Yes, sir. Well, if it is him, I've found out where he lives. They were in that tenement for over two hours, sir, and I hung about in the shadows for all that time without being seen, I think. When they came out they seemed to be having some sort of quarrel. I followed them back to Merrion Square, and then I followed him for a short while, but he kept looking round, so I fell back, and then I lost him, sir.'

'It doesn't matter. You've done well, lad, very well indeed.' Kee drummed his fingers on the table. 'We'll raid this place tonight, when we can be sure he's at home. Now hop off and write your report, there's a good lad. I've got some thinking to do.'

About what the devil I tell Radford about this girl. If anything, Kee thought. He had set up this surveillance without Radford's permission, and now it had borne fruit. In fact it was a hot political potato. Her daddy's not going to be pleased about this. Not one little bit.

As Foster stood up to go, Kee said: 'Oh, about your report. This is a hush-hush one. Don't give it to the girls to type. Davis will do it for you, if you can't manage the machine yourself.'

'I'll have a go myself, sir,' said Foster conscientiously. 'I've always thought I'd master it, if I kept up the practice.'

14

A NDREW SAT IN the lounge of the Lambert Hotel, smoking and reading the *Irish Independent*. There was a tale of atrocities in Bolshevik Russia: two Irish nurses had spent four days in a cellar crammed with counts and countesses waiting to be shot in the courtyard behind. The Red Army had started to invade Poland. In the United States 2,700 suspected communists had been arrested, and there was discussion of amending the constitution to ban the sale of alcohol. Bernard Shaw's *Heartbreak House* was still running in London. Salome was the hot favourite for the 500 Guineas in Phoenix Park.

He sat by the window with a clear view of the street and the entrance hall. Outside, part of the road was blocked by a lorry delivering vegetables. Cyclists swirled past, ringing their bells derisively, and swerving to avoid the dung left by a horse-drawn cab. The proprietor of the hotel was persuading the doorman to cast aside his dignity and sweep it up. A group of boys in shabby, outsize clothes hung around the back of the vegetable lorry, just out of reach of the delivery men, hoping to pick up dropped fruit.

One of the oldest couples in the Lambert Hotel came down the main staircase in their pre-war finery: the man in top hat, frock coat, and trousers caught with elastic under his boots; his wife in a mauve silk dress that came down to the ground, and a feathered hat the size of a cartwheel. Some special occasion, no doubt, but the clothes looked quite absurd today. The street urchins stared, began to nudge each other, and wolf-whistle; the hotel proprietor scurried about, trying to bow, smile, chastise the boys, and order a cab all at once; and Patrick Daly strode into the lounge.

Andrew stood up to greet him. He bowed, clicked his heels, and indicated a chair opposite him. 'Will you take coffee?'

'No thanks.' Daly frowned at him, then grinned. 'Come on. You're in luck. He wants to see you.'

'Mr Collins?'

'Hush.'

Andrew picked up his brown leather bag and followed Daly past the pantomime in the hall. Daly took his arm briefly to show which way to go. 'It's in Donnybrook. We'll take the tram.'

They caught the tram at the end of the street and sat side by side on the top deck. Andrew sat slightly stiffly. He hoped Daly would think that was the way German officers always sat; but in fact it was because he had his hunting knife strapped to his belt, in the small of his back. He probably wouldn't need it, with two loaded automatic pistols to take out of his bag and show Collins; but he had put it on as a last resort anyway.

Daly seemed in sunny mood, pointing out the city sights.

'That's the GPO on your right, where they hoisted the flag in '16. Patrick Pearse stood on those very steps here and read out the proclamation. Have you been to Dublin before, Mr Hessel?'

'No. It is my first visit. Thank you.' Andrew smiled and nodded, but within him the tension was wound tight. He recognized the symptoms of excitement: slightly brighter colours, heightened sensitivity to small sounds, a great awareness of everything relevant to his survival, and a distancing, almost obliteration, of everything else. Time had not begun to slow down yet, but he knew that would come, when the moment for action came closer.

As they left the centre and trundled along Leeson Street and Morehampton Road towards Donnybrook, Daly fell silent. Andrew scanned the streets anxiously for signs of the police or army. A Tin Lizzie snorted past, its armoured turret and machine gun looking menacing and out of place in the city streets, but it was going in the opposite direction, and there were no others.

'We get off here,' Daly said.

Andrew followed him down the winding stairs at the

back of the tram, and stood in the street expectantly. Daly looked up and down, considering each passer-by in turn. Apparently satisfied, he crossed the road and turned to his right, with Andrew following.

Brendan Road itself would be the hardest, Andrew knew. Radford or one of his officers had to be somewhere here, watching. It turned out to be a quiet, residential street, perhaps a little over a hundred yards long, the hardest kind to loiter casually in. The houses were two-storey red-brick semidetached villas with gardens front and rear, and coloured glass in the doorways. There was a window-cleaner halfway down, he noticed, some children playing football with a bundle of rags, a young woman pushing a perambulator. No one else at all.

Thank God for that.

Daly relaxed slightly, and quickened his pace.

'A nice quiet place, you see, Mr Hessel,' he said. 'You'll not be having anyone bother you in your negotiations here.'

'I am glad to hear it.'

Just before they reached the young woman with the perambulator, Daly opened a small garden gate, walked down the path, and knocked on the front door. It was the first house in the street, Andrew noticed, but quite a way down because of the unusually large back garden of the house on the corner of Morehampton Road. He glanced up and down the street again. About thirty-five yards further on a small road came in from the left, and fifty yards beyond that, Brendan Road itself turned left too. In the other direction, the way they had come, a cyclist had just turned into the road, wobbling unsteadily with a large load of groceries in the basket over his front wheel. But he couldn't be a policeman, surely? For one thing, he was far too young.

Wherever he was, Radford had managed to show far more discretion than Andrew had expected.

The door opened, and they stepped into a narrow hall, cluttered with two bicycles. Daly led him through to a room with a table, six chairs, a sideboard, a large wooden chest in the corner and a spinning wheel. The table was covered with papers and a typewriter. Two young men looked up from it as he came in.

'This is the German officer, come to see Mick,' said Daly. 'Two of my men, Mr Hessel.'

Andrew clicked his heels and bowed.

'Mr Collins's office is upstairs, Mr Hessel,' Daly explained. 'I'll take you there in a moment. But first, Seamus and Frank here would like to see the pistols you've brought.'

Andrew thought furiously. Yesterday, the two pistols had been empty; today, they were fully loaded. He didn't want Daly to see that. Nor did he want to lose the man's trust by seeming awkward. Or by hesitating.

'A pleasure,' he said. He put the leather bag on the table, opened it, and lifted out the long Parabellum. As he did so, a telephone began to ring in another room. Daly looked flustered.

'Is anyone in the office?' he asked.

One of the young men shook his head. 'I'll go, then,' Daly said. 'I've had the demonstration already.' He went out and closed the door behind him. So he can't suspect anything, Andrew thought.

The two men looked at the gun in his hands, impressed. 'That's a big weapon,' Frank murmured. 'What does it fire?'

'Nine-millimetre cartridges, like the smaller Parabellum,' Andrew said. He showed them how the helical snail magazine worked, and where the safety catch was. Then he put the gun back in his bag. He took out the Mauser and unwrapped that in turn. 'This uses 9-mm too.' Keep talking, he thought; then perhaps they won't ask to touch this one either. 'Both guns were very effective at the front,' he continued. 'It was possible to hit targets twenty or thirty metres away, even for ordinary young officers. You could do the same in the streets here.' He began to put the second gun back in his bag. 'I hope very much Mr Collins will like them. I want to show him all the details first. Where is he, please?'

The young men looked disappointed, but the guns were safely back in the bag. Andrew kept his hand inside it on the butt of the Mauser. This is the crucial moment, he thought. Either they protest, and take the guns away from me, or they show me through into Collins's room with two loaded automatics in my bag. Either way, someone's going to die in the next few minutes.

One young man picked up a piece of paper, and the other turned back to his typewriter. 'Paddy'll show you,' he said, indifferently, as Daly came back into the room.

Daly smiled, and held the door open to the corridor. 'Certainly I will. Follow me, Mr Hessel, and I'll show you where you can meet the Minister of Finance.'

Andrew followed him upstairs. Time was moving very slowly now. In a few moments, he thought, I'll be sitting right in front of the man. After a few minutes' talk I'll show him the photograph of the Maxim gun, and then, when he's absorbed in that, I'll take a pistol out of the bag and shoot him. If Daly stays I'll shoot him too. Easy.

And then?

At the top of the stairs they turned and went back along a little landing to a bedroom at the front of the house. Andrew thought: That makes it easier. Radford's bound to hear the shots from there, and if he doesn't, I'll smash the window and jump out.

Daly opened the door and showed him inside. The room was light and spacious, overlooking the road. There was a double bed in a corner, and a table and two chairs near the wall. There were some shelves and a couple of boxes of papers. There was no carpet on the floorboards. And there was no one in the room at all.

Shocked, Andrew spun round and stared at Daly.

'But – where is he?' he asked.

There was a wicked grin on the Irishman's face. 'Sure and he'll be along in a moment or two, Mr Hessel. You can never tell with our Michael from one minute to the next. Just sit down there and wait a while, would you now.'

He closed the door, and Andrew heard his footsteps clattering away down the stairs.

The woman with the perambulator continued slowly along Brendan Road towards Morehampton Road. She had, in fact, walked her baby all the way down Brendan Road already once this morning, and had been preparing to buy a few vegetables in the shops on Morehampton Road and then walk back again, if necessary. But this time, when she turned left into Morehampton Road, she speeded up her pace quite noticeably. After about twenty yards she turned left again, into Auburn Avenue. A few yards along this street two men sat in a parked car, reading newspapers.

As she passed them she said: 'Number one. He's in there now.'

Then she walked on, her pace gradually slowing. The baby began to grizzle, and she bent down and gave it a rattle.

'It's all right, sweetie,' she said. 'We'll soon be in the park now. Mummy's done her work for this morning.'

In the car, Radford folded his newspaper and nodded to his driver. The car turned left into Morehampton Road, and very quickly right, into Belmont Avenue. This road formed part of a crescent, the other end of which came out almost opposite Brendan Road. At the bottom of the crescent was Kee, waiting with eight detectives in two cars. Four of them were in the first car with Kee, three in another with Davis. Radford had kept them down here, so that there was no chance of the woman being seen talking to a large group of men who later turned out to be police. His driver pulled up beside Kee's car. Radford got out.

'Right, gentlemen,' he said. 'This is a raid on number 1 Brendan Road. I want you all to get up there immediately I tell you. Davis, you drive straight down the road and block it off at the first junction. Kee, park your car at the top and walk down. Wait in the street, out of sight of the house, until you get orders from me. If someone leaves the premises, arrest them. When we go in, I don't want a single person to get away. Understood?'

Kee said: 'Yes, sir.'

Davis said: 'Who is it we're after, Mr Radford, sir?'

'Michael Collins, I hope!' said Radford briskly. As he turned to get back into his own car, he thought Davis looked curiously shocked. Surely *he* wasn't going to start being nervous, too? Radford had had enough of that in this force. He got back into the car. 'Press your damned throttle, man,' he said to the driver.

It was only a few minutes since he had got the message, but he was haunted by the thought that Andrew might already have come out, with no one there to see him. But then, the man can't have it both ways, he thought. He asked me to keep out of sight and that's what I've done. None of these officers had a clue what was happening until I told them just now. This is one operation that hasn't been betrayed.

So let's just hope it works.

Sean was overcome by a mixture of depression and rage. I did it, he thought, I broke with her as it was my duty to do. It could never have gone on anyway, it was foolishness from the beginning. Now I've put a stop to it. I'm free again to be a soldier for my country and not ...

Not ever run my fingers down her thighs again *stop that! Don't even think that ever again, Sean Brennan*. Not ever again – Christ! He braked violently and swerved his bicycle on to the pavement to avoid a man staggering from the back of a dray with a load of tins. The man swore virulently as half the tins dropped out of his arms into the gutter. Sean had been looking at him for the last half minute as he pedalled up the road, but the sight had not registered with his brain as having any meaning. He was still reliving the scene earlier that morning, when they had met by accident in the street as she was on her way to the university. He had said he thought it was best that it was over between them for the time being, and she had said yes she was sure he wanted to get back to playing at little boy revolutionaries, and she was sorry she had distracted him.

As he pushed the bike back into the road, Sean saw the back of a young woman in a blue dress going into a haberdasher's and for a second he was sure – but no; the shape of the hips and the hands were quite, quite different from Catherine's. God – how coarse other women seemed in comparison with her! Like a grotesque parody of perfection, a sick joke almost.

Catherine is not perfection either, Sean boy, he told himself. She may look the part all right but she is riddled with lust and vanity and all the things that should never – that I should never . . .

Want.

He stopped the bike at a crossroads and squeezed the brakes so tight that his hands whitened and he thought the handlebars might snap off altogether. I wanted her and I wanted to do those things and it was wonderful, he thought, *but it can't go on*. We're not right for each other, the way she spoke to me this morning shows it. And it was taking my mind off the things I should be doing; the way I lost that German the other night shows it. And then Paddy Daly shouting at me and all the boys laughing; it made me look such a fool – she should understand that. And the priest was right too in his way, though sod all he knows about how it feels. But if we're not right for each other and never could be married then it is a sin, for all it feels so wonderful – and it was foul what she did to stop the child.

It was sensible but it was foul and sordid at the same time. Sean didn't understand his own attitude about this but it outraged him even to think of it. Of course we couldn't have cared for a child but you can't do those things, he told himself as he pedalled furiously out towards the south side of the city where he would meet Daly for the lunchtime briefing. When you start doing things like that it all becomes so sordid that it *has* to be wrong. There's no beauty or love left in it at all.

The girl has all the wrong emotions surely. She led me on in the first place and now, when we break up, she should have wept and there was nothing like that. Just anger and scorn as though it was *me* that was to blame. Sean thought if she had wept this morning things might have been different. He would have held her and dried her tears on his shoulder and explained how it was all for the good and he would visit her sometimes; but to show rage as she had done – that had unsettled him deeply. It only goes to show how right I was, he thought; we're two different species entirely. Two different classes. Whatever her sympathy for the new Ireland, she doesn't understand the right way to behave at all. She's grown up thinking the world belongs to people like her and it won't, soon. It doesn't already.

She's just got to learn.

None of these thoughts did anything except fill him with more rage and misery. He felt like whipping his back with thorns as he had read the Muslims did, but all he could do was pedal as hard as he possibly could so that he was out of breath and some of the anger dissipated that way.

He was coming along Morehampton Road when he saw three cars pull out suddenly in front of him, about a hundred yards ahead. Something about them caught his attention. They pulled out urgently, angrily almost.

Fools, he thought. They must have lost their women too. Then two of the cars stopped and six or seven men got out.

An alarm bell started to jangle in Sean's brain.

The cars had parked very quickly and the men were running towards Brendan Road. The third car drove straight down it.

It looks like a bank robbery, Sean thought. But there are no banks in Brendan Road, no shops even, nothing but quiet residential houses like the one I'm going to. Number 1. Where I'm going to meet Paddy Daly and Michael Collins comes too, most days about lunchtime.

Sean stopped his bicycle thirty yards away from the parked cars and hesitated, wondering what to do. He could see two of the men standing at the end of the street. They looked keyed up, tense. A middle-aged man started to walk down Brendan Road and they grabbed him and started to question him fiercely. The man looked shocked, and began to protest in a loud voice. A small crowd gathered.

Sean thought: It's a police raid.

He wondered what to do. The anger he had felt against Catherine surged along new channels, fuelling his hatred of the police. These are the same devils who had arrested half of the best republicans over the past year, and locked them away in Mountjoy Gaol or sent them overseas to rot in England, all on the say-so of Lord bloody high and mighty French. And now here they are about to catch Paddy and Michael Collins.

They will, too, unless I do something.

What?

Sean had a pistol in his pocket but the police were surely armed too and there were six or seven of them at least. If I go up there and start shooting I may hit one or two but I'll never hit them all. If I stand and fight they'll kill me. But what else is there to do? At least the shots'll warn anyone who's in the house. And it's more important to warn Michael than to save my skin.

I'll do it.

I'll cycle right up to the one who's holding the old man, take out the pistol and shoot him in the chest. Then I'll shoot the other one. After that I'll ride straight down Brendan Road and shoot as many of the others as I can. At the very least it'll make a terrible noise and put them off their raid. I can either cycle straight through, or, if I've killed these two and there are too many down there, I can turn round and ride back out this end.

And there won't be any more snide comments about little boy revolutionaries from Catherine, either. She'll read about this in tomorrow's paper and know I'm in a real war all right.

He took the pistol out of his pocket and flipped the butt open to check the magazine was full. Then he snapped it shut, took the safety catch off, put the pistol back in his pocket, and glanced over his shoulder before he cycled away from the pavement.

A bread van came past. Behind the bread van, the road was clear. Except for a cyclist about seventy yards away.

There was something familiar about the cyclist. A big, burly man, bare-headed, pedalling energetically with his knees slightly turned out. Maybe a slight frown on his face, though it was hard to see at this distance.

It was Michael Collins.

With a whoop, Sean did a U-turn and belted back down the road towards him. As he came near he crossed to the wrong side of the road, yelling and waving his arms madly.

'Hey, Mick! Hey! Stop!'

Collins saw him, waved, and braked.

'Sean! What's all the rush, boy?'

'It's the police! They're raiding Brendan Road! They're after you, I'm sure of it!' Sean told him quickly what he had seen, pointing to the parked cars and the crowd that was still gathering round the end of the street. 'Thank the Lord you're here, Michael! I was sure you were in the house already – I was going to ride down the road and shoot at them, to give our lads a warning!'

Collins looked at him, a slight smile on his broad, cheery face. He put a hand on Sean's shoulder.

'A brave thought, Sean, but don't do it now. There's too many people up there, someone might get hurt. Anyway, I can't afford to lose you.'

Sean said: 'I thought we might be about to lose you, which would have been much worse. Come on, we'd best get away.' He was anxious about the noise he had made already; one of the detectives might look down the road at any moment and see them. One of them might even have the photograph they stole from his room.

'Ah, now, wait a moment. There's no great rush now, is

there?' Collins was looking curiously up the road, a twinkle of amusement in his eyes. 'There's a biggish crowd up there now, I see. Why don't you and I cycle up quietly and join it? It'll be highly educational for a young lad like you to see what the British police get up to in this country of ours, now won't it? Come to that, I'd like to find out myself.'

And to Sean's great surprise, Collins began to pedal sedately on up Morehampton Road, towards the crowd and the police.

Sean pedalled nervously after him.

Kee was incensed by the sound of the scuffle that had broken out behind him, at the top of Brendan Road. He was already angry with Radford, for not telling him anything about this operation until a couple of minutes ago. After working together like brothers, almost, for so many years, it rankled to be ordered to bring a group of detectives to this part of the city to stand in a road for over an hour without the faintest hint of why they were there. It was the way he himself might treat a junior constable, perhaps; it was hardly the way for an Assistant Commissioner to treat a Detective Inspector, especially one who was an old friend.

Apart from that, it was unprofessional. If Radford had trusted him, he could have surveyed this road beforehand, and made up his mind exactly where to dispose his men to cover all exits. As it was, he didn't even know whether number 1 was on the right or the left, or what the bloody road looked like further down, or whether there was a back exit. Not to mention how many people had been seen entering and leaving the building, or who it belonged to, and what the neighbours were like. And where had Radford got the information about this place anyway?

The scuffle behind him seemed to have something to do with a man who wanted to come down the street. The man was making a lot of noise, and attracting a small crowd. Exactly what we don't want, Kee thought. What am I supposed to do now – stand around outside number 1 waiting for orders, while the crowd gets bigger by the second? Already half a dozen young boys had stepped past them, and were following his little group of detectives down the road at a safe distance. They'll start throwing stones soon.

'Shall I go in straight away, sir?' Kee asked. 'It looks like the only way now, if you want it to be a surprise.'

Radford hesitated, and glanced at his watch. Could he wait outside this house for fifteen minutes, pretending to look inconspicuous, as though waiting for a nonexistent tram? He glanced up and down the street. Ahead of him, Davis had parked his car assertively in the middle of the road, and was standing with his arms folded beside it. Behind him, the second of his detectives was striding across the road towards the boys who were following Radford. As he did so, however, two men wheeled their bicycles into the street, and the detective strode towards them instead, anxiously waving his arms. Radford looked at number 1, and thought he saw a face disappear as a curtain was drawn back.

God knows what is going on in there, he thought. It must be at least ten minutes since Butler went in; he might be in trouble.

Kee was right. It was impossible to delay any longer.

Radford strode briskly towards the front door of the house. 'Come on,' he said to Kee. 'You lead the way.' He beckoned to his driver and the other detective accompanying Kee. 'Come on, lads, we're going in now. Brace yourselves for trouble.'

The last thing Andrew had expected was to be shown into an empty room. As Daly went downstairs, the shock hit him with a sudden surge of sickness in the stomach, instantly repressed. His mind, keyed up for violent action, began to race like a car engine thrown out of gear at full throttle.

What were the possibilities? Daly might have realized all along that he was a British agent, and shut him in here as a prisoner until he decided what to do with him. The wicked grin on the man's face seemed to point to that. But then, he had not locked the door — Andrew got up and tested it — and he had left him in here fully armed with two pistols.

Daly did not know they were loaded, of course. But if he thought Andrew was a British agent, he would *expect* them to be loaded, wouldn't he? Or at least he would have thought they *might* be, and taken the trouble to check. In fact, if he had wanted to make Andrew a prisoner, his best chance would have been downstairs, with two strong men to help him.

It didn't make sense. Maybe Collins was just late and Daly had other things to do.

Other things more important than guarding a suspected British agent?

He sat down at the table, put his leather bag on top of

the papers, and opened it. The feel of the heavy Mauser inside comforted him. But where *was* Collins? He thought he heard a noise outside, and walked over to the window to pull down the net curtains and peer out.

The road looked busier than before. There was a group of men walking down it, looking at the house as they came towards it. One of them was Radford.

Hell's bloody teeth, Andrew thought. There they are walking down the middle of the road — not even on the *pavement*, for Christ's sake! — as though they're thinking of buying the place. Even a child could see they don't belong here; in fact, those kids are staring at them with their eyes popping out. They're not making the slightest attempt at disguise. Any moment someone in this building is going to look out of the window and see them.

And then what? Then Daly will know I'm a British agent because it's too much of a coincidence that a house like this would be raided just at the moment when I come to it. Maybe that's what he was waiting for — he got me here early to see if anyone turned up before Collins arrived. And now they have.

How do I get out of this?

The solution came to him as he saw Radford begin an earnest, anxious discussion with one of the other detectives. They're going to be seen any second, Andrew realized. It's no good waiting for Collins. If he isn't in this building already, he couldn't get in if he wanted. There's only one thing for it.

He strode to the bedroom door, opened it, and hurried down the stairs. 'Daly!' he shouted. 'Mr Daly, where are you? *Achtung — schnell!* There is danger!'

He was halfway down the stairs when Daly and the two young men came into the hall at once.

'What the devil is it?' Daly asked. 'Your man's not here yet, he'll –'

'No, it's not that!' Andrew said. 'There are men outside in the street – I think they are the police!'

'What?' Daly and the others dashed through to the front downstairs room, and peered out. Andrew heard a voice say: 'Jesus, Mary and Joseph, the man's right!' Then they were back in the hall. Shocked, Daly gave Andrew a swift, appraising glance, but it was one more of gratitude than suspicion. Now I've proved my credentials, Andrew thought, but where the hell is Collins?

It's too late for that now.

The front door opened at the same time as Daly said: 'We must get out the back. Frank! Seamus! Quick!'

The next few minutes were very chaotic. Kee came through the front door very fast and grabbed the first man he saw, which was Andrew. He slammed Andrew against the wall hard, and the violence of the impact did two things. First, it winded Andrew, and second, it decided him which way to fight. Out of sheer frustration he resisted, and then, when Kee tried to turn him round, Andrew kneed him in the groin, jerked his hands free and hit him a short, clumsy punch to the side of the head. The two of them reeled back and forth in the narrow hall, wrestling without any clear advantage. Andrew was aware of other detectives trying to push past, and without really meaning to he knew he had stopped them. Then a second detective grabbed his right arm from behind and shoved it painfully up his back, and someone else hit him hard with something heavy on the side of the head, below the ear.

Kee said: 'At least we got one of the buggers, anyway.'

Sean was stunned when Michael Collins wheeled his bicycle boldly into Brendan Road, and when the detective saw them and came striding straight towards them, Sean was appalled. They've got my photograph, he thought, and surely to God they must know what Michael looks like, too. But it seemed they did not. Almost immediately his anxiety turned to amazement, and then delight.

Collins smiled at the policeman cheerfully. Before the harassed detective could speak, he said: 'Excuse me, officer, but I wonder, are you in need of any help?'

'What?'

'Well, I believe you are policemen, are you not, and as I live in this road I wondered if you were in need of any assistance. Who is it you are after?'

The detective gazed at him uncertainly. Collins's friendly, open countenance was a vast relief after the protests and sullen name-calling of the crowd. He said: 'We're after Michael Collins and the damned Shinners, that's who. I just wish these people would stand back, for the love of God. There's likely to be some shooting if they put up a fight.'

Over the policeman's shoulder Sean could see some of the other detectives involved in an anxious conference opposite the door of number 1. The gaggle of young boys were about fifteen yards behind them, egging each other on to see who would come the closest. The detective glanced at them anxiously.

Collins said: 'Is that a fact? Well, those young boys ought to be out of the way for a start. Would you like me to have a word with them for you, officer? I know one or two of the little devils myself.'

The detective looked vastly relieved. 'That'd be a great help, mister. Tell them to get right back, away from number 1, would you? That's where it's going to start.'

He left them to go to the assistance of his colleague. Collins got on his bike and cycled slowly down the street. As he came abreast of the boys he shouted to them to keep back, but his eyes, like Sean's, were on number 1 where the detectives were pouring in through the front door. As he cycled past they heard shots from the rear of the building.

'Will we go in, Michael?' Sean asked.

Collins shook his head. 'No, no, it would do no good. They'll get out the back if they're quick.'

By now people were looking out of their windows all along the street, and a little crowd had gathered around the police car at the junction halfway along. As Sean and Collins approached it one of the detectives stepped forward. Collins smiled at him.

'Good morning, officer,' he said. 'I hear your friends are after Michael Collins.'

Davis grinned, his face a curious mixture of tension and relief. 'True,' he said. 'But he's a terrible hard man to catch.'

'I wish you luck,' Collins said. 'It's a nasty job you boys have to do. How do they know he's using that house, do you think?'

The two men's eyes met. Davis said: 'I've no idea at all. But no doubt I'll find out, before the day is over.'

For a moment they stood together, without speaking, and Sean had a sense that they could have said much more, in another place or time. Then Sean and Collins moved quietly to the back of the crowd, and watched, until at last the detectives came out, bringing their one prisoner.

He was a man neither Sean Brennan nor Michael Collins had ever seen before.

15

RADFORD CAME INTO the front room in Brendan Road behind Kee, and shut the door behind him. He was hot, breathing heavily.

'Damn!' he said. 'Damn them all to perdition! They got away!'

'All except this one,' Kee said.

Radford glared at Kee, and the handcuffed figure of

Andrew Butler. He said: 'They all got away, Tom. Every last one of them. He's one of ours.'

'What?' Kee was appalled. 'In here, and you didn't tell me? I could have —'

'Shut up, Tom. Not now, please. I've got to think.' He looked at Andrew. 'What happened? Was Collins here?'

Andrew began to shake his head, then stopped because of the pain. 'No,' he said. 'Never came.'

'Why not?'

'How the hell should I know?' Andrew felt himself trembling with frustration and rage. 'Ask this big oaf here — perhaps he scared him off, walking down the middle of the street!'

'That's enough of that!' Radford snapped. 'Do they know who you are?'

'Not unless you've told them. Or he did.' Andrew tried to get a grip on himself, realizing that Radford was trying to salvage what he could from the fiasco. At least he had had the sense to shut the door, to keep the others out. But what did it matter now?

Radford turned to Kee. 'Look, Tom, as far as you're concerned, this man is a German officer, right? He's an important catch. Keep him handcuffed and take him to HQ. Only you and I are to interview him. Got that?'

'Got it.' Kee said. 'But I wish you'd told me.'

'Just get him outside, Tom, will you?' Radford answered. 'I'll explain later. I want to search this place first.'

He opened the door and went out.

'Come on, then, Hermann,' said Kee. 'On your feet.

German officer, eh?' He hauled Andrew out of the front door, and dragged him past the sullen, muttering crowd to where Davis and his driver stood by their car.

'*Scheisskopf,*' Andrew said, for their benefit.

Standing quietly with his bicycle, Sean Brennan saw the two men coming towards him, and recognized one as the detective who had chased him in the church. He drew his cap down over his eyes, and stepped slowly to the back of the crowd.

But Michael Collins stood quite calmly, looking for all the world like a bank clerk who has never seen anything so exciting in all his life.

Later that evening, Andrew and Radford sat together in an interview room in the cellars of Brunswick Street. It was a cold stone room with nothing on the walls. It contained two upright chairs and a table. Radford held out a sheet of paper.

'That's it,' he said. 'There's your cover note.'

Andrew read it slowly.

Acting on information received, detectives of the DMP G Division raided a private house in Brendan Road this afternoon. In the house the officers found a number of men, whom they believe to be members of the Irish Republican Army responsible for several recent outrages, including the attempted assassination of Lord French at Ashtown Cross. Unfortunately, the men were apparently warned of the raid a few minutes before it happened, and, after a fierce interchange in which a

number of shots were fired, all but one managed to make
their escape through the back garden.

The police did, however, arrest one occupant of the
house — a former German Army officer, whom they
believe to be in Dublin with the aim of selling arms to the
Sinn Feiners. The German has been taken to Dublin
Castle for interrogation, and he will either be tried under
the Defence of the Realm Act or deported within the
next few days. Lord French is prepared to issue the
strongest possible protest to the government in Berlin.

Andrew tossed it back. 'You'll release this to the press?'

'That's right. It looks good for us. A small propaganda
triumph, even if we did miss Collins himself. And the
beauty of it is, the Sinn Feiners may protest, but for once
they know it's really true. They *were* trying to buy
arms from a German officer. Or at least they think they
were.'

Andrew's lips tightened. He rubbed the back of his head
irritably, trying to mask the pain. It was a long time since
he had felt such a sense of waste, of anticlimax. 'I didn't get
into this to make propaganda points,' he said.

Radford sighed. 'Nor did I. But it's the best we can do,
just now. Why do you think he didn't turn up, anyway?'

'If I knew that, I'd know everything.' Andrew pushed his
chair back, and stood up. 'I've been round and round
it in my mind, but I can see no purpose in it. Bloody
Irish inefficiency, probably. Unless they knew you were
coming.'

Radford flushed. 'I've told you twice already, haven't I?
No one knew — no one at all — until after you were in that

building. That's why we made such a botch of the raid; I hadn't time to get the lads in place. It makes us all look stupid, leaving the back door unguarded. But they couldn't have known — I'll swear it on anything you like!'

Andrew gazed back at him in silence, cold, dispassionate, with that air of distant unconcern which had always irritated Radford about the aristocracy. In the end he said: 'All right, I believe you. But from now on, operations with the police are a dead duck. When are you going to let me out of this place?'

Radford sighed, and stood up. He fished a pair of handcuffs out of his pocket, and clipped one of the bracelets around his own left wrist. 'Now, if you like,' he said. 'I'll walk you over to Dublin Castle, so the lads can see, and then you can slip out the back door any time you like. That suit you?'

Andrew shrugged. 'It'll have to, won't it?'

Radford fastened the other bracelet round Andrew's right wrist, and unlocked the cell door.

Not for the first time that evening, Detective Constable Dick Davis stopped typing, and scowled at the filing cabinet in the corner of his office. There was something missing from this report which he was typing out, and he didn't understand why.

Nearly all confidential reports in G Division — those which could not be entrusted to female secretaries — were handwritten first, and then given to Davis to type. This was partly because he was simply more proficient than anyone else with a typewriter, and partly because, unlike everyone else, he didn't seem to mind using one. As a result he had a highly developed sense of what such a report should include, because he had read them all, word by word.

This report, compiled jointly by Radford and Kee, was very detailed about the events during the raid on the house in Brendan Road, the way the suspects had escaped out of the back garden, and the files, guns, and paperwork that had been found. It did not, so far, include a report of the interrogation of the German officer who had been arrested, but no doubt that would follow in due course. Davis had seen Radford escorting the man over to Dublin Castle a couple of hours ago. He had hoped he might be involved in the interrogation himself, but it seemed that Radford and Kee were keeping that task to themselves.

But the thing which puzzled Davis most was how Radford had found out about Brendan Road in the first place.

It was a vital piece of information, and it was simply missing from the report. '*Acting on information received*', it said, and that was all. For the twelfth time that night, Davis sat back in his chair, picked up his cigarette, and blew a cloud of foul-smelling smoke at the grey filing cabinet. Information received by whom? By Radford himself, it seemed. And anyone else? Davis doubted it. Even Radford's Ulster confederate, Tom Kee, had seemed in the dark this morning. Kee had tried to hide it, but it was Davis's impression that he was pretty annoyed. So either Kee was a consummate actor, or he had been frozen out.

Why? To this there was an obvious answer, and it was

one which sent a chill through Davis's bloodstream. Radford didn't dare share his information with anyone, because he was afraid it was being passed on to the IRA. Davis smoothed the paper in his typewriter thoughtfully, making sure that the extra carbon — the one for Michael Collins — was in line with the others.

I should really finish this report soon, he thought, before that beggar comes back and starts checking up on me. Because if he's afraid that information is being passed to the IRA, his next move is going to be to find out who's doing the passing.

Radford's an Ulsterman, for heaven's sake, Davis thought; he'd hardly been in this city until two months ago. He doesn't know the difference between Donnybrook and Drumcondra. Who's he been in touch with?

It has to be someone within the movement itself, he decided. And that, to Davis, was the most frightening thought of all. Because if someone within the republican movement was passing on high-quality information to Radford, then there was no knowing what that information might contain. It might contain, for instance, the name of the detective in G Division who was working for the IRA. The informer might even come across one of the flimsy carbons from Davis's typewriter in the republicans' files, and show it to Radford. It would be easy enough to check which typewriter the report had been typed on — each machine had its own distinctive faults in the way the letters came out on the page.

The informer might even have heard of the time when Michael Collins had been spirited into Brunswick Square itself, and sat all night at the desk of Radford's predecessor, reading through the files which Davis brought him. At the time, Davis had thought it his proudest moment, but he was not particularly anxious to explain his pride to a British judge, or to spend the next ten years remembering it in a cell. They would probably send him to a prison in England, Davis thought. English prison officers did not like Irish republicans, or bent police officers.

He shivered, and looked round to see if someone was coming in, or if the window had been opened. No. The building was quiet, as it usually was in the early part of the evening.

I'm getting jumpy, he thought. Time to finish this report. I need a drink, a bite to eat and a breath of fresh air.

He stubbed out his cigarette, and for ten more minutes his fingers hammered hard on the keys.

But as he unwound the completed report from the machine, he thought: Wherever he gets his information from, that man Radford is becoming a menace.

He'll have to go.

Sir Jonathan was pleased with the afternoon at the races. It had been one of those fine, crisp days that come sometimes in midwinter, when the sky clears, the sun shines down out of a blue sky, and for a few hours everyone can unbutton their topcoats and remember what it can be like in summer. The atmosphere consoled him a little after the fiasco of Andrew Butler's failure, which he had learnt about the previous night.

To his delight, Catherine gave at least an appearance of

enjoying herself. She had been a lover of horses since she could walk, and as they paraded in the paddock she gazed at their silken, gleaming flanks with close attention. In the twelve thirty she had picked an outsider, Scheherazade, who had come in by a short head at fifteen to one; and from then on her advice had been sought on all sides. Colonel Roberts and his wife, who had just come over from England, were delighted, as was MacQuarry, a tall, thin Scotsman who worked in the official solicitor's department at Dublin Castle.

The young men were less of a success, so far. MacQuarry's son, David, the heir to several Highland grouse moors and trout streams, had even turned up with a young lady of his own, who looked likely to become his fiancée at any moment. The other, Simon le Fanu, a short, powerfully built captain in the Inniskillings, seemed so uncharacteristically pale and morose that Sir Jonathan wondered if he was ill.

Sir Jonathan stood beside him as they took their places in the stand for the penultimate race in the day, the three o'clock. It was a novice handicap over a mile and two furlongs, once round the course.

'Have you got any money on this, young Simon?' he asked.

The young man shrugged. 'A couple of quid on Shangri-La, for the name. But I've no idea really.'

Sir Jonathan grunted, offended by the lack of enthusiasm. In his opinion racing could be enjoyed only if pursued with passion, even by those without knowledge. He considered the scene around him, still lit by the declining rays of a sun which shone miraculously out of a clear blue western sky. What he knew about young Simon could be summed up in five facts: he had served for two years in Flanders; he had been wounded; he had won the Military Cross; he was the heir to 5,000 acres in west Meath; and he was unmarried. All of these, so far as Sir Jonathan was concerned, were positive recommendations.

He tried a different tack. He said: 'There was a time, eighteen months ago, when I thought I'd never see a sight like this again. I dare say you felt the same, eh?'

Simon shivered. 'True enough. The nearest we got to it was when some troopers organized a racecourse for the rats, along the duckboards in a communication trench. They used to shoot them as they came through the finishing post.'

Sir Jonathan laughed. 'Never keep an Irishman from a bet, eh? If you put some of these fellows in a hole in the ground, they'd bet on something.'

'That's what we did, didn't we?' said Simon. 'They kept a book on the new recruits, once, till I put a stop to it. Two to one they wouldn't last a fortnight.'

'My God,' said Sir Jonathan, horrified. 'Hardly cricket, that. Court-martialling offence, I should think. Was there a charge?'

'No.' Simon did not elaborate, and in a moment the excitement of the race was upon them, and the story forgotten. Only much later, when they had returned to Merrion Square, and the butler, Keneally, was carrying round a tray of drinks in the main drawing room, did Sir Jonathan think of it again. He noticed le Fanu standing politely by himself on the edge of the hearth, took his daughter firmly by the arm, and steered her across the room.

'Cathy, my dear, come and talk to young Simon here. He didn't have much luck this afternoon – I think he's been a bit put off betting by some of the things that happened to him in Flanders. Perhaps you can cheer him up.'

'I doubt it, if he's thinking of the war.' Catherine had purposely been avoiding Simon all afternoon, precisely because she understood her father's designs in inviting him. But a few words could scarcely hurt. Indeed, they might even have a healing effect. All afternoon, she had been aware of a dull ache in her chest, which had threatened to break out into agony once or twice, when she had seen a hand or the side of a face in the crowd that might have been Sean's, until she looked closer and saw it was not. The only relief, as she had found with other types of pain in her childhood, was to throw herself with relentless determination into a bright, brittle surface appearance of energy and laughter. She might atone for it later, she thought, with floods of tears into her pillow; but not now, not in front of these people. She had too much pride, and her pride gave her strength.

'What happened to you then, Simon?' she said lightly. 'Did you see the error of your ways, and wish you were at home, fighting for Ireland instead?'

'I *was* fighting for Ireland,' said Simon stolidly. 'I volunteered; we all did. Ten thousand of us at least.'

'There were nearly the same number of Englishmen stationed behind in the old country, to keep us all in order. Poor mathematics, was it not?'

Simon flushed. 'I didn't know you were a Sinn Feiner, Miss O'Connell-Gort. I should have thought with your family —'

'I should have had different views. Yes, I know.' She smiled at him sweetly, thinking: It's funny how one man can be devastatingly attractive, and another, roughly the same size and shape, can look ugly as a toad. When that flush spread upwards, I'm sure the veins in his neck began to swell, and the pimple on his forehead looked as if it was about to burst. The thought amused her, and she said: 'I'm sorry, I'm eccentric, that's all. I just do it to tease. Now, what was it Father was saying you bet about, in Flanders?'

Whatever it was, she never learned, for Keneally coughed importantly at the door, and announced another guest.

'Ladies and gentlemen, Major Andrew Butler.'

Catherine glanced around curiously. She remembered that her father had threatened to inflict three of these absurd suitors on her, but he had said that the third might not be able to come. Here he was, apparently. A dark-haired man in civilian clothes. Tall, broad-shouldered, rather athletic. And — sweet Christ! — his face was disfigured by the most horrendous scar. A livid line of white like a snake down the side of his face. Where did Father dig up these horrors?

The man caught her staring at him, bowed ironically, and stared back. She flushed, realizing how rude she must seem, and then another thought struck her. When he looked straight at her most of the scar was hidden, and the rest of the face, the undamaged part, was really rather attractive. Slim, strong, with a short military moustache, dark, slightly shadowed eyes that surveyed the room with a sort of . . .

What, exactly?

Whatever it was, there was something about them that had to be more interesting than gazing at the pimple on Simon le Fanu's forehead, or talking to that emaciated stork David MacQuarry, who had so hilariously turned up with his own cheerful bouncing fiancée-to-be. No, she had to hand it to Father, this monster did at least look interesting. So when her father went forward to shake the new arrival's hand and then turned to look for her, she did none of the things, like turning her back or striking up a passionate conversation with Mrs MacQuarry about furniture covers, which she might have resorted to if she had wished.

Instead, she smiled brightly, held out her hand and, feeling the ache in her heart sharpen, decided to challenge him unmercifully, in order to help herself forget Sean.

'I'm so glad you could come, Major Butler. Father said you were a busy man. Forgive me, but you *are* in the army, aren't you?'

'Yes, I am.' Andrew accepted a drink from Keneally, and frowned at her. 'Oh, I see. The clothes, you mean. Well, we don't have to wear uniform all the time.'

'I didn't mean that,' she said. 'I meant, if you're in the army, I don't see how you could possibly be so busy as to pass up an afternoon at the races. Most of the rest of our Imperial garrison was there.'

Andrew looked at her for the first time. He had declined Sir Jonathan's ridiculous invitation to the races for obvious reasons: anyone might see him there, including Patrick Daly and the other three who had escaped from Brendan Road. He had only decided to come here tonight because he was bored, because there was very little danger of discovery, and because the Collins mission was almost certainly blown anyway. Tomorrow, or the next day, he would leave Dublin and go back to Ardmore, and see if he could patch up one of the cottages to live in.

And then decide what to do with the rest of his life.

In the meantime, for some reason, he was at a dinner party. He gazed at the young woman in front of him, trying to take in the fact that she, and the others in the room, were real, and not just passers-by in the street whom he could ignore. A delicate, sylphlike face, short black pageboy hair, red lips, wide dark hypnotic eyes. He remembered she had said something to him.

'Sorry. What did you say?'

Catherine was piqued. Her dart did not seem to have got through. 'I said, I don't understand why anyone in the army can claim to have anything really useful to do.'

'Oh, I see.' With a shock, he realized that she was actually trying to be rude to him. The shock was compounded by a realization that he had not been in a situation remotely resembling this for a very long time indeed. There had been mixed evenings in the officers' mess at Aldershot, before demobilization, but that had been almost a year ago. And there had been that month in London, when he had visited almost every high-class brothel he could find, in an attempt to exorcise the German girl, Elsie, from his mind. He thought he had succeeded.

Since he came back to Ardmore he had lived the life of a recluse, a celibate. There had been women around, of course, but only cooks and servant girls – he had kept his distance from them.

He thought he had closed that door in his mind and locked it.

Now, quite suddenly, he was faced with an attractive young woman of his own class. A quite remarkably attractive one, in fact. Fairly tall, slender, in a loose green silk dress which showed off a considerable area of neck and shoulder. A hint of a body that was lithe, athletic, overpoweringly feminine.

But it was the scent that really aroused him. She was wearing some kind of perfume that he had not smelt for a very long time, and which took him back, irresistibly, to Elsie, and the way she had unbuttoned a similar, cheaper dress, very slowly and suggestively, and then pulled it down, smiling as he watched, all the way down to her hips . . .

Something about his gaze caused the young woman in front of him to flush a light pink, and he thought *for Christ's sake, get a grip – this is a dinner party in Dublin, not a whorehouse.*

And this girl's probably a silly little Irish virgin.

Nonetheless he said: 'Why are you being rude to me? Are you frightened of my scar?'

And Catherine, who had got quite a shock at the wolfish, yearning look in the man's eyes as they travelled down her bare shoulders, said: 'I couldn't care less about your scar. If you join the army you must expect to get hurt, mustn't you?'

Andrew was stunned. No young woman had ever said anything like that to him before. And truly, she did not look revolted. Only challenging, almost deliberately provocative. He said: 'Why are you being rude, then?'

She shrugged. 'Because — I don't like the army, I suppose.'

'So what *do* you like?'

'Oh, I don't know. Horses, for one thing. You should have been there this afternoon.'

'Why?'

'It was a fine day. And I won fifty pounds.'

Andrew laughed. 'Bully for you. What are you going to spend it on?'

'Books, perhaps. Or some new paintings for this room. It needs some more, don't you think?'

Andrew looked around the room vaguely. There were several large ancient portraits of noble ancestors, most of them turning a uniform mud colour under many years' exposure to firesmoke and sunlight; and at the end of the room a slightly more cheerful one of a huntsman, with his horse and hounds, sitting proudly in front of a quite phenomenal heap of dead pheasants, ducks, partridges, rabbits and deer. It reminded him of a similar one in the dining room at Ardmore, and for the first time it dawned on him that this young woman might actually own this house one day.

'Yes, surely,' he said. 'What are you thinking of buying?'

'I don't know. Something different from these, anyway. Perhaps a portrait of myself by Augustus John. Or a nude man by Modigliani — if he did any men.'

'Now you're trying to shock me.'

'Would you be shocked to see a picture of a naked man on the wall? I see plenty of nude women, and I'm told it's fine art.'

'Yes, but – not in the living room, surely?'

For answer, she pointed across the room to a table by the window. On it was a sculpture, about two feet high, of an athlete throwing a discus. He was clothed only in a flat Grecian sunhat.

Andrew laughed. 'All right, all right, I have no arguments. Install a life-size oil painting of a male nude over your mantelpiece if you like. I'll come along and watch the faces of your guests, if I may.'

The laugh had an effect on them both. Catherine thought it attractive – cheerful, manly, a point in his favour. Andrew realized, dimly, that it was the first time anyone had made him laugh like that since – since at least before the fire.

But the ache in Catherine became sharper too. It was foolish to talk like that about naked men. She knew who she would want to model for any such portrait, and it was no one here in this room.

Andrew said: 'You're an unusual young woman, Miss – Catherine, isn't it?'

'Yes. Am I? It's probably because I'm a medical student, and used to thinking about bodies. Also I've spent a lot of time on my own, in the country, so I'm used to thinking for myself. And I'm a Catholic, like my mother. And a nationalist – a Sinn Feiner, in fact. So I would seem unusual to you, I suppose. In fact, I'm hardly suitable for you to talk to at all.'

He had expected a boring evening, full of tedious social

chit-chat. Not a full-blooded attack from his hostess the moment he came in the door. He looked at her closely, thinking: Why is she doing this? He remembered a nervous young lieutenant who had talked like this to keep his courage up, the night before battle.

He said: 'Are you afraid of me?'

I would be, she thought, if I met you alone on a dark night, and you were looking for a woman. The eyes – it was the expression in them that set him apart. They were bright, watching her intently, but from somewhere very distant, deep within himself. Yes, I am afraid of you, she thought, but I have to face you down.

She said: 'I expect I can shoot as well as you.'

Again, he laughed, and this time Sir Jonathan looked over, pleased. He had felt sure that Andrew would be a match for his wilful daughter; he had not guessed she would manage to amuse him.

'With a pistol, I mean,' she went on. 'My brothers taught me to use one when I was twelve. I could outshoot them.'

He said: 'I'll take you on, then, one day, and we'll see. Come to my estate, at Ardmore. The house is burnt down, but I still have a shooting range, and you can bring your own pistol, if you like. But it would have to be for a bet – something serious on both sides. You choose first, and I'll match it.'

'All right, then,' she said. Her eyes held his, boldly. In her stomach, excitement flickered like an adder's tongue. 'But first I have to learn a little bit more about you, so I can decide what you would most hate to lose.'

'Really?' He raised an eyebrow, the scar whitening on his cheek. 'Ask away then.'

She considered, pleased at the way her policy of aggression was paying off. 'First, tell me why your house burned down.'

He began to tell her, briefly, but then Keneally announced that supper was served. At the table, it became obvious he would have to tell the whole party. It was a tale which expressed the inner fears of every Anglo-Irish landlord, surrounded as they were by a sea of poverty, envy, and Roman superstition.

Colonel Roberts, recently arrived from England, was appalled. 'It sounds more like something out of the Punjab than the United Kingdom,' he said. 'Are you positive it was the Sinn Feiners who did it? These things can sometimes happen by accident, you know.'

Andrew smiled grimly. 'All I know is, at least one of them was there on the night, and I'd marched them out of the house at gunpoint two days before. That house had stood for two hundred years before that.'

The solicitor MacQuarry, who, in addition to his moors in Scotland, had an estate in County Wexford, mentioned a similar tale he had heard of a house that had nearly been burnt there; and Simon le Fanu had heard of Unionist farmers' crops being burnt, and the tails of their cows docked in the night.

'So we have to show them,' said Sir Jonathan. 'Firm government action is the only way, plus a determination on our part not to be intimidated.' He fixed Catherine firmly with his eye, trying to quell the explosion before it could erupt.

But she had made her views known to the Viceroy; she did not want to fight that fight over again tonight. She was more intrigued to learn about Andrew.

'Where are you going to live, then?' she asked.

'I'll rebuild the house, one day. Until then, I have a place here in town, and some cottages on the estate where I can camp.'

'Why not leave, sell it all up, and go to England?'

'Where to? It's my home.'

'Will you have the money to rebuild it?'

'Not now.' He looked at her coldly, with more distaste than before. She wondered what she would do if her own home were burnt down. But then it was not her own home yet; not until she had an approved husband. I wonder if I look like a good catch to you, she thought; a young girl with lots of money and a compliant father. And a Sinn Fein lover in the slums.

Ex-lover.

The talk drifted on, to the political situation and what Lloyd George should do. There was talk of English recruits coming over to strengthen the police; of a thorough overhaul of Dublin Castle; of how the Home Rule Bill might defuse it all. To her father's great relief, Catherine let it drift over her. It's all a charade, she thought, there's no point in arguing with them. Words mean nothing. Sean is right, action is the only way.

And that will mean death, and war, and burning all over the country. Do I want that?

I want Sean.

I'll go back and find him again. I was crazy to walk out like that. It's what we do that matters. What we do when we're together, not what we say. Oh Sean, I need you.

Andrew had been watching her, fascinated by her proud slender beauty. For much of the time she seemed withdrawn, drifting away inside herself. At the end of the evening he said: 'You went very quiet, young lady. I thought you might argue with us, if you are a nationalist, as you say.'

'There's no point. Words change nothing. Only action does.'

'True.' Just as failed action only makes things worse, Andrew thought. What would this girl be saying now, if Michael Collins had kept his appointment yesterday? He shrugged and said: 'Well, what's it to be?'

'I beg your pardon?'

'Your prize. If you win the shooting match.'

'Oh, that.' She had forgotten all about it.

'Yes. It has to be something serious, remember.'

She wondered how to put him off. The man had interested her for a few moments, no more. She had no intention of going out to the country with him for some bet. But she didn't want to back down. So she said: 'All right. If I win, your ruined house belongs to me. How about that?'

His lips tightened. This girl is lethal, he thought; she only strikes at the heart. She watched him coolly, her eyes wide, dark, distant.

He said: 'That's a big bet, young lady. I shall have to think what to take from you in exchange.' He held her gaze for a moment, then turned abruptly and went down the steps into the street. 'I'll let you know in a few days,' he said. 'Better practise your shooting.'

Then he was gone, crossing the square quickly, his heels clicking on the pavement. She stood on the doorstep and watched for a moment, wondering if a young man in a flat cap would appear under the streetlight on the corner, where she had kissed Sean.

But there was no one there.

16

IT WAS QUIET in the library. Davis always treasured his visits here; it was like dropping into a pool of silence, after the glare and bustle of the streets outside. Here there was only the flicker and rustle of pages, like leaves in the wind, and the breath of whispered, apologetic conversations.

He came here regularly. He had acquired a reputation, in the force, as being something of a reader; apart from cars it was his main interest, so far as anyone knew, outside his work.

The young man behind the counter had seen him coming. At the moment he was dealing with an insistent old woman, who wanted the definitive book on wedding etiquette, and refused to be satisfied with the only one he could find. Davis met his eyes, briefly, then picked up a book idly, resigning himself to wait.

As he read, he took a copy of the transcript of Radford's interview with the German officer and slipped it between the pages, like a bookmark. It was, he thought, very disturbing. In the first place, the raid had foiled what might have been a highly successful arms purchase for the Volunteers. In the second place, the police now knew all about it, and would no doubt use it as evidence to convince the higher command that far tougher measures were necessary against the IRA.

This man Radford was becoming a menace. He was too effective; he made Davis nervous. Not only had he found out about the Brendan Road rendezvous; he had got all this information out of the German in a couple of days. He must be a powerful interrogator, Davis thought; and his mouth went dry for a moment as he imagined himself sitting across the table from the Ulsterman, not as a colleague, but as a suspected traitor.

The old lady was satisfied at last. She left, clutching a large volume open at a page full of illustrations of wedding dresses and veils. Davis looked around him, and then stepped up to the counter. He smiled at the young man, and passed him the book. The report stuck out a fraction of an inch from the end of it.

'Would you put that one back on the shelves for me?'

'Surely, sir. Is there anything else I can help you with?' As he spoke, the young man bent down and put the book into a rack under the counter, deftly abstracting the paper as he did so.

'Not at the moment. How are things here?'

'Peaceful enough. But we've a couple of new volumes in that might interest you. I made a note of them. Here.'

He passed over a folded sheet of paper. It said, simply: 'Need to see you. Donegan's, tonight. D.'

He nodded. 'Thanks,' he said. 'They look very interesting.'

He wandered slowly away to the shelves on engineering and transport, chose a book at random, took it to the counter to be issued, and walked out.

Donegan's was a small tobacconist's in Aungier Street, halfway between Dublin Castle and St Stephen's Green. It was the sort of place where men were dropping in all day for cigarettes and a chat; like the kiosk that Thomas Clarke, the first signatory of the Republic, had had in Parnell Street before the Rising. But, as Davis knew, more came out of Donegan's than tobacco. In the little room at the back, there was a complete printing press, where the republican newspaper, *An tOglach*, was printed.

Davis hoped he was the only member of the DMP who knew this.

As he stepped inside, the proprietor, Donegan, looked up with a cheerful grin.

'Ah. Mr Davis, would it be? There was a fellow here looking for you just now. Wait now while I close this door, would you?'

He locked the door behind Davis, and then led him through to the room at the back. Here, two men sat quietly reading. One was Patrick Daly and the other was Michael Collins himself.

Collins got up quickly, and pumped him by the hand.

'Dick! Good to see you, my boy! Have a chair, have a chair. Have you got much time?'

'An hour or so.'

'Good. That's great. We should be through by then.' He sat down, and looked at Davis intently. As always, Davis felt overawed by the sheer energy and ebullience of the man; but at the same time vastly reassured, to feel that the affairs of the revolution were in such hugely capable hands.

'You look worried, Dick.' Collins grinned. 'Is the crime wave wearing you down?'

'Hardly. The police are becoming very efficient these past days. You saw that in Brendan Road, didn't you?'

Collins frowned. 'I know. Because of your new boss, Radford. I've read the reports you send us. The man's too damned efficient for his own good.' He paused. Davis met Daly's eyes and knew what was coming. Collins said: 'We're going to get rid of him.'

'How?' Davis felt a surge of excitement, almost sexual in its intensity. It was for this, as much as for his political beliefs, that he did this work. The sense of power that enabled him to look at his colleagues, and know almost for certain that this day would be their last on earth. And that he, Dick Davis, had a hand in it.

'That's what we need you for,' said Collins. 'Where does the man live?'

'In the Standard Hotel, in Harcourt Street. I think he's going to move into the Castle soon, but they haven't found him a room yet. Everyone wants one.'

'We'll save them the trouble. What time does he usually go to the hotel?'

'It varies. Six, seven in the evening, maybe, for dinner. He's not that regular.'

'Do you go with him?'

'Sometimes. More often he goes with his friend, Kee.'

'I don't want Kee yet,' Collins said. 'With luck he'll go back to Belfast when his master's dead. But our problem is, we're not absolutely sure what Radford looks like. The last thing I want is to shoot the wrong man.'

Davis began to describe him, but Daly interrupted.

'That's no good. You can never be sure from what someone says. Look, we want you to point him out to us. Some time tomorrow if you can. Where are you likely to be with him?'

Davis thought. 'In HQ in Brunswick Street, I suppose.'

'All right.' Daly nodded. 'Well, at some time during the day, I want you to come out of the front door with him. We'll be watching it. If you come out together with Radford, do something – take your hat off, fiddle around with the lining or something. If you're with anyone else, keep your hat on.'

Davis considered the idea. 'Are you going to shoot him there and then? I'd have to try and defend him, you know.'

Daly shook his head. 'No, no. We just want to get a good look at him, so we don't make a mistake later.'

'All right.' It didn't sound too good to Davis, but he couldn't think of anything else. 'There's one other thing you ought to know,' he said.

'What's that?'

'He wears body armour. Some kind of bullet-proof vest. I've seen him put it on. It makes him look stouter than he is.'

Daly smiled. 'He's worried already, then. We'll get him, Dick, don't you worry.'

Collins stood up. 'We could go out and have a pint together, Dick, but I don't think it would do your reputation any good.'

'To be seen with you? No.' Davis left. As he walked along the street outside he took off his hat and looked at it curiously. One touch of this, and I sign a man's death warrant, he thought.

The sense of power coursed through him. Then, unbidden, the voice of his old school chaplain came into his mind, saying: 'And Judas Iscariot betrayed our Lord with a kiss.'

Davis cursed, jammed the hat back on his head, and put the thought resolutely out of his mind. That was nothing like it, quite different entirely. That was religion, this was a matter of real life, politics, freeing the nation from oppression.

He strode on briskly down the street, until he came to a pub called Rafferty's, near the tram stop for his journey home. He went inside, bought a large double gin, and drank Michael Collins's health, all alone at the bar.

* * *

Sean awoke, sweating. For a moment he was disoriented. The clean, white walls, flowery chintz curtains, the crucifix at the foot of the bed, the painting of the Sacred Heart — where was he? There were people moving around downstairs, talking quietly, laughing. No shouts or brawls or stench; in fact, a tempting smell of frying bacon drifted in. Then one of the voices spoke more clearly — a woman's voice — and he remembered. He was in Mrs O'Hagan's, the new lodging house Paddy Daly had found for him.

He got out of bed, stripped, and washed from the ewer and basin on the table in the corner. The water was ice-cold, and goose pimples rose along his skin. But he persisted, splashing himself all over with the flannel, trying to raise a lather with the small cake of soap, until his skin was red raw and his teeth were chattering uncontrollably. Still he went on, rinsing the soap off, dunking his head in the basin, even putting his feet in it one at a time to clean them. Every part of him must be clean, especially there, between the legs, and if it was cold and hurt, so much the better. The towel he found was not large, and it was soon sodden, but he rubbed himself hard with it, vigorously, until his skin became pink and warm. His feet ached on the cold wet floor.

He saw the crucifix on the wall and thought: Now I am clean of her, now I am free. I will confess it all later today and then I will be free of her completely. And now I am cleansed and pure to do whatever duty has to be done.

The breakfast room was small, with a crisp white

tablecloth and gleaming cutlery. There were two other young men already sitting there; both were lodgers in the house, Sean knew, and part-time members of the Volunteers. But they had jobs to go to in the day, as Martin had once had, and both were already eating quickly, with one eye on the clock. They nodded to him. Mrs O'Hagan had had a paper delivered, and one boy had it propped on the table in front of him.

'Look at that, boys!' he said exultantly. 'We must have won nearly every blasted seat in the country!' He jabbed with his fork at the results of the local elections on the centre page. 'A Sinn Fein council in every town in the land! Now whose country is it?'

'Same as before,' said the other lad morosely. 'Voting won't change a thing.'

Mrs O'Hagan came in smiling – a round cheerful woman in an apron, her grey hair covered under a white cap. She put a steaming plate of bacon, kidneys, fried egg, mushrooms, tomatoes, and fried potatoes in front of him, and stood back proudly. 'There now.'

'Mother of God!' He looked up and caught the frown on her face. 'I'm sorry, Mrs O'Hagan, I didn't mean to swear, but – do you eat like this every day?'

'Of course we do. You boys are doing your bit for the country, and that's my contribution – to send you out fit and strong as you can be. Now you eat it up – I don't want a bit left, mind – while I fetch you a fresh pot of tea. Come on, Seamus, now – your tram'll be leaving in a quarter of an hour.'

The other two laughed at Sean's evident surprise. 'You've fallen on your feet here, Sean,' said Seamus, grinning, as he hurriedly forked the last of his bacon into his mouth.

'I have that, too.' And yesterday I woke up in a slum where I had to scavenge for every scrap like a dog, he thought. The others left and Sean began to eat. Daly arrived twenty minutes later while Sean was drinking his third cup of tea and munching toast, engrossed in the newspaper. He heard the front door open, and then a heavy hand slapped him on the back.

'Well! And how do you like the life of O'Rahilly, then? Better than your last billet, eh, Sean boy?'

'It is, surely.'

Daly sat down, his genial face turning quickly serious. 'Well, don't get too used to it. You're on the run, the peelers could learn about this place any time. Enjoy it while you can.'

'I know. What's our job for today?'

'Aren't you the keen one? Nothing too strenuous this morning. I thought we'd stand in the street and watch a few policemen. Would that suit you?'

Sean flushed, remembering what had happened outside the Lambert Hotel. 'You know I'm not too good at that.'

'I know, lad. That's why I'll be there this time, to hold your hand. Anyway, that's only part of it. Let me tell you now.'

He poured himself a cup of tea, and began to explain.

Sean had guessed that Davis was working for the Volunteers when he saw him with Collins in Brendan Road. He had not realized, until today, how close that cooperation was.

Daly said: 'When he touches the man with his hat, walk up as close as you can. Don't let him see you, but make sure the man's face is stuck in your mind. We don't want any mistakes later.'

The moment came around midday. They were loitering inside a friendly newsagent's opposite the police headquarters in Brunswick Street. They had been there for most of the morning, examining each paper closely as though they might one day consider buying it. Quite suddenly, Davis came out of the front door. Behind him was another man, a little shorter, a rather stocky, genial figure, unusually broad in the chest. As soon as he was outside on the pavement, Davis snatched his hat from his head and began to fiddle ostentatiously with the rim. He held it almost at arm's length, as though there was something inside it that offended him.

'Steady on, now, no need to overdo it,' Daly muttered. 'The man's making a bloody pantomime of it!' He clutched Sean's arm to make sure he had seen too. There was only one man with Davis, so there was little chance of confusion. Nonetheless, as they came forward to cross the street, Davis made some remark to Radford, and slapped him on the chest with the hat. Radford looked mildly surprised. They crossed the road at an angle to where Sean and Daly were standing, and set off towards the city centre.

Sean hurried after them, leaving Daly a little behind, as they had agreed. Walking briskly, he passed the two men, and by the next junction he guessed he was a dozen or so yards ahead. He stood here, looking up and down, as though uncertain which way to go. Then he turned round. The two detectives were a couple of yards behind him.

Radford was looking straight at him. He smiled. Sean thought: *My God he knows who I am! He must have seen the photograph what do I do now?*

Then he went past. The smile was not for Sean. Radford was talking to Davis, in a strong Belfast accent, about rugby. Sean stood where he was, until Daly came up.

'Jesus, Mary and Joseph, boy, you were close enough! You don't think he recognized you?'

'If he did, he's done nothing about it.'

Daly looked around. The street was busy, but the two detectives were nowhere to be seen. He began to relax. 'True. Well, we've seen his face now. There's no way you can forget it?'

Sean shook his head. Every detail of Radford's face was imprinted in his mind. The heavy, firm jaw, quick, intelligent eyes, sandy moustache, the creases in the cheeks. There had been a pleasant, bluff, open air about the man – that was what disturbed him most. A bit like one of his housemasters at school, the one who had taught maths and hurling. He and Sean had had arguments in their time, but he had been a decent enough sort, in his way.

But this Radford was a policeman from Belfast. He's not a schoolmaster, Sean thought, don't think it. He can put me or Paddy or Michael Collins or any of us in a little stone cell for years if he wants to. That's his job. That's what he's come to our city to do. Maybe he's got a nice smile and is fond of dogs and children. Forget all that. It's not personal. It's not going to be done out of hatred, as the priest said. It's my duty as a soldier. A blood sacrifice for my country. That's all there is to it.

The afternoon was long and slow. Sean wished the time would move faster. He and Daly shared a pie and a pint in a pub, and then walked across the city to Harcourt Street. They checked the entrances to the Standard Hotel, and then walked back along the street to the Castle, thinking which way someone might choose from there to the hotel. If Radford was going to visit the Castle at all today. It was probable, but not certain. They had no way of knowing. In the end they decided to stand as near as they could to the hotel, and walk down the road towards the man when they saw him coming. A quick shot in the head should do it. There was no shortage of ways to escape afterwards.

The bellboy in the hotel was one of Collins's informants, and he told Daly that dinner was not served until six thirty in the evening, and most of the British officers didn't return to the hotel much before then. So then there was nothing to do but wait. Daly decided that it was pointless, indeed dangerous, to hang about in the street all afternoon, so they split up and agreed to meet again at half past five.

Sean walked towards the church, with half an idea of making his confession. As he washed himself, this morning, it had seemed a good idea. Then he had felt pure, clear, certain; now his emotions were more violent, unsettled. I need to be in control of what I feel, he thought. But I don't think a priest can do that for me now. Not now. Not today, with what I have to do.

He went to St Stephen's Green and strolled around the park, his hands thrust deep into the pockets of his coat. It was a cold, cloudy afternoon, and the place was full of

mothers and nannies with prams and little children, out for
a breath of fresh air and a chance to feed the ducks. Sean
felt a great surge of unfocused anger, so that he had to walk
quickly, scowling, to release the energy of it. I must get a
grip on this, he thought. I must use it and control it or I'll
make a mess of the killing this evening. And it mustn't be in
hatred, the priest said that.

The worst of it was, he wasn't sure what he was angry
about. Catherine's face rose up before him in a daydream,
unwanted, smiling lasciviously, and then scornful, waving
the piece of sponge which she – ah, what did that matter? It
was her idea but I wanted it too, how can I blame her for
taking precautions, even if . . . ? She should have told me.

I didn't want to know. I still don't want to know.

He began to realize he was angry with himself, for
wanting what he had no right to have, what she had no
right to give him. And he thought: Why? Why shouldn't
we have it?

Because it's just wrong. To do that in a squalid slum,
with people quarrelling all round, and babies climbing up
the stairs and crawling in the gutters outside . . . Now that
the magic was broken it seemed he had done something
dirty, disgusting. And with a fine well-brought up girl like
that who used to think of me as some kind of hero. Well,
she wanted it too. Maybe they're all like that, depraved
from too many centuries of lording it over the peasantry,
longing to be thrown on their backs by some farmer's
boy . . .

He noticed a clock outside a hotel. Four twenty-five.
You mustn't think like this, Sean, he told himself. I mustn't
think of this at all. I'm not some ignorant farmer's boy,

she'll see that tomorrow in the papers, and Catherine doesn't matter to me anyway. What matters is to do my duty well and cleanly and think of every possible thing that can go wrong so that I'm ready for it.

He had checked his pistol three times already. It was cleaned and loaded. All he had to do was pull back the safety catch, cock it, and fire. No problem there.

Radford was known to wear body armour so it would have to be a shot in the head from close up. They would walk quickly towards the man from the same direction, so that they didn't fire at each other by mistake.

What if he wasn't alone?

If there were two men they would take one each, Daly had said. If there were more than two they would call it off.

If the street was crowded with women and children?

It won't be, Daly had said. Not at that time of day. But if it is, we call it off.

What if Radford smiles at me, as he did this morning, and I think he's just like my old schoolmaster?

If he does that I'll kill him all the same. It's not personal, I don't hate him. We all have to die one day. He's an old man anyway, nearly fifty by the looks. And Martin died, because of men like him.

And if my hand shakes and I can't do it?

You will. It's easy. Just like giving an injection or slipping a scalpel into a corpse. I'd be doing that today if I wasn't busy here. Unpleasant the first time but easy after that, like cutting butter. All you have to do is hold yourself still inside, forget Catherine and everything else, and just think of the policeman's face and your hand on the trigger and bring the two together and that's it.

Bang.

Finish. Walk away.

Sean glanced at the clock again and decided it was time to return to Harcourt Street. He strode purposefully across the park, a fresh-faced, handsome young man in a brown coat and flat cap, frowning slightly in concentration. Once a couple of toddlers blocked the path, staggering energetically after a duck. The smallest, a little boy, fell flat on his face in front of Sean's feet, and started to cry. Sean bent down and picked him up.

Surprised, the child stopped crying. He stared, wide-eyed, at the face of the stranger who was trying to set him back on his feet. Sean gave him a winning smile. The boy smiled hesitantly back.

Then the mother came and took the little boy's hand. Sean touched his cap, thrust his hand back deep into his coat pocket where it clutched the butt of the 9-mm Parabellum, and strode briskly away.

That evening, Tom Kee sat in the downstairs bar of the Standard Hotel. He was in a corner by himself, with a nearly untouched pint in front of him, looking out of the window. He didn't want to be disturbed. In a few minutes he was going to have to tell Bill Radford about the failure of the raid on the tenement, and he wasn't looking forward to it.

For most of their working life, he and Radford had been close and shared everything together. The discovery that Radford had kept an important secret from him had hurt Kee deeply.

It grew worse the more he thought about it. He could understand that Butler, the agent, hadn't trusted G Division. That was good sense; it showed the man knew his job, and had a healthy understanding of the dangers of trusting *anyone* in this benighted city. But nevertheless Radford should have known, beyond any doubt at all, that he, Tom Kee, *could* keep the secret. Not only that, but he needed to know about it, so that he could take the basic precautions to ensure that the raid was a success. Instead of charging into the street at the last minute and bungling it, like the Keystone Kops.

That hurt. Radford hadn't trusted him, and the raid had been bodged.

But worse still, in Kee's opinion, were the underlying reasons for it. He remembered the conversation he had had with Radford and the army colonel before Christmas, about the idea of working with agents from Military Intelligence. Kee hadn't liked it, then or now. Maybe the Sinn Feiners thought they were fighting a war, but in fact they were criminal murderers who should be arrested and put on trial. Going out to deliberately shoot them was wrong.

Kee was absolutely sure about this. Of course, he himself carried a gun, and he was quite prepared to shoot if he had to. But there was a clear distinction between that and going out with the deliberate intention of killing someone. Policemen did the first; soldiers, spies, assassins and murderers did the second.

What hurt Kee was the belief that the man Butler had not been sent to arrest Collins, but to kill him.

The more he thought about it, the more convinced he was that Radford hadn't told him about Butler's plans because he knew he wouldn't approve. Radford hadn't cared too much about the details of the raid, because he thought they were going to find dead IRA Volunteers in the house, who wouldn't need to be arrested.

Why else had Butler taken a leather bag to the house, with two loaded automatic pistols?

Kee looked at his watch, and took a sip of his beer. He was going to confront his old friend and superior with his suspicions tonight, and his mouth was dry with apprehension. Their friendship had lasted for many years, and he hoped it would survive the confrontation. But if it didn't, it wouldn't be worth keeping. What sort of friendship would we have, he thought, if one of us was afraid to speak up when he thought the other was stepping over the line between daring police work, and conspiracy to murder?

Kee had hoped he would be able to impress Radford at the same time with the results of orthodox police work. At midnight last night he had raided the tenement, together with the young detective Foster and a platoon of soldiers. He had to take the soldiers; it would have been madness not to. Half of them had been posted outside, to watch the back and front of the building, and make sure no one escaped over the roof. The rest had come in with him, banging on the doors of the inhabitants, herding them into terrified little groups in the middle of their squalid rooms, guarded by Tommies with tin hats and rifles. While Kee and Foster raced up the stairs, trying door after door to see which room Brennan would be in.

He had been in none of them.

The room they had finally identified as his was quite empty. It had been little more than a large cupboard, with a creaky bed by the wall, a fireplace, a table and chair, a scrap of carpet on the floor, a window. Kee had looked out of the window. A twenty-foot drop to a concrete yard with an open drain and some dustbins. No escape there. And there were no possessions in the room – only a burnt saucepan, some holey blankets on the bed, a pillow and mattress that must have been old when Queen Victoria was born, and a pile of sticks, newspaper and coal. The ashes in the fireplace were cold.

Kee had sat on the bed, sick with disappointment, and tried to imagine the proud, beautiful young girl from Merrion Square in this room. He couldn't. It was too squalid. And yet Foster had been adamant and Kee believed him. There must be something seriously wrong in that girl's mind, he thought.

But that was beside the point. Brennan was still at large. Ordinary police work had failed again. Kee had kept the details of the operation back from Radford, hoping to surprise him. Now he would just look devious, and the rift between them would widen.

So now he sat in the bar of the Standard Hotel and waited for Radford. It was already twenty past six. He looked out of the window. In the semidarkness, an army lorry rumbled past, followed by a tram that clanked to a stop opposite the hotel, its bell jingling eerily. It was misty outside, he noticed; he could only see the tram indistinctly, through swathes of vapour tinged yellow and orange by the gaslights. If it got much worse no one would be able to see anything, and all traffic would seize up for the night. The combination of a still, damp, windless night, and over a million coal fires, could produce a Dublin fog to rival any 'London particular'.

If Radford doesn't come soon, Kee thought, he may not make it at all.

The gradually thickening yellow fog made Sean nervous. On the one hand, of course, it was a good thing, because it made their continued presence in Harcourt Street much less obvious to anyone who might be watching. By six thirty, visibility was down to twenty yards. But on the other hand, it was making it harder to keep a lookout for Radford.

He and Paddy had worked out a system. One of them would stand quietly in a doorway about ten yards from the hotel. The dripping brass plate on the door showed that the house was used by a dentist, and he appeared to have gone home by now. The other one would stroll slowly along the pavement away from the hotel, in the direction of Dublin Castle, until he was nearly out of sight of the first. Then he would cross the road, walk back on the other side, and they would change places.

If the man on the pavement saw someone who might be Radford, he was to signal it to the other by taking out a handkerchief and blowing his nose. Then he was to wait until the suspect came up, and if it was Radford, shoot him in the head. The man in the doorway was to come up as fast as he could, to help finish him off, if necessary. If there were too many passers-by, the first man was to engage

Radford in conversation until the other people had gone on, while the second man walked casually up and shot him.

If Radford approached the hotel from the wrong end of the street, then at least the man in the doorway was near enough to the hotel to see him go in. Then they could both go home.

Sean thought about the plan as he paced slowly down the pavement. The fog seemed to fill the street with so many strange noises which he didn't usually notice. Some were muffled, some sharpened and magnified out of all proportion. He knew there was a tram somewhere, because the dinging of its bell was as clear in his head as though he were on it. Yet he couldn't see the machine, or hear its engine; he wasn't even sure which direction it was coming from. There were bicycle bells too, and the clip of a horse's hooves coming quite surprisingly fast. From down by the river, the hoot of a foghorn boomed every half-minute; and occasionally the chatter of conversation carried to him, disconcertingly, out of shops and doorways he couldn't quite see.

The twenty yards' walk away from Paddy had come to seem like some frightening odyssey into the unknown. The further he got from Paddy, the more lonely he felt. Apart from the sounds, there were the shapes: strange, indeterminate thickenings of the mist under the gaslights, which suddenly coalesced into something meaningful – a tram, a bicycle, a pedestrian. And if it was a pedestrian, there was so little time, in twenty yards, to know if it was Radford or not. Only a quarter of an hour ago they had nearly killed the wrong man: only at the last minute had Sean seen

Paddy waving energetically from behind the victim, and realized the mistake. Same height, same build, wrong face.

He had lowered the pistol to his side and by some freak the pedestrian appeared not to have noticed it. They had watched him, and he had not gone into the hotel.

But although they had both been shaken, they had not given up.

'Not yet,' Paddy had said. 'Tonight's the best chance we'll have, if we just keep our nerve. Another half-hour and he must come.'

And Sean had agreed.

It would be terrible to give up now. All day he had spent nerving himself for it; to give up and walk away now would be a waste, impossible. Before the near mistake he had felt as clear in his mind as he ever had; quite cold, concentrated on the one thing he had to do, empty of all other thoughts. There was something almost religious, mystical about it.

Now the feeling was a little more ragged, fraying like a flag that has been flying in the storm too long; but he still thought he could hold out for another ten minutes. Radford *must* come soon.

He reached the end of his beat, and looked back. Paddy was only partly visible — a dark shape beside a blur that was a doorway, with the mist behind him glowing from the invisible hotel lights beyond. Time to cross the road and go back. The noises were more eerie than ever. It sounded as though the foghorn had come closer, and there was the clanking of a bell that was quite unlike a tram. Sean peered into the mist ahead, and then stepped out into the road.

Halfway across, a dark shape began to loom towards

him. A bell clanked and a foghorn groaned. It was this, he realized, that was making the noises. Whatever was it? He reached the other pavement, and waited.

Jesus, Mary and Joseph – it looked like a horse with horns! Sean shuddered and almost crossed himself – on a night like this the banshee and God knows what else could not be entirely dismissed. He stared at it wildly and then realized. Right here in the middle of the city at six o'clock some desperate peasant was driving a dogcart down Harcourt Street with a cow between the shafts! A cow with a bell hanging on its chest, for Christ's sake!

Sean didn't know whether to laugh or cry. He turned to check Paddy and the rest of the street and then he heard the voice.

'Are you lost then, Seamus?'

'Damn the bit of it, sir. I do be taking me short cut home, is all!'

'Good luck to you then!'

The voice that had asked the question – it was the same one he had heard this morning! Radford – but where was he?'

Sean looked beside the cart and saw him. A stocky, energetic man, striding along beside the cart and laughing at the absurdity of the sight as he overtook it. He was only about five yards away from Sean.

Sean took out his handkerchief with his left hand and waved it. Radford stopped, and stared at him in surprise.

In the next minute everything seemed to happen very slowly.

Sean dropped the handkerchief and pulled the Parabellum out of his pocket with his right hand. He looked at

Radford and saw the smile fading from his face. As Sean lifted the Parabellum Radford began to move, ever so slowly at first it seemed, to his right. Sean had the pistol up and the barrel followed Radford's head all the way. Sean thought nothing at all, only: Now.

He fired.

Radford jerked convulsively sideways, and collapsed on the ground in front of a shop window. But he wasn't dead, not at all. He writhed and kicked and got himself up on his knees, and Sean saw him tugging at something in his pocket. The butt of a revolver came out.

Sean fired again.

Radford's nose disappeared. In its place was a black hole. His mouth was open too in a wide O just beneath it. He was blown back on his knees so that the back of his head hit the shop window and left a great smear of blood and brains across it. Then he slumped anyhow to the ground like a broken doll.

The cow bellowed, and jerked the dogcart out into the middle of the road. It nearly knocked down Paddy Daly as he sprinted across, pistol in hand. From somewhere a long way away Sean heard another eerie noise. It was the sound of the farmer screaming: 'Mother Mary, God, Jesus Christ Almighty! Murder! Murder! Help! He's killed him! Will you shake a leg now, you foolish beast!'

And much nearer there was Paddy's voice in his ear, saying: 'You did it, then. You got the devil right enough. Come on now, Sean, boy. Put the gun in your pocket and walk away with me. No need to run. Just walk briskly and we'll be out of sight in a couple of seconds.'

Sean did exactly as he was told, and in less than a minute he and Paddy had faded into the fog, just two more eerie shadows in the thickening gloom.

Kee heard the shots and was up and halfway across the bar before anyone else moved. Then an army captain and a major got off their stools and the three of them came down the front steps of the hotel together.

Dear God, Kee was thinking, *don't let it be Bill, please let it not be him* ...

But of course it was.

By the time they had got past the terrified screaming ludicrous farmer and crossed the street to where the body was lying, there was already a small crowd around it. Kee pushed through and saw it but the face was unrecognizable. Only the hair and the clothes told him.

Kee looked up and down the street and tried to take charge.

'Which way?' he yelled. 'Which way did they go?'

But the people in the little crowd shook their heads and backed away, as though they were already regretting their involvement. The nearest, a man in a soft hat and smart coat, actually turned to go. Kee seized him by the lapels and slammed him against a lamppost, yelling: 'Which way, damn you? Which way did the swine go?'

Shocked, the man stuttered: 'I don't know. I didn't see ...'

Kee threw him away in disgust. 'Damned liar!' He turned to the others. 'Who saw it? Which way?'

But they shook their heads, backing away, and when

Kee strode towards them the army major said: 'I say, steady on, old chap.'

Then a woman said: 'I came from St Stephen's Green and saw no one running or anything, so I think they must have gone up there.' She pointed past the hotel, towards Adelaide Road.

Kee grabbed the major and said: 'You round these people up. Don't let any of them go.' Then he shouted to the younger one, the captain: 'You come along with me!' He sprinted off up the road into the fog, drawing his service revolver from his pocket and cocking it as he ran. But after ten yards he knew it was hopeless. Shadowy figures appeared out of the gloom, on either side of the road. He ran from one to the other, pistol in hand, peering into frightened, indignant, baffled faces; there was no possibility it was any of them. He ran on, into the fog, thinking: They'll be running, too. I'll stop anyone who's running.

But no one was.

When he reached the junction with Adelaide Road, he stopped in the middle of the street, baffled. Cars, bicycles and pedestrians came and went in and out of the fog from every direction, looking at him oddly or ringing their bells to make him get out of the way. It was futile.

He turned to walk back.

The army captain who had followed him said: 'It's no go, I'm afraid. Are you a police officer?'

Kee nodded. But I'm not behaving like one, he thought. I need witnesses. I hope that other chap has rounded them up. He started to walk back down the street. His legs felt like lead.

'Who was he, do you think?' the captain asked.

Kee said: 'He was my friend.'

Then he walked on very quickly and when he found the other officer had only collected two witnesses he cursed him for an incompetent fool and then almost immediately apologized and wondered if he was going to crack up completely. He ran out with the captain and brought in the farmer, then he rang Brunswick Street, then he began to interview them in the hotel.

None of them was any good as a witness except the farmer and he was drunk. It was a young lad, he said, he came out of the mist like a divil and then he was gone. Kee showed him the photograph of Sean Brennan, and the farmer said it was very like him exactly, sorr, but he would have needed to see the boy's face to be absolutely sure, and that was one thing he hadn't got a peep at. Then he said: 'It was a pity ye went on down the street with the soldier when ye did, sorr, because the boy who did the shooting went the other way entirely, I had thought to mention it but there was all that trouble with the cow.' At that point Kee got up and went out of the room.

He found Davis and Foster and a couple of other detectives in the foyer.

'Go in and take a statement from that fool,' he said. 'If I stay near him a moment longer I swear I'll strangle him.'

Then he went out to see what was happening to the body and when that was sorted out he came back into the bar for a drink.

Investigations went on all night but there was no useful evidence at all.

It was the worst night of Kee's life.

Some time towards morning, when the first hint of dirty grey light began to appear in the east, Kee stood on the steps outside the Standard Hotel and said: 'I'll find them for you, Bill. I'll find them if I have to stay in this heathen town for the rest of my natural life.'

17

'IT WAS GOOD of you to come.' Sir Jonathan shook Andrew firmly by the hand. 'Come this way. Keneally, show Mr Harrison straight through when he arrives, would you.'

He led Andrew up a single flight of stairs into his study. It was a pleasant, masculine room: leather-bound armchairs, a desk with a stack of papers weighed down by a shell-case, rows of books, and a large stuffed pike in a glass case over the fireplace. And on the wall, a number of framed photographs.

Andrew looked at the photographs curiously. One was of a young man on a horse in a hunting coat, surrounded by a pack of hounds; another of a similar young man, slightly broader in the face, sitting quietly at a desk, a pen poised in his hand. There was another of both young men standing proudly together in army battledress. Their hair was immaculately brushed, their eyes alight with hope, the leather of their Sam Browne belts gleaming.

There was a photograph of me like that in Mother's bedroom at Ardmore, Andrew thought. It went up in flames a month ago. Like everything it stood for.

Sir Jonathan saw him looking. 'My sons,' he said. 'Richard was killed at Vimy Ridge, John at Passchendaele.'

Andrew nodded. There was no need for sympathy. They had both been there. A million young men like that had been dismembered in the mud. Andrew wondered what his own eyes would look like now, if a photographer ever sat him down.

He said: 'There's no picture of your daughter.'

'No. Well, I've still got her with me. More or less.'

Andrew wondered vaguely what that meant. He said: 'It was a pleasant evening the other night.' That was what one said, wasn't it? The uses of polite society were very distant for him.

'Glad you enjoyed it. Drink?'

'Whiskey and water, please. Small one.'

While Sir Jonathan was pouring the drinks he said: 'I've asked Harrison to come but we may as well start. We both had a talk with Radford before he was killed, poor chap.

He felt pretty bad about the way your mission failed at the last leap. Felt most of it was his fault, in some way.'

Andrew took the whiskey and held the cut-glass tumbler thoughtfully between himself and the fire. The flames were refracted into strange orange shapes in the peaty liquid. 'He was right, too,' he said calmly.

Sir Jonathan frowned. The arrogant self-assurance of this young man was one of the least attractive things about him. But it was also one of the reasons why he had been chosen for this job. He reminded himself of the medals Andrew had won, the success of his escape from behind German lines, the devastating fury he had unleashed in the trenches. If the man felt fear, Sir Jonathan thought, he seemed drawn to confront it.

Keneally knocked at the door. 'Mr Harrison, sir,' he said.

The drab little man with the pebble spectacles came in, carrying a briefcase. He nodded to Sir Jonathan, and held out a hand for Andrew to shake. The hand was soft, clammy.

Sir Jonathan poured him a drink and they all sat down. Harrison leaned forward on the edge of his chair, peering carefully at Andrew. 'You've been unlucky,' he said.

'Yes. So was Radford.'

'Quite. Which makes it more urgent than ever to deal with Collins and his murderers. We wanted this meeting to know what your plans are now.'

'Now?' Andrew raised an eyebrow at them both in faint surprise. 'To go back to Ardmore, that's all.'

'But what about Collins?'

'The German officer, Count von Hessel, has been

deported. You don't expect me to bring him back to life again, do you?'

'Why not?'

'Why not? Mr Harrison, these men may be bog Irishmen, but they're not completely stupid. They're probably deeply suspicious about the whole story already. What do you want me to tell them – I knocked out my guards at Dun Laoghaire, caught the first train back, and now here I am ready to do the arms deal all over again?'

'It's a possibility. We could supply you with a cover story. Plant a tale in the newspapers to say that you'd escaped.'

Andrew thought, and said: 'No. There would be too many people involved. Somebody would be bound to tell Collins.'

There was a silence. Sir Jonathan asked: 'So what do you intend to do, then?'

'Nothing. I tried, the police cocked it up. It's finished.'

'And Bill Radford? Don't you want to avenge him?'

'He knew the risks. The same could have happened to me.'

Sir Jonathan frowned. 'I expected more of you than that, my boy.'

Andrew looked at him, and said nothing.

Harrison coughed. 'Before you, er, decide to drop out of the whole business, something came to my attention the other day which perhaps you should see.' He fiddled with the locks of his briefcase, opened it, and passed across a slim manila folder with two typed sheets of paper inside. 'Have a look at those, would you. I've marked the relevant paragraphs in the margin.'

The sheets of paper were police reports about an investigation into the deaths of three young men who had been found in the river Blackwater with their car two weeks ago. At first it had been thought they had drowned, but the pathologist's report showed that one had been shot, one had been stabbed to death, and the third had had his skull crushed by several blows to the head. Two, it seemed, had had some connection with Sinn Fein, but the third had not. The RIC were treating the deaths as murder.

Harrison had marked two paragraphs. The first stated that two of the dead men were connected with another investigation into a fire at Ardmore House, which was now being treated as arson. Servants stated that the men had been seen there on the night in question, and that they had apparently had a quarrel with the owner, Major Butler, some days before. There was therefore some suspicion that these men might have started the blaze.

The second marked paragraph referred to a witness – a Dr Scartan – who had driven across the bridge on the afternoon when it was believed the murders took place. He had met a fisherman there, who was just packing up his tackle to leave. He had had a short conversation with the man, and offered him a lift, but the fisherman had declined. The police were most anxious to meet this fisherman, and Dr Scartan was quite convinced he would recognize him if he met him, or if he saw a photograph.

Andrew read both paragraphs carefully, and then handed the folder back. 'So?' he said. 'I don't see the connection.'

The huge eyes peered at him carefully from behind the

thick spectacles. 'Well, Mr Butler, the point is really this. The local police are anxious to solve this crime, and it would appear that you, as the owner of Ardmore House, would have had at least some motive for wishing these men dead. Now if Dr Scartan were to see this photograph of you...' He fumbled in the briefcase again, and brought out a small black-and-white print of Andrew in army battledress, not unlike the one on the wall of Sir Jonathan's two sons. '... together with a description of the wound on your face, then he might possibly identify you as the fisherman. Which would be strong circumstantial evidence to link you with the unfortunate deaths of these three young men. Do you get my drift?'

Andrew sipped his drink, and contemplated him scornfully. 'It's hardly proof, though, is it? A decent barrister would make mincemeat of it in five minutes.'

'I quite agree. In ... normal circumstances. But if this case were brought before a jury, say, in the city of Cork, perhaps – there are unfortunately very strong prejudices at present against landlords with an army background, such as yourself, and in favour of what are misguidedly seen as innocent young Sinn Feiners. An Irish jury might not have quite the same grasp on logic and the rules of evidence that you might hope for.'

There was silence in the room. A clock chimed loudly somewhere outside. Andrew said: 'Are you saying that if I don't go on with this Collins business, you'll throw me to the wolves?'

Harrison coughed apologetically. 'I wouldn't put it quite as crudely as that, Major Butler, but yes, that is the general idea.'

'You're forgetting something. I have a document in my possession which states quite clearly that I will be paid £10,000 for the arrest of Michael Collins, dead or alive. It was signed by Sir Jonathan in the presence of yourself and Commissioner Radford. If I were on trial, I could produce that in court.'

'That would, indeed, be very embarrassing. Sir Jonathan and I would say it was a forgery, of course, but we would rather not have to. But you see, Major Butler, even if it brought us down, it would scarcely do you any good. One glance at a document like that, and your guilt in the eyes of the jury would be established. And the penalty for murder is still hanging. Even for the murder of Sinn Feiners.'

Andrew looked incredulous. 'So you are saying that the only way you will save me from hanging for the murder of three Sinn Feiners, is to carry on and murder some more. Is that it?'

'Precisely, Major Butler. And one Sinn Feiner in particular.'

There was another silence. Sir Jonathan had been looking stern, but increasingly embarrassed throughout the previous conversation. When Andrew glanced at him, he cleared his throat and said: 'And of course, when you do kill Collins, the reward will be paid in full. You have my word on that. It's just that we can't afford any backsliding now, you see.'

'I see,' Andrew said thoughtfully. 'So much for the concept of honour.'

'Yes, well.' Sir Jonathan's face, Andrew noticed curiously, was actually quite red. Clearly this attempt at blackmail wasn't Sir Jonathan's idea, Andrew thought.

But he's going along with it, nevertheless. Now I know who's running the show, anyway.

He turned back to the small, bug-eyed figure of Harrison. 'And do I have your word that this RIC investigation goes no further, if I agree to carry on?'

'Of course. We have no interest in harming you, only in defeating the enemy. It's a war, you see, just a different kind of one. Everyone supports the troops when they're fighting. But if they turn away, they get shot.'

'My God.' What do you know about fighting? Andrew thought. Or do they have wars under the stones, too, where the slugs are?

Sir Jonathan interrupted, clearly still embarrassed. 'Our only interest is in defeating these swine before they ruin the country completely. If Lloyd George would give us martial law, we wouldn't need this sort of cloak-and-dagger stuff. But he won't, so it's up to us to fight the Shinners by their own methods, that's all. I'm sure you see that, Andrew, don't you?'

'Oh yes,' said Andrew softly. 'I see it absolutely.'

'Good. So you'll do it?'

'I'll carry on, yes. But you can't expect me to come up with a new plan, just like that.'

'No, of course not. But you may want to carry on with the one Harrison put to you before? Resurrecting Count von Hessel?'

'Perhaps. I'll think about it. But no silly stories about him escaping at Dun Laoghaire. If he comes back, it's from Germany. And that'll take time.'

'In that case it may be best that you drop out of sight for a few days,' Sir Jonathan said. 'I was thinking that before you came. We don't want you seen walking around Dublin if you're supposed to have been deported, do we?'

'They may already have seen me,' said Andrew bitterly. Though on reflection he thought it unlikely; he had been out of the house in Nelson Street only three times since the raid on Brendan Road. Once to buy food, and twice to come here.

'Let's hope not. But the longer you stay, the greater the risk. And as Harrison says, it might be unwise for you to go back to Ardmore at the moment. Why not go down to my house in Galway for a few days? There are none of Collins's men there. You could relax, ride, breathe the sea air. Good shooting, too.'

Andrew did not particularly want to be beholden to Sir Jonathan for a home, but the prospect of staying alone in the house in Nelson Street, indoors most of the time to avoid a chance meeting with Daly, was beginning to pall. And Ardmore was just the contemplation of ruin, and now, it seemed, awkward interviews with the local RIC. At least, if Harrison knew he was in Galway, he couldn't pressure him for instant results.

'All right,' he said gracelessly. 'Why not?'

Harrison left, but Sir Jonathan asked if Andrew would mind staying behind for half an hour. 'I have some letters and bills to send to Ferguson, my estate manager at Killrath,' he said. 'And with the posts so unreliable as they are, I would be grateful if you could take them with you.'

'By all means.' Andrew settled down in a corner to smoke, when the door of Sir Jonathan's study opened and Catherine looked in. She saw Andrew and hesitated, her hand on the doorknob. 'Oh, I'm sorry, Father. If you're busy it can keep for another time.'

Andrew got to his feet – slowly, as though it was a thing he had just remembered to do, rather than an automatic courtesy. She looked pale, he thought, more tired than before, with dark smudges round her eyes that were not artificial at all. He said: 'No, please don't leave on my account. I was hoping to see you and pay my respects or whatever one does, after the other evening.'

'Thank you.'

Sir Jonathan looked up. 'Catherine, don't go. I'm just writing a couple of letters for Major Butler to take to Killrath. Could you entertain him for half an hour or so while he waits?'

Catherine was not sure she wanted to be bothered with this. But then, what else was there? With Sean gone, everything seemed drab, wearisome. At least this man had brought a little colour to the other evening, for an hour or so. So she said: 'Of course,' took him to the drawing room downstairs, and ordered tea.

There was something incongruous about this man in a flowered armchair. He looked tense, ill at ease, angry. When the muscles of his jaw moved, the livid scar on his cheek writhed like a snake. Catherine had the impression he was far away in his own mind, unaware of her. Keneally brought tea and she poured it, feeling foolish and annoyed by the silences that fell between them. Being a society hostess was a role that bored her, and she particularly hated being forced to do it and then ignored.

'Well,' she said suddenly. 'Have you made up your mind yet?'

'What do you mean?'

'About your half of the bet. As I remember, the other night you said I could have your ruined house, Ardmore, if I could shoot better than you.'

She was gratified to see that she had his full attention. The hard dark eyes focused on her coldly. He said: 'As I remember it was the other way around. You decided you wanted it.'

'Perhaps.' She sipped her tea coolly. 'I can't imagine it's worth much now anyway.'

Not to you perhaps, Andrew thought. Something about her eyes — dark, intense, determined — reminded him of the way Sir Jonathan had looked at him as they discussed their deal upstairs. It annoyed him. These people held all the cards, suddenly.

He said: 'That house is my life, young lady. It would be stupid for me to bet about it unless you were ready to offer something equally valuable to you in return. Which you aren't.'

She flushed. 'Aren't I? Try me.'

'All right then.' Andrew was annoyed now, but the situation amused him, too. At least, if he had to do what Sir Jonathan wanted, he could still take this high-and-mighty girl down a peg or two. He said: 'Let's pretend we're in a fairy tale. If you win, you get the ruins of Ardmore; if I win, you still get them.'

'What?'

'As a wife, dear girl. I need one, and you seem to be reasonably well brought up, and able to pour the tea without spilling it. I offer the house, you offer yourself. Then you get Ardmore whatever happens.'

Despite herself, Catherine flushed bright red. Then she laughed. The laugh sounded forced even to her. My bluff has been called, she thought.

'What's the matter? My face is so unsightly you wouldn't even consider it, I suppose.'

'Oh no.' She put her teacup down and stood up, feeling the blush mercifully drain away. 'Your scar is the most attractive thing about you, as far as I can see. It's not very gentlemanly, though, to compare me to a ruin. I'll get the pistol now.'

'Now?' Surely the stupid girl didn't mean it?

'Why not? There's a small walled garden behind the house. That'll do.'

Stunned, he followed her out into the corridor. There was a locked cupboard round a corner, which she opened, and took out a Webley revolver. Deftly, she loaded six cartridges into it. 'Three shots each. We'll need something for the marks.' She gave him the pistol, walked through to the kitchen, and came back with two sheets of paper, a pencil, some small nails, and a hammer.

The garden was about thirty feet long, surrounded by high walls, with a terrace, a small lawn, and some espaliered trees and rockeries around the edge. Catherine drew a thick pencilled cross in the middle of each sheet of paper, with a circle about two inches in diameter around the point where the lines met. Then she walked down the garden and nailed them to the branches of a tree. She walked back and looked at him with a slight, cool grin on her face, pushing a strand of her short black hair away from her face with a finger.

'Will you shoot first or will I?'

Andrew burst out laughing. 'All right, you're mad, I admit it. Don't worry, I won't hold you to it against your will.'

The small, tight smile had not changed. 'Then I don't get the house.'

'It's only a ruin anyway. Go on, you shoot first.'

'All right.' She took the pistol from him, cocked it, and held up a finger for a moment to test the breeze. Then she lifted the gun slowly. He thought it might be too heavy for her but he saw it was not. She held it in one hand, her right arm straight out from her shoulder. He saw it was quite still, rock steady.

The three shots came very swiftly, in almost as many seconds. The sound in the little walled garden echoed deafeningly.

Andrew could see one shot near the centre of the cross. There was another towards the edge of the pencilled circle. From this distance he could not see the third at all.

She handed the revolver to him. It was light, he noticed, a smaller model than the one he had used in the war. It had been one of his pastimes, in the long, boring weeks in the billets and trenches, to set up makeshift targets – food tins, paper, dead mice and rats pinned to a door by their tails – and knock holes in them. Once he had drawn the face of a German officer and drilled holes in its eyes, nostrils, and teeth from ten yards.

He lifted the gun, sighted, and fired.

As the echoes rang in their ears, a door opened behind them and Sir Jonathan came out. 'What the devil . . . ?'

'It's all right, Father,' Catherine said. 'You asked me to entertain him so we're having a shooting match.'

'Good God, I thought we were being attacked!'

'No such luck, I'm afraid.' Andrew noticed with amusement that the Colonel had his own revolver holster unbuttoned, and his hand on the butt of the pistol inside.

Catherine and Andrew walked down to the end of the garden together. Andrew looked at Catherine's target first. He had thought her third shot had gone wide, but to his surprise he saw it had clipped the hole of the first, so that there was one single large hole within half an inch of the intersection of pencil lines in the middle of the paper. The third shot was about an inch away, to the upper left, just touching the circle she had drawn.

His own shots were grouped closer, in a cluster less than an inch wide straddling the intersection.

He held the two sheets of paper together. Their eyes met. Andrew said: 'I win, I think, Mrs Butler.'

He was pleased to see that a slight flush had returned to her face. She said: 'You're a better shot than I thought. Well, when I'm a ruin like your house, you shall have me.'

Then she turned and walked back into the house.

As Sir Jonathan gave him the letters he said: 'She's not used to being beaten, you know. Did you have a bet on it, or what?'

'Nothing serious,' Andrew said. 'Just a game, that's all.'

It was the end of the next day when Andrew saw Killrath.

All day, as the train wound its way steadily westwards, through Tullamore, Athlone, Ballinasloe, and on to the town of Galway itself, he had sat at the window of the first-class carriage, sunk in depression. This retreat to the west was a combination of all the things he most hated.

It was a mark of defeat, first of all. He had failed to find Collins, or kill him. Instead, he was now hunted himself.

He was angry, too. Very angry at Harrison, for the threat of blackmail. For all its clumsiness, Andrew was forced to accept it as a possibility. The little man was clearly ruthless in his own way, devoid of scruples. If he has to throw me before the courts, he will, Andrew thought. Probably his own job only hangs by a thread. If the Shinners' campaign goes on, and he can point to no successes against it, that thread will be cut; and then he'll drag me down into the mud with him. Certainly Sir Jonathan believed it was possible. He's got no love for the little slug, either.

For the hundredth time, Andrew searched for a better method of approaching Collins. But he had considered and rejected all of them before; they were as full of holes as a colander. Even if he had not been scarred, Daly had seen his face. They knew who he was: he was a German officer, Count von Hessel. Andrew hoped, fervently, that they still believed that. If they did, he still had a remote chance of success. A chance that would be totally dissipated if he were to turn up claiming to be someone else.

So Count von Hessel would have to re-establish contact. After all, von Hessel warned Daly of the approach of the police; he fought the police; he was arrested and deported. Hessel was a stubborn fellow: he would come back to Dublin and try again. There's no reason why Collins should think it was not true.

He hoped not, anyway. He had been through all this last night, sitting in his study in Nelson Street. What would a German count do, he had asked himself, if he were rash enough to come back a second time?

He would write them a really harsh letter, complaining of their lack of security. He would be outraged that Collins hadn't kept his appointment on time. He would demand better security, and better guarantees, in future.

So that was what Andrew had done. He had written a letter on a sheet of paper embossed with his grandparents' German address; and early this morning, before leaving to catch the train, he had delivered it to Sir Jonathan in Merrion Square.

Sir Jonathan had been surprised. 'Why are you giving it to me?' he had asked.

'Two reasons. First, because I'm not a professional forger and I need you to find one. I want the correct German postage stamp put on it, a perfect facsimile of a German franking mark. Can that be done?'

Sir Jonathan had only hesitated for a moment. 'Yes, I think so. There's a fellow called Smythe in the Castle who's obsessed with that kind of thing. He'd make a perfect job, I'm sure.'

'Good. Only for heaven's sake make sure he keeps his mouth shut. I don't want anyone to know about this unless they need to. Neither do you, I suppose.'

'No,' Sir Jonathan had agreed. 'And the other reason?'

'I want the letter inserted into the incoming international mail. Can that be arranged?'

Sir Jonathan tapped the letter against his palm. 'I don't see why not.' It was addressed to Mr Michael Collins, c/o Dáil Eireann, The Mansion House, Dublin. The Sinn Fein postal workers would abstract it, and pass it on to an address which neither of them knew. 'When do you want it posted?'

That was the hard part. 'I think about two weeks from now,' Andrew said. 'That should give Hessel time to get back to Germany and return. Can I stay down at Killrath until then?'

'Of course. My dear chap, the place is yours.'

A car met him at the station in Galway. The chauffeur, a slim young man of about eighteen, took Andrew's only suitcase and threw it carelessly in the boot of the large bull-nosed Morris.

'My name's David Ferguson,' he said, without being asked. 'My father's the agent here. I expect Sir Jonathan told you. We more or less run the place for him while he's away.'

'No, he didn't say.'

'Did he not? That's strange.' The young man steered the car carefully through the crowded streets. 'I'm sorry about all this. It's market day today. We'll get out on the open road eventually.' He waited while a jam of horse-drawn carts, cars, and two large motor lorries sorted itself out. 'Sir Jonathan said you were in the Guards with him in France.'

'That's right.'

'Jolly good show. I'd have gone too, if I'd been old enough. Though it can't have been much of a picnic, especially the last year, I suppose. Did you get the face wound there?'

'Yes.' Andrew did not want to make conversation, especially about the war. But he could see some response was necessary. As the traffic eased, and they drew out of the town, he said: 'Tell me about Killrath, then. What should Sir Jonathan have told me?'

It was a fortunate question. The young man, clearly hurt by Andrew's initial monosyllabic response, brightened instantly.

'Ah, well, it's one of the great houses of the district, no question. The first part of it was built in 1656, by Sebastian Gort — one of Cromwell's men, a colonel, I think. He took the land from the O'Flahertys — there was a great tribe of them round here then. They were mostly killed or pushed out to the islands in the far west. But the house itself was all extended in the 1720s. That's the part you can see today. They had a German-born architect, I think. Has Sir Jonathan not told you any of this?'

'No, no. He didn't mention it. How big is the place?'

'Oh, I don't know. Thirty-odd bedrooms, I suppose.'

Much bigger than Ardmore, then, Andrew thought. He hadn't considered this. 'And the estate?'

'Well, it's quite large. About 80,000 acres, though half of that's bog and mountain. There are thirty moderate-sized tenant farms, a hundred or so crofters, and we run the rest. That's what my father spends most of his time doing. It's a lot of work.'

'I imagine so.' Andrew remembered the wide-eyed, insolent young woman and her silly shooting match. 'And — forgive me — is Miss Catherine the heir to all this?'

The young man glanced at Andrew speculatively, then

returned his eyes to the road as they negotiated a series of steep bends. 'Unfortunately, yes. I mean, don't get me wrong, I've got nothing against her, of course, but she had two brothers who were both killed in the war. The elder one, Richard, he was always expected to succeed Sir Jonathan. A lovely chap, he was. Taught me to ride when I was eight. I felt really sick when I heard.'

The car had been climbing for some time, winding through a series of small lakes and little rocky mountains. As they came to the top of a rise they could see the broad Atlantic on their left, blue and grey under high cumulus clouds. There was a rocky coast, dotted here and there with little islands. Inland, there was a mixture of poor farmland and bright-green bog.

'Another three miles or so yet. The estate proper begins at the side of the mountain there.' David Ferguson pointed some distance ahead. 'That's the O'Connell part of it, anyway.'

'The O'Connell part?'

'Yes. The O'Connells have always been the other main family round here, apart from the Gorts. They're Roman Catholics, you see, native Irish. God knows how they managed to hold on to their land all that time, through the penal laws and everything, but they did. Clever lawyers, letting one of the family pretend to convert, sheer tenacity – I don't know how, but they did. Then about forty years ago the last couple of O'Connells had only one child – a daughter, Maeve – and Sir Jonathan married her. That's why it's called the O'Connell-Gort estate. There was a terrible fuss at the time, I think: the O'Connell grandparents wanted the children brought up as Catholics, but they weren't — not the boys, anyway. I think Miss Catherine still is, of a sort. It upset their mother. I wonder sometimes if that's why she went mad, you know, in the end.' The young man shrugged. 'I don't suppose Sir Jonathan would want me to talk about that.'

'Probably not.' It's a whole world of its own, Andrew thought. They were passing through a rocky area of little fields, laboriously enclosed by stone walls, with small one- or two-roomed farm cottages dotted here and there amongst them. Paddy Daly would have trouble tracing me here, he thought. Nonetheless, there might easily be sympathies for Sinn Fein.

'Have you had any troubles out here?' he asked.

The young man shook his head. 'Nothing serious. A few of the smaller farmers have had their cattle maimed, that's all. But the RIC are still pretty much in control, thank God.'

He looked as though he would have asked about the situation in Dublin, but at that moment they swung over another ridge of small hills, and there was Killrath in front of them. It was a long, square, three-storey building on a low headland, facing southwest over the Atlantic. The sun was low in the west, far out to sea, and the red light was reflected off the windows like flame. For a second Andrew caught his breath, as he remembered the fire at Ardmore; but this was beauty, not destruction. A stepped garden led down towards the cliff in front of the house, with a sort of ornamental pond, and rows of low, windswept trees planted to give protection from the gales. At the foot of the headland was a long, wide, sandy beach stretching for miles. It was low tide, and there was no wind. The hard wet sand gleamed in the reflected sunlight, and little sparkling breakers curled and broke into floods of orange and gold. In the distance, the minuscule figure of a fisherman was pulling his tiny coracle ashore.

David Ferguson glanced at his passenger proudly.

'Welcome to Killrath, Mr Butler,' he said.

18

H E WASN'T IN the tenement. When Catherine turned up there, a slatternly woman met her on the stairs and told her about the police raid. The woman wore an old stained dress and torn slippers, and was feeding a baby at her breast as she spoke. Two other children with bare bottoms tugged at her skirts and crawled around her feet. She looked frightened, bitter, and suspicious.

'They dragged us out of our beds in the middle of the night. With guns and steel helmets, they were. Laughing at us till I thought me last day had come. But it was your Sean they were interested in, that's all they would ask about. And himself long gone, God rot 'em!'

The woman shivered, and looked at Catherine's fine coat with something between contempt and envy. 'Left you, has he? They're all the same. You drop him, girl, he's not worth it.'

'Do you know where he's gone?'

The woman laughed, throwing back her scrawny head and showing a line of brown, rotten teeth. 'You think he'd tell the likes of me? You've a lot to learn, girl. Why? Left you a bun in the oven, has he?'

'No, of course not.' Catherine flushed, fumbled in her purse and held out a pound note. 'Here. I'm sorry you were troubled. Buy some food for the children.'

The gift made her feel worse rather than better. As she came out into the street she felt eyes on her all around — children, mothers hanging washing across the street, unemployed men smoking on doorsteps. She had not come here in the daytime before; it was a bad mistake. She didn't feel safe until she was back in the main thoroughfare of Amiens Street.

The relief from openly staring eyes was immense.

She did not notice the tall young detective, twenty paces behind on the opposite side of the road. He never stared. Whenever possible, he watched her reflection in shop windows. Sometimes he strolled ahead of her, guessing which way she was going.

Foster knew her quite well now. He wasn't surprised when she went to the university. Sean wasn't there, either. Foster saw her talking to Professor O'Connor after a lecture. The professor shook his head. Catherine gave him a letter. She spent a couple of hours in the library and then she went home. Foster knew that sooner or later she would come out and go to Parnell Square.

So he hung around outside her house, and waited.

Sean wasn't at the Irish class in Parnell Square, either. Catherine sat through it in a daze, unable to concentrate. She hated herself for sending the letter, but she hadn't been able to sleep until she'd written it. All it said was:

> *Sean,*
> *I need to see you again so we can talk. It's too cruel to end like this. I had good reason to lose my temper but I wish I hadn't, now.*
> *   Catherine.*

The third sentence had cost her three hours of bitter self-reflection. She didn't often apologize, and she didn't intend to make a habit of it now. There had been a much longer letter explaining how she really felt, but she had torn it up and thrown it in the fire.

Love is like physical addiction to tobacco, she thought. People try to give it up but they say they can't because it hurts too much. He's a vain, stupid boy but I can't stop thinking about him and the longer this silence goes on the more it hurts.

She went to the university again next day. The Professor had no message. Dejected, she went home in the afternoon to study.

She sat in her room and found she was drawing a series of curves on her lecture notes which reminded her of Sean's buttocks. She scribbled them out irritably, and tried to concentrate.

I thought taking a lover was something to do with freedom, she thought, but it's not. It's got more to do with slavery.

Keneally, the butler, knocked on the door. He had a disapproving frown on his face.

'There is a young man to see you, Miss Catherine. One of your fellow students, he says.'

'Yes? Well, what's his name?'

'A Mr Brennan, Miss Catherine.' Keneally sniffed. It was clear there was something quite unsuitable about the visitor.

'Well, go on then. Show him up! I'll meet him in here!'

When Keneally had gone she found she had already stood up to welcome Sean and had knocked a pile of notes fluttering to the floor. I mustn't look eager, she thought. Especially not in front of the servants.

But I can't help it, I love him! And he's here!

Outside, Foster could not believe his luck. Brennan had simply stepped out through the gate of the park in the square, crossed the broad street, knocked on the front door, and gone in.

He knew the young man was Brennan because he had taken his cap off before he knocked, and Foster had had a clear sight of his face. It was just like the photograph. There was no doubt at all.

He wondered what to do now. I've got to get this right, he thought. There'll never be a chance as good as this.

The simplest thing is to go up to the house and arrest him there. What will happen?

I'll knock, the butler will open the door, and I'll explain who I am. He'll be surprised, but he'll let me in. I'll tell him Brennan is an IRA murderer.

He won't believe me.

He'll make some kind of fuss and want to ask Miss Catherine's advice, or we'll have a long argument in the hall, or he'll want me to ring Dublin Castle and speak to Sir Jonathan. One way or another Brennan will hear the noise, and be warned.

Then there'll be a shooting match inside the house. I don't know my way around the house and probably Brennan doesn't either, but Miss Catherine does and she may help him. The servants will be flustered and get in the way.

It's too risky. Easier to arrest him when he comes out. He's not very big; if I get a grip on him I should be able to hold him, snap the handcuffs on.

But I can't stand right outside the house, or he'll see me and go out the back. And if I stand too far back, I may have to chase him. Then he'll disappear in the streets and get away, or there'll be a shooting match and passers-by will get hurt.

I need support.

There was a telephone box just down the road, opposite Leinster House. Foster rang from it.

Davis answered.

'Who? Kee? The poor man's just fallen asleep on the bed in his office. I'll wake him if you like but he's not been asleep for two days. Can I take a message?'

Keneally showed him in and shut the door. Sean stood just inside the room, looking at her. She stared at him, quite silent. She saw that same wide, quizzical smile, slightly nervous perhaps, in the boyish open face. A single unruly strand of the dark smooth combed-back hair fell forward over his forehead, and she longed to brush it back. But it was his eyes that upset her. They had always been so open, alive, sparkling – it was one of the things she had loved him for. Now they were dark, troubled, unwilling to meet her gaze.

He looked away from her, around the room. He had his coat on and his cap in his hands, and he was twisting it like a farmhand. Then he realized what he was doing and threw it on a chair.

She said: 'Didn't Keneally offer to take your coat?'

'I wouldn't let him. There's a gun in the pocket.' He smiled, and then felt crass. The room intimidated him: the beautiful patterned green and gold wallpaper, the two inlaid desks, the window seat, the pictures, the tasteful, stylish armchairs. She looks a natural part of it all, Sean thought. That delicate haughty face with those dark haunting eyes; that hard slender body in a turquoise silk dress that cost more than father could earn in a month – she could have stepped straight out of one of those portraits I passed on the stairs. She belongs here; I'm a clod.

Catherine said: 'Well, you may as well take your coat off now. Unless you're just staying for a moment, that is.' *Now why did I say that? Please don't go now, Sean – not now, not after all these long hours!* But she had her pride. It shielded her like invisible armour. She did not want it. It just came.

He took his coat off. *Thank God.*

'You got my note then?'

'I did that.' He didn't come to her and embrace her. He walked over to the fire and held out his hands to that instead. He felt a need to take possession of the room. He put a foot on the seat of one of the armchairs, and sat on its arm. 'You need to talk, you said?'

'We need to talk.' All that helpless addictive longing for him, and now he was here, she found it difficult to control her anger. 'Where are you staying?'

'A nice clean place. Landlady, home cooking.'

'*Where*, Sean?'

He gazed at her, stubborn, not answering. Then he said: 'We can't go on, Cathy, it's no good. We made a mistake – it was all too fast, and the wrong time. We can't go on like that!'

'Because I won't get pregnant – is that what you mean? You think the wrong way round, Sean!'

'No! It's not that. I've thought about that and I can see ... some sense in it. Not that it's decent, mind, but I – I was at fault too, there.'

She thought: Where's the fault? There wasn't any fault, Sean; just two of us, together. It was beautiful. But in her pride she said sarcastically: 'Really? You surprise me.'

'I've thought a lot, Cathy. We went too far, too soon. It was my fault too, but it was wrong. What could it lead to? Look around you, at this room, this house. We can't get involved, you and me.'

'We *are* involved, Sean Brennan.' She didn't want to cry, so she said it with unusual force, as though rebuking a child. It was the wrong tone to adopt, she vaguely saw that. It went with the house, her wealth, her control of the servants – everything that worried him. She tried again.

'And if I *had* been pregnant, Sean love. What then?'

'God knows.' He stood up and began to pace the room. 'That just shows it, doesn't it? If you were a girl of my class we could get married, but you're not, not at all . . .'

'Sean.' She took his arm, stopped him pacing, looked into his eyes. It was the first time they had touched. 'I'll marry you if you want, you great fool. And then I *will* be of your class.'

'What?'

She had never meant to say that, but now she had it was an immense relief. There, I can forget my pride if I choose, just step out of it like my clothes, she thought. She took his hands, led him to the ottoman, and told him of her father's conditions for inheritance. 'So if I married you, I'd be Cinderella in reverse.'

Then she remembered the woman she had seen in the tenement yesterday morning, and shuddered. Perhaps because of the shudder, he misunderstood.

'You prove my point. Anyway.' The proximity of her face, the touch of her hands on his, was too unsettling. He stood up abruptly. 'Any talk about that, all that is premature now. There's a war on now, Cathy, I'm a soldier in it. I can't be tied down. When the British have left the country, if you're still here. Maybe then.'

She felt her fingers shaking and couldn't stop them. So now I've said I'll marry him and he's refused, she thought. I offer to break my father's heart and throw away my inheritance, and he rejects me. That I could sink so low. Anger flooded through her, saving her from tears.

What had he said? If you're still here, when the British are gone? The insufferable male arrogance of it! 'All that's make-believe, Sean. Look what happens. You can't even shoot Lord French.'

'Read your newspaper.'

'What do you mean?'

He saw a newspaper on the floor, and picked it up. It was yesterday's. There was an odd look on his face; that wide smile that she so loved, proud, but slightly twisted, somehow. And the eyes; dark, troubled. He held the paper out. 'Go on, look.'

'I've read it.' She was dazed; it was hard to follow what he was saying. A sick feeling came into her stomach. 'The police commissioner? The one who was shot in Harcourt Street?'

'Yes.'

How could she have read it and not thought of Sean? She knew that he would support the killing, of course; she had even imagined them discussing it, and agreeing it was a regrettable necessity. But it had been a particularly unpleasant murder, this one – nothing open or daring about it like Ashtown.

'You did this?'

He went to his coat and took out the Parabellum. 'The gun itself.' He held it out, flat, in the palm of his hand. The strong smooth fingers that had stroked her breast. 'Now do you say it's all make-believe? Little boy revolutionaries?'

He was proud, definitely. Of course the killings were necessary, for the freedom of the country. Once, on the beach at Sandymount, she had said she would like to see Lord French dead. That was all words now. The words of a silly young girl. I don't want anyone dead. Not at Sean's hands, she thought. Not shot in the street like that.

She picked up the gun and held it.

Dead in the street with no nose. She felt sick. She handed the gun back. 'Put it away, Sean,' she said.

She felt immeasurably sorry for him, somehow. As though he were a child who had scribbled on a priceless painting and brought it proudly to show her. Yet he was still beautiful, still the Sean she had loved.

The odd, slightly twisted smile remained on his face. 'Do you see now? I'm not just making it up. This is important work I'm doing. I have to give my whole mind to it.'

'Yes.' She stood up, brushing her hands on her skirt. This was the worst of it. He cared everything for this and nothing for the love they had made together, at all. 'Will you go now, Sean, please?'

He stood up too and reached out to embrace her. Now, for the first time since he had come in, as though showing her the gun had made it possible. She turned her head so that the kiss was only on her cheek. He stepped back and picked up his coat and cap.

'Maybe when the country is free. I'll see you then.'

'Maybe.' She pulled the bell rope by her desk. When Sean opened the door, Keneally was outside.

'Mr Brennan is leaving now, Keneally. Show him out, please.'

'Certainly, miss. Step this way, sir, if you would.'

Catherine closed the door, sat down on the ottoman, put her head in her hands, and waited for the tears to come.

Davis was terrified.

He put down the phone with a shaking hand and looked around the room. There were four desks, littered with papers, files, ashtrays; but he was alone. He had just come in here, to the main office, when the phone rang, and he had picked it up.

Thank God it was me, he thought. If anyone else had taken the message Brennan would be doomed for sure. I can do something.

But what?

His brain refused to function. All that went round and round in his head was the thought: Foster's trapped Brennan. Brennan killed Radford and I helped him set it up!

He lit a cigarette to calm his nerves. I've got to stop this, he thought. If they arrest Brennan and lean on him he'll implicate me, and then ... A vision came before him of ten years in a British gaol, slopping out his filthy bucket every morning, shuffling along the metal landings like a chimpanzee in a zoo, pushed and prodded by gaolers who would have no sympathy, none at all, for an Irish policeman who had betrayed his colleagues. Neither would the other prisoners. He would have to beg for solitary confinement for his own protection, and even then, there would be mistakes. Oh, sorry, Paddy, I thought he was your friend. Hurt your face now, has he? Dear, dear ...

The longer he sat here, the more chance there was of Brennan coming out before help arrived. Davis decided not to wake Kee. The man deserved a rest. He would go out in a moment and find one of his other colleagues, and they would walk to Merrion Square, that was it, so that there was every chance they would arrive too late. Finish the cigarette first.

But what if Foster arrests him anyway? With a jolt, Davis remembered how keen young Foster was, and how unusually fit and strong. He was a wing three-quarter in the DMP rugby team. If he got hold of Brennan before the lad could draw a gun, there was every chance he would bring him in on his own.

There was a phone in a little tobacconist's round the corner in King Street which Davis used for emergencies. He stubbed out his cigarette and stood up, meaning to put on his coat and go there. He could ring Daly and perhaps some boys of the Dublin Squad could get to Merrion Square in time to deal with Foster. Yes, that was it. Then with luck, they would get rid of another dangerous policeman at the same time. Disaster would turn to triumph. I'll do that, he thought.

With his coat half on, he hesitated. Every minute counted now. The office was still half-empty. Why not ring from here? He would never normally do it, but this was an emergency. In case anyone overheard, he could speak to Daly as though he was confirming the details with Foster. They would understand, at the other end. He had a second, compelling vision of the athletic, bulky figure of young Foster striding back to Merrion Square, and Sean Brennan, even now, coming out of a door in front of him.

Davis took out his pocket book, checked the number, and lifted the moutpiece. As he was about to speak to the operator he turned round to check that he was still alone.

He wasn't.

Kee was standing in the doorway looking at him.

Their eyes met. Davis felt the blood drain from his face. He put the phone down carefully. *How long has he been there?* he thought. *How much did he hear?* And then: *Come on, Dick, for God's sake get a grip – the man can't read your mind.*

Kee said: 'What was that about Brennan?'

'Sorry, sir?' He didn't hear it all, Davis thought. Come on, Dick, stall – there must be some way out of this.

'You were talking about Brennan on the phone a couple of minutes ago. It woke me up. Come on, Dick, spit it out!' Kee had just woken from the first half-hour's sleep he had had in two days; his head hurt, and his mouth felt like the inside of an ashtray. He was not in the mood to be messed about. 'You were talking about him on the phone – who to?'

The shock was too great for Davis. He searched for a lie

but his brain wouldn't work. Despairingly, he said: 'Foster, sir.'

'Why? Has he found him?'

'Yes, sir. At least he thinks he has. In Merrion Square.'

'Then what the hell are you waiting for? Come on, grab your coat! Is there a car downstairs?'

As Sean walked down the steps it was still light. There were bushes and grass in front of him and he walked along a path between them, aiming for the far side of the square.

He thought: I did it. She's lovely but she can't touch me now. I kissed her and it meant nothing; I'm free.

A man in a top hat walked past, glanced at Sean disapprovingly, and made for one of the big houses on the north side. Sean thought: Don't patronize me, slob. I've been in one of your big houses and fucked one of your posh neighbours' daughters naked in a slum and I could do it again if I wanted but I don't. And don't call the police because I can kill them too.

He felt as though he was walking on air.

A man stepped out from behind a tree and seized his arm. Sean tugged away but someone else seized his other arm and forced it up his back. Sean struggled, and the three of them lurched sideways across the path. Then he felt something hard and cold under his ear and a voice said: 'Stay still or I'll blow your brains out!'

Sean stopped struggling. The voice said: 'Kneel!'

One man kicked him in the back of the legs and he was forced down on his knees. His wrists were cuffed together behind his back. Hands searched his pockets rapidly and pulled out the Parabellum. He was jerked to his feet. 'Walk!'

There seemed to be at least three of them. One on each side with an arm linked through his. A third behind with a pistol.

Sean looked wildly from side to side but he could see no escape. They were walking very quickly and when he tried to drag his feet the man behind kicked him, hard. 'Move, laddie! Fast!'

On the north side of the square there was a car waiting. Two of the men got in the back with Sean in the middle, and the third one drove.

Sean asked: 'Where are we going?'

'To Britannia's dungeons, boy,' said the man on his left. 'Say goodbye to the sunlight.'

Sean looked at the man for the first time. The shock jerked him upright. He recognized him. It was the man who Collins had spoken to in Brendan Road; the man who had identified Radford for them. A vast wave of relief surged through him.

'But you're —' he began.

The man punched him in the mouth. 'Shut it,' he growled. 'From now on, you speak when you're spoken to. Understood?'

Sean gaped, and said nothing.

19

ANOTHER TWO WORDS from the boy, Davis thought, and I'd have been on the way to the hangman with him. He sat staring rigidly ahead, all the way to Brunswick Street. No one said anything.

Kee marched Sean straight past the desk sergeant and down to the cells. In the interrogation room he thrust him into a chair, his hands still fastened behind him. There was one other chair and a table in the room. There was nothing else. No bed. A door. Four walls. A small barred window high in the wall.

Sean's face was white. I expect mine is too, Davis thought. So far, Kee and Foster didn't seem to have noticed.

Kee sat down in the other chair.

'Right,' he said. 'First things first. Your name?'

Sean said nothing. Kee slapped him across the face.

'Your name, boy. What is it?'

'Sean.'

'Sean what?'

'Brennan.'

'Address?'

No answer. Kee grabbed him by the collar, dragging his face forward across the table. With his arms behind him, Sean couldn't protect himself.

Sean gave the address of the tenement.

'That's not true. You've left it. Where do you live now?'

Sean spat in Kee's face.

Kee roared. He dragged the boy to his feet, knocking over the table, and punched him in the stomach. All the air went out of Sean in a loud gasp. He doubled up and fell forward, banging his head on the floor. He lay there, hunched in a foetal position, hands pinioned behind his back. Kee wiped his face, and sat down.

'All right, Brennan,' Kee said. 'Let's start again.'

Ten minutes later they had an address, which Kee was far from convinced was correct, an admission that Sean was 'a soldier of the Republic' and very little else. Kee was feeling tired and disgusted with himself. Once again his anger and frustration had got the better of him, and he had been led into behaviour he regretted. He did not, as a rule, beat up his prisoners; indeed, he instructed young constables strictly against it. Now he had broken his own rules, and got precious little for it.

It was because of the shock of Radford's death. These bastards bring out the worst in us all, he thought.

He got up, jerked his head to his colleagues, and went outside. They went upstairs to his office.

'We'll raid that address,' he said. 'Wait till later tonight, when the devils are likely to be at home. We'll want a full platoon of soldiers – do it properly, seal the house back and front. No more cock-ups this time. See to it, Davis, will you?'

'Sir.'

'In the meantime, we'll charge Brennan with illegal possession of a firearm with intent to endanger life, and attempted murder of Lord French. That should put him away for a long time.' He sighed. 'And we'll bring in the girl. Maybe she can tell us what he can't.'

Catherine had been sitting at her desk for two hours trying to read one of her medical textbooks, but the words made no sense. She had read the same page four times, and had no idea what it was about. Human beings were made up of all these bits and pieces, she thought; bone and muscle and sinew and nerve, but there is no way of understanding why they act as they do. I love him, but he doesn't love me. He's just in love with killing and his idea of himself as a soldier of the Republic. He wants me to be submissive and chaste and to wait for him until he chooses to come back and to feel guilty because I'm rich. *I'm not like that, Sean!*

She seized the book by its spine and flung it across the room. It hit the edge of the ottoman and flopped to the floor, lying open at an expensive, coloured picture of a naked man, which could be opened out, layer by layer, to display the various organs within. The top layer had been ripped by the throw.

She picked it up, slammed it shut, and stuffed it into a bookcase.

He doesn't know me at all, she thought. He doesn't want to know me. That gun he showed me meant more to him than I ever did. He thinks I'll worship him because he made a hole in a policeman's face. He's a fool. Of course the cause is vital but it's not everything, we shouldn't have to deny everything else because of it. What sort of a country will it be if you have to forget about love to fight for it?

It's not that. He's not denying love. He never felt it.

She slumped down on the ottoman with her head in her hands and thought: I wish I had someone to talk to. What would my mother have said? Would she have understood me now?

Someone knocked at the door. She straightened up, and dabbed at her face with a handkerchief. 'Yes?'

Keneally came in. 'Two gentlemen to see you, madam. They say they are detectives.'

'Oh.' She felt faint, as though a hand had squeezed her heart. 'Er, not here, Keneally. Ask them to wait in the downstairs drawing room, will you.'

'Very good, madam.' The old butler hesitated, a look of puzzled concern on his face. 'One is the same man, I think, who came here some weeks ago.'

'I see. Thank you.' Now there was no doubt. It was Sean they were after. She remembered the odd, twisted smile on his face as he had shown her the gun. But that didn't matter now. However foul the murder had been, however much it had damaged Sean, she had to protect him. She sat at her dressing table, blotted away the signs of tears, dabbed on powder, shook her hair and combed it carefully. She mustn't look perturbed. Short dark hair, pretty innocent face, simple elegant turquoise dress. It would do. She gave herself a firm, tight smile, stood up, and took a deep breath. Training. No emotions in front of the servants, no scenes in public. It was only for Sean that she had divested herself of that invisible armour.

She went calmly downstairs and into the drawing room.

The same burly, middle-aged detective was there, with his coat on and his hat in his hand. By the window was a very tall, well-built young man in his early twenties. Catherine had a vague feeling she had seen him once or twice in the street.

'Good afternoon, gentlemen. Can I help you?'

'Yes, miss.' Kee took a card from his wallet and held it out for her to look at. 'Detective Inspector Kee. We've met before. And this is DC Foster. We'd like you to accompany us to police HQ in Brunswick Street.'

'I beg your pardon?'

Kee repeated himself. 'We've a young man there we'd like you to identify for us.'

'Oh my God.' Her left hand gripped the back of an armchair for support. Then she realized they were watching her and forced herself to be calm. 'Is he alive?'

'Oh yes, miss. He's just under arrest. We've a car outside.'

'But – how long is this likely to take? My father will be home soon.' Catherine thought perhaps her father would be able to protect her, then immediately realized that his presence would make things worse. Much worse.

'I really can't say, miss. But it is rather urgent. So if you could fetch a coat.' He advanced on her in a way that suggested he might take her arm if she refused.

She resented it. 'You're not arresting me, I take it?'

'No, miss. I've no reason to do that at the moment. But I am investigating some very serious crimes.'

'Then I can give you an hour. No more.' She went out into the hall, got a coat, and left a message with Keneally to tell her father when she would be back.

Foster drove. Kee sat beside her in the back. He said nothing. He wanted to shock her first, with the sight of Sean.

She *was* shocked.

They had taken the handcuffs off him. They had also taken away his tie, belt and shoelaces, so he had to clutch at his trousers when he stood up. There was a bruise on his right cheek, and his normally smooth hair was ruffled and untidy.

The cell was small – eight feet by five, perhaps – and there was nothing in it but a narrow bed, a table, and a chamberpot. The walls were stone, and there was a small barred window high up over the bed. Sean stood up and looked at her.

She whispered: 'Hello, Sean.' She forgot how his rejection had hurt her. She wanted to fling her arms around him, kiss his bruised cheek, smooth his ruffled hair. But not in front of these men. They had a purpose in bringing her here; it was important to defy them.

Sean said: 'Who is this?'

Her heart stopped. *Not here Sean not now please not again!* But Sean went on, remorselessly, looking her straight in the eye: 'I don't know her. What do you bring her in here for? This isn't a women's prison – or a zoo, is it, for posh girls to come and gape at? Get her out of here!'

Foster said: 'You came out of her house, Brennan. I saw you. You fucked her in a tenement, as well. A filthy stinking tenement off Amiens Street, with an open drain in the back yard.'

'Shut your mouth!' Sean leapt forward and tried to grab Foster's throat. But Kee caught him by the right arm, Foster by the left, and they slammed him back against the wall. Catherine burst into tears.

Kee shouted: 'This is Sean Brennan, isn't it, young woman? Do you agree?'

Catherine nodded, hopelessly. 'Yes, yes. Let him go!'

'And you're his mistress, aren't you? You go to see him and he makes love to you.'

'That's none of your business!'

'But it's true, isn't it?' Kee caught Sean by the hair and pulled his head back, so that she couldn't avoid staring him in the face. 'Look at him. It's true, isn't it – this is your lover!'

'So what if he is? That's not a crime, is it? Let him go, I tell you!'

She tried to tear Kee's hands away from Sean's arm. Kee let go of Sean's hair with his left hand and tried to brush her away, but she held on, wrestling with him and trying to scratch his face. Sean struggled to get free, and the four of them lurched back and forth in the confined space. Then Foster got hold of both of Sean's arms, and Kee bundled Catherine out of the door.

'You bully!' she said. 'Torturer! You've torn my coat!'

Foster came out of the cell. Kee took Catherine's arm, and half led, half dragged her along the corridor. 'Come on, this way. Allan, get one of the secretaries down here, will you. I think it's time you answered a few questions, young lady.'

He took her up a flight of stairs, and into a slightly larger interview room. A few minutes later Foster reappeared with one of the young lady typists. He brought in a chair for her and she sat by the door. Kee sat opposite Catherine at the table.

'What's she here for?' Catherine asked.

'Regulations. So you don't go out saying we molested you.'

'You already have. You tore my coat.' Catherine stood up and showed the typist where her fur collar had been ripped loose along the seam. 'See that? This man did it.' The typist, a woman in her late twenties, looked embarrassed.

Kee waited until Catherine sat down again. He said: 'All right. We know you've been seeing him, and we know where. You went to the tenement off Amiens Street, you went to the Gaelic League in Parnell Square with him, and he came to your house. We know all that. What we don't know is, why?'

Catherine took a deep breath, considering her answer. I must get hold of myself, she thought, I must recover my poise. I need it now; whatever Sean has done, whatever he feels about me, these men are enemies of the state. They're doing all this deliberately, to unsettle me.

She said: 'That's none of your business.'

'Perhaps you don't know what he's done. Did you know he had an automatic pistol in his pocket when he came to see you today?'

'Yes. He showed it to me.'

'And did he tell you what he used it for?'

'He needs it to protect the country against foreign policemen, I believe.'

'So you agree he's a murderer?'

'I didn't say that.'

'The only thing a gun can do, young lady, is kill people. I would have thought a medical student would know that. So if he uses the gun against policemen, that means he kills them.'

And as he kills people, it changes him, she thought. It twists that beautiful smile and takes him away from me. But it doesn't matter now, that's the price we both have to pay for freedom.

She looked Kee straight in the eye and said: 'There's a war in this country. Only last week, every city in the land voted for Sinn Fein, but the British soldiers still don't go home. People get killed in wars.'

'Who has Sean Brennan killed?'

'I've no idea.'

'Listen, young lady. You don't deny that you are in love with this young man, do you? Or that you have gone so far as to ... take off your clothes and go to bed with him. Do you?'

Kee found it actually hard to say the words. She seemed so young, so ... slender and childish in her body still. But as a young bride in a white dress, he realized, she would be celebrated in every society newspaper in the country.

She said: 'I'm proud of it.' And I wish he loved me, she thought. Without that it's all wasted. Involuntarily, her eyes filled with tears. She ignored them.

Kee said: 'In that case, I find it impossible to believe that he didn't tell you who he killed. He did tell you, didn't he?'

'No.'

Kee sighed. 'All right, we'll take it slowly, then. You remember the assassination attempt at Ashtown Cross. Sean Brennan was there, wasn't he? You looked out of the window and saw him.'

If I don't get control of this I'll convict Sean out my own mouth, Catherine thought. Whatever he's done I couldn't live with that. These people are my enemies, anyway. She pushed back her chair and stood up. 'I'm sorry, Inspector,' she said. 'I agreed to give you an hour and that time's up. As far as I can understand I'm not under arrest so I'm going home now. Excuse me.'

She stepped towards the door.

Kee stood up to bar her way.

The door opened and Sir Jonathan came in.

Catherine gasped. She hadn't known you could feel panic and elation at the same time.

Sir Jonathan said: 'Would someone tell me just what the devil is going on?'

Kee was incensed. He suggested to Sir Jonathan that they talk in another room, but Catherine said: 'No! He's going to talk to you about me, Father, and I want to hear what he says. He's a brute and a bully. Look, he's torn my coat.'

Sir Jonathan glared at Kee. 'Is this true?'

'I really think, sir, it would be better ...'

'Listen to me, man. My daughter is a lady, and should be treated as such. Any allegations you have to make you can make in front of us both, as she says. But first of all I want to know why she was brought here without my knowledge. Well?'

This is intolerable, Kee thought. This is a police investigation and an army colonel thinks he can just barge in here and throw his weight about. But the trouble was, Sir Jonathan was very well placed in Dublin Castle.

Kee swallowed his bile and said: 'She agreed to come, sir.'

'That doesn't answer the question. If you have any charges against my daughter I ought to be the first to know, damn you!'

'There are no charges, sir. She was just helping us with identification and answering some questions.'

'I'm glad to hear it. Is that why you tore her coat?'

'I'm sorry about that, sir. She got upset and tried to scratch my face.'

Sir Jonathan looked round him, trying to assess the situation. He noticed the embarrassed typist on her chair and realized she must be a female chaperone. Behind Kee was a big, young, stolid-looking detective, standing motionless like a sentry. Kee himself was holding his emotions in, but obviously angry — whether with Catherine or himself, Sir Jonathan was not quite sure. Catherine appeared to have been crying; but there was a sharp, defiant light in her moist eyes, which Sir Jonathan recognized, together with her straight back and slightly lifted chin, as the signal for a major argument. It also, probably, meant that she was guilty of something dreadful.

'Right,' he said. 'Tell me from the beginning.'

The bald facts of the story that Kee told him hit Sir Jonathan like a series of blows in the stomach. Throughout it he stood quite still, rigid almost, like a man on parade. He watched Catherine's face and saw that the story was true; and a sense of vast desolation and weariness seeped through him. His right leg trembled, and for a moment he thought he would have to sit down; but that would be too humiliating. He stood stiffly, and anger began to flood through him and give him strength.

He confronted Kee first. 'You have known this for over three weeks, and never told me?'

'Suspected, sir. We weren't sure until a couple of days ago, and we only arrested the young man this afternoon.'

'That's not the point. You have had spies following my daughter for over three weeks, while all these alleged events took place, and yet you never saw fit to inform me, her father.'

'I'm sorry, sir. But my duty is to catch Sinn Feiners, which is what I've done.'

Kee felt some sympathy for the man. He imagined how appalled he himself would feel in a similar situation. But it would never arise, he thought. Not with my children. Never.

Sir Jonathan turned to Catherine. Her very silence so far was an admission of guilt. 'It's all true, then, I take it?'

She said: 'I love him. I've nothing to be ashamed of. He's a brave man and an Irish hero.'

No one spoke, and it seemed to Catherine that the words

echoed unnaturally loud in the little room, mocking her. Do I believe a single word of that now? she wondered. But if I don't, there is nothing left. I'll go mad, like Mother.

And I believed we were coming closer, Sir Jonathan thought. It's all there in that face: the defiance, the illogical hatred of England with which Maeve used to confront me. But Catherine has a stubborn strength of will that Maeve never had. The determination behind those dark, haunted eyes – that's mine, not Maeve's.

He said: 'We won't discuss that here. Inspector, she has identified the young man, you said. Do you have any more questions for her now?'

'Yes, sir. It's my belief that Brennan must have told her something of his plans, and who he tried to kill.'

'Did he?' Sir Jonathan asked Catherine.

'No. He wouldn't be so foolish. Anyway, I don't intend to answer any more questions. I was about to leave when you came in, Father. Unless I am under arrest, that is what I shall do.'

She looked at them, and then made a step towards the door.

'Catherine!'

'Yes, Father.'

'The Assistant Commissioner was murdered the other night. Shot down in cold blood in the street. Would your Sean Brennan have had anything to do with that?'

'I really couldn't say, Father.'

'Could you love a man who had done that? Shot an unarmed man in the street like a coward?'

Her eyes filled with tears. She didn't answer. After a

pause she took another couple of steps towards the door. Her father grabbed her arm and turned her to face him.

'Did he do it, girl? Did this Brennan kill Radford?'

'No!'

For a moment the two of them stared into each other's eyes, defiantly. Sir Jonathan let go of her arm. She put her hand on the door handle, but Foster's hand closed over hers.

'Am I under arrest?'

Kee shook his head. Foster took his hand away, and Catherine walked out into the corridor, alone.

Davis had been busy. He had contacted the Royal Barracks in Benburb Street and arranged for a platoon of soldiers to be ready for a search operation under the direction of Detective Inspector Kee later that evening. They had asked him for the address but he had said that for security reasons the Detective Inspector would only tell them that when he arrived to take charge. The major on the other end of the line had been a little huffy, but Davis had been adamant. There were too many security leaks these days, he said. Procedure must be followed strictly.

Then he had walked around the corner into the small newsagent's shop in King Street. There was a phone in the back office which Davis was free to use any time. He asked for one of the numbers which Paddy Daly had given him. A woman's voice answered.

'Hello. Clancy's Joiners and Decorators.'

'Good afternoon. Is Mr Daly there, please?'

'Just a moment. Who shall I say is calling?'

'Mr Hanover. It's about a new job I need a price for.'

There was a pause. The line crackled. A man's voice came on the line. 'Paddy Daly here.'

'Oh, hello, Patrick, this is George Hanover.' They had settled on the name of the English king as a code word long ago, to show that the message was about a raid. Clancy's office, at the other end of the line, had a notice outside saying that all kinds of household decorations were undertaken. Davis tried to make all his calls sound like those of a customer placing an order.

'Yes, Mr Hanover, sir. What can we do for you?'

'There's a house in Phibsborough I'd like you to look at: 47 Berkeley Street.' That was the address Sean had given Kee. Davis was worried that there were probably other Sinn Feiners living there who Kee would arrest when it was raided. Files, too, perhaps; arms. 'Could you go there today and give me a quotation?'

'Today is it? We're a bit pushed. What sort of time?'

'My friends will be visiting the place in the evening. If you could have checked it out before then I would be most grateful.'

Daly caught the urgency in his voice. 'Right sir, we'll do that for you. Is it every room you want seeing to?'

'Every room. And Paddy, there's another thing. I've got a young friend of yours staying with me. He's likely to be with us for a few days, I should think.'

There was a sharp intake of breath at the other end. Then Daly said: 'Who would that be, then?'

There was no code for this sort of message. Davis said: 'Brennan, Sean Brennan.'

'Holy Mary Mother of God.' Davis imagined the distress at the other end. When he had recovered, Daly said: 'Well, give the poor lad my blessing. We'll try to arrange a visit as soon as we can. Would you be able to get round for a chat some time?'

'I'll do that,' Davis said. 'I can't give you a time now, though. We're very busy here.'

'Sure you will be. Oh, one more thing, Mr Hanover.'

'Yes?'

'Our friend that's visiting you. Brennan. He doesn't live in Berkeley Street, you know. It's another place entirely. Tell him his place'll be empty by this evening, too, will you?'

David heaved a sigh of relief. The address Sean had given Kee was a false one, anyway.

'I'll do that, Patrick.' He hung up, left a few coins by the phone, and walked back through the newsagent's into the street. If he had time, he thought, he might be able to see Sean before Kee had finished interrogating the girl.

Catherine stood with her father in the downstairs drawing room. Like the dining room, in which she had made her bargain with him all those months ago, it had once been used as a ward for wounded soldiers. Then it had been dirty, carpetless, defaced by the blood, graffiti and despair of those who had used it as a hospital. Now the carpets were thick and soft, the walls were repapered in crimson and cream, the portraits gazed down again with their ponderous gloom. There was a harp and a piano in the corner, and a bright fire blazed in the grate.

Sir Jonathan stood with one hand on the mantelpiece and glared at her. He was still in uniform. The firelight gleamed on his polished leather belt and riding boots, and lit the little coloured flashes of medal ribbons. His back was straight and his face was hard with anger, but Catherine had the sense that underneath it all he was tired, tired to death as she was.

She sat as far away from him as she could, on a music stool in the corner by the harp. She had deliberately not lit the lamp, so she was half in shadow.

'You were my last child,' Sir Jonathan was saying. 'You have defied me enough times before but this time we made a bargain which I thought you would keep. I did not marry Sarah Maidment, I have made everything over to you in my will, and now I find that all this time you have been going behind my back, like a – street girl, it seems. Sleeping with a murderer.'

'He's not a murderer, Father, he's a soldier. He fights for his country like you did. And Richard and John, too. They killed Germans, didn't they? Wasn't that murder as well?'

That hurt. When she saw his pain she wished she had not said it. But she was in too much despair to think clearly.

'If you think that, Catherine, you must be as mad as your mother was,' he said quietly. 'Your two brothers were fighting in uniform in the most terrible war the world has ever seen. They gave their lives for king and country. You cannot compare them for a moment with swine who skulk around in back streets in plain clothes, and dash out like cowards to shoot men in the back.'

'Sean's not a coward.'

'Of course he is, they all are. Cowardly murderers who stab us all in the back, like Pearse and his rabble did in '16. No better than Whiteboys who cut off the tails of cattle. If he wasn't a coward he'd have joined up to fight for his country.'

'Father, this *is* his country. That's what he's fighting for – they all are.'

'And you think Ireland will be a better place when it's ruled by a bunch of murderers, do you? Is that what you think?'

'I think it already is run by murderers.'

She had thought that at that point he would end the conversation entirely, and perhaps throw her out into the street, to take her chance with such of Sean's colleagues as she could find. She had thought of that possibility on the way home, and wondered if she should go to Parnell Square and throw herself on the mercy of whoever she could find. But she had her pride still. Only Sean, in the movement, had really accepted her. Once. Without him there seemed no point. There was a terrible loneliness in leaving the only home she had, with nowhere to go. So she had come back here, more out of inertia than anything else.

She felt enormously tired now. The day had been too full of shocks: the discovery of what Sean had done, his rejection of her, his arrest, and now this. Despite it all she bore her father no ill will: he had even tried to protect her, in his way. It was just that he was so utterly, hopelessly wrong.

To her surprise he flushed, as if embarrassed at the last point. 'If he did kill someone he'll be hanged, you know.'

'That's what I mean.'

To his surprise she did not cry at the thought of Sean hanging. She swept her hands idly, irritatingly across the strings of the harp, then stilled the sound with her arm. She stared at him out of the shadows, still clasping the instrument, which he knew she had never learnt to play. Her arms, in the sleeveless turquoise dress, were bare, and the line of her neck and shoulders was quite slender and beautiful. Her small, delicate face, framed by the short dark hair, watched him so seriously; pale, intent, determined. He thought she would make a marvellous portrait, just like that, if any artist could capture it. A portrait of what, exactly? Of a new type of young woman that I can't understand or control at all, it seems.

How did I get a daughter like this? She had that look on her as a child of four or five, I remember. And she would scream and kick the house down if she didn't get what she wanted then, too.

But, by God, she can't have what she wants this time.

He said: 'I take it the story the police told me was true.'

'The details were true. They missed out the fact that it was all done in love. I don't expect policemen can understand that.'

'No one could understand a girl like you falling in love with a murderer.'

'He's not – Father, you don't *know* he is a murderer.'

Sir Jonathan said nothing. He moved away from the fire, and stood looking down at her. The firelight flickered on her smooth, defiant face. He felt an immeasurable sense of desolation.

He said: '*You* know, though. Don't you, Cathy?'

She turned her eyes away.

He walked to a cabinet in the corner and poured himself a whiskey. For a while neither of them spoke. Sir Jonathan was glad the room was dark. If his daughter was crying he didn't want to see. He hoped she was. It would be some small sign of decency, of shared human values.

But I have sinned, too, he thought. I must have done, to have all this inflicted on me. I betrayed her mother, and that was done for love. The boys understood that but this child never forgave me. Now she is all I have left. And she has betrayed me. Perhaps that is my punishment.

I have a duty to try again.

He said: 'If he is a murderer, that policeman could lock you up as an accomplice. You realize that, don't you?'

'He's got no evidence.' Her voice was quite dull and flat.

'*Did* you help him, Cathy? Did you help this man to kill a policeman?'

She shook her head. 'He wouldn't have let me if I'd asked.' Then she looked up at him suddenly. He was sitting on the arm of a chair quite close to her, gazing down into the whiskey glass. His shoulders sagged: he looked utterly forlorn. Catherine saw how he might look as an old man. She put her hand on his shoulder.

'No, Father, I didn't help him kill anyone.'

She took her hand away, stood up, and walked across the room. 'Now, if you don't mind, I'm going to bed. I can't talk about this any more today. I'll go mad.'

Like your mother, he thought, as she went out of the door. *I'll go mad* – that's what Maeve said, and she did it, too.

He poured himself another whiskey, and sat staring

gloomily into the fire. At least my daughter is not a murderess, he told himself; I'm sure she was telling the truth then. Is that what life has come to – to be glad I can believe a thing like that?

20

S EAN SAT ON his bed in his cell, and confronted his fears. There were a number of them. He was afraid that he might be beaten and tortured; he was afraid that he might betray his friends; he was afraid that he might be shut in here for life; he was afraid the police would find out about the murder of Radford; he was afraid that he would be hanged.

He sat on the narrow, hard bed and forced his brain to examine these one by one. He had heard many stories of beatings and torture; all the Volunteers had. Men had had their arms twisted, fingernails crushed with pincers, fingers bent and broken, pistols held to their heads; in the hunger strikes in Belfast prisoners had been hosed down and had their hands fastened behind their backs for weeks, so that they were unable to undo their trousers to use their chamberpots.

So far little of this had happened to Sean. He had been punched and beaten on the first day, but since then the Ulster detective had behaved with reasonable correctness. He had shouted at him certainly, and repeated the same questions again and again with wearisome regularity, but no more. So long as this man was in charge, then, it seemed likely there would be nothing worse.

And without torture he would not betray his friends or admit to the shooting of Radford. There was no need for it. He had found the right formula. 'I am a soldier of the Irish Republic; I refuse to answer that question.' He had said that for two days. He believed he could keep on saying it for ever.

So there remained the fears of being shut in, and of being hanged.

Others have been imprisoned for Ireland before me, Sean thought – all the greatest men of our nation. Parnell, though in a much better cell than this; Wolfe Tone, Napper Tandy, Robert Emmet, O'Donovan Rossa, Padraig Pearse, Thomas Clarke, Sean MacBride . . . the list went on and on. The heroes of 1916 had died in Kilmainham, but others had suffered in Mountjoy. Sean felt proud to be in such illustrious company; already he had found several names carved on the cell wall, and begun to add his own. But it was the living death, year after year in a stone tomb, with the walls closing around him, that he feared. Still, others had survived it: Thomas Clarke had been in gaol for fifteen years, breaking stone, sometimes forced to lap his food from the floor with his hands behind his back – but he had come out, to marry, run his newsagent's in Amiens Street, and be the first signatory of the Declaration of the Republic in 1916.

And then be court-martialled and shot.

If he could face it, Sean thought, so can I. It is an honour and a duty, the other side of what I have prepared for. Outside, I had to be ready to face death and kill for the Republic; in here, I must suffer. Become a martyr if necessary. 'From the graves of patriot men and women spring living nations,' Pearse said. The side that can suffer longest will win in the end.

The key to survival was to accept your fate, not fight it. It would be easier without choices and hope. He could choose, he realized, to hang or to be imprisoned. If he admitted nothing they were unlikely to hang him, because they had no evidence. But if he wanted to die, all he had to do was tell them that he had killed Radford. When the heavy cell door closed on him, and he thought of all the years he might spend here, he was tempted.

But then there were the hopes. In a few short years the British might be thrown out of Ireland, and then he would be freed, a national hero. That was a fine hope, for it involved no action on his part. The other hope was more practical. It was the possibility that one of the detectives might arrange an escape.

The man – Davis, he was called – had come to see him on the first evening, when Sean was still in the police cells. He had come in hurriedly, and gabbled his message in a low murmur.

'You'll know my face, boy, so you'll know I didn't like hitting you, believe me, but it had to be done, or you'd have betrayed me, and let us both down, likely. Do you see that now?'

'Maybe.' Sean had been cautious, reluctant to commit himself. His jaw and stomach had both been aching badly, he had been sick on the floor, and they had left his hands fastened behind his back. He had not cared greatly whether he betrayed this detective or not, at the time. The man was agitated, sweating profusely.

'Well, you'd better see it. It's a bloody dangerous job I do here, I can tell you. So you keep your damn mouth shut or I'll tell them all I know about you, and then you'll swing and no mistake.'

Davis had illustrated his point graphically by seizing Sean's collar and pulling it tight around his neck, so that he found it hard to breathe. Sean's contempt for the man increased.

'But if you just keep mum there's a chance we can get you out, boy. It's been done before and it may be done again. I've already told Paddy Daly you're here and they'll be having a meeting to decide what can be done. So you've a chance yet.'

Perhaps, Sean had thought. The leap of hope had made him more than ever conscious of the squalor and pain, and an urgent longing had arisen in him to be free and out of here immediately, cycling through the cold crisp air by the Liffey.

'Will you take off my cuffs, then?' he had asked.

'Don't be daft, I can't do that. That'd be the first way of getting a finger pointed at me. I'm not supposed to be in here at all, let alone cleaning you up and making you look nice. When we do the interrogations I'll be the hardest cop of all if I can, just to avoid suspicion. You'll have to put up with that. Just keep your mouth shut, now, boy — remember that!'

By the afternoon of the third day he had determined to abandon all hope, and resign himself to a long sentence, if he could. If he could not, he had only to admit the shooting of Radford, and the British would send him to heaven, to shake the hand of Padraig Pearse, Thomas Clarke, James Connolly, and all the other angels . . .

He was elaborating this thought in his mind when a key clanked in the lock. A warder stood with his back to the open door. 'Out!' he said.

Sean stood up. 'Where to now?' he asked.

No answer. The man clamped one handcuff bracelet round Sean's wrist, the other round his own, and led him out into the long, echoing corridor. As they went down a staircase Sean thought wearily: Another interrogation, more questions — 'Do you know him? Did you do this?' 'I am a soldier of the Irish Republic, I have nothing to say' — again and again and again. Or had the detective, Davis, managed something at last?

There it was — the niggling, irritating weakness of hope, followed always by the disappointment which made him weaker than before. I must suppress it, he thought. I'm a martyr; I'll never get out. Think that, and be strong.

Kee was in the interview room, as he had expected.

So was Catherine.

She was wearing a pale-pink dress with white lace at the throat and a single pearl on a gold chain round her neck. Her eyes were wide and shining as though she might have been crying. She smiled at him.

'Hello, Sean.'

Sean had been so obsessed with his own fears that he had scarcely thought about her consciously for three days. She had surfaced only in his dreams, and in those last moments before he fell asleep. Even then he had tried to suppress the memories as being unnecessary, likely to weaken him when he needed all his strength. Now he was stunned by the femininity of her body, the tantalizing scent that came from her, the thought that he had kissed that face, that neck, the breasts under that dress...

He looked away from her, to Kee, and saw a broad, cunning grin on the man's face. Damn him, Sean thought, he knows exactly what I'm thinking. The man's enjoying this.

Kee said: 'Miss O'Connell-Gort has come to visit you. You have ten minutes. The warder will stay with you but I will spare you my presence. I hope she persuades you to tell the truth.'

He went out and closed the door. The warder sat down on a chair by the wall. Sean sat at a table facing Catherine.

'Sean. How are you? Have they hurt you?'

She reached out her hands across the table to touch his. The warder coughed loudly. 'No physical contact, miss. Regulations.'

'How stupid and cruel.' She laid her hands flat on the table, a few inches from his.

Sean said: 'Why did you come?'

'Why? To see you, of course. I've been asking permission for the last three days.' She studied him, sensing his anger but misinterpreting it. 'Believe me, Sean – I'd have come earlier if they'd let me.'

Sean remembered Kee's last words. 'What have you told them?'

'Nothing. No more than they knew already.' She smiled. 'I told them I was proud, Sean.'

'Proud of what, for Christ's sake?'

'Proud that you'd been my lover. Proud even of what you'd done.'

'*What* did you tell them I'd done?'

She was shocked by his vehemence. The smile on her face faded to something harder. 'I told you, Sean – nothing. If you think for one moment I'd betray you, you're wrong.'

'You may have said something without realizing it.'

She did not answer. Sean realized that the warder could hardly fail to hear every word. It would be madness to talk about details. He looked at her for a long moment, taking in every detail of the delicate, proud face, the slender neck, the rise of the small breasts under the dress, the slim, fine-boned hands that had scored lines in his buttocks and back as he thrust inside her. He said, very coldly and clearly: 'It was good of you to come, *a ghra*, but you must never do it again. Promise me that, will you?'

Tears rose to her eyes. 'But *why*, Sean?'

'Because, Cathy. That's all. Just because.'

'But I can help you. Bring you comfort, take messages. Tell the papers if you're being ill-treated.'

'No. You said it yourself. We were lovers once, but we're not any more, and we never can be now. It weakens me, for God's sake, to see you here, all soft and . . . It gives them a handle over me, helps them put pressure on. I want you to go right away and stay away. I'm a martyr now, I'm dead to the world.'

'But you might get out, Sean! You might . . .'

'Escape, you mean?' He glanced meaningly at the warder. 'Not a chance. Now go now, will you? Go! Forget I ever was.'

She sat there, stricken, not moving. With an impatient jerk he got to his feet, scraping the wooden chair back across the stone floor. She stood up too. He meant to walk away without a word, but somehow, without ever intending to, he took her hand for a second and pressed it.

It was a great mistake. The touch only lasted for an instant before the warder stopped it, but the soft human femininity of it destroyed his belief in everything he had said. He wanted to hold her, to kiss her, do all those things they had done together before, again and again forever . . .

The warder snatched his hand away, clipped the bracelet on his wrist, and marched him roughly to the door.

Back in his cell, he lay face down on his bed and wept. Then he prayed, desperately, that Davis would get him out before the walls closed in and drove him mad.

The one thing Catherine could not do was take second place to others. She had not been brought up to it. As a child she had fought her elder brothers all the way, to prove that she was better than them: she rode better, learned to read sooner, could paint and draw better, even row a boat as well as they could. The country folk around Killrath had a stock of tales of her leaping her pony over stone walls at breakneck speed, climbing cliffs to steal gulls' eggs, capsizing a dinghy in the surf.

Then the boys were sent away for long periods to boarding school, her father took up with Sarah Maidment, and her mother began her long slide towards insanity. For all that time Catherine had been left alone with a series of governesses, feeling her own pain, triumph and confusion as the centre of the world. She learned *about* the world, but was not part of it. She knew how to challenge, dare, defy, and command, but not how to cooperate.

As a student, she had continued her isolation without feeling it abnormal. Most of the others she had met had been sympathetic to the cause of Irish nationalism, but not actively involved. Sean had been her one real friend – her link with the world where these things were actually happening. Now he had rejected her, and she did not know what to do.

She had told Professor O'Connor about Sean's arrest and he had been sympathetic, but he implied that the Volunteers already knew, and were doing all they could. He wondered if she would like to join the women's movement, Cumman na mBann, but she saw no point. She was sure they would disapprove of her. She could not face the discipline of running messages, taking orders, waiting, cooking, cleaning, and supporting the men which she was sure it would involve. Such things demanded an acceptance of comradeship and subordination which were no part of her nature. So she refused, and went miserably home to her green and gold sitting room in Merrion Square, to sit and think.

She tried to study, but the words slithered meaninglessly around on the page, defying her to make sense of them. She had nothing else to do. She sat on the green window seat overlooking the gardens of the square, and tried to sketch a portrait of Sean which she had planned, but after a few strokes of the charcoal she smudged it, and flung it face down on the floor. She wept, and wondered if this was the way her mother had felt. At least her father had left her mother for another woman; was that better, or worse, than being rejected in favour of an ideal?

Evening came. The fire died down to a few smouldering ashes, and the only light in the room came from the misty yellow gas lamps in the square. A cold, sleety drizzle was falling outside. Catherine sat motionless in the window seat, her knees drawn up to her chin, gazing moodily out at the ghostly trees and scurrying pedestrians.

There was a knock at the door. When she did not answer, it opened, and her father came in.

He said: 'I thought I might see you at dinner.'

'I'm not hungry. I told Keneally that, hours ago.'

'He told me you ate nothing for lunch, either.'

'So?'

Sir Jonathan sighed. He considered lighting a lamp, but decided it would provoke an outburst he did not want. He sat down quietly on a sofa, thinking how pale, almost white, its normal lemon colour appeared in the semi-darkness. The room was cold, he thought, but oddly restful.

He said: 'That inspector from G Division phoned. He told me you visited Brennan in gaol today.'

'Yes. He was there, smirking.'

'Brennan's to be charged with illegal possession of firearms and membership of Sinn Fein, that's all. They've no evidence for anything else.'

'Good.'

'It'll still put him away for four or five years. Damn good thing too.'

No answer. Sir Jonathan shivered. This room was really very cold. No wonder she was hunched up like that. He bent down and put a few small logs on the fire, carefully, in a pyramid over the embers, so that they would blaze up as soon as possible. He watched the flames begin to lick upwards, and held out his hands to them, wondering how best to put what he had to say. His anger had faded over the last two days, leaving a slight sense of pity, and a calm determination that he had been right all along, and that things were going to go his way. It was like that moment in breaking a young horse, when the trainer senses the fight will be won.

He said: 'I want you to go to Killrath tomorrow.'

'What?' Catherine sounded confused, as though she had been thinking of something else entirely.

'You heard. I've rung Ferguson already. He's expecting you.'

'What are you talking about? I can't go to Killrath.'

'Of course you can. You're doing no good here. I doubt if you're studying much, and you don't even eat. A breath of sea air will do you good. Also –'

'Father, I'm not going!'

The outburst was brief, as he had expected. Defiant, but without the strength of will which he had known in her. He continued, stolidly: 'Also, I've come to an arrangement with that Inspector Kee. He could quite easily charge you with aiding and abetting, you realize that, don't you? But if I agree to take responsibility for keeping you somewhere out of the city for a while, he'll drop all charges and leave you alone. No more interrogations, either.'

'I'm not afraid of him, Father. Anyway, I can't go. I've got lectures to attend, books to read. It's nonsense.'

'Take your books with you, by all means.' The fire was blazing nicely now, the flames sending out a little colour into the room. Sir Jonathan stood up to warm his backside in front of it. In the firelight his legs made huge, dancing shadows on the opposite wall.

'Anyway,' he said. 'There's another thing, far more important than all of that. I've deliberately left it alone for the last two days because I could see you were in shock, and upset. But it's time to settle it clearly. *You listen to me, now!*'

He had not meant to shout, but she had turned her head away to stare out of the window. It was like the way she had put her hands over her ears, as a little child – it had made him furious then. He controlled himself with an effort, and went on.

'We made a deal about your inheritance, and by your relationship with this young Sinn Feiner, you clearly broke it. I don't want to hear any more about what you did or didn't do with him; I'm a man of the world, I suppose, and can imagine for myself. The point is, you should have done nothing. Now, the main part of our deal was that if you did not live up to expectations, you would be disinherited, and the estate would be settled on someone who better deserved it. *I can still do that, you understand!* I can order Keneally to throw you out of the house tomorrow, and you can find your own accommodation with your Sinn Fein friends. And by God I swear I will do it, Catherine, unless you change your ways immediately. *Do you understand me?*'

There was a silence. He wondered if he had sounded hysterical rather than firm. But if he had learnt one thing in life about how to deal with horses, soldiers, and children, it was that you should never make a threat unless you are prepared to carry it out. He had not been a good parent to Catherine, he knew, but he hoped she had seen enough of him to know he meant what he said.

'Change my ways how, exactly?'

He breathed a small sigh of relief. If she had not answered, he might have lost her. But now she had taken one small step in his direction, he could lead her where he wanted her to go.

'First, go to Killrath. Second, agree that you will not see this young Brennan again.'

There was another long silence. It was the second thing he thought she would find hardest. He was prepared to agree to allow her to write to him, if necessary. He could not prevent it anyway.

She swung her legs off the window seat to the floor, and sat staring at him bleakly, her arms holding the seat by her sides.

'All right, father. What time is the train?'

If he had been a demonstrative man he might have hugged her, and that might have made a difference. But he was not, so he said: 'The train leaves at 9.30. I'll come with you to the station. Be sure you are ready.' And left the room.

This is the end of it all, she thought.

21

KILLRATH, IT SEEMED to Catherine, had been invaded. All the way down from Dublin on the train, she had thought of the great house ahead of her as a refuge. She would be able to sleep again in the room she had had as a child, ride Grainne along the cliffs and sands, wander the great rooms and gardens at peace, with only the wind to disturb her. The pain of the past weeks in Dublin would fade, the Atlantic gales would clear her mind.

That was what she hoped. She had known Andrew Butler would be there but she had not thought about him at all, all the long day in the train. But when she came out of the station at Galway there he was, lounging against the bonnet of her father's car.

It was a cold, blustery day. He wore a long belted Burberry coat with the collar turned up, leather gauntlets and a motoring helmet with the goggles pushed up on to his forehead. She saw that despite the weather, the canvas roof of the car was rolled back.

He smiled at her, teeth gleaming white under the scarred cheek and thin moustache, and made a mock salute.

'Good afternoon, Miss Catherine.' He took her suitcase, put it in the car boot, and held open the front passenger door. She stepped round to it, then hesitated.

'Where's David Ferguson?'

'He's at home. When your father telephoned I offered to drive down and fetch you instead. I thought you might prefer it.'

Home, she thought. How on earth could this man speak of Killrath as home? It was her home, no one else's – even the Fergusons lived in a house in the grounds. A worm of fear crawled in her stomach. She glanced at the car irritably.

'Why is the roof down? Can't you put it up?'

'I can if you like, but I prefer the fresh air. Don't you?'

'Not when I'm dressed like this.' She was wearing a three-quarter-length pale-blue woollen coat, button boots, and a matching wide-brimmed hat secured with a pin. It would quite obviously blow away in the wind. 'Put it up, please.'

She watched as he dragged the hood forward and clipped it in place. If he thinks he can mock me, she thought, I won't have that. There was something offensively relaxed and confident about his manner. It jarred with her mood. I'd forgotten about this, she thought. Did father realize it, when he sent me down?

She got in and sat quietly, staring straight ahead. He drove out of the town, whistling softly between his teeth and glancing at her from time to time. She felt his presence overbearing, an intrusion. All day she had been turned in on herself, thinking how foolish she had been with Sean, how cheap and tarnished she must look to the world. Andrew's cheerfulness was intolerable.

'Can't you keep quiet?' she said at last.

He raised his eyebrows. 'I haven't said a word.'

'You keep whistling. It's getting on my nerves.'

'My deepest apologies.'

They drove on in silence. As they reached the coast a storm blew in off the sea, splattering the windscreen with hailstones. She thought he would stop but he drove on, peering through the little gap made by the wiper and rubbing the mist of their breath away with his glove. As the storm eased he went faster. She wondered if he was driving deliberately fast in order to impress her. If so, she didn't care. He could kill them both if he liked.

He glanced at her briefly. 'Your father told me you'd had a bad time in Dublin but he didn't explain how.'

'Good. I don't want to talk about it.'

'Fair enough. But I hope a few days down here will blow it away. It's a beautiful part of the country.'

'I do know that, Major Butler. I was born here.'

'And you think I'm intruding, obviously.' As they approached the rocky hilltop where they would catch their first glimpse of Killrath, he slowed the car and stopped. The hailstorm had just passed, and a dark indigo cloud covered the mountains inland. The house itself, still wet from the storm, sparkled in the pale evening sunlight. Andrew switched off the engine.

'Why have you stopped?'

'Just to enjoy the view for a second.' He got out of the car, walked round to the front, leaned against the bonnet, and bent his head over his cupped hands to light a cigarette.

'Damn you,' Catherine muttered softly to herself. She wished she could drive but she had never learnt. She felt a fool just sitting there, waiting on his pleasure, her view obscured by the misty windscreen and his broad back leaning against the bonnet. What made it worse was that it was a view she had always loved herself. She got out of the car and walked a little way down the road, so that she could lean with her back against a rock out of the blustering wind.

There was a moderate sea, and cloud shadows chased each other across it, turning the waves various shades from a deep midnight blue to a cold steel grey. Whitecaps were bursting quite far out, and a cluster of seagulls followed an intrepid fishing coracle as it made its way precariously inshore.

'You're a lucky girl, to inherit all this.'

She looked round and saw with annoyance that he had walked down the road to join her. He leaned one arm against the rock, so that he could look at her and the view at the same time. He took a deep drag on his cigarette and the scent of the tobacco mingled not unpleasantly with that of the damp heather and spray.

She said: 'It would have gone to one of my brothers, if they had lived.'

'Your father told me. They were brave men, but unlucky.'

She turned on him angrily. 'What do you know about it?'

'I was there, remember? Not with your brothers, but at the front. Most men were unlucky, Catherine. Millions of them.'

'So why were you spared?'

'Who knows?' He took another drag of the cigarette. 'All I know is I spent a lot of time thinking about Ardmore, which is a place not as grand as this, but prettier, as your brothers must have sat in their billets and remembered this view here.'

It was not something she could argue about. 'They wrote about it too,' Catherine agreed after a while. 'I used to send them photographs and news of what was happening here.'

'My parents did that as well. Did I tell you, they both died while I was away?' He flung the cigarette down on to the road, and watched the wind blow the last breath out of it on the gravel.

'I'm sorry.' It was the first time she had thought about anyone else all day, apart from her own misery and Sean's imprisonment. The death of Andrew Butler's unknown parents seemed trivial in comparison to that; but she remembered the loss and loneliness she had felt at her three funerals: first her two brothers, then her mother, Maeve. No doubt he had felt like that. 'Do you have any other family?' she asked.

He shook his head. 'So we're matched, you and I. Sole inheritors of great estates. Even if mine's just a pile of ashes in a park. Come on, you look cold.'

He strode back to the car and started the engine. She followed, slowly. This is not going to be a stay in Killrath on my own, she thought. This man is going to invade every part of it.

He appeared to be well in with the Fergusons, too. The son, David, met them at the house with a broad smile on his face and an assurance that dinner would be ready in an hour and Miss Catherine's room aired *as Major Butler had ordered*, and Catherine had the odd sense that David paid more attention to Andrew than to her. This was more marked when the father appeared ten minutes later. Ever since she had realized she might inherit Killrath, Catherine had known that dealing with her father's agent, Arthur Ferguson, would be her hardest trial. He had not forgotten her defiance over the evictions, nor did he appear to have changed his opinion that women had no understanding of the business of estate management. He greeted her with crusty politeness, as usual, but with Andrew he was almost cheerful. Catherine watched in pensive silence while the two men discussed the arrangements for winter feed. Andrew's manner was easy, relaxed, controlled. It reminded her of something or someone that she couldn't quite place. Whatever it was, the elusive memory made her distrust him deeply.

She confronted him at dinner. They sat together at a polished table in the smaller family dining room. Oil lamps glowed in the corners of the room, and a fire crackled in the hearth. Occasional gusts of wind rattled the windows and sent draughts stirring the curtains. The butler came in to serve the soup.

When they were alone Catherine said: 'You seem to have made yourself at home here.'

'It's like Ardmore, only larger. Your father has chosen good staff.' He sipped his soup. 'Why are you so angry about it?'

'Because it's my home and you have no place in it.'

It hurt. He had been fascinated by their sparring at their last meeting, and had been glad when her father had rung to say she would be coming down. He hoped she might feel the same. He had made some efforts to make her arrival pleasant. There was more to it for Andrew than the relief of boredom. He thought of her, quite coolly, as the first girl he had met who had both enough fire in her belly to satisfy him and enough money to rebuild Ardmore.

He saw himself as breaking in a young filly. He must expect kicks; he must not allow her to get away with them. He said: 'I don't bite, you know. Besides, I don't have a home of my own.'

'That's not my fault.'

'No. But it's no reason to start throwing your father's guests out. Or have you seen the light, and decided to evict all your tenants when you're mistress here?'

Catherine flushed. There was a knowing grin on his face which enraged her. 'Have you been talking to Ferguson about me?'

'He did say you had a disagreement a few years ago, yes.'

'Well, I hope he told you that he was wrong! It was Ferguson who wanted to evict the tenants then — I never shall! All that man ever thinks of is cattle, rents, and profit.'

'Which have made people like you very rich. And me, I once thought. Don't despise your servants, Catherine.'

At this point the butler came in with two housemaids to clear the soup plates, carve the meat, lay out the warm dishes of vegetables, and pour the wine. Catherine waited until they had gone, letting her temper cool, seeking the most wounding phrase she could find.

'I'm used to servants, I never despise them. What I do despise are self-appointed schoolteachers.'

It was not a fortunate choice. He raised his glass to her and laughed, which was not the result she had hoped for at all.

'I never had a sister, Miss Catherine, so perhaps I'm unused to the domestic life of the fair sex. But if I were your schoolteacher, I think I'd have bent you across my knee and given you a hearty spanking long ago.'

And you'd have liked it, too, he thought, as he saw the flush rise across her face and her eyes widen with anger. He remembered the chases he had had with Elsie in the Schwarzwald, and the rough, vicious, thrilling wrestling matches with which they had ended. Both of them had been covered with love bites and bruises everywhere. He had not known love could be like that; he had seldom thought of it any other way, afterwards. This girl was slimmer and more finely built than Elsie but from the graceful, assertive way she moved he had had little doubt that her body was hard and athletic as well as beautiful. I could see you lying below me in the pine needles, he thought, kicking and scratching like a hellcat. Except that it's winter here and there's only heather or sand or bogland. Perhaps it'll have to be indoors. Could I manage it, in a week?

He leaned forward and watched her over the table, cradling his wineglass in both hands. Catherine was shocked. She remembered the same fear and fascination she had felt for him when they had first met, only a week ago – could it be such a short time? This was a man quite unlike any others she knew. Self-contained, dreamy, with an arrogant self-confidence quite equal to her own, and something more, that frightened her. As though, when he looked at her, he did not see a person at all. Like a hawk looking down at a vole.

She said: 'I don't think you know very much about women. If you tried to spank me I'd scratch your eyes out.'

The burst of delighted laughter which greeted that remark unsettled her even more than before.

Next day she suggested, rather as a way of putting him in his place, that they ride around the estate together. She wanted to take control, and show that both Killrath and the initiative belonged to her, which was the way she liked it.

Also, he would give her something else to think about. His insolence last night had made her angry, but it was a welcome anger. It had stopped her thinking about herself and Sean for nearly an hour, and that could only be good.

They rode along the clifftops to the west. Catherine rode Grainne, sitting side-saddle in a long brown skirt, slim black riding jacket and small round hat. Andrew was mounted on Simla, a big bay cob that her father used for hunting. The animal played up at first, and it became clear to her after a mile or so that Andrew was a competent horseman, no more. He was a little hard on the beast's mouth, impatient and rough when it was not needed.

'He's lively,' he shouted across to her. 'Feeling his oats. Isn't there some open ground where we can have a gallop, steam some of it off?'

'In half a mile or so.' First they had to go along a narrow path with only four or five yards between the stone wall on their right and the cliff-edge on their left. For most of the way the cliff was a steep grassy slope, going down a couple of hundred feet or more to an outcrop of black rocks just above the sea; but there was a passage of a hundred yards or so round an indented bay where the cliffs dropped sheer into the water. Catherine led the way on Grainne, who picked her steps daintily along the narrow path. Looking down to her left, Catherine could see gulls and kittiwakes launch themselves off ledges into space, floating effortlessly in the updraught over the grey waves below. Her parents had forbidden her to ride along here as a child, and even her brothers had refused to do it when she dared them. That was why she had brought Andrew. It was a place that tested the nerves of both horse and rider; there was no room for fear or mistakes.

Catherine had always enjoyed heights, and she had absolute confidence in Grainne.

When she was halfway round the bay she reined the mare in, and glanced back over her shoulder. Simla was about fifteen yards behind, plodding along steadily, lifting his head with a jerk and snorting every now and then as though aware of the danger. Andrew was talking to him and the horse had one ear back to listen, the other cocked forward towards Catherine and Grainne.

A black-backed gull swooped down between them, soaring sideways on the wind that rushed up over the cliff. As it neared Simla it screamed loudly, and bent its three-foot wings to sweep upwards within a foot of the horse's head. The cob checked, snorted, and tossed its head from side to side to try to see where the bird had gone. Andrew dragged at its mouth sharply and kicked it forward. Alarmed, Simla broke into a trot. Catherine could see that in a few seconds he would be up with Grainne on the narrow path, and there was no room to pass.

She nudged the mare forward into a quiet walk. Even she had never trotted along here and it seemed a mad thing to do. She heard a snort and a sharp curse from behind her, and felt the hunter nudge her horse's rump. She looked round quickly. Andrew was holding Simla's head in hard, and the animal was straining, its eyes white, its ears sharply back.

Andrew yelled: 'Go ahead, can't you? He wants to trot — the bird's spooked him.'

Catherine ignored him. A few yards ahead the gap between the stone wall and the cliff edge was at its narrowest, less than two yards wide. Grainne picked her way daintily towards it, refusing to be flustered by the fuss behind her. Catherine knew that Grainne could see off most of the other horses when they were out together in the field; it was unlikely that Simla would have the nerve to try to push his way past her.

And if Andrew Butler did fall off the cliff because he was a bad horseman, that would be very unfortunate. A great waste of a good horse.

They reached the narrow place and Grainne stepped quietly through it. There was a snort and a clatter behind. Catherine glanced back over her shoulder. Andrew had reined Simla in and was trying to force him to stand. The horse danced nervously and sidewalked in a half-circle. Catherine had the impression that Andrew's face was paler than usual.

She walked Grainne on to the far side of the bay, where the grass at the clifftop widened. Then she turned the mare and waited until the other two came up to her. She smiled and pointed.

'Look,' she said. 'You can see where we were from here. Dramatic, isn't it?'

The narrow section was on an overhang, and the cliff edge went down quite vertically beneath it for fifty feet, then sloped inwards. At the bottom, about two hundred feet below, a wave surged forward and burst over a line of jagged black rocks.

'We call them the Devil's Teeth,' she said. 'They say the Vikings used to throw monks down on to them, years ago.'

Andrew shouted: 'Why the hell didn't you trot when I said?'

She smiled, as though she had forgotten it, and said: 'It's dangerous. You need to keep the horses calm in a place like that. Come on. Didn't you want a gallop?'

She nudged Grainne into a trot, put her straight at the stone wall, and leapt neatly over. On the far side was a field grazed more or less smooth by sheep. She cantered down it, leapt the gate at the bottom, and crossed several more small, rocky, stone-walled fields in the same way. She reined in at the edge of a small lake, dismounted, and sat on a rock, holding the reins loosely in her hand so that the mare could graze.

Andrew came up a few minutes later. Simla was sweating and foaming slightly at the mouth.

She watched him critically as he dismounted. Perhaps there'll be a little less arrogance now, she thought.

She asked: 'Did you enjoy that?'

At first he did not answer. She had unsettled him and he was not used to that. He walked down to the edge of the lake, picked up a stone and skimmed it across the water. Then he sat down on a rock, took out a cigarette and lit it. As he exhaled the first breath, he said: 'Do you always ride like that?'

'Like what?'

'Like – someone who's afraid of nothing.'

'You don't have to be afraid if you trust the horse. I've had Grainne since she was a filly. Why? Did Simla scare you?'

'A little. He hasn't got any wings, as far as I can see.'

She laughed. And that was progress, he thought. There was no fear in the laugh, it was a shared thing. He didn't want a girl who was afraid of him all the time. After last night's conversation he had wondered if he might have made her too nervous; after this morning's ride he wondered if she would ever be afraid of him again. Elsie had been afraid of him, a little, he remembered. That had added spice to it – the knowledge that he could do what he wanted, that in the end she would always submit. But too much fear would have made her a quivering jelly, like those girls in the brothels. No fight, no fun at all.

For Catherine, the laugh was a relief too. She had been so bound up in herself, she had not thought she ever would find anything funny again. But the exercise, the pleasure she got from feeling Grainne so perfectly at one with her, had released her tension more than anything that could have happened in Dublin. And now she had cut the man down to size a bit, he seemed more human.

A storm was darkening the sky a mile or so out to sea. Catherine said: 'Since we're here, would you like to see the family Ferguson wanted to evict?'

Andrew shrugged. 'Why – are they paragons of peasant virtue?'

'Hardly. That's the whole point.'

As they rode round the side of the mountain and down a narrow lane, the rain caught up with them. At first it was a thin drizzle, sweeping out of the west under a gloomy sky. Then there was a flash of lightning and the rumble of thunder out at sea.

The rebuilt cottage was much as Catherine remembered it. Rough stone walls, with moss and plants clinging to them on the south and west; thatch that needed renewing, muddy footpaths through a garden full of stalky cabbages and undug rows of potatoes. A thin line of peat smoke came from the chimney, and there was a cow and a donkey in one field. Two young men, about fourteen and sixteen, were digging in the other.

'Hello, Brian,' Catherine called out. 'Is your mother home?'

'Sure and where else in the world would she be?'

A thin, dirty, dark-haired woman of about forty came to the door of the house, a scowl on her face, her children lurking in the background. When she saw who it was she wiped her face with the back of her hand, and the scowl changed into a grimace which might have been meant as a smile. 'Is it yourself back again among us then, Miss Catherine?'

'I am that, Josie.'

'It's the best place for you.' The woman came down to the gate, pulling a shawl over her head against the sweeping rain. 'That Dublin'll be no place for a girl like you, what with all the shootings and murdering that's going on there now. Is it true what they say, that even the Viceroy himself is shut shivering in his bedroom for fear of the boys that's running round the town now?'

'Not exactly, Josie.' Catherine thought of Sean, locked alone in his tiny cell. 'But those boys are doing their best. They'll have the country free yet, you wait and see.'

The woman turned her head and spat expressively into the mud. 'I wouldn't have no truck with them. It's them my Kevin went off to join, likely, when he said he was after taking the King's shilling. And where's the money he's supposed to send me from their stinking republic, eh? You tell me that!'

Catherine shook her head. 'Kevin probably didn't go to either of them, Josie. But the Republic will come and it'll make things better for everyone, you wait and see.'

'Nah.' Josie waved her arm dismissively. 'You're a good girl, Miss Catherine, but you're filling your head with moonshine if you believe that. There's no one in this country but you and your mother ever did me a good turn, and that's never a thing to do with soldier boys one side or the other. Will you come in out of the rain and take a dish of tay?'

Catherine glanced at Andrew and shook her head. 'No thanks, Josie, I'm showing Major Butler around the estate. But I'll look in again another day if I can.'

As they rode off up the lane, Andrew laughed. 'So much for your support for Sinn Fein,' he said. 'Even that filthy old hag can see they're a bunch of murderers. Wasn't it women like her who threw horse dung on the traitors in 1916, because their service pensions couldn't be paid during the Rising?'

The rain was coming down in sheets now, and a flash of lightning made the horses frisk nervously. Grainne danced round in a circle. Catherine yelled: 'She's just an ignorant old woman who doesn't know any better. It doesn't mean the Republic's wrong – it's coming, like it or not. You'll see!'

Then the rain and the thunder made it too hard to talk. They trotted up the lane towards Killrath. Catherine was soaked, and the rain made her skirt cling to her. Andrew grinned in appreciation as he watched her slim back and haunches move at the trot. But the incident puzzled him. There were peasant families like that at Ardmore. All landlords suffered them, but they brought no conceivable benefit to the world that Andrew could see. He understood Ferguson's irritation with the girl better now. A girl of her class needed such woolly sentiment knocked out of her.

He wondered if he were the man to do it.

The following afternoon, Catherine wrote to Sean.

A ghra,
This may be the last letter you ever get from me, and I
shall not know if you've received it because I don't want
you to reply.

You told me not to try to see you again so I won't, but
I have to say these things because they are so clear in my
mind now and you must know them.

The times we were together were the most wonderful
in my life. I will remember them always, every moment.
I did what I did because I loved you and I believed you
loved me, for a while. But you've told me you don't love
me, now. I believe you because of the way you told me —
before the detectives came. I won't beg. You wouldn't
want a girl who did that, anyway. It was the cruellest
thing anyone has ever said to me. I shall never forget it.

I hope one day you learn what it is to love as much as I
loved you. For your sake, I hope she loves you too.

You would agree with my father; he wants me to
marry a man of my own class as you said. I may not be
able to resist it, but it will be a sad cruel heartless
business, like sending a mare to the stud, the way he
thinks of it. Nothing like what we had.

You don't understand my free speaking perhaps but
that is what the world needs more of. If the Republic
comes and women are not free to choose as men are it
will be a poor thing, not what James Connolly died
for.

I miss the touch of you, Sean. More than anything.

Never lose your courage.

Your lover,

Catherine.

She wanted to tell him what she thought about his killing the policeman but that might be to condemn him with her own hand. As it was the thought of prison warders reading the letter hurt, but that was a thing for them to be ashamed of, she thought, rather than her. If what she felt was true, it should be said.

Alone in his room, Andrew washed, shaved, and changed into dry clothes. Then he paced up and down distractedly. This was not supposed to happen, but the girl was getting under his skin. And into his mind, too, so that he could think of nothing else.

In part it was the enforced idleness, he thought – the empty time waiting for the next stage of the operation. He couldn't stay in Dublin, or go back to Ardmore. But that he could cope with on his own. With this girl here, it was a different matter.

In a way what she had said was true. He did not know a lot about women. He had made love to a dozen or more – mostly high-class whores in officers' brothels in France and London. But there was not a lot to understand in that. He had paid his money, bought them drinks, been forceful and manly, and always it had been over too soon. Most had failed to hide their obvious repugnance at the sight of his face. Then, when he had tried the tricks he had learnt with Elsie, they had been terrified. Only with Elsie had he had a relationship. And she had not been a normal girl either.

Catherine was not very much like Elsie. Elsie had been much more buxom, more earthy, broader and stronger in the face and the body. She had not been well educated or intelligent; in fact she had been simple and mildly insane. And he had never, even when he was wildly in love, considered marrying her.

Catherine was like Elsie in only two ways. She did things that were quite unpredictable and exciting; and Andrew had fallen in love with her.

He tried to analyse how this could possibly have happened. When he had met her everything had been going wrong for him. Ardmore had burnt down, his mission against Collins had failed, he had had no clear plan for the future. That was not unlike the time he had stumbled on Elsie's cottage in the Schwarzwald, exhausted, starving, near to giving himself up. At that moment Catherine, like Elsie, had done something quite unexpected, challenged him in a way that forced him to take notice of her.

So whenever I'm in a mess I fall in love with the first woman I see, he thought. Or do women force themselves on me *because* I'm in a mess?

There was a lot more to it than that.

There was the fact that she seemed unaffected by the sight of his scar. She could be callous about it, cruel, but she was not horrified. That made him feel a man again, rather than a leper.

There was the fact that both women had had something that Andrew badly needed: in Elsie's case, food and shelter, in Catherine's, a lot of money and a very big estate. So I'm a mercenary bastard, Andrew thought. Well, he could admit that.

But that wasn't the whole story either. Although Andrew could be both cynical and ruthless, he was not unfeeling. Certain emotions could take him over completely, and then he would put all his energy and ruthlessness at their service. Anger and a desire for revenge, for instance, in dealing with a German machine-gun nest or the men who had burnt down Ardmore. Love – or was it lust? – in staying with Elsie for over two months, much longer than he had needed to.

And now, with Catherine Maeve O'Connell-Gort, what?

It seemed to Andrew like everything he had ever heard about love. He could still remember the first time he had seen her, down to the last detail of the cool, appraising look on her face. There had been something behind that look, some stronger emotion which she was trying to hide. Perhaps it was that emotion which had driven her to challenge him. Perhaps – *oh God I hope not* – perhaps there was a similarity with Elsie here too.

Perhaps Catherine was waiting for a Hans, as Elsie had been.

Oh Christ I hope not, Andrew thought. But now the idea had come to him it made a lot of sense. That was the reason why she seemed, underneath that hard, brittle surface, so unhappy and self-absorbed. It might be the reason why she had come down from Dublin – to get away from a lover who had jilted her. Perhaps her father had even sent her away because the young man was unsuitable. And that was the reason why, most of the time, she seemed scarcely aware of his existence at all.

An obsession like that will be hard to get rid of, Andrew realized. I have to make her notice me and respond to me. I have to make her as obsessed with me as I – God help me – am with her.

He had no clear idea how to do that. If he could get her in bed he imagined – he hoped – he could get her to enjoy the sort of games he had played with Elsie. The sight of those lips parted as she gasped her orgasm would be worth – well, it would be worth a lot.

Especially if the inheritance of Killrath came with it.

When Catherine came downstairs for dinner she felt fresh, clean, empty. She had soaked for an hour in a hot bath, washed her hair, and put on a soft, loose-fitting green dress. She was pleasantly tired from the ride, relaxed and glowing from the bath.

Feelings that Sean would probably never have again.

She felt like a traitress.

But Sean didn't want her, didn't need her. That was all over now. She must forget him, or she would go mad.

Only there was nothing else in the world to think about.

Andrew was in the room too, smoking and reading a newspaper by the fire. He looked up, admiring the way her skirt swung as she crossed the room. She ignored him, walked straight across to the table in the corner, and poured herself a large glass of sherry.

He smiled, the scar twisting on his cheek. 'The curse of the idle rich.'

'What?' She gulped the drink, and frowned at him as he sat staring at her over the top of the newspaper.

'Drink. The curse of Ireland – especially those with too much money and not enough to do. I didn't think you were like that.'

'It's none of your business.'

She refilled the glass and went past him to curl up in the window seat. She had to wipe the windowpane with her hand to peer out at the driving rain and low, scudding clouds.

'That's the other curse of this country — foul weather.'

She ignored him. He stood up, with his back to the fire, apparently amused, persistent. He had seldom seen a girl quite so haunted, so at odds with the world. Perhaps if she started drinking, some of her ghosts might come to the surface.

'You still haven't told me why you came down here.'

'I was ordered to. By my father.' She sipped the sherry without looking at him.

Progress, he thought. Play the fish gently and it may come to land. He strolled over to the drinks table and poured himself a small whiskey with plenty of soda.

'I saw you as someone more independent than that.'

'Did you?'

'Certainly. You're a medical student, aren't you?'

The man was a pest, there was no doubt about it. But he was an irritation she could use, perhaps, to distract herself from her own grief. Left on her own, she felt at times it would drown her.

'Look, Major Butler —'

'Can't you drop that? Call me Andrew, please — it sounds so stupid with just the two of us.'

'All right, Andrew.' It sounded such a civilized name for such a hard, damaged face. 'My life is for me to lead, wouldn't you agree? If I choose to study medicine, that's my business.'

'Of course. But I'd have thought you'd be proud of it, not prickly as hell.'

'I've always been prickly. If I'm not, I don't get what I want.' And even when I do, I still lose it, she thought. I wasn't prickly with Sean, surely — or was I?

He perched himself on the arm of a chair, and considered her. 'You know what? I don't think you know what you *do* want.'

'What do you mean?'

'Well, look round you at this house, and your other home in Merrion Square. You'll inherit both, now that your brothers are dead. If I were in your position I'd spend all my time learning to manage them, not running off to Dublin to train as a doctor.'

'Well, you aren't in my position, are you?' She crossed the room to pour herself a third glass of sherry.

'No, I'm not, but I could be.'

'Oh yes?' She turned, leaning against the drinks table, and raised her glass to him mockingly. 'Is my father going to adopt you as a new son? Congratulations.'

'Of course not. But he might consider me as a possible son-in-law. Given that I've already won you in a shooting match.'

The shock of it stunned Catherine so that she could not speak for a moment. But it made perfect sense, she realized. This was why her father had sent her down here — not just to get her away from Sean and the police, but because he knew this — this stud — was here. Perhaps they had already discussed it, even arranged the terms of the marriage contract behind her back. This was how it felt, then — this was how daughters were bought and sold to keep family estates together.

She took a long, slow sip of her sherry, then put it down and walked across the room towards him. She stood about as close to him as it was possible to stand without touching. He was nearly four inches taller than her, much bigger and stronger than Sean, she realized. Close to, his eyes were steel grey, the scar livid, his face very decisive and hard. Nothing gentle or foolish about it at all. He made no attempt to move or smile.

She said: 'I told you you had no place here. This is my house and I want you to go.'

'That's not a very ladylike reply.'

'I meant it.'

'Catherine.' He caught hold of her wrist. She tried to pull it away but his grip was surprisingly strong. He lifted it to his lips and kissed it with a mock flourish. 'I'm sorry. It wasn't a very polite way to ask but I meant what I said. We're two of a kind, you and I. Think about it, please.'

'Let go!'

'I have.'

She stepped back, shaken, rubbing her wrist. She wondered if she should hit him but she had the feeling, quite clearly, that he would hit her back. She was furious.

'I said you knew nothing about women. You can't even be trusted to behave in decent society, it seems.'

In an isolated cottage in the Black Forest he might have pushed matters further, but here there were servants outside the door, ready at any moment to knock and announce with a polite cough that dinner was served. Also, the purpose of the game was to make her like him as well as fight. Andrew decided to change his tactics. He sat down, to seem less of a threat.

'I'm sorry. You're probably right. I haven't seen many young women recently and you're a remarkably beautiful one, though you may not realize it.'

'It's a bit late for flattery.'

'Is it? Maybe, if you say so. Look – sit down, can't you?'

She perched on the window seat, well out of his reach.

'What's so wrong with the idea, anyway? You've got this big estate, and you need a husband to run it. You're a very attractive girl, and despite my face you can see I'm not a hunchback –'

'You *have* been talking to my father, haven't you?'

'Not about this. I'm just trying to talk sense.'

'Well listen, Major Butler . . .'

'Andrew.'

'. . . it may sound sense to you, but I can assure you, it just isn't going to happen. So just put it out of your mind, will you, and then we can have a reasonably civilized existence here for the rest of your stay.'

'I don't think you want a civilized existence.'

'What?'

'I think you, like me, are the sort of person who needs a certain amount of excitement all the time to keep them sane.'

'I don't know what you're talking about.'

'No? Then why did you lead me along that cliff edge today? No one in their right mind would do that on horseback, if they didn't enjoy danger. Why did you challenge me to a shooting match? Not one girl in a hundred would think of a thing like that.'

'I don't care what other girls do.'

'I know. That's why I like you. That's why —'

There was a discreet knock at the door. The butler stood there. 'Supper is served, Miss Catherine. Major Butler.'

'Thank you, Brophy. We'll come through.' As she walked to the dining room, Catherine's fury subsided slightly to the level where she was conscious of a challenge. She felt a revival of the interest which he had sparked in her the first time they met. There was something dangerous in him which had to be faced and defeated, but she need not deny him altogether.

Andrew saw the heightened colour in her face and congratulated himself. He sat down opposite her quietly, willing her to take up the conversation, rather than him. That would be another small victory.

She picked up her soup spoon and said: 'That's why what?'

'That's why I said what I did. Not because of anything your father may have said. But because I need a wife, you need a husband, and I've never met a girl I could admire more.'

She said carefully: 'Look, Andrew, I can't think why you admire me but there are a few things that ought to be said. First, as I've said twice before, you obviously don't know a lot about women or you'd realize that it's not very normal for any man to try to choose a wife on the basis of two or three days' acquaintance. And second, you're making a very big presumption. If you say you need a wife, I suppose it may be true, but I have no need whatsoever of a husband.'

And so we're into the negotiation, he thought. At least the bait's not being ignored now. He said: 'I disagree. No, hear me out. In the first place I would never expect either you or me to do the normal thing in a matter of this sort – in fact I'd expect you to be highly impulsive and do exactly the opposite. And second, of course you need a husband.'

The man's a madman, she thought. But something inside her had begun to respond to the insanity of it all – an imp of laughter that might burst out into hysterics at any moment if she thought of Sean. But that's over now. Over for ever . . .

'Why do I need a husband? Tell me.'

Now there's a question you don't ask if you're not just a little interested, Andrew thought. He looked at her carefully across the shining table, taking in the slightly heightened colour of the face, the wide dark eyes, the pride and tension in the set of her chin. He had the impression she might do anything at any moment, and that she would not know what it was until it happened.

He said: 'You need a husband for the same reason that every hot-blooded young woman needs a husband. And because –'

'That's enough. No – a few more minutes, Brophy.' She waited until the butler went out again. 'That's a pretty common, cheap reason. One minute you tell me we're unique special people, and then you say I need to be mated like a mare. Well, if I want a stallion I can find my own, Andrew Butler, thank you.'

And look where that led me, she thought. *Oh, Sean, Sean.*

'And also because you need someone to share the

running of this estate with you. Maybe you could do it on your own if you worked at it, but what's the point?'

'That's what we pay Ferguson for. There. Poor Andrew, your argument fails on both points. So now what?'

He sat back in his chair and smiled, and was enchanted to get a smile back. Oh, we've moved a long way already, he thought. Just keep playing the game gently now, gently.

'Now,' he said. 'We call Brophy, and have the fish.'

By the end of the meal they had consumed a bottle of wine between them, and Catherine was quite drunk. They had even laughed together twice: once when he had told her of his early attempts to ride his father's hunter, and once when she had told him of the ghost she and her brothers had tracked in the west wing, which had turned out to be an equally frightened parlourmaid. There was the sense of a drawn battle, a shared conspiracy, between them.

They moved back into the drawing room where the fire had been made up to blaze brighter than before. She knelt down and held out her hands to the fire, a slim dark-haired girl in a loose green dress. On the wall above the mantelpiece was a portrait of an arrogant young woman in eighteenth-century clothes, sitting side-saddle on a bay hunter. He said: 'There should be a picture of you here, too.'

'Why?'

'Because time passes and one day you may be a respected matron, but you will never again be quite what you are now.'

She smiled briefly, and said: 'If you had started like that, we might have got on a little better before.'

'No we wouldn't.' He poured out two glasses of brandy, and was surprised and encouraged when she took one.

She said: 'Apart from making absurd proposals to me, why are you here?'

'How do you mean?'

'You're a soldier, aren't you? Why aren't you busy fighting the mad Irish, like my father?'

'I had some leave due.' This was not a line of conversation Andrew wanted to follow. He was ready to return to Dublin next weekend, and take up where he had left off before. Within a day or two of that, he hoped to be either totally successful, or dead. Until then, he did not want to think about it.

Since he was far from sure of coming back, he wanted to seduce Catherine before then. The talk of marriage might become a reality for him later, if he survived. If not, it wouldn't matter.

He watched her sip her brandy, and wondered why she had started to drink. She had been very abstemious the night he had first met her in Merrion Square. Was tonight's binge because of him or that unknown Hans? Certainly she had started with the sherry well before this marriage business had come up.

'So why didn't you go to Ardmore, if you love it so much?'

He sighed. 'Because. Because it's lonely looking at ruins. I will build it up but I need money and someone to do it with me.'

A silence fell between them. It seemed to Andrew a companionable sort of silence, something he remembered with Elsie. They sat either side of the fire, and stared into the flames. Then she sipped the brandy, and said: 'Well, I may have the money, but I'm no good at building, you know. As you say, I like excitement, and it's pretty dull piling bricks on top of each other.'

'You don't understand. That place is what I fought the war for. It would be a victory to build it up again.'

'And what would you do with it then?'

'Bring my wife home to it. Breed racehorses and sons to ride them.'

'Very dull.'

'It wouldn't be. I meant what I said, you know.'

'So did I.' She drained her glass and stood up suddenly. She swayed slightly and held on to the chair back for support. 'Listen, Andrew Butler, I'm going to bed. Where I will give your proposal the five minutes' serious thought it deserves, before I fall asleep.'

He stood up too, like a gentleman. This is the moment, he thought, if there is one. To his surprise, she seemed to read his mind. She wagged a finger tipsily.

'And I am going to bed *alone*. I can't think otherwise. But don't get your hopes up. There is in fact no hope for your stupid plan at all.'

Oh yes, there is, he thought, as he bowed and watched her make her way across the room towards the door. When she reached the door she even turned back and glanced at him, as though surprised that he had not tried to follow. Oh yes, there is hope all right, young lady. Quite a lot of it, in fact.

Not tonight, but soon. Maybe tomorrow or the next day. Go to sleep now. And please, dream about me.

As I shall dream of you.

22

Kee slumped back in the chair behind his desk in Brunswick Street, and thought. His hands were clasped tightly together under his chin, his legs stretched out in front of him. On the desk were a half-finished, cold cup of coffee, a brown manila folder and the photograph of Sean Brennan.

The photograph was mounted in a frame with a little folding leg to prop it up. Kee stood it there each morning as an aid to thought. It disturbed him. That wide, confident mouth, smart suit, clean-shaven chin, neatly brushed hair, clear, apparently honest eyes gazing straight at the camera. What could make such a man a murderer, an assassin? Perhaps there was an arrogance in the face too, a mockery, a conviction that he could not be wrong. Sometimes the face infuriated Kee, so that he wanted to slam it face downwards on the table; but he resisted the temptation, as he had resisted, after the first day, the temptation to drive his fist into the real face in the prison cell.

That was not Kee's way. He knew it went on, he knew

that other men did it, he knew now, since Radford's death, the powerful urge that made the desire for revenge almost irresistible. It was the smugness of the face, above all, that outraged him. The look that said: 'I am right to kill you, and you are a fool and a tyrant not to see it. I am one of the best young men of my generation, and the future lies with me.' And what had that led to? A hole the size of a golf ball in Bill Radford's face, his brains spattered over a shop window.

Kee thought of the phrase the lad repeated endlessly during interrogation: 'I am a soldier of the Irish Republican Army. I refuse to answer any more questions.' It brought out the worst in him. He wanted to scream at the boy, beat his choirboy face until it was a mass of blood, stick a revolver barrel up his nose until it bled and then see what he answered.

But he didn't. Because Kee believed he himself was right and the boy was evil. And he had just enough self-control and intelligence left to realize that once he did those things, he would be playing the game the Sinn Feiners wanted. Reinforcing the stereotype of brutal police tyranny which made these young men seem noble, heroic. Making another martyr to add to the long list the Fenians probably muttered to over their rosary beads.

His only hope was to bring the lad to court, unmarked, and with such evidence of his guilt that no jury could fail to convict him. Which was where the manila folder came in.

The manila folder contained a forensic report on Brennan's gun. It was a German Parabellum automatic, firing 9-mm ammunition; Kee knew that already. The pistol had been carefully cleaned, so it was not possible to say when it had last been fired. Four of the bullets in the magazine clip were copper-cased, round-nosed ones; the other four were flat-nosed with a nickel casing. When these bullets had been fired in the laboratory, they had developed six grooves on the outside. These grooves corresponded with the grooves in the barrel, which was rifled.

So far, so good. The flat-nosed bullets, it appeared, had been manufactured like that; the scientist did not think they had been interfered with since. Nonetheless, a flat-nosed bullet would cause immensely greater damage inside a body than the others. They were, Kee thought, outlawed in war. He had read that most of the original ammunition supplied to the Volunteers at the Howth gun-running in 1912 had been of this dum-dum type, and the leaders of those days had refused to issue it. So much had things changed.

The scientist had also examined a bullet which had been retrieved from Harcourt Street where Radford had died. Two shots had been fired, but only one bullet had been recovered. This bullet, also, was of 9-mm calibre. It was misshapen by its impact with Radford's body and the wall of the shop, but it was nonetheless possible to observe four or five grooves along its sides, which were exactly the same distance apart as those on the bullets fired in the laboratory.

Thus it was possible to conclude that the bullets had been fired from precisely the same type of pistol. The scientist regretted, however, that his science had not yet advanced to the state where it was possible to say whether the bullets had come from the same individual weapon.

Kee pondered this. It was good evidence, but not conclusive. If he had had one witness who had seen Brennan in the area, it would have been almost conclusive. But the witnesses were useless.

The only other possible evidence was a confession. And that could be got out of the boy only by torture. There was simply no other way.

Or was there?

Kee slipped the folder into a drawer, locked it, stood up, and put on his coat. It was not far, and it was a fairly fine day.

He would walk to Mountjoy Prison.

Sean was surprised and annoyed to be moved to a different cell. His meditations, his careful self-control, had made him familiar with every detail of the cell he had been in for the last three days. He knew every knothole in the hard wooden bed, the different lumps on the whitewashed stone wall, the graffiti which he had found and added to. He had even begun to take an interest in a spider which inhabited the window recess.

All these things brought him comfort. Now he had been moved, for no reason, and would have to begin again.

The cell he was moved to was slightly larger. But it had two beds, one above the other. And there was a man on the bottom bunk.

The man jerked upright as he came in. 'What the hell's this? What's he doing in here?' he yelled at the warder. But the door slammed behind Sean without an answer.

Sean looked at him. 'I'm sorry,' he said. 'They didn't ask me either. He said something about a new set of arrests and needing the room, that's all.'

The man on the bunk was small, with thin pointed ears and straggly hair that stuck up in a peak at the back. He said: 'It's not your fault, boy. They brought me here an hour ago. I thought it was the de luxe treatment until you came in.'

'Thanks,' Sean said. 'Will I take the top bunk?'

'Unless you're one of the hard men who lie on the floor. Not that there's much difference, with beds like these.'

Sean climbed up on the bunk. But there was nothing much to see there – just a grey blanket and a space of a couple of feet between it and the stone ceiling. He shuddered, came down again, and perched on one of the two stools.

The two men looked at each other. 'What are you in for?' the man with straggly hair asked.

'I'm in the IRA. They caught me with a pistol in my pocket.'

The little man stuck out his hand. 'Daniel O'Rourke, F Company, Dublin Volunteers,' he said. 'They dragged me out of bed two weeks ago, in the big sweep after the attack on Lord French.'

Sean gripped his hand firmly. 'Sean Brennan. I was in D Company but now I'm in the Squad. I was at Ashtown myself.'

The sense of companionship, after such a long time alone, was overwhelming. The two men clasped hands and did not let go for nearly a minute. Then, eagerly, impulsively, they began to talk.

* * *

For Kee, it worked like a dream. He sat in the cell on the floor above, with the technician who had set it all up. In front of him, on the table, the reels of magnetized piano-wire steel turned slowly. The technician had assured him that the modified Poulsen telegraphone would record everything that was said. Whether it did or not, Kee could hear the words of the two men through the loudspeaker in front of it. They were blurred and crackly, but it was still possible to make out what was said. Kee made notes swiftly. The microphone was in the small ventilation grille a few feet above the men's heads. They were unlikely to see it; the cell was poorly lit at the best of times, and at night they had only a small candle.

But long before dusk, Sean had admitted to shooting Radford. O'Rourke was delighted: he was proud to be sharing a cell with such a man, he said. In return he detailed all his own most daring exploits. They were not as grand as Sean's, but they were a lot more interesting than the things he had told his interrogators.

Kee had only recently discovered these machines, and had not used them before. But he was an instant convert. He would have them installed in every police station in Belfast, he thought. The only slight problem was, would a judge accept it as evidence?

Davis sat in the upstairs room of Clancy's Joiners and Decorators. There was no sign in here of any interest in carpentry or wallpaper. Instead, there were three desks, a telephone, and files and books neatly ordered in shelves along a wall. Davis imagined that policemen more inquisitive than he was would have found their contents very interesting. And he knew that Kee would have found his own presence here more interesting still.

In front of him, Michael Collins paced the narrow floor space between the desks. Every few minutes, his left hand pushed back the lock of black hair which fell forward over his forehead. His right hand was alternately thrust deep into his trousers pocket, and taken out to bang frenziedly against the edge of a desk.

'We've got to get him out, Paddy!' he was saying. 'The country needs no more martyrs, especially young lads like him. The boy's put his life on the line for us – we owe it to him to try!'

'The country doesn't need any more corpses either, Mick,' said Paddy cautiously. 'If we do mount a rescue attempt, it's got to have a ninety per cent chance of working.'

'Of course. And it will. Who do you think you're preaching to now, Patrick? Wasn't it me that sprang twenty men over the wall at Mountjoy a year ago? *And* we lifted de Valera out of Lincoln Gaol. It's the details that make it all work. Every single detail has to be right. Then all you need is the daring to carry it through.'

He swung himself impulsively on to a desk, and sat there glaring at them.

'Sure and I agree with you about all that,' said Daly calmly. 'We've had the armoured car under observation for three days now. It never varies. But what I'm not happy about is these papers.'

'That's why Dick's here now.' Collins looked at Davis. 'Who would have the authority to call the boy out of his cell?'

Davis thought carefully. 'The prison governor himself. Or Kee, who's running the investigation. And Military Intelligence, possibly, though Kee would be wild about it if they did.'

'That's all?'

'Unless we had an order signed by Lord French, for instance. But there's no reason for that – they'd be so surprised they might ring up to check.'

'Could you sign for him yourself?'

This was the question Davis had been dreading. 'I suppose I could, yes, and they'd almost certainly accept it. But then, how would I account for it? Kee's conducting the whole investigation himself. He knows I have no reason for removing the boy.'

'So then your cover would be blown and they'd know you were working for us.' Collins looked at him thoughtfully. Davis wondered what he was thinking. Was it shameful to fear imprisonment, to worry about his pension, to hope desperately that there was some safer way of getting the boy out? Or was Collins thinking that one active soldier like Brennan was worth a dozen undercover police agents? If so, he was wrong – he must be wrong! What I do, Davis thought, has to be worth ten times the contribution of a boy who just throws bombs and pulls the trigger.

Collins nodded slowly. 'No, we couldn't have that, Dick. But can't you get papers signed by Military Intelligence, perhaps? That would seem to be our best bet.'

Davis relaxed, relieved. 'We've got copies of that sort of thing, certainly. There's nothing particularly unusual about the form itself. I can find out who's the right officer to sign it, too, and copy the signature; but I can't get you the original. Can you get your printers to mock one up?'

Collins's voice was very quiet, gentle, as it always was when asking someone to do something harder than usual. 'The original is what we need, Dick. Plus a sight of the man's signature so that we can forge it. Remember, every little detail counts. Surely you can do that for us, now?'

Davis sighed. There were times when he felt like a piece of grain, ground between two massive granite wheels. The further on he went, the harder were the things he was asked to do. I hope the Republic recognizes the danger I've run, he thought. When it's all over, there should be a special pension and a medal for me alone.

'I'll try, Mick,' he said. 'I have a few contacts in MI. I can't promise anything but I'll give it a try.'

Davis was relieved to find that his contact, Captain Smythe, appeared pleased to see him. He sat at a desk in an office on the second floor overlooking the courtyard of Dublin Castle, his desk a mass of papers from reports of raids in the city last night. He was a thin, intense man in spectacles, with sparse, mousy-coloured hair. He wore a neatly tailored uniform which was stained with ash from a large briar pipe which he was puffing energetically.

'Good to see you, Dick. What can I do for you, old chap? You sounded pretty cagey on the phone.'

'We have to be, now. For all I know there's a Shinner working on the exchange in Brunswick Street.'

'God forbid. It's high time you fellows moved in here. After the death of your assistant commissioner I'd have thought they'd put that at the top of the priority list.'

'I hope they do,' said Davis. He took off his overcoat and hung it with his hat on the stand by the door. There was an agreeable fug in the room from the fumes of Smythe's pipe and the blaze of a little coal fire in the grate. 'It's getting far too dangerous in the city.'

'Quite. I take my hat off to you fellows for sticking it out.' Smythe leaned back in his chair and puffed more energetically at his pipe than ever. 'Now, how can I help you?'

'Well, two things really.' Davis had worked this out very carefully in his mind before he came here, but it still seemed to him unlikely that he would succeed. He could see the pad of order forms on Smythe's desk, half hidden by a spreading pile of papers, with the vital rubber stamp beside it. He and Daly had consulted the printer of *An tOglach* with a similar order form that Davis had borrowed from police files.

The printer had told them that the memo pad could be forged easily enough – Davis had a blank sheet of the same type of paper in his pocket – but that the official Dublin Castle stamp, with the complicated swirling lines of its imperial heraldic crest, would take days to get right. An approximation could be mocked up more quickly, but men who were used to seeing the real thing could easily spot it. If there was any doubt, the prison governor would probably have two or three documents franked by the genuine stamp lying around on his desk, to compare it with. As Collins said, details were vital.

So Davis had to get hold of that stamp. And to do that, he had to distract Smythe. Get him out of his own office.

He said: 'The first thing is, Kee thinks he's arrested one of Radford's killers.'

'Get away! So soon! Damn good show, what!'

'Surely. Name of Brennan – Sean Brennan. But we want to pin as much on him as we can, obviously. So I was wondering if I could check through your files and see if you've got anything under that name, or if he figures in connection with any of the other members of Collins's squad.' Davis nodded hopefully at the two large filing cabinets at the back of the room.

Smythe puffed thoughtfully. 'Hm. I suppose there's no harm. Forgive me for being cautious, training I suppose. Still, you've helped me in the past. Yes, go ahead – so long as I'm here and you don't take anything away. What's the other thing?'

'The other thing is this.' Davis reached inside his jacket pocket and passed over an envelope. Inside were a number of documents in Michael Collins's own handwriting. There was a letter to the commandant of the Kilkenny Brigade of the Volunteers, complaining about the lack of recent reports and action; there was a list of possible people in the Kilkenny district who should be approached for contributions to the Loan; and there was a copy of orders apparently sent to the commandant of the adjoining brigade, authorizing him to attack a particular police barracks on the border of the two districts during the coming week, alone if necessary, or with the cooperation of the Kilkenny Brigade if it could be obtained. The date for the attack was not mentioned, but suggested routes for approach and escape were discussed.

Smythe read with interest, and growing astonishment. At the end he took his pipe out of his mouth, and fumbled for the ashtray, without taking his eyes off the papers.

'Great Scott!' he said. 'Wherever did you get these?'

'One of the few loyal postmen took them out of the mail and handed them on. They're getting so cocky they use the regular postal service these days. It didn't pay off this time.'

'So they're genuine, you think?'

'Absolutely. So far as I can tell.' Certainly the paper and the handwriting were genuine. Davis knew that, because he had seen Michael Collins write them himself. The information in them was another matter. The names and addresses of those who were likely to contribute to the Loan were in fact composed of those who had annoyed the Kilkenny Volunteers; and a covering letter had been sent out to the two commandants, ordering them on no account to attack the police barracks in question for at least two weeks. No doubt the RIC in the barracks would have a few sleepless nights, and might draft in reinforcements. So other barracks should be attacked, the ones the reinforcements might have come from.

'That's marvellous,' said Smythe. 'Can I keep them?'

Davis appeared to hesitate. 'Unfortunately, no. Not everyone is happy about our just handing over information, you know. But I don't see why you shouldn't make copies. One good turn deserves another, after all.'

This was the crucial point which Davis had been banking on. Smythe was a meticulous officer, very keen to keep all his paperwork in order, and fascinated by technical gadgets. On previous visits he had proudly shown Davis his photographic copying machine: a camera mounted at the precise distance to take perfect pictures of any form of written document. He had explained how to calculate the different levels of lighting dependent on the shade of the paper and blackness of the ink, and demonstrated his small portable darkroom and developing equipment.

'A perfect copy in under twenty minutes!' he had boasted enthusiastically. 'Or ten copies if you want. Amazingly useful. If I ever leave the army I might set up in business to mass-produce smaller versions of this, for the office of the future.'

All this equipment, Davis knew, was in a room at the other end of the corridor. He looked at Smythe, and waited.

It worked like a charm.

Smythe got to his feet, grinning with enthusiasm. 'Don't worry,' he said. 'No problem with copies here. Do you want to come along and watch?'

Davis glanced at the clock on the wall. 'I'd love to, but I don't have a lot of time. Do you mind if I ... ?' He nodded at the filing cabinets.

'Yes, of course. Go ahead. Just mind you put everything back neatly, won't you. If you need any copies, just ask. My eye! This'll be a feather in our caps, and no mistake.'

When he had gone out, Davis waited a few moments, then opened the door softly to check that everything was quiet in the corridor outside. It was. He shut the door walked swiftly over to the desk, took the forged order out of his pocket, inked the rubber pad, and pressed it on to the paper carefully. The coat of arms of Dublin Castle stood out clearly. On impulse, he took a genuine sheet of paper, and stamped that too. Why use forged paper at all, if I don't need to? he thought. Then he folded both sheets, put them back in his pocket, and began to search through the filing cabinets. He didn't particularly need information on Brennan, but there was bound to be something interesting in these records, all the same.

When he came back, Smythe was delighted. He had the originals under his arm, and he held three wet, shining photographs by his fingertips.

'There you are, see – perfect! Not a word you can't read! Did you find what you wanted?'

'A few things, yes.' Davis showed a page of notes he had made. 'Nothing decisive, but it all adds up.'

'That's it exactly.' Smythe put the gleaming photographs on his desk, gave him back the original letters, and picked up his pipe to relight it. Between puffs, he went on: 'One thing I learned ... as intelligence officer ... nothing so small you can ignore it ... all pieces of a jigsaw that comes together in time.' When the pipe was fully lit he took it out of his mouth, glanced at it critically, and waved the match up and down vigorously to put it out. 'By Jove, Dick, on days like this I begin to feel the tide is turning and we've got these swine on the run. Don't you know?'

'Maybe.' Davis picked up his notes and prepared to go. 'We have good days and bad days.'

'Course. But you've got this lad Brennan, and we're going to make hay in Kilkenny. *And* there's this German plot. I wouldn't be surprised if we're seeing the last days of old Michael Collins, you know. Off to join the old pantheon of Irish heroes in the sky, what? High time, too.'

Davis paused as he shrugged on his coat. 'What German plot?'

'Oh, don't you know?' Smythe's eyes twinkled, as if he had half expected this response. He puffed at his pipe tantalizingly. 'No, probably you wouldn't. All hush-hush. Forget I spoke.'

'But what . . . ?'

Smythe tapped the side of his nose. 'No, sorry, old chap. Absolutely top secret, all under wraps. Shouldn't have mentioned it. Just keep your eyes peeled over the next couple of weeks, and you may get a nice surprise. Big thing, I promise you. But don't breathe a word.'

Davis was intrigued. He turned over in his mind whether he should stay, and try to press the man to explain himself. But he decided against it. He had got what he came for, and that was more than enough. Not only that, but Smythe still trusted him. That was something to store up for the future.

Still, he thought, as he walked briskly across the Castle yard, why a *German* plot?

There was a connection there somewhere. But a connection with what?

When Sean awoke, Catherine was standing at the basin washing herself. She had her back to him, and she was quite naked. She bent forward and scooped water out of the bowl to wash her face, and then her neck and behind her ears and under her arms. He wondered if she were soaping her breasts but he couldn't see that. Her movements were very brisk as though she were in a hurry to be clean. It was so cold in the room. The fire had died down and her breath steamed. She must have goose pimples everywhere, he thought, how can she bear the cold? He tried to get up but he couldn't persuade himself to move; he was too warm in the bed and his erection was as hard as a rock. Then she lifted her leg to put her foot in the bowl and wash her leg and he knew it must be a dream because he had never seen her do anything like that. He had not even seen her wash before. But before he could wake up she turned round. Drops of water were running off her body like tears but her face was smiling. Her hair was damp around her face, her eyes shone with happiness, and she stretched out her dripping arms to embrace the man who stepped from the shadows behind Sean.

Sean could see nothing of this man in his dream except that he was fully clothed. His big male hand gripped her naked buttock and her face, which Sean could see over the man's shoulder, laughed with pleasure.

He woke up then, sweating.

He did have an erection and he was lying on a hard bed under a grey blanket with a grimy stone ceiling eighteen inches above his head. There was an unpleasant stench in the room, and a snuffling grunt from the bunk below him which Sean recognized as being the sleeping sounds of O'Rourke. There was grey light in the small barred window to his right. It was the beginning of another day in Mountjoy Gaol.

Sean was sleeping fully clothed to keep warm. As he moved, the letter in his breast pocket crackled. She shouldn't have written to me, he thought, then I wouldn't have had these dreams. He thought of tearing up the letter and stuffing the bits into the foetid chamberpot under O'Rourke's bunk, but he couldn't do it. That was the trouble: it was a link with the outside, with the life that might have been.

She has every right to go to someone else, he thought. I had my chance — I had her, even, as much as any man could have — and I rejected her. If I had behaved differently I would have had a right to be jealous. For the last two days, since he had received the letter, he had relived in his mind everything that had happened between himself and Catherine. He had wanted to blame her but there had come a time, late last night, when he had realized that it was unjust. She would almost certainly have stayed by him, if he had wanted her to.

The trouble was that it was only now, when he knew he was going to die, that he could admit to himself how much he needed her.

He had realized he was going to die yesterday when Kee had charged him with the murder of Assistant Commissioner Radford. The Ulster detective had been quite cold, hard, correct, with the light of utter certainty in his eyes.

'You have the right to stay silent if you choose,' he had said. 'But anything you do say will be taken down and used in evidence. The trial should take place next month.'

Kee had been quite calm, watching Sean intently to see what his reaction would be. Sean had been stunned.

'How do you know that?' he had said.

'You admit it then?'

Kee had been sitting, while Sean stood to attention in front of him. The young detective, Foster, had been standing behind Kee, watching Sean. Sean had looked from one to the other of them, searching for words. Why not admit it? he thought. It was an act of war – I'm proud of what I've done. But he wanted to live, too.

So instead, he had said: 'What evidence do you have?'

'Forensic evidence. The bullets in your gun match exactly those taken from the body of Radford.'

'I don't believe you. That's impossible to prove.'

'We'll see about that in court. Do you want a lawyer?'

'I'm a soldier of the Irish Republic. I don't recognize British courts in Ireland.'

'You'll get a lawyer anyway. Even back-street murderers are entitled to a fair trial.'

'It wasn't murder, it was an act of war! *He* had a gun, too.'

There had been a long, shattering silence. Kee and Foster had stared at him, and Sean began to realize what he had said.

Kee had asked, quite gently: 'How did you know he had a gun, Sean?'

'I read it in the newspapers.'

'I see.' No one in the room believed that. It had been a sort of relief to Sean that they now all accepted what had happened. He thought of the confessional, the relief that came after admitting sins, the welcome back to the fold of humanity.

'Who was the other fellow with you?'

It was the wrong question. At that moment Sean might have admitted the killing if he had been asked directly, but he would not betray a colleague. There was no answer.

Kee sighed. 'There's just a couple of things that still puzzle me about this, Sean. How could you be sure you'd shoot the right man? It was a foggy night – you could have killed anyone. How could you be sure what he looked like, and which hotel he was staying in?'

Kee had not expected answers to these questions, and none had come. But he had planted them deliberately in Sean's mind, so that later, when he was back in his cell, he would think about them.

And then discuss them with O'Rourke.

Kee's plan nearly failed. For most of the afternoon, Sean and O'Rourke debated whether it was really possible to prove that a particular bullet had come from a particular gun. Neither knew, but both doubted it. But the only way Sean would be able to challenge such evidence would be to accept a lawyer and recognize the existence of the court. That Sean refused to do. None of the martyrs of 1916 had done it: he could not do it now, when the Republic was even more in being than then. The British legal system would win, therefore, by default.

'But since I did it anyway,' Sean said, 'I suppose it doesn't make much difference.'

There had followed a long silence while he had considered how he would die. O'Rourke, sensing the direction of his thoughts, began to talk of the heroism of the earlier martyrs: of Thomas Clarke, who had sighed with relief when he knew he would not have to endure another long prison sentence; of the Pearse brothers; of MacDonagh, who had died 'like a prince'; of James Connolly, white with pain from his smashed ankle, who had had to be sat up on his stretcher to be shot. All of them had faced the firing squad with pride. Sean would be hanged, like Robert Emmet in 1803.

Upstairs, Kee yawned, and drummed his fingers on the table with frustration. It was not until five thirty in the afternoon that he heard Sean say: 'At least they're puzzled about one thing.'

'What's that then?'

'How I could recognize Radford and know what time he would go back to his hotel.'

'How did you?'

Sean laughed. 'One of his own bloody detectives, that's what. He identified the fellow for us. He'll do the same for Kee before long, I bet you.'

O'Rourke was delighted. 'You mean we have our boys right in there among the peelers?'

'We do that. Not that I like the fellow all that much, mind. He did the job for us, all the same.' He paused, and then, to Kee's intense frustration, added: 'But you'd best keep quiet about that, Dan. It must be a dangerous business, and if the word got out they'd be setting up the devil's own hunt for the boy.'

'Surely,' O'Rourke agreed. 'Me lips are sealed. And if you don't tell me his name, I couldn't pick him out if they stuck pins in me, could I now?'

And with that, Kee had to be content.

Lieutenant Alan Wilson sat in the front seat of the Peerless armoured car and picked his teeth. It was a difficult operation, for the front seat was narrow and cramped, and the driving of Private Garside, beside him, was never of the smoothest, but it expressed his boredom and contempt for the situation in which he found himself.

He had joined the army two years ago, just in time to see a month's action in France before the armistice. Since then, army life, which he had hoped would give him opportunities for excitement and adventure, had deteriorated into an ever more dispiriting round of training, bull, and routine. He had hoped to be sent to Mesopotamia, where there was still action of the traditional sort, with the Imperial Army sorting out rebellions of colourful, factious tribesmen. He might have seen the Pyramids, made love to a belly dancer, driven his armoured car full tilt across the desert in pursuit of fleeing Arabs on camels. That would have been something to write home about, he thought. Instead, every morning at ten thirty, he drove half a mile along the North Circular Road to collect a dead cow.

Or sometimes a pig, he thought gloomily. Today it was three sheep. The job he had been given was the meat run. With a driver, Private Garside, and a gunner, Corporal MacNair, he had to drive to the Corporation Abattoir to pick up the day's meat ration. It was typical, he thought: the bloody Irish were so disaffected and incompetent that they couldn't even be trusted to deliver a load of mutton to the barracks without an armoured car to carry it.

It annoyed Lieutenant Wilson particularly because he was proud of the Tin Annie. His father had owned a garage, and had worked hard to put his son through a minor public school. Young Alan had always been fascinated by things mechanical, and had volunteered for the motorized armour division because of it. All the three vehicles under his command were serviced once a week, kept in faultless mechanical condition and spotlessly clean. Yet the back of this one, despite all his efforts, stank like a butcher's van. It humiliated him. And so, to show his disgust for the whole performance, he picked his teeth and yawned.

It was raining, and although the massive bonnet of the car was heavily armoured in steel plate, the driver and the Lieutenant sat with their heads open to the elements. There was a bullet-proof screen that they could pull down in front of them, but they normally drove with it lifted up to increase visibility. Both wore capes, and the rain pinged on their tin helmets noisily, adding to Lieutenant Wilson's misery and sense of humiliation. Not even an Irish gunman would be dim enough to attack a vehicle like this, he was sure, yet regulations insisted they take all necessary precautions.

Behind and above them was an armoured turret with a Browning machine gun in it. Young Corporal MacNair swivelled it enthusiastically from side to side, aiming at anyone who might look remotely suspicious. At the last road junction he had shocked the life out of a group of middle-aged men and women, who had found themselves staring down the barrel at five yards' range. They had scurried off down a side street, shaking their fists and shouting incomprehensibly.

And why not? the Lieutenant thought vindictively. It was their children who threw stones and horse dung at the car every day on patrol – it was people like them who had caused the army to be here in the first place, instead of lying on a beach in Egypt, or driving along the shores of the Red Sea. It was people like them who forced him to drive back to the barracks every day with animal carcasses in the flatbed part of the car behind the turret, where troops and equipment were usually carried. He had been tempted, more than once, to dress up the carcasses to look like dead Irishmen, and would have done it, too, if his CO had had more of a sense of humour.

They reached the abattoir, swung into the yard, and parked. Lieutenant Wilson climbed out of his seat and stretched, wrinkling his nose at the appalling stench, as he always did. Leaving the private and the corporal in the car, he tramped through the puddles towards the office, the rain streaming off his cape. The windows of the office were steamed up, but there was a welcome glow of light from a fire inside. He opened the door and went in.

The manager, Ryan, stood behind the desk with one of his assistants. Both looked as pale as their aprons and had smiles on their faces; rather stiff, glazed smiles, Wilson thought. But all the Irish were cracked; he had no desire to understand them. He fumbled with his hand under his cape to bring out the order.

Something prodded him in the back. A voice said: 'I'd leave that, boyo, if I were you.'

He turned to look behind him, but before he could succeed his arms were seized and he was propelled forward against a wall. His tin helmet banged against the plaster and tilted back over his head. His arms were forced up painfully behind his back. Something very narrow and hard prodded him under his right ear.

A voice said: 'Stand still, Tommy, and you won't be killed.'

Someone reached around his waist and took his pistol out of its holster. Then a voice said: 'Stay facing the wall. Start getting undressed.'

'What?'

'You heard. Take the helmet and cape off first. Then the rest of it.' His arms were released slowly. 'Any monkey business and we'll undress you ourselves. But I'll put a hole in your head before I start.'

Shaking with shock and humiliation, he did as he was told. Stupidly, he said: 'You won't get away with this. There's an armoured car and a machine gun outside.' As soon as he'd said it, he felt a fool.

'Is that so, sorr? And there's me thinking you fetched the meat on a bike.'

When he was down to his underwear, someone seized his wrists and tied them tightly together behind his back. Then he was made to sit down on a chair and his hands were tied to the strut between the back legs, too, so that he had to sit up stiff and upright. He was still facing the wall. He heard the door open and close behind him. Any minute now it'll happen, he thought. MacNair will open up with the Browning and these bastards will be unstitched all over the pavement.

But instead there was a shout and a single revolver shot. Then the door opened again, and he heard heavy breathing and curses as several people came in.

He risked a glance behind him over his shoulder. His driver, Private Garside, was shoved into the middle of the room with his helmet knocked sideways. Wilson noticed the manager and his assistant, still standing with those sheet-white faces, and he realized their hands were tied behind them. They must have been like that when he came in, and he hadn't noticed. The same voice that had spoken to him told Garside to face the wall and strip.

Another voice said: 'What happened?'

'We carried the meat out like you said but the stupid sod in the turret wouldn't get down to help me. He started swivelling the bloody gun around so I got up on the car and shot him.'

'All right. Lug his body out of the car. Then Seamus'll put these clothes on and we'll get going.'

A couple of minutes later Garside was tied to a chair as well. Lieutenant Wilson heard the engine of the armoured car start up, and then a horrible grinding and clashing of gears. When he thought of what driving like that would do to the gearbox, and what the whole episode would do to his army career, Lieutenant Wilson felt a horrible cold empty feeling rise inside him, as though he were about to cry.

A little way along the North Circular Road, the armoured car pulled into a side road and stopped. Paddy Daly, in the full uniform of a major of the 1st Wiltshire Regiment, stepped out of a house, smiling.

'Well done, me boys – just what the doctor ordered. Now, you've got ten minutes to get inside and smarten up. Then we'll have a full inspection. Come on, you 'orrible shower – jump to it!'

He slapped his swagger stick against his boot, grinning broadly. Then he swung himself casually up into the turret of the armoured car, and began to examine the machine gun. He did not intend to use it, but there was no harm in having it ready. Also, he could cover the street with it if by ill luck a British army patrol should come down here while the boys were preparing.

His stomach crawled inside him as the minutes ticked by.

At last ten minutes had gone, and the four men reappeared on the pavement. They stood stiffly to attention, and he climbed down and examined them critically. This was no routine inspection. Any one of a host of tiny details, invisible to the casual civilian, could easily blare a warning to the military mind. Daly himself had never been in the British Army, and he had spent most of yesterday alternately observing the Wiltshires in the street outside the Royal Barracks, and trying to read up on details of cap badges and uniform in the city library.

Seamus Kelly and Brendan O'Reardan were wearing the uniforms stripped from the lieutenant and private at the abattoir, so at least the details of them should be all right. O'Reardan had obviously had considerable trouble squeezing his 44-inch chest inside the battledress blouse, but it would do, at a glance. The lieutenant's uniform appeared to fit Kelly perfectly. The other two wore bits and pieces assembled from stores that the Squad happened to have. One was impersonating a private, one a corporal. Daly could see no difference between them and the others, but...

He could wait no longer. Time was another vital detail. Kelly had locked the two soldiers, the manager and his assistant in their office, and the other men in the abattoir had been tipped off to take no notice, but they would work their way free eventually. Then the soldiers would ring the Royal Barracks, and a search would begin. Not yet, probably, but soon.

'Right, you lads,' he said. 'Climb on board.' He spent a few more precious minutes in the turret, pointing out to Kelly and O'Reardan things he had noticed about the Browning. Daly would have dearly loved to operate the thing himself, if need be; but none of the armoured cars he had observed around the city had had anyone of the rank of major in the turret. Anyway, his was the more important job, of carrying the bluff through. He squeezed himself into the front seat beside Kelly and the driver, Clancy.

'Right, Tom,' he muttered. 'Mountjoy Prison it is.'

There was no trouble at the gates. By the time they had reached them, Clancy had managed three gear changes in a row without turning every head in the street, and the mere sight of an armoured car sent one of the two sentries scurrying to open the heavy iron-studded gates. The other one saluted Daly smartly.

'Escort party from the Castle, come to pick up prisoner Brennan,' Daly said, in his best English accent. He pulled some papers casually from his front pocket and handed them over.

This is the first test, he thought. He drummed his fingers casually on the flap of his revolver holster.

The sentry gave the papers a cursory glance, handed them back, and saluted again.

'Very good, sir. Go straight ahead.'

So that's the first step, Daly thought.

Clancy let the car into gear with an unfortunate jerk, and drove through the open gates into the prison yard. *Where the hell do we park?* Daly wondered. He scanned the yard quickly. The most obvious entrance seemed to be straight ahead of them, slightly to the left. 'Swing it round to face the exit,' he said to Clancy quietly. 'We don't want any fancy manoeuvres on the way out.'

There was no sentry at all outside this entrance. *Is it the right one?* Daly thought. *I don't want to make a fool of myself and walk into the kitchens.* But there seemed to be no other choice.

As planned, Clancy and Kelly stayed in the car; one to drive it, one to lounge in the machine-gun turret and give them a chance of beating off any attack. The other two, without a word, got down and followed Daly in.

Inside the door there was a corridor and an office, with two prison warders in it. Daly marched up to them smartly.

'Detail to take prisoner Brennan to Dublin Castle,' he said. 'Can you fetch him for me, please?' He handed over the folded order with the official stamp of Dublin Castle.

One of the warders took it and examined it gravely. Then he handed it back, taking in Daly's badges of rank as he did so.

'Right, Major. You'll have to take this to the governor's office to get it stamped. We'll bring the prisoner there, too. I'll show you the way.'

Suppressing all signs of hesitation, the three IRA men marched smartly behind him, into the heart of the prison.

Sean was annoyed. He had asked for pencil and paper so

that he could write a reply to Catherine, and he had been given one single sheet. For two hours he had written nothing, trying out phrase after phrase in his mind and then discarding it. When he had finally begun, he had seen after a few lines that he had struck the wrong tone – still too proud, too full of self-justification. But he had no rubber and no more paper, so he began again on the back.

The cell door opened and two warders stood there.

'Brennan. Out!'

He folded the paper and stuffed it into his shirt pocket, together with the pencil. He walked out onto the landing, holding out his wrists to be handcuffed. I am like a trained animal, he thought.

To his surprise they did not turn left at the foot of the steel staircase. 'Where are we going?' he asked.

'Governor's office,' said one of the warders shortly.

It'll be the lawyer, he thought. They've got a lawyer for me and they're going to try to persuade me to accept him. I won't.

He was taken up a flight of stone stairs and shown into a large room with carpets on the floor and books and pictures on the walls. A grey-haired man in civilian clothes was sitting behind a large desk, studying a piece of paper. Facing him was a British army officer and two soldiers.

The governor glanced up briefly as Sean came in. Then he spoke to the army officer.

'Signed by Captain Smythe, I see,' he said in a conversational tone. 'I thought all this was being handled by the DMP and Inspector Kee?'

'I don't know anything about that, sir,' the Major answered. 'My orders are just to come and get him.'

'Quite.' The governor perused the order again. 'I'd have thought if a *captain* in the intelligence service wanted to interview someone, he'd have come and got him himself, rather than sending a *major* to do his dirty work for him, wouldn't you?'

Daly hadn't thought of that. Damn the bloody British Army and its hierarchies. He said: 'I thought so too, sir, but I didn't like the idea of putting anyone else in charge of my armoured cars. The streets are pretty dangerous now and most of these intelligence wallahs have no experience of how to actually handle men in combat.'

'Wallahs' was a good touch, despite the residual traces of a Dublin accent. The Wiltshires had been in India; Daly had checked.

'Maybe not,' said the governor. He inked a rubber stamp, pressed it firmly on to both copies of the forged order, handed one back, and dropped the other into a tray. 'Though the sooner we get you fellows off the streets the better, I say. Anyway, there he is. He's all yours.'

The short conversation had given Sean a few precious seconds to adjust to the shock of hearing Daly's voice. When Daly and the other two turned towards him Sean gave them a swift glance and then stared straight past them, up at the wall over the governor's head where there was a wooden plaque with the gold-inscribed names of previous governors. He felt the muscles of his face twitching desperately and bit the insides of his lips to control them.

The warder beside him unlocked his handcuffs and the soldiers took Sean's arms and propelled him through the door. Outside, a warder coughed discreetly.

'No handcuffs, Major?' he asked, looking at Sean pointedly.

'What?' *That's the second mistake*, Daly thought. He gave what he hoped was a calm smile. 'No, no need. I've got four men and they're all armed. There'll be no trouble.'

'He may look pretty, but he is charged with murdering a policeman and trying to put a bomb under the Viceroy, you know, sir.'

'I'm well aware of that, thank you.' Daly unbuttoned his holster, took out a Webley revolver, and cocked it. It made him feel much more comfortable. He pointed it at Sean, but it could just as easily cover the prison warders. 'One false move out of him, and I'll save the hangman a job.'

The warder appeared satisfied. They marched, six of them – Sean, three soldiers, two warders – down the stone staircase and along a corridor. The sound of their boots echoed around them. There was a large closed door at the end of the corridor. Sean concentrated all his attention on it, willing it to open.

They reached the door and halted. The warder spoke to his colleague at the reception desk. The three soldiers and their captive stood unmoving. Almost like statues, if statues could have a pulse that beat like thunder in their throats.

The warder unlocked the door. The detail marched through. There was an armoured car outside. One of the soldiers got into the front seat beside the driver, tugging Sean in beside him. There was just room for Daly on the outside.

Daly saluted the prison warder, and then got in beside

Sean. The warder stood on the steps, watching them, frowning as though something was wrong.

Clancy turned the keys of the armoured car. It wouldn't start. He tried again. Still nothing. The warder came slowly down the steps towards the front of the car.

'Give it some choke!' Daly hissed out of the side of his mouth. Clancy pulled out the choke and tried again. The engine fired. He let the gears in with a sharp jerk and the car lurched bumpily across the yard towards the gate.

Sean saw the warder open his mouth as though to say something, then change his mind and step out of the way.

The warders at the main gate saluted as they went out. Clancy turned left into the traffic, narrowly missing a pony and trap. Nobody said a word. After about fifty yards Daly craned his neck round to shout to Kelly and O'Reardan in the machine-gun turret.

'What're they doing?' he yelled.

'Closing the gates, Commandant!' Kelly yelled. 'They just saluted and closed the gates behind us!'

'We did it!'

A great yell of triumph erupted from every man in the car simultaneously. Daly grabbed Sean by the hand and thumped him on the back, the other man pummelled him in the stomach, and Clancy, the driver, reached across to ruffle his hair. Kelly and O'Reardan burst into a full-throated verse of the 'Soldier's Song':

> *'I'll sing you a song, a soldier's song*
> *With a rousing cheering chorus . . .'*

Daly shouted at them to be quiet, but as they lurched along the Phibsborough Road towards the city centre he found it hard to imagine that any other armoured car in the city was crewed by men with such broad, triumphant grins on their faces.

23

CATHERINE LAY IN the bath and thought of her mother. The three bathrooms on the first floor at Killrath had been fully equipped and installed at the turn of the century under the orders of her mother, who was then in her early thirties. The bath Catherine was in was a massive iron tub eight feet long and nearly three feet deep, which had been specially commissioned from an ironworks in Belfast. It had feet like lion's claws, and a fitted shower cabinet made of teak and brass at the tap end, with its own special mirror, taps, and a shower head a foot wide at the top. The rest of the room was of matching magnificence. There was an equally massive washbasin, cork matting on the floor, bamboo and cane easy chairs, a large mirror decorated with twining stained-glass leaves and flowers, and a sculptured ceiling where dolphins and mermaids could be seen sporting gaily.

Catherine lay back in one and a half feet of steaming, soapy water, and looked at them. People had confidence in those days, she thought.

She remembered how she and her brothers had admired the tall, distant, beautiful figure of their mother. She had been one of the most striking women in the west of Ireland. People had come to Killrath to write poems and songs about her, paint her portrait, vie for her attention. Catherine and her brothers had been brought in by their Irish-speaking nanny to sing at the parties, ride on the picnics, stand by their mother's side in the photographs.

When did it all end? By the time she was twelve the parties were fewer, her mother more erratic, sometimes even dishevelled in her dress. Doctors began to come more frequently than artists. And by the time the war began her mother was clearly going insane.

Why? Because Father rejected her and took up with another woman. She must have been as lonely and unhappy as I am now, Catherine thought. And there was nothing she could do.

Catherine wondered if her mother had felt the same about her father as she herself did about Sean. Objectively, there ought to be no comparison. Her mother had been rejected for another woman; she, Catherine, had been rejected for ... what? A soldier's life? Sean's heroic vision of himself? The attractions of a secret brotherhood? The glory of assassination? Of secret murder?

It was the first time she had thought of Sean as a murderer. She knew and loved all the arguments – the fight against the foreign oppressor, the service of the old woman of Ireland, the Shan Van Vocht, the Fenian vision, the torch handed down over the generations, the unending struggle, the glorious rhetoric of the Republic. But the look of triumph on Sean's face as he had shown her his gun had besmirched it all. Perhaps because he was rejecting her at the time. Perhaps because of the way he had used it – to blow away half a policeman's face on a dark night before the man had time to fight back.

The worst of it was that she still loved him. That was it, that was the link with what her mother had felt. Sean did not need her any more, but she could not get him out of her head. And now that he did not want her, the world was an empty desert.

When Mother felt like this she gave up, Catherine thought. The fog of depression entered her brain and she went mad. That won't happen to me. I'm not like Mother, I won't let it. There must be other choices.

She slid down to the tap end of the bath to turn on the hot tap, and then, on impulse, stood up and looked at herself in the mirror. She wiped the condensation away with her hand, and saw a nude girl with steam rising around her, like Venus. I am as beautiful as Mother once was, she thought. Men could make poems and paintings of me. Other men. Not just Sean.

She turned the tap off and lay down again to soak. She had read somewhere that a woman would always love the man who took away her virginity. Later she had thought: That can't be true, it wouldn't be fair. What if you're attacked, raped by a monster? Yet here she was, obsessed by the memory of Sean, her own first lover, when it was all over between them.

How could she break free?

Maybe there's some truth in this myth. Maybe you can't forget your first lover so long as he's the only one. Maybe it's a sort of medical problem of the mind that needs treating. How?

By taking another lover.

The thought appalled and thrilled her. She believed strongly in the idea that women should be as free to take lovers as men, and that no harm was done so long as no one was hurt and there were no unwanted babies. As an idea it seemed simple, translucent, obvious; but it was turning out harder than she had expected. The memory of Sean was like a bacillus that had invaded her bloodstream, and needed to be cleared out.

She thought about Andrew Butler.

He was an arrogant, supercilious pest, but he was obviously attracted to her. He must be, to stand up to all the rebuffs she gave him. Perhaps he is actually suffering, as I am suffering about Sean, she thought. The idea amused her. She did not love him, but he fascinated her. And men use women who fascinate them, she thought. They exploit them for their own pleasure, to get whatever they think they need. Why shouldn't a woman do the same?

Could I?

It would be an utterly unprincipled, wicked thing to do. But then, perhaps such values are old-fashioned, out of date, blown away in the tempest of the war. Women who stick to them turn in on themselves and go mad, like my mother. That won't happen to me.

She stepped out of the bath and stood on the cork matting in front of the large decorated wall mirror, watching the soap suds trickle down her body to the floor. I look nervous, she thought. I look like a sacrifice. But that's what I was before

This time it's different. I'll be the one who's in control. Because I don't really want him as much as he wants me.

I won't be the sacrifice. He will.

Andrew remembered the pattern of the past three evenings.

They would meet in the drawing room, she would drink more sherry than him, they would begin an argument which would carry on throughout the meal, and she would leave him early to go to bed.

Every evening he would try to gauge whether she liked him a little more. And he would be transfixed by her beauty, and wonder what he could do about it.

Tonight it was different. She poured herself a sherry but she didn't freeze him out or start a quarrel. She didn't sit down on the window seat as she usually did. She sat down in a chair by the fire and smiled at him.

'That's a change,' he said. He was quite taken aback. 'What is?'

'A smile.'

'Don't I usually smile then?'

'Not until you've told me to leave the house, or tried to ride me over a cliff, no.'

'I'm sorry.' She took a deep breath. 'I've been very shut up in myself. It makes me rude and — what did you call it? — prickly.'

There was a certain speculative amusement in the way she looked at him, he thought, as though she wondered what effect this new approach would have. He wondered himself. He said: 'Well, I'm glad that I shall see you with your hackles down for once, before I leave. It should be an interesting sight.'

'You're leaving?' Her plan would fail completely if he left.

'Are you so concerned? Yes, on Wednesday, if I can get a train. My leave doesn't last for ever, you know.'

'No, I suppose not.' Wednesday. The day after tomorrow. There was still time, then.

Their meal was curiously subdued. They talked a little about the fishing, the inevitable rain, the awful news from Russia and Poland, the introduction of Prohibition in America, and the proposed attempt to cross the Atlantic in one of Zeppelin's airships. When they had finished they went back to the drawing room. Brophy, the butler, served them coffee and brandy, and Catherine thanked him and said he could go to bed.

There was a steady rattle of rain on the windows, and an occasional gust of wind blew smoke back down the chimney. Andrew was surprised that Catherine had not gone to bed immediately after the meal, as she usually did, and he wondered again at the curious way she looked at him. She knelt on the rug in front of the fire, watching the flames through the brandy glass. Her skin glowed, her short dark hair was smooth, soft in the firelight.

He said: 'I still haven't had a straight answer.'

'To what?'

'My proposal.'

'Yes, you have. The answer is no, Andrew, the same as it was yesterday and the day before. I can't help it if you're deaf.'

'You're a cruel woman.'

'I'm sorry. Why don't you just forget about it? There are other ways for people to relate to each other, without getting married, after all.'

'Such as?'

Again that strange, speculative look. There was a hint of mischief in her eyes, a ghost of a smile around her lips. 'I don't know. You're older than me, and a man of the world. Surely you must have been on friendly terms with other women.'

On friendly terms. That was not quite the phrase he would have used. 'One or two, yes,' he said.

'But you didn't marry them.'

'Of course not. You may think I'm just being flippant but I've never met anyone I wanted to marry before.'

'All right then, tell me about it. I'm interested in the psychology of it. What does a man think when he has an affair with a girl who he's not going to marry?'

He was used to her frankness and unpredictability by

now. It was part of her, but tonight it annoyed him. She thinks she can mock and refuse and tease without realizing the effect it has, he thought. She's a virgin; she'll grow up to be an old maid.

'He thinks, I suppose, about her body, and the pleasure she can give him. And whether she's exciting and fun to be with.'

'And don't you think women think like that about men?'

'Some do, perhaps. I don't know.'

This isn't working, she thought. He looks too morose, angry almost. She put her brandy glass down carefully on the hearth, and got to her feet, holding out her hands to the fire. Without looking at him, she said: 'If I ever married a man I would want to know everything about him first.'

'I could get an accountant to draw up a list of assets, such as they are; show you a copy of my war record, if that would help.'

'Idiot. I don't mean that at all.'

'Well, what then?'

She turned round to face him. He was still sitting in the chair, nursing his brandy, scowling. She took a deep breath. *Oh, Sean, Sean, forgive me.* Trembling slightly, she said: 'Stand up.'

'What?'

'Please.'

He put the glass down and stood up, facing her. If ever a man was made a fool of, he thought, it's me. 'Is that all right?'

'Kiss me.'

He did. She slid her arms around his neck and it was very

tentative at first; his lips were sullen, frozen. Oh, come on, she thought, I can't do this all alone. His moustache tickled, there was a nice, bristly feel to it. She put her hand on his cheek, and without meaning to, touched his scar. It felt hard, inanimate, gristly. Then suddenly his resistance snapped and he crushed her to him, kissing hard, earnestly.

A long time later they paused for breath. She loosened his hands gently, saying: 'There. Now I know how you kiss.'

He said: 'My God. I don't understand.'

'No? And you a man of the world, too.' Now we'll see, she thought. *Oh, Sean, Sean.* Forget him.

'I'm going to bed,' she said. 'Stay there alone if you like.'

It was a long, lonely walk to the door. Catherine must have walked those ten yards across that room hundreds of times before in her life but this was the first time she could ever remember feeling self-conscious about every step. It's not going to work, she thought, that was an utterly cheap and crazy thing to say, I'll never be able to face him again, I must look a complete fool walking like this . . .

'Catherine.'

'Yes.' She turned, her hand on the doorknob.

He crossed the room, put his hands on her arms. 'Do you know what you're saying? Do you mean it?'

'Of course.'

He bent forward and kissed her, more gently this time, almost reverently, as though she were a child. His moustache tickled, his breath smelt of brandy. The kiss ended and she stood in front of him, very cool and quizzical, trembling like a leaf inside.

'Wait here, then. Come up in five minutes.'

Andrew had imagined several ways that it might happen but none of them had been like this. He had thought he might surprise her after a ride, all flushed and warm in the stable, and lay her on her back in the hay; he had thought he might go into her room when she was asleep in the middle of the night; he had considered getting her really drunk, and seducing her on the sofa in the big drawing room when all the servants had gone to bed.

It had never occurred to him that *she* might seduce *him*.

When he came into her room, it was lit by a soft oil lamp in the corner, and a wood and peat fire in the grate. It was a large room, with two pink armchairs near the fire, a carved dressing table and a screen in the corner, a vast wardrobe with a full-length mirror, and a four-poster bed with pale yellow curtains. At first he did not see her, then he saw she was leaning against the pillows in her bed, wearing a cream-coloured nightgown with buttons down the front. She smiled.

'Hurry up. These sheets are cold. I need you to warm them.'

He took off his jacket and flung it over a chair. Then he hesitated. This was all too cool, too deliberate.

'If you're shy you can get undressed behind the screen. It's over there.'

'All right.' He picked up his jacket and went behind it. I don't think I've ever done it like this before, he thought. It's all wrong. I'm supposed to be in charge, not her.

Her clothes were behind the screen too; a dress, a

brassiere, soft silk camiknickers. He realized he would have to walk across the room towards her, quite erect and naked.

Her eyes widened slightly when she saw him.

He was not used to being looked at. Since his face had been wounded he had been ashamed of his body. But there was no look of horror on her face; more of excitement, determination. She was right, the sheets were cold.

'How many lords and ladies have been in this bed before us then, Miss O'Connell-Gort?' he said.

'Oh, dozens.' It's going to work, she thought. It's really going to work. She held out her arms and drew him to her.

This time, the kiss was rougher, more passionate and insistent. She moaned and ran her fingers through his hair. He kissed her neck and fumbled with the buttons of her nightdress.

'It's all right. I'll take it off.'

She tugged it over her head and then gasped as he sucked her breasts — hard, much harder than Sean had ever done. It hurt, but it did something to her stomach as well and she felt her loins warm and moist. She parted her thighs and kissed him again, rubbing her hands down his back to press him on to her.

'Oh yes, yes. Go on.'

And then he was thrusting into her and it was another man, she was really doing it with another man and it was all right, he was good and strong and she needed it so much and . . .

And it was all over.

She felt him go limp inside her and kissed his cheek

gently and felt his arms and back with her hands and thought how heavy he was, smooth hard muscles under the skin. There was soft fur on his buttocks and the small of his back, and a ridged line like a scar on his left side.

He rolled off her and lay on his side with his head propped on his elbow, gazing at her. His face in the lamplight was shadowy, the expression hard to interpret.

'I've wanted to do that since I first saw you,' he said.

'Have you, Sir Galahad?' She thought how strange his face was after Sean's; older, rough, a cruel face to look at close to. The way he had thrust into her had been quite brutal. She felt aroused, annoyed that it had been so swift. She shouldn't be thinking of Sean: the whole purpose was to forget him.

She rubbed both hands along his back, and said: 'So what is your next ambition, then?'

Andrew was amazed; shocked even. Not even Elsie had been quite so brazen. He leaned forward and kissed the little brown nipples and she closed her eyes and moaned. He kissed them harder, feeling his erection return, and then her hands were all over him, clinging to him, pulling him down on to her. He didn't like it. He felt used, exploited. I've got to show this girl who's master, he thought. He remembered Elsie, and as he thrust inside her he caught her wrists and forced them down over her head so that she had to look up at him as he thrust slowly, deliberately.

'What?' She tried to clasp him to her with her thighs, drumming her heels hard against his buttocks. 'Come *on*, Andrew.'

But he took his time, watching her, enjoying the moment

of control. She was lithe and slim as he had imagined; the struggle excited him. The bedclothes fell on the floor, but he was too heavy for her. She could not throw him off, even if she wanted to. Then he began to thrust faster and faster and her eyes closed and she stopped struggling and began to move with him and he saw her gasp and cry out just before he did so himself.

Afterwards they lay quietly in each other's arms.

She thought: I never thought it would be like that. He's a brute and a pig but I've done it and I don't feel guilty. I didn't promise to marry him, I just wanted to do it with another man and that's what I've done. There was no love here, only lust, but that's all right. I like lust. You can do it just as well without love *Oh God why do I feel so lonely?*

She had a sudden disturbing picture of Sean, alone in his cell. But he seemed very distant now, tiny, a little man in a stone box that grew smaller and smaller and fell out of sight in her mind like a matchbox thrown into the sea.

Tears prickled in her eyes. She realized Andrew had fallen asleep. She got up quietly to blow out the oil lamp, crept back into bed, and lay on her back watching the flickering shadows on the roof of the bed, caused by the dying embers of the fire.

Andrew woke later while it was still dark. The wind outside was stronger, and gusts rattled rain against the windows. He listened to her breathing softly beside him, and stroked her smooth dark hair with his fingers. A log fell in the grate, and he raised himself on his elbow and watched the warm firelight bathe her face.

He thought: I am here but I have not mastered her. There is more courage and spirit in that slim soft face than in any woman I have ever met. He wondered if she dreamed of him at all, or if, like Elsie, she was far away. He wanted to stay with her for ever.

Then he remembered Michael Collins. A gust of wind blew smoke down the chimney and for the first time he was afraid. His skin was sensitive and tender all over as though he had just been born; he did not want to be hurt now. But it had to be risked. He looked at her with immense gratitude and then quietly got out of bed, collected his clothes, and went back to his room.

At first it was too cold to sleep there. For a long time he lay, watching the grey dawn light creep through the curtains, and thought of Ardmore. Tomorrow, he thought, before I go to Dublin I will ask her again. And then when Collins is dead I will have the money to rebuild Ardmore and we will sleep in my mother's room together and she will bear my sons.

You and I are too much alike, Catherine O'Connell-Gort. I won't let you back out now.

In the morning Catherine woke up early and wondered for a moment where she was. The room was the same but there was something missing from it. Then she turned and saw the pillow crushed beside her own and remembered.

She got up, ran a bath, and brushed her hair in front of the decorated mirror in the bathroom. This is where I had my great idea, she thought. I look just the same. I am the same, really, it doesn't touch you much inside if you don't let it. All that's a myth.

But although she smiled she felt like weeping and kept thinking of Sean. I've abandoned him, she thought. I've abandoned all that now.

She went downstairs to the breakfast room. There was no one there. She gazed out of the window at the rain sweeping in from the sea. Raindrops were splashing like smoke on the stone paths in the garden, and the wind was lashing the bent shrubs and bushes this way and that. But far out to sea a pale sun was shining on silvery-grey, whitecapped waves, and she could see the edge of the dark clouds coming nearer. She thought she would go out for a ride later, when the storm had passed.

Brophy brought her bacon and eggs, and she ate hungrily, scanning the headlines of the *Irish Times*, which he had laid out in front of her. She had glanced at him anxiously when he brought it, but it was all right, he was his usual avuncular, cheerful self. There was no hint of shock or disapproval in his eyes.

It's all fine, Catherine thought, it's all right. My body isn't hurt and my mind is clear and everything is straightforward now. He made love to me and it was coarse and brutal, like the pig of a man he is. But in its way it was thrilling too, in a quite different way than with Sean. Like riding a new skittish hunter for the first time and being thrown; frightening but compulsive too, so you want to do it again and control it. Perhaps I was like that for Sean. Forget Sean. I was right – it's a medical thing like an inoculation in reverse. The second man immunizes you against an obsession with the first and brings health. I can do it with Andrew again if I like, whenever I like, or not at all if I don't want to. It's my life again, I'm free and in control.

She realized Andrew would probably ask her about marriage again, and she wondered if every night would be like that, or whether she could tame him. She had led him to her bed, after all; now she knew what to expect. But anyway there was no hurry; it didn't seem an important problem at the moment.

The rain was easing off. Andrew seems to be sleeping late, she thought, with a secret smile. He must be tired. She poured herself some tea, buttered some toast, and scanned the newspaper idly. A headline caught her eye.

SINN FEINER CHARGED WITH RADFORD'S MURDER
TRIAL LIKELY IN TWO WEEKS

A sick, fluttery feeling invaded her stomach. She bent her head closer to read.

Dublin Castle confirmed yesterday that a man has been charged with the murder of Assistant Commissioner Radford of the DMP, who was murdered in Harcourt Street last week. The accused man was named last night as Sean Brennan, aged 20, a medical student at University College, Dublin. It is understood he was arrested in Merrion Square last week, and is currently being held in Mountjoy Prison.

The government is anxious to bring the case to court as soon as possible, and the trial is scheduled to take place within the next two weeks. Assistant Commissioner Radford was shot at point-blank range in

Harcourt Street, and eye-witnesses at the time reported
that two armed men ran off into a side street . . .

There followed details of what little was known of the murder, but Catherine did not read them. She was too shocked. She put the paper down, her hand shaking. Sean must have been charged yesterday, perhaps while she was lying in her bath thinking of seducing Andrew. They probably tortured him, beat him until he confessed. Perhaps last night, while Andrew and I were . . .

And if they find him guilty, he'll hang.

'Ah, there you are! Good morning.' It was Andrew. He came in, walked round to her side of the table, and kissed her neck.

She shrank away. 'No. Please don't.'

'Why not?' His hands stroked her shoulders softly. A few minutes ago she might have liked it. Now it seemed a violation.

'Leave me alone, please.'

'What's the matter?' This was worse than he had thought.

'Oh, it's nothing. I'm sorry, it's not your fault. Just something I read in the paper, that's all.'

'Really? What is it? Show me.' He sat down facing her across a corner of the table, and poured himself a cup of tea.

'It's none of your business.'

He drank the tea thoughtfully, and stared at her. More monkey tricks. He had thought at least this morning she would be pleased, happy as he was. Instead, here was the old arrogance back again. Did she think she could summon him to her room at night, and then slap him in the face the next morning?

He said, mildly enough: 'You say there's something printed in the paper and yet it's none of my business?'

'Yes. Oh, to hell with it. Look there then, if you must.'

She flung the newspaper across, pointing to the article. He read it. 'So?'

'So?' She pushed her chair back and walked to the window, running her hands distractedly through her hair. 'So Sean Brennan was my lover and now he's going to hang.'

'Oh.' Andrew couldn't think of anything to say. He felt ill, wasted, as though his blood had turned to ashes. As he had felt the day after Ardmore had burnt, when he had gone back to stare at the smoking ruins. And, just like then, something small began to smoulder within himself, and he knew that later, when he had recovered, the anger would flare and consume him.

He said, stupidly: 'He was your lover? When?'

'In Dublin. We were students at UCD together.'

'And you did – let me get this straight, Catherine.' He stood up suddenly, strode to the window, and spun her round to face him. 'You did with a dirty little Sinn Feiner what you did with me?'

She stared at him, then shook her head. 'Please, Andrew!'

'Don't please Andrew me! I want to know! Did you?'

'Yes!' She stood quite still and glared at him, then relented slightly. 'It was all over before I came down here. That was why I came.'

His face was very grim and hard, like her father's when she had done something wrong. But there was pain there, too, in the lines round the eyes. She looked away; she didn't want to see that. At least Andrew would live; he wasn't going to hang.

She walked to the door at the far end of the room and said: 'I'm going back to Dublin. I've got to see him.'

Andrew stared at her. 'Why? You said it was all over. And if he's a murderer, for Christ's sake!'

She looked at him wearily. 'I loved him.'

'And you don't love me?'

'Oh, for God's sake, Andrew! Look, I'm sorry. I said I *loved* him, not that I love him now. And if he's going to die...'

Very carefully he said: 'I thought after last night that you must feel something for me as well.'

'Oh.' She shook her head, trying to remember the feelings she had brought into this room, only a few minutes ago. Then she walked back down the room and took his hand. 'I didn't make any promises, Andrew, did I? Anyway I don't want to talk about that now. I just want to go to Dublin and see Sean.'

'I may as well come with you then. I was going tomorrow anyway.'

'If you like.' She didn't like it but she could see no way of resisting.

'I'll get David Ferguson to run us down in the car. There's a train about eleven.'

When she got to her room there was a maid there, cleaning out the ashes from the grate. The maid asked if she should go but Catherine told her to carry on. Then she flung a few clothes and books into a bag and sat distractedly at her dressing table staring into the mirror. Her face was slightly paler than usual, the eyes wider and darker-ringed, but otherwise there was little to show the pain and guilt she felt. No tears, just that sick, empty feeling inside.

The maid interrupted her thoughts. 'Is this yours, my lady? I found it on the floor beneath that chair.'

It was a folded, typewritten letter. The first time Catherine read it it made no sense at all. She forced herself to concentrate and read it again.

> *Dáil Eireann*
> *c/o The Mansion House*
> *Dublin*

14 January 1920

Count Manfred von Hessel
Lambert Hotel

Dear Count von Hessel,
I have received your proposal which is, on face value, very interesting to me. I will meet you within the next few days. The arrangements will be made by the bearer of this, whom you may trust absolutely.
Michael Collins
Minister of Finance.

Catherine was stunned. What on earth was it? Michael Collins! A letter signed by him, here at Killrath! And to

Manfred von Hessel – who could he possibly be? And how could it have got under a chair in her bedroom? No one came in here except herself and the servants, and she doubted if most of them could read.

So how? She had a sudden vision of Andrew coming into her room, grinning lecherously as he looked at her, and throwing his jacket casually across the chair before he undressed behind the screen. It could have fallen out of the pocket. It must be his.

But . . .

She tried to focus her bruised mind on the problem. There was something wrong here. Terribly wrong.

Andrew was an army officer, he must hate and despise Collins, and the letter was not addressed to him. So how could he have it? He must have stolen it from someone. He must be a spy, a member of the British Intelligence Service. That's it, she thought. That's why he's an army officer but doesn't wear uniform. That's why he works with Father. That's why he won't tell me what he does.

Oh, God, I haven't just betrayed Sean with another man. I've betrayed him with a bloody spy!

She sank her head in her hands, and then realized that she couldn't cry, because the wretched housemaid was still busying herself with the grate. She took a deep breath, dabbed at her eyes with a handkerchief, and began to brush her hair.

She couldn't meet her own eyes in the mirror. I'm a fool, she thought. I try to break free and I just tangle myself more in a net. If I give this letter back to Andrew I'm colluding in his bloody spying. Anyway, why should I?

What was the letter about, exactly? She read it again, carefully. It didn't make much sense. A meeting, a proposal, trust the bearer. And dated 14 January, more than ten days ago, so the meeting must have taken place already. Perhaps Andrew had tried to catch this Hessel, whoever he was, at the Lambert Hotel.

Then she noticed something else, at the foot of the letter, a light pencilled scrawl. Breedan — what did it say? — Brendan Road.

It meant nothing to her. Then a memory surfaced in her mind — something she had read in the newspaper a week or two ago. Hadn't there been a police raid in Brendan Road? Yes, that was it — a raid on a house, and someone had been arrested. But who?

She turned to the maid. 'Molly?'

'Yes, miss.'

'You know the old newspapers. Do you know what Brophy does with them each day?'

'Oh, I don't know, miss. Uses them to light fires, mostly. The rest he keeps in a heap out the back of the kitchen, I think.'

'Thank you.' It suddenly became very important to try to find the article, and trace the name of the man who had been arrested. My God, perhaps Andrew did this — Andrew betrayed him! Was anybody killed? She couldn't remember.

David Ferguson hadn't turned up with the car yet. She left her bag in the hall and hurried through to the kitchen.

The newspapers were where Molly had said, in a cupboard at the back of the kitchen. The cook looked at her curiously, but Catherine took no notice. Most of the newspapers were torn, bits missing. It probably wasn't here. She spread them out on the floor; 15 January, 16 January – no, nothing. Ah, here it was – Saturday, 17 January. She read eagerly, hurriedly.

POLICE RAID ON HOUSE
GERMAN ARMS DEALER CAUGHT
COLLINS ESCAPES AGAIN

Shots were fired yesterday in a police raid on a house in Brendan Road, Donnybrook. Acting on information received, detectives from the DMP G Division raided the house which was believed to be a headquarters for the Sinn Fein 'murder gang'. After an exchange of shots, all of the occupants except one escaped by the back door.

The arrested man appears to be a former German officer, who had apparently come to Dublin in the hope of selling arms to the IRA. He is currently being interrogated in Dublin Castle, and is then likely to be deported, with a strong protest from the Viceroy.

Our correspondent understands that the police were particularly disappointed in this raid, as the house is believed to be one frequented by top members of the so-called Sinn Fein 'government', including Mr Michael Collins, and it is quite possible that the German officer had gone there in hopes of meeting him. Mr Collins, however, was not arrested.

She was right, then: if the German officer was called Hessel, then Andrew must have betrayed him. That was why he had this letter in his pocket. But when had he got it?

Before Hessel read it, or after? And how would he get hold of such a thing? Catherine had no idea.

She walked back into the hall and found Andrew waiting, with David Ferguson standing beside him, holding a suitcase.

'I'd hoped we'd have you here for a little longer this time, Miss Catherine.'

'Yes. It's a pity, David, but I've got to get back. Look after Grainne for me, will you?'

The rain had cleared as she had expected, and it was a beautiful, cold, clear morning with a light wind. Ideal for a ride. The tide was far out, and a few small figures of coracle men trudged across the shining wet sand, looking like beetles with their boats upturned over their heads.

The drive into Galway was silent, strained. Catherine sat beside David in the front seat, staring out of the window. David tried to carry on a shouted conversation with Andrew in the back, but in the end the noise of the car and Andrew's brief dismissive replies discouraged him, and he fell silent.

Not until they had settled into a first-class compartment, and the train had begun to pull slowly out of Galway station with a whistle and chunter of thick, black smoke, did they begin to speak. Catherine handed him the letter.

'I think this must be yours,' she said.

She watched him closely as he read it. It didn't take long – clearly he had seen it before. He put it in his pocket and glanced at her with affected unconcern. 'Yes.'

She waited a full half-minute for an explanation. Then, when none came, she said: 'Who is von Hessel?'

The reaction this time was slightly more than when he

had first seen the letter. His eyes held hers, very cold and steady, but he could not quite control the whitening of the skin, the general overall increase in the tension of every facial muscle. Parts of the scar went red, by contrast. An interesting medical observation, she thought.

He took his time before answering, as though weighing all the implications. 'Von Hessel was a German officer. Ex-officer. He tried to sell guns to Collins. He was arrested and deported.'

So he *was* the man in the newspaper. 'And that letter?'

'It's to do with my work.'

Another long silence. Fields with bare, leafless trees flashed past the window. A herd of ponies galloped madly, startled by the train. A steward pushed a trolley down the corridor and opened the sliding doors. 'Coffee, madam? Sir?'

'No, thank you.'

'Yes, please.' Catherine smiled sweetly. She felt cool: angry, but in control. When the steward had gone, she stirred cream into her coffee and said: 'You're a British spy, Andrew, aren't you?'

Andrew was trying desperately to work out what to do. Last night he had thought he could master the girl; this morning she not only seemed indifferent to him, but had found out something that could endanger his whole plan, if she understood it. She had a Sinn Fein lover, no doubt she had other contacts in the movement. It was bad, but not disastrous. She didn't know that he was Hessel, and was planning to meet Collins again.

He said: 'I'm like your father, I work in Military Intelligence. Does that make me a spy?'

'I think so.'

'That's because you have different political views. I support the Union, and the rule of law.'

Catherine ignored that. She was beginning to enjoy her role as interrogator. She said: 'Hessel was arrested by the police, not the army. Did you get hold of that letter *before* the arrest, and give it to the police, or did they give it to you afterwards?'

'Don't be silly. I can't tell you things like that.'

'Only, if you got it before, then it means you must have known Hessel – in fact you must have shown it to him yourself. And if it was afterwards – I can't see what you would need it for afterwards, can you?'

Andrew laughed. Neither of them thought the laugh sounded very relaxed or convincing. 'Look, Catherine, you're not a detective, so don't try and play at being one. The fact is, this letter has been left in my pocket by mistake, when I should have thrown it away. Hessel's been deported. I don't need it – look.'

He took the letter out of his pocket, lit it with a match, held it between finger and thumb until it was burnt, and ground the ashes to powder under his shoe. 'There. End of mystery.'

But it's not, he thought. I can't have you walking round Dublin for the next few days. Somehow, that has to be stopped. He said: 'I'm more interested in talking about you and me.'

She sighed. 'Not now, Andrew, please.'

'Will I see you when you're in Dublin?'

'I don't know.'

'Look – surely after last night? It wasn't that bad, was it?'

'Last night was fine. It was just what I needed. But it was before I knew Sean was going to be tried for murder, and that you were a British spy, Andrew.'

He was silent. *Just what she needed.* The words settled slowly into his mind like a cloud of gas drifting over a trench. One part of phosgene in a million parts of air could change everything inside a man utterly, and for ever. Not at once; it took a day before the inevitable death. So it was with only a few words. They settled into his mind, quietly, peacefully, and began to work.

He began to realize that he had been used. There had been no love in it as he had hoped. Just something to satisfy her own transient desires. He had not thought women could be like that.

They talked little throughout the afternoon. When they reached Athlone the carriage filled up, with two officers and a businessman and his family, so further personal conversation was impossible. But when the train was already beginning to slow on its final approach to Dublin, he said: 'You'll be going back to Merrion Square, I suppose?'

'Yes, of course.'

'There's something I want to show you before you go home, if you can spare the time.'

She shrugged. 'Go ahead.'

'It's not here. It's in my house.'

'Ardmore?'

'No. I have a small house in Dublin. It won't take more than a few minutes, but it's quite important. It's about that letter.' He glanced at the ashes on the floor, which were now scattered under the shoes of the businessman's wife.

She thought about it. She was tired, but the letter intrigued her. If she found out more about it, it might help the movement; and also, if she knew where he lived she could tell Sean, or Professor O'Connor, perhaps. Oh no. She remembered the description of the dead police commissioner. I don't want to encourage any more of that, she thought. Not to Andrew. Not to anyone.

'I don't want to know where your house is,' she said. 'It's best if I don't.'

'Please,' he said. 'It won't matter to me if anyone does know — I won't be staying there. And it is important, really.'

'Oh, all right.' For the moment she was too tired to resist. But even as they walked out of the station and called a cab, she was thinking: There's something wrong about this. I thought it was clever at first to interrogate him about the letter but now I'm getting in deeper than I should. But she was too concerned with Sean to think it through. It would only take a moment, Andrew had said. And it was on the way anyhow.

The cab took them down a narrow road of tall, not very prosperous terraced houses. There were some children playing with a hoop at one end of the street and a barrow boy selling vegetables. It was a poorer area than she had expected.

He paid off the cab outside the door.

'I thought you said it would only take a moment?'

'Oh, I'll help you call another cab. There's no shortage.'

They went in. The house had a musty, unlived-in smell

to it. There was a patch of damp in one corner of the hall and dust on some of the paintings. It was cold; there were no fires lit.

'Welcome,' he said. 'Let me take your hat and coat.'

'No thanks. I'll keep them on. Heavens, Andrew, do you live here?'

'Only when I have to. It was my parents' town house.'

'You want someone in to clean it up, give it a bit of life.'

'Yes.' He looked at her strangely.

I shouldn't have come, she thought. This is a waste of time. 'All right. Where is this thing that's so important?'

'It's in the cellar, I'm afraid. It's rather big.'

'In the *cellar*?'

'Yes.' He opened a door at the back of the hall. Some steps inside led down. He lit an oil lamp and led the way. Mystified, she followed. He opened a door at the bottom and went in.

The cellar was almost empty. Catherine looked round and saw an old bicycle, a couple of trunks, some bottles of wine covered in cobwebs, a stack of chopped wood in the corner, a broken sofa with the springs hanging out of the bottom.

'What's all this?' she said. 'Andrew, there's nothing interesting here.'

'Only one interesting thing.'

'What's that?'

'You.'

He had put the lamp down in the middle of the floor, and stepped back to be between her and the door. She stared at him. His face was lit oddly from below because of where he had put the lamp, so that the shadows were in the bottom of his eyesockets instead of the top. There was an odd, bitter smile on his face.

'What *is* this, Andrew?'

'I suppose you could call it a kidnapping,' he said. 'Would you push that sofa over against the wall, please.'

'Certainly not!'

'Please. I insist.' He took an automatic pistol out of his pocket and pointed it at her.

'You wouldn't shoot me!' She took a brisk step towards him. He cocked the pistol. She took another step, then stopped.

'Move the sofa,' he said.

'Move it yourself.'

He took a step backwards, kicked the door shut behind him, pointed the pistol at the ground, and fired. The noise in the cellar was shattering. Catherine screamed and put her hands over her ears. Her head seemed to be ringing as if it were inside a huge bell. She looked down. A chip had been blown out of the concrete floor three inches from her toe. She gaped at Andrew, aghast.

'Please,' he said. 'I don't want to fight, and I don't want to hit you. But I will if have to. You'd get bruised, and hurt.'

She turned and pushed the sofa against the wall.

'Now sit on it.'

She sat.

He walked over to the bicycle and took a chain and padlock from the saddlebag. Then he bent down at the far end of the sofa, by the wall. She saw there was an iron heating pipe running along the edge of the wall. He slipped the chain around the pipe, and then passed one end of the chain through the large ring in its other end. He said: 'Come and sit here. Take your boot off and stretch your leg out.'

'Why?'

'Just do it.'

She did it. He looped the free end of the chain around her ankle and fastened it tightly with the padlock. Then he stood up. 'There. I'll bring you food and water in a moment.'

'You mean you're going to leave me here?'

'I'm afraid so. Just for a day or two. It's what I *need you for*, you see.' He emphasized the words oddly.

'You're mad. I'll scream, anyway. People will come and rescue me.'

'Do you think I'd have fired this gun in here if any sound could get out? You'll just give yourself a sore throat.'

'But *why*, Andrew?'

He shrugged. 'Work it out for yourself. I'm sorry, my dear. I was quite fond of you last night. But as you say, I'm a British spy, and they're very nasty people. It's much better to trust Sinn Feiners. Good night.'

He walked out of the door, and she heard the sound of the bolts being shoved to behind it. She wasn't sure, but she thought he locked the door at the top of the cellar stairs, as well.

24

'Moved? Moved where?'

'To Dublin Castle. He was requisitioned by order of Military Intelligence this morning.'

Kee couldn't believe it. He stared at the prison governor as if he were some sort of five-headed leprechaun who had just popped up through the floorboards. 'By whose orders?' he said at last.

'Captain Smythe, I believe.' The governor frowned. He searched amongst the papers on his desk, found the order form, and passed it over. 'Yes, that's it. Didn't he tell you?'

'No he damn well did not.' Kee examined the order form with care. It was the right paper, correctly stamped both at Dublin Castle and here in Mountjoy Prison. It was signed by a Captain Smythe. Kee wasn't familiar with the signature but it looked all right. He tried to think who Smythe was. A vague image of a small, pipe-smoking, pompous individual came to mind. What the hell did he want with Brennan?

'Do you mind if I borrow your phone?'

'Go ahead.' Kee picked up the phone, asked for the number, and waited. A clipped, brusque English accent came on the line.

'Smythe here. Intelligence.'

Interference, more like, Kee thought. He said: 'This is Detective Inspector Kee of the Dublin Metropolitan Police. I'm ringing from Mountjoy Prison.'

'Oh yes. Morning, Kee. What can I do for you?'

'You can start by telling me what the hell's going on.'

'Sorry, old chap. I don't quite get you.'

Kee took a deep breath. 'What I mean, Smythe, is why the hell have you requisitioned my prisoner? That man has been charged, and it's my investigation. He's got nothing to do with you.'

The voice at the other end sounded puzzled. 'I say, steady on, old chap. You seem to have got your wires crossed. Which prisoner are you talking about exactly?'

'You know damn well which prisoner. Sean Brennan, that's who. I'm here in the governor's office at Mountjoy with a warrant signed by you for his transfer to Dublin Castle. Your soldiers came and took him . . .' He glanced at the governor. 'When?'

'Half an hour ago.'

'Half an hour ago. So where is he now?'

There was a silence. Then the voice on the telephone said: 'A warrant signed by me, you say?'

'Yes!' Kee roared. If I had him here I'd take that bloody pipe and stuff it down his throat, he thought. I suppose they think they can get secrets out of him which I can't.

'Sorry, old boy, there must be some mistake. I haven't

signed an order requisitioning any prisoner for days. Certainly not one for anyone called – what was it?'

'Brennan. Sean Brennan.'

'No. Definitely not.'

'But I've got the form here in my hand!' Kee looked at it again. It was all genuine, he was sure of it. Sure of everything except the signature, that is. He met the governor's eyes, and a dreadful suspicion began to drain the blood from their faces simultaneously. The voice crackled irritatingly in his ear.

'Listen, Kee, old chap, this is a serious accusation you're making. I assure you on my word of honour that I have not requisitioned any prisoner by the name Brennan from Mountjoy Gaol. So if you've got an order bearing my name, it must be a forgery. Why don't you bring it down here and let me have a squint?'

'Yes. All right. I'll do that.' Kee put the phone down. His hand was shaking so he did it clumsily. Brennan was Bill Radford's murderer – he was the one man in his whole career whom Kee had ever truly wanted to see hang. *Where was he?*

He turned to the governor. 'What was the name of the officer who collected him? He must have signed something, mustn't he?'

'I don't remember. Yes, here it is.' The governor passed over another sheet of paper. The signature at the bottom was nearly illegible. 'Dawson? Deasy? Dickson? It could be anything. He was a major in the Wiltshires, I know that. They're stationed in the Royal Barracks, near Phoenix Park. I'll ring them, if you like.'

While the governor phoned, Kee paced up and down the room, his clenched fist banging softly against his thighs. It was his fault, it had to be. If only he had been here an hour earlier, as he usually was. But other things had been piling up. Davis had come to him that morning with a pile of reports and unanswered queries which he seemed desperate to have answered. Kee had to direct the office as well, now that Bill Radford was dead.

'Dead, you say?' The governor's voice echoed Kee's thoughts. 'My God. I see.' The governor listened some more, then put the phone down, shaken. 'I'm afraid no armoured car was sent here, but one was stolen at the Corporation Abattoir this morning. One soldier was shot dead, and two others stripped and bound. I'm afraid we've been conned, Inspector.'

'An armoured car! Great God!' Kee sat down on a chair for a moment, stunned. 'Is nothing safe from these murderous thugs?'

'Apparently not.' The governor glanced at him, then dialled another number. 'I'll put out an alarm round the city.'

But Kee had his face in his hands, and was fighting back tears of frustration. I had him, Bill, old friend, he thought. I had him here in my hands; and now he's slipped free, like water.

I'll never leave this blasted town. I meant what I said. If I don't catch the bastards, I'll die here.

Daly had dropped off Sean and Seamus Kelly in Drumcondra before heading out into the country to strip the Tin Annie of its machine gun. Kelly took Sean to a house where two old grey-haired sisters insisted on giving the boys a meal. So it was late afternoon when, with caps pulled down jauntily over their eyes, they pedalled back into the city.

'Big Michael himself'll be wanting to see you,' said Kelly. 'Sure you're the living proof of the invincibility of the Dublin Squad!'

They both laughed. The exhilaration of the morning's escapade was bubbling out of Kelly, and all the time the joy was growing in Sean, too, like a seed that is about to germinate. Already he was able to laugh; soon that laughter would no longer be anxious or desperate, and he would really believe he was free again.

The city was growing dark, and a soft evening rain was sweeping in from the sea. Sean rejoiced in the feel of it on his face. The sulphurous smell of coal fires, the rattle of trams and bicycle bells, the hiss of the gas lamps being lit, everything delighted him. He had resigned himself to seeing none of it again, now he could do what he liked: buy a newspaper, go for a pint in a pub, ride a tram, even cycle straight out into the country if he chose. Not today, perhaps, but then he did not need to do everything today. The rest of his life stretched out in front of him, with all those unlimited summers and winters that it had always had, and that he had never appreciated before.

He thought about Catherine's letter. '*The times we had together were the most wonderful in my life.*' In prison he had admitted to himself that some of the things he had said to her had been wrong. Now, perhaps, he could see her again, try to explain.

Tonight when he was alone in bed he would think if he really wanted to do that. And if so, how. Almost certainly, the police would guess at the possibility, and be watching her home.

It won't be possible for some time, he thought.

Then he saw her.

They were cycling along the North Circular Road when Kelly spotted a detachment of soldiers getting out of a lorry ahead of them and searching young men on the pavement. He pointed them out to Sean, and the two of them turned left down a side street, and left again. It was an area that had once been prosperous, and was becoming less so. They saw some women talking, children playing with hoops in the street, and a barrow selling vegetables. Further on, a man and a woman were getting out of a cab.

The woman was Catherine.

Sean was certain of it, though she was twenty yards ahead of him. It was dark and smoky in the street, but in order to get into the house the man and woman had to pass under the yellow, spitting glow of a gas streetlight. No one else had a back quite so lithe and slender as that, quite the same jaunty flick of the head. Even at that distance, he could not be wrong. And then, as she turned back to speak to the man who was paying off the cab, he saw her face briefly in profile, and every atom of his body ached for her.

But by the time he had recovered from the shock and decided to pedal quickly forwards, she had gone up the steps to the front door of the house. The man had unlocked the door, put his arm on her shoulders briefly to show her in, and they were gone.

Sean stopped outside the door, gazing at it hopelessly. Kelly went on, then realized Sean was no longer with him, and came back.

'What's up? Come on, Sean boy. This isn't the place at all.'

'No.' Number 16. What had she said in the letter? *'My father wants me to marry a man of my own class as you said. I may not be able to resist it, but it will be a sad cruel heartless business, like sending a mare to the stud . . .'* Was this where it happened, then? So soon, so soon after I was sent to gaol.

He thought for a moment of bursting in and throttling the man with his bare hands. But Kelly had a hand on his shoulder.

'Come on, Sean boy, we can't hang around here. Those soldiers are probably out looking for you. And there's a curfew since you were arrested, you know – we haven't a lot of time. Pedal down here after me and we'll give them the slip, right enough.'

So Sean followed. As they turned out of the street he noticed its name – Nelson Street. But the joy had gone out of his release completely. When they met some soldiers, he pedalled past them quite calmly, hardly caring whether they recognized him or not. He remembered some words from a poem he had once read at school: *'Stone walls do not a prison make/Nor iron bars a cage'.* No, he thought. It's in our minds that we are free or not, depressed or joyful. If I've got the freedom of the whole city, and no love, what's the point?

Catherine had tried to tell him that before.

* * *

'It's quite like mine, old boy. I'll grant you that.' Captain Smythe sucked at his pipe to keep it alight. 'But I'll swear by anything you like I never signed it. Let's have a closer squint.'

He pulled a large magnifying glass out of a drawer, and examined the signature minutely. Kee sighed with exasperation. Who did the idiot think he was – Sherlock Holmes? 'I'll accept your word for it –' he began.

But Smythe was waxing enthusiastic. 'There, see! Take a look at that loop on the *y*! It's not a single curve, it's two. The pen's not run straight on as it should. It's stopped, and the fellow's had to go back and join it on with another stroke. I'd never do that, you see. This is how I dash off the old autograph...' He signed his name on a scrap of paper with a flourish. 'Now these fellows couldn't do that – probably traced my signature and then went over it in pen. But they couldn't quite carry it through in one go.' He straightened up. 'Fascinating stuff, y'know.'

No wonder we don't cooperate with these clowns, Kee thought. He said: 'The question is not whether it's forged or not, but who did it. Who is in a position to get hold of your signature *and* a copy of a correct order form with a genuine stamp on it?'

Smythe puffed at his pipe furiously. 'Well now, the question we have to ask first, surely, is whether the paper and the stamp are genuine or not. First things first, you know, Inspector.'

'They look real enough to me.' Kee groaned inwardly, bracing himself for another session with the magnifying glass. But to his surprise Smythe picked up the paper and took it to the window.

'There's a watermark on all of these forms,' he said, as he held it up. 'Not many people know about that. Good Lord. Yes, well, that's there all right.' A little of his enthusiam seemed to be dented. 'The other thing is, each individual sheet has a number. Printed in invisible ink at the bottom – my own invention, matter of fact. They'll never have forged that, you know. Just add a few drops from this bottle and . . . Oh dear. Oh dear me.'

'What's the matter?'

'We only print these numbers on order forms for Intelligence. For this very reason, in fact.' The man seemed distracted. He hunted around on his desk for his own order pad, looked at it, and sighed. 'Yes. Look there, Inspector. The number on the top sheet is only two digits on from the one on this form of yours. That clinches it, I'm afraid. God knows how, but someone has managed to pinch a genuine order form off this very pad here on my desk.'

Smythe sat down abruptly in his chair as though someone had hit him behind the knees. He stared at Kee across the litter of papers on his desk. The measure of his surprise was obvious from the fact that his pipe, which he had put down for a moment, was left to smoulder slowly in the ashtray until it began to go out.

'So who could have done that?' Kee asked.

'I really have no idea.'

Smythe might have no idea, but Kee had. There was already the damning evidence he had heard in Mountjoy. How had Brennan known what Radford looked like, and where he lived? 'One of his own bloody detectives, that's what,' Brennan had said. 'Not that I liked the fellow much.' Ever since Kee and Radford had come to Dublin from Belfast, they had been acutely conscious that the very force they had come to command was penetrated by Collins's agents. Only a very few men in G Division had seemed worthy of trust. Men like Davis, and the young detective Foster, who were always ready to volunteer for any assignment, type out any report. And now this.

Kee asked, casually: 'I don't suppose any of my men has been to see you in the last few days?'

Smythe thought. 'Well, yes, now you come to mention it. One of your chaps called Davis. Very good sort for an Irishman, you know. Had some rather useful information. I say . . .' Light began to dawn. 'You're not suggesting he could have had anything to do with this, are you?'

'Was there any time at all when he was alone in your office?'

Smythe had picked up his pipe again, but he paused in the act of opening a matchbox. A faint tinge of pink began to spread across his face. 'Well, as a matter of fact, old chap, I'm awfully sorry to say this, but there was.'

Michael Collins was vastly pleased to see Sean. The big man shook him fervently by the hand, punched him playfully on the shoulder, and seemed almost about to indulge in a wrestling match, before something of the reserve in Sean's demeanour stopped him.

'Well, Sean boy, it must have been a hard time indeed. Sit down now. I want to hear about what happened – all of it.'

They were in the drawing room of a lodging house in Donnybrook. Sean sat down uneasily in one of the comfortable flowery armchairs, with Seamus Kelly grinning opposite him.

'I don't really want to talk about it, Mick,' he said.

'So you may not, but it's necessary, I promise you. I didn't go to all the trouble of getting you out of the cells of Brunswick Street and the Joy without expecting a soldier's report, you know. We need to know everything we can. Did they hurt you badly?'

For all his bluff, boisterous nature, Collins could be amazingly sensitive at times. His voice as he spoke the last words was gentle; as Sean looked up he thought he saw the shining of tears in his eyes.

He shook his head. 'Only on the first day. Kee hit me then – so did our man Davis. But it wasn't that bad. Just a lot of questions, again and again, and no time to sleep.'

Collins looked surprised and relieved. 'That's a wonder, then. Take me through it all, though, will you, Sean? From the beginning when you were arrested.'

So Sean told him. The hardest thing was to explain why he had been in Merrion Square at all; Collins had known about Catherine, even met her once or twice, but the act of going to the house was pure foolishness. Sean tried to skate over the moment when they had let Catherine see him inside Brunswick Street, but even so, Collins became thoughtful. 'They could have charged the girl along with you if they'd wanted, Sean boy,' he said. 'If they didn't, it's probably because of her father, or it could be that she told them what she knew. Either way, it's best that you're finished with her now. She's not a risk that a soldier like you should be running, especially now that you're out. If that girl looks behind her in the next few days she'll probably see six shadows, and five of them'll be working for the British and looking for you.'

Sean understood Collins's logic, but he could not bear it. Throughout the rest of the conversation only half his mind was on what he was saying; the other half replayed, again and again, the vision of Catherine entering the house in Nelson Street, the other man's arm reaching familiarly round her shoulders ...

Perhaps I should tell him, Sean thought, as his story came to an end. Mick Collins has a big heart, he'll understand. But even as he opened his mouth the front door slammed, and there were shouts and laughter in the corridor. Paddy Daly burst in, with Clancy and O'Reardan from the armoured car.

'Sure here they are now! We fetched them for you, Michael! Sean Brennan and the Browning as well!'

In the ensuing pandemonium of back-slapping, laughter, and celebration, there was no place for any sensitive consideration of Sean's feelings towards Catherine. There was a moment when Collins and Daly, each trying to lift the other off the floor in a bearhug, collapsed with him on to a delicate bow-legged wooden chair which promptly splintered into matchwood beneath them. For Sean, after the tension and silence of the prison cell, it was overpowering. After an hour or so Collins noticed this, and said: 'You look tired, young Sean. What you need is a good night's sleep. Seamus — take him up to meet the landlady. As for the rest of ye, clear off out of it now, and take care with the curfew. Can't you see this row is making your uncle Patrick and me tired? And the pair of us with state business to discuss, as well!'

The younger members of the group shuffled out, grinning widely. It was well known that Collins worked harder and made more noise than any other three men put together, and his changes of mood were equally sudden and disconcerting. When they had gone, Collins turned to business. He pulled a letter from his pocket. 'I've had another of these, Paddy,' he said. 'I thought we might.'

Daly took the letter and read it. It was handwritten this time, on embossed, printed notepaper.

> *Schloss Hessel*
> *Altenkirchen*
> *Sauerland*

Dear Mr Collins,
You will know very well that I was arrested and deported after failing to meet you in Dublin last week. Unfortunately it was impossible to fully disguise from the police my intentions, because of the guns and papers I then on my person had. I am most angry about this, since I had full trust in your organization and was most badly betrayed.

Nevertheless, the machinery we discussed is still in my possession, and I would like you to see it and if possible agree to buy. I am a man of determination and I hope that you also are such. I intend to return to Dublin and shall be as before in the Lambert Hotel resident for one

day only, on 5 February. To stay longer, I dare not. If you or your representative can meet me there and arrange a secure place for negotiation, I shall be happy to make your acquaintance. If not, I shall be disappointed in you, as indeed my countryman Captain Spindler in 1916 was.
Yours sincerely,
Manfred von Hessel.

'What do you think of it?' Collins asked.

Daly examined the letter carefully, as though the paper itself might give him some clue. He said: 'How did it come?'

'Intercepted in the post and passed to one of our boys on the North Wall. Here's the envelope.'

Daly examined that too. He grunted. 'It seems genuine enough. But the man's mad, to come back for a second try.'

'Surely.' Collins raised an eyebrow. 'And so are you and I, to think of springing young Sean out of the Joy. But it worked.'

'That's different, Mick.'

'Every action is different in some way or another. The man seems determined enough – what do you think?'

Daly scratched his head, thinking back to the two meetings he had had with Hessel; one in the Lambert Hotel, the other escorting him to Brendan Road. 'Sure he was an impressive man. Tall, hard sort of fellow. Would put up a good fight in a corner.'

'He did that, you say, when the police came to Brendan Road.'

Daly grinned. 'There was a deal of banging and cursing, to be sure. He gave us time to get away – and he spotted the peelers first, from the window.'

'So you wouldn't say he was a fraud, then?' Collins looked at him curiously, an odd half-smile on his face.

Daly considered the question. 'He didn't act like it, surely. And he had two fine German army pistols to show you. I suppose the police have got them now.'

'I suppose so.' Collins pushed a lock of loose black hair away from his forehead, and drummed his fingers thoughtfully on the chair arm. 'I've asked Dick Davis about that raid. He knew nothing about it before, and it was Kee and Radford who interrogated the German. Davis couldn't get to see him. It seems Kee's like that – he kept young Sean mostly to himself, too.'

'So?'

'So he's a good detective. It doesn't help us with Hessel. What I want to know is, do I see him, or not?'

Daly pondered. It was not often that Michael Collins seemed uncertain, or asked his advice so directly. 'I'd say no, Mick.'

'Why? We could do with the guns, couldn't we?'

'We could, and that's a fact. But look – he's a known man, the police have arrested him, and he's more or less told them his plans. They've only got to see him stepping ashore to set a man on to follow him. And there's another thing. When Davis got that paper stamped by the Intelligence man in Dublin Castle, he was boasting about some kind of "German plot". Don't you remember?'

'I do that.' Collins grinned and scratched his chin. 'You mean this fellow could be something to do with it?'

'He's German, isn't he?'

'I know. And his countrymen have given us more help than any others in our generation. Remember Spindler and the *Aud* in 1916? He brought a shipload of guns all through the British blockade. If only the lads in Kerry had been in position when he was, we could have had a rising all over the country. The man's right about that, at least.'

Collins still had that provoking half-smile on his face. Daly felt as though Collins were playing with him, teasing him, holding something back. He felt annoyed, and protective, like a father with a wilful, brilliant child. He said: 'And what if he's just a spy, trying to lead the police to you?'

Collins shrugged. 'He didn't behave like that in Brendan Road, you say. You even let him into my room with two pistols.'

'True, but ...' *I didn't even check they weren't loaded*, Daly remembered with a rush of cold sweat. 'But I don't trust a man who avoids the police so easily, and then comes back.'

'All the more credit to him, I'd say. If half our boys dared as much, we'd have had a republic years ago. Are you really telling me, Paddy Daly, that you can't arrange a meeting for me with this fellow without a G man hanging round the corner? I know Radford was there last time, but we've taken care of him.'

Daly was stung. 'Sure we can do it, Mick. I can guard him with some of our best boys, and take him for a walk halfway round the city first. That way no one would get within a mile of you.'

'Then do that.' Collins was no longer asking for advice. His mind was made up. 'It seems to me that if there's a fellow with such nerve that he can come all the way back from Germany for a second try, the least I can do is see him. And ... if you think he's a fraud, search him before you bring him in to me, will you? I only want to talk about guns, not see them demonstrated.'

Daly grinned. After the rescue of Sean, everything seemed easy to him. He himself had captured a Browning machine gun today – perhaps the German would really bring them twenty Maxims. 'All right then,' he said. 'Perhaps today was a lucky omen.'

Collins grinned back. 'Luck be damned. It's all down to brilliance, guts, and good planning. Now, where shall we meet this fellow?'

Davis was typing out a report when Kee came in. It was a result of all the paperwork he had presented Kee with early that morning, in order to ensure that Kee did not go up to the Joy too soon. It also created an impression of industriousness on his own part. Before Christmas he had thought Kee was highly impressed with him, but recently he had been less sure. He felt he was being deliberately excluded from things, and that worried him. This Ulsterman was far more paranoid than his dead colleague Radford. And after today's escape, Davis thought, Kee would be livid. Possibly he would collapse and turn in on himself, give up because of the treachery all round him. If he did that it would be a great victory. But if he did not, and carried on as he had been, he would have to go, too.

Davis felt a secret surge of excitement as Kee came in. It was like the thrill he had felt when he had said goodbye to Radford for the last time – casually, as though they would meet the next day, when all the time Davis had known they would not. It was like being the author of a play, he thought, sitting on stage and manipulating his characters while they spoke to him. Only Davis knew what had really happened today: everyone else, Kee included, was still guessing and reacting to the shock. Davis looked up, interested, to see what Kee's reaction would be.

Kee came in and sat on the desk opposite. He was disappointingly calm, Davis thought. He had expected histrionics, anger, frustration. Instead there was a grim, collected, withdrawn look to the man. He didn't even speak for a half a minute. Davis glanced down at the paper, and typed a few more words. He realized that Foster had come in too, and was standing behind him.

'Busy, Dick?' Kee said at last.

'I am that. All these reports.' Davis lifted the pile of papers from his desk, to show how many pages were left.

'You're good at paperwork. I'll say that for you.' But there was something distinctly odd about the *way* he said it. Davis looked up, and an alarm bell began to ring in his mind. Why wasn't Kee talking about Brennan's escape?

Kee took a paper from his pocket. 'Seen that before, Dick?'

Davis took it. It was the order for the release of Sean Brennan. His stomach fluttered. He passed it back. 'No.'

'You won't have seen this either.' Kee passed over a typewritten sheet, the transcript of the recorded conversations between Brennan and O'Rourke.

Davis read it slowly. When he got to the remarks about *one of his own bloody detectives* his hand began to shake. He put the paper down carefully on the typewriter.

'Brennan said this?'

'He did.'

'That's dreadful.' Davis decided to play it out to the end. Perhaps he was misinterpreting that look on Kee's face. There were a dozen detectives in G Division. *How could they possibly know it was him?* He said: 'It would explain why so many things go wrong.'

'You're right there, you bastard.' Kee stood up, his big hands clenching and unclenching at his sides. 'It would explain why so many detectives have died. Including Bill Radford.'

That was when Davis got up. He stood up quickly, and in the same movement turned for the door, drawing his arm back to punch Foster in the stomach. But the big young man was ready for him. He seized Davis's arm at the wrist, and forced the arm downwards and back so that it nearly cracked at the elbow. In a brief struggle, Davis's head got cracked against the doorpost, and Kee and Foster managed to pin his arms behind him in handcuffs. Kee shoved him roughly back into his chair. He glared at Davis, panting.

'If I had a rope, I'd hang you right now.'

'But why, for God's sake? You're mad, both of you!'

'Are we?' Kee waved the order form in Davis's face. 'You know what this is, don't you? I've just come from Captain Smythe, and he told me exactly how you got him out of his office and confirmed that the form came from his notepad. So you can forget about sitting there all sweet-faced with your typing. That's why you came to me this morning with all those details, wasn't it? To keep me busy while your friends got the bastard out!'

A sudden impulse seized him. 'I'll bet you send copies of this to your murderous friends, too, don't you?' He ripped the report out of the typewriter, and riffled through the sheets. One carbon copy, two, three, *four*. Davis groaned. In a few minutes they would search him, too. And in his jacket pocket there were three neatly folded carbons of the other reports he had typed that afternoon. There was no escaping them, now.

He looked past Kee, out of the window. It was the last one without bars which he was likely to see for a very long time.

There were no windows at all in the cellar. Just a metal grille high in the wall which, presumably, provided some ventilation. But there was not much air. There was an unpleasant, musty, stuffy smell, and Catherine began to think that the oil lamp might be using up as much oxygen as she was.

After Andrew had left she had tried hard to remove the chain from her ankle. It was not so very tight; there was no restriction on her circulation. With her boot off the chain hung down like an ugly anklet. She pointed her toe and forced the chain down, a millimetre at a time, until it was almost, almost over her heel.

Almost, but not quite. The harder she pushed it, the more the links pressed into her skin. The pain became intense. And there was still a point beyond which it simply would not go.

Infuriated, she pulled it back to where it hung loose again, massaged her aching ankle, and turned her attention to the pipe that ran along the wall. It was fastened to the wall by metal bolts every two or three feet. Perhaps they could be loosened. Certainly they were old and rusty, and looked as though they had been there for some time. But after ten minutes of ferociously pulling, tugging, and jerking the chain on it this way and that, Catherine gave up. The pipe was rock solid. It hadn't moved a fraction of an inch in any direction. She was stuck.

She sat back on the dusty, ancient sofa, and for the first time allowed herself to think of what had happened. She had been kidnapped, clearly, but why? Last night she had made love to the man, tonight he had locked her in a filthy cellar. The logic of it eluded her. She knew he was a British spy. So what? She hadn't known where his house was, until he had shown her himself. She didn't know what his plans were. She didn't even have a photograph of him to give the Volunteers so that they could identify him.

And in any case, she had not seriously intended to betray him. There had been enough killing, she wanted nothing more to do with it. Only last night she had taken him to her bed, and if he had behaved like a brute there, he had given her pleasure too. Did Andrew think she was such an unfeeling monster that she could make love to him one night, and then hand him over to be shot the next? The man must be mad to think that.

Perhaps he *was* mad.

She remembered his eyes, in that moment of appalling, ear-splitting echoes after he had fired the gun. The eyes had been hard, cold, with an expression of delight in them too, of pleasure in what he had done. That was why she had obeyed him. Because in that moment she had truly believed he would shoot her next.

She began to shiver, and wondered if she would freeze to death, starve, or suffocate from lack of air. If Andrew was really mad, perhaps he would leave her here for ever.

Then he came in with a tray of food. It was not very appetizing: fried egg, bacon burnt at the edges, a slice of bread, a cup of tea. He set it on the sofa beside her.

'I'm no great cook, I'm afraid. But it's what I could find.'

'Andrew. When are you going to set me free?'

He considered the question, standing a yard or so in front of her, out of reach. 'Maybe tomorrow evening, if all goes well.'

'You mean you're going to leave me here all night? But why, for heaven's sake?'

She thought he smiled, though his face was dark, shadowy. 'I thought you liked the unexpected.'

'I think you're mad.' It was a statement, not a challenge.

'No. Just determined. I have a job to do, and you know enough to spoil it. As soon as it's over you'll be free, I promise.'

'What are you talking about? What do I know?'

Instead of answering, he glanced round the room and shivered. 'It's cold in here. You should eat your food while it's hot. I'll bring you down some blankets and pillows, and a bucket.'

Then he was gone. She ignored the food. He returned a

few minutes later with a pile of blankets and pillows which he dumped on the floor. He put a metal bucket there too, with a newspaper in it. All the time he stayed at a distance, just out of her reach.

She asked: 'What the hell do I need a bucket for?'

'That's not a very ladylike question. I'll bring you a bowl of water in the morning, if you want to wash.'

He really does mean it, she thought. Shivering, she sipped the tea. She realized he would go again in a minute and she didn't want that. She tried to make her voice calmer, more friendly.

'Andrew. I don't understand anything at all about this. Can't you at least have the decency to explain?'

He sat down on one of the old trunks. To her anger, he seemed more amused than anything else; certainly not embarrassed.

'It's a bit of change from Killrath, isn't it? My apologies, Catherine. I'd rather keep you in a bedroom upstairs, if I could. But then you'd scream, or throw something out of the window, and people would come. So this is the only place. No one knows you're here, no one can hear you, and you can't get out. Just resign yourself to it. I'll bring you anything you need, within reason.'

'What I need is to get out of here and go to see Sean Brennan. That's what I came to Dublin for – you know that!'

He stood up. 'Yes. Even after last night all you can think of is Sean Brennan. Well, I'm sorry, Miss O'Connell-Gort, but that is exactly the reason why you have to stay here. At least you can share part of the little murderer's fate, if not his presence.' He picked up the oil lamp, and put it down within her reach, with a box of matches. 'I should blow this thing out at night; it doesn't feel full.' Then he walked to the door and went out.

'Andrew!' But she heard the sound of the bolts being rammed home, and his feet climbing the stairs. 'Come back, you pig,' she whispered to herself.

But he didn't. Gloomily, she picked up the plate of rapidly cooling food, and began to eat.

He's right. This is what it is like for Sean, she thought.

Sean dreamed about the hangman. He himself was standing on a trapdoor, his hands bound behind him, with a noose around his neck. There was a priest beside him, muttering prayers, who held out a crucifix for him to kiss. But Sean's eyes were on the hangman who had a black hood over his head, with two slits in it for his eyes. The hangman stepped back, pulled a lever, and Sean fell through the trap. There was a sudden, terrible pain, then darkness, and then *he was still in the room!* His body was hanging there but he, Sean, was somewhere above, looking down at the little group of people who busied themselves around it.

The hangman cut his body down, laid it in a coffin, and walked away, out of the prison, still wearing the black hood over his head. Sean followed him, watching. The hangman rode a bicycle at first, but no one took any special notice of him. He bought some fruit in a greengrocer's and put it in the basket on the handlebars of his bike. He went into a pub and drank a pint of porter at the bar. Sean went up close to try to see his face, but all he could see was two grey cold eyes through the slits, and a line of froth where the mouth was, as if he somehow strained the porter through the cloth. It was very important for Sean to see the face but each time he came close the hangman waved his arm and Sean felt himself brushed away, like a troublesome, invisible fly.

Then the hangman went out and this time he didn't take his bike, he took a cab. The cab went along the North Circular Road and turned left and Sean became very agitated. He knew he was tossing and turning in his bed but he couldn't wake up. The cab stopped outside the house in Nelson Street and the hangman got out, his black mask still over his face, the brown paper bag of fruit in his hand. Sean moaned and said: 'No! No! Please no!' but no one could hear him because he had no body or voice to shout with. The hangman knocked at the door and Catherine opened it. She was slim and naked and she smiled seductively at the hangman. He held out the bag of fruit and she took a red apple, and while she was biting it he bent forward and kissed her neck through his mask. Sean saw the hangman's hairy hands slide down her back and stroke her thighs, and the other apples spilled out of the bag and bounced wildly down the steps. Then Sean woke up, sweating.

There was a grey dawn light seeping through the window. There were white net curtains and a crucifix on the wall opposite with the body of Christ visible faintly against the dark wood. In the bed next to him Seamus Kelly was snoring gently. He could hear the rattle of a tram through the window, and the murmur of women's voices somewhere downstairs.

Sean realized he was free. He could get up if he liked and

walk out of the room and no one would stop him. He could have a wash in a clean basin and walk down the garden to the privy on his own and read the newspaper and help the landlady wash the dishes if he chose. He could watch the hurling on Saturday or ride out to the country with Seamus to try to snare rabbits. Maybe Collins would send him to join a country unit and attack an RIC barracks.

Before he did any of that he had to see Catherine.

He tried to clear the dream out of his mind but bits of it began to come back. There was something about the hangman, the way he had walked, that was familiar. In his dream he had had the impression that if only he could get the hood off he would see a face he would recognize.

But that was all nonsense. The truth was that he had seen Catherine visiting a house in Nelson Street. It was far too dangerous for Sean to try to contact her at the house in Merrion Square or even at the university, but if he kept an eye on the house in Nelson Street he might see her. He might even find out who the man was. He could ask the neighbours who owned the house.

What he would say if he met her he had no idea. But whatever plans Collins or Daly might have for him, this was something he had to do first.

He lay quietly for a while, watching the dawn light grow in the windows, and then he drifted off to sleep.

25

ANDREW SPENT THE night in a bedroom upstairs in Nelson Street. It was cold there too, and the sheets were damp. He remembered the heat of their bodies last night at Killrath, and wished he could think of some way of bringing Catherine upstairs to bed with him. But she would fight him every inch of the way, and probably try to escape or even kill him the moment he fell asleep. He could not risk that. Nor did he want it.

In the past two weeks at Killrath he had felt his anger, his hatred for the Fenians, slipping away. He had thought almost entirely about Catherine, and scarcely about Collins at all. He remembered that moment last night after they had made love – a minute, an hour perhaps, he had no idea – in which he had just lain there, stroking her tousled hair, watching her sleeping face in the firelight and imagining her at Ardmore. He wanted to control her, but could not conceive of seriously hurting her. And when he had woken alone this morning he had wondered for a while who he was. His hatred of the Fenians had seemed to him distant, unimportant, beside the one marvellous thing that had happened.

But in a few short minutes this morning she had told him that she loved Sean Brennan, and that she despised him for being a British spy. And Andrew's anger had returned.

Catherine had caused the anger but he did not direct it against her. He was convinced that she could be made to love him when her mind was cleared of this madness. He would have gone out and shot Sean Brennan himself had the government not arranged to have him hanged. And when Brennan was dead Catherine would forget. In the meantime, Andrew focused his rage upon Collins, the head of the IRB, the most important Fenian of them all. Collins's men had burned Ardmore and taken Catherine from him. Andrew rejoiced in his anger and tamped it down inside him, nursing it so that it would last and flare when he needed it. Tomorrow or the next day he would meet Collins and then the man would just be a lump of clothes and meat on the floor.

In the morning he took a bowl of warm water and a towel down to Catherine. He lit the oil lamp and looked at her. She lay on the sofa, hunched underneath the blankets, her button boots neatly on the concrete floor in front of her. She sat up, cold, grumpy, miserable, and rubbed her chained ankle, which was red with cold.

This was not how he had wanted to treat her, but it was only for a day – she was tough enough to survive that. Anyway, she deserved it. He put the bowl of water on the floor, and asked: 'Did you sleep well?'

'That's a damn stupid question. Of course I didn't.'

'I'm sorry about this. It's not what I wanted to happen.'

Catherine glared at him. He had an odd, irritating smile on his face. The cold had made her ache all over, right through to her bones. She said: 'I suppose it's just an accident then. You chained me up and fired a gun at me by mistake.'

'I had to. You'll be free by tonight, perhaps sooner.'

'Why not free me now?'

'I've got an appointment to keep first. And besides, I care for you. I want to keep us both out of danger.'

She summoned up all her reserves of self-control. Despite his obvious madness, he had to be better company than stone walls. If she continued to insult him, he would just go away and leave her alone for hours and hours in the cold and the dark.

'Look, Andrew,' she said. 'I think I deserve an explanation, don't you?' It sounded so reasonable, like a conversation over the supper table. But then look what those had led to, at Killrath. 'Can't you at least tell me why all this is happening?'

He sat down on the chest. 'I could. But you won't like it.'

'Please. Please tell me.'

He nodded at the bowl. 'The water's getting cold. Aren't you going to wash?'

'In a minute. Not in front of you.'

Silence. 'Strange, isn't it, that you can take all your clothes off in front of me one day, and be ashamed to wash when I'm here, the next.'

The remark frightened her, almost more than anything else that had happened so far. It was the cold, distant way he said it. And the thought that he had a gun, and controlled her food and water, and could force her to wash in front of him, do anything he wanted, if he were mad and determined enough.

She sat and watched him, and said nothing.

He said: 'I thought we should be married. I still hope we will, when this is over. I shall at least be richer then.'

'Why richer?'

'Your father promised me £10,000 to kill Michael Collins.'

'My father? You *are* mad.'

'No.' He was watching her closely. That spirit he so admired was still there, then, unbroken. He hoped, at the end of it, she would be impressed, even understand. 'I've got a document, signed by him, upstairs in a safe. That's why I've got to keep you here. Just until Collins is dead. Later today, I expect.'

'But what in the world has that got to do with me, Andrew?'

'You know things about me that might spoil it. About von Hessel, for instance.'

'Only that you helped arrest him.'

Again that irritating, distant smile. 'Not exactly. Let me tell you. As you say, you've a right to an explanation.'

He told her, simply and clearly, what had happened in Brendan Road, and what he planned to do today. He showed her his gun and the knife he had decided to strap inside his left sleeve, along his forearm so he could draw it swiftly. All the time he watched her, carefully, wondering about the effect his words would have. Searching for the slightest sign that she might care about him.

When he had finished there was a long silence.

She said: 'You're a murderer, then.'

'Call it that if you like. A soldier would be nearer the truth.'

'That's what Sean said. They're going to hang him.'

'Michael Collins'll probably do the same to me, if I get this wrong. The world is a cruel place, Catherine.'

'And you think that if I got out of here, I'd go straight to someone in Sinn Fein and tell them, just so that you'd be killed?'

He nodded. He hadn't frightened her, he saw. She was angry now, rather than afraid.

'Well, you're damn well right, Andrew Butler. I would!'

He stood up. What else could I expect, he thought. But afterwards, what will she say then? He went to the door.

'That's what I thought. You have your wash, and I'll bring your breakfast. Then you can sit here and wish me luck for the rest of the day.'

Sir Jonathan telephoned Killrath at ten o'clock. He was sitting in his office at the Viceregal Lodge, looking out of the window at the deer in Phoenix Park. Some men were spreading hay from a cart under the trees, and the deer were coming out daintily to feed. It was a pleasant sight, which he had enjoyed on more than one morning when he had nothing better to do.

Today, he knew, Andrew would be arriving at the Lambert Hotel to make contact with Collins. Later today or tomorrow he would hear the news. Either a sensational victory, with the main enemy of the state dead in the streets; or Andrew facing a similar fate; or, all too probably, another frustrating failure. With Andrew, he thought, at least that was less likely than with most men.

Certainly the government needed a success, after yesterday's fiasco at Mountjoy. He remembered the cries of the news vendors last night: 'Read all about it! Sinn Feiner breaks out of Joy! Daring escape!' This morning, as his chauffeur drove him in, he had seen a defiant perkiness in the faces on the pavement; he even thought he had heard a man on a street corner singing an instantly manufactured song – *The Ballad of Sean Brennan*, no less. That man Collins makes us all look fools, he thought. It's insufferable.

God knew what Catherine would do, when she heard. She would read about it in the newspapers this morning. But perhaps, just perhaps, the week at Killrath with Andrew Butler had begun to have the desired effect, and she would not care any more about this wretch Brennan. Sir Jonathan hoped so, but he did not think it likely. He decided to try to speak to his daughter, if he could.

He picked up the telephone and asked the operator to connect him to Killrath House.

The Lambert Hotel still made Paddy Daly nervous. Not nervous because he was afraid of anything that might happen there, but nervous because he felt out of place. The old-fashioned gentility of it, the profusion of potted plants, the frail, overdressed old ladies and gentlemen made him feel clumsy, a big Mick with hobnailed boots who was likely to break something at any moment.

But perhaps that was the attraction of it from the German gun-runner's point of view. No one would think of looking for him here. It showed a sense of discretion which was vital if they were not to be detected, especially after the police had arrested him once.

If he *was* genuine, that is.

Paddy had his doubts about that. Dick Davis's remarks about the 'German plot' had begun to prey on his mind. If I were in British intelligence, he thought, what would I do? I might try and tempt Michael Collins to a meeting, where he could be shot or arrested. Well, the meeting place was all right. He should be able to lead the German there without any detectives following. He knew most of the G men by sight, and over the past year he had become an expert at losing them in the city streets.

There was one other possibility that had occurred to him. Last time, at Brendan Road, he had let Hessel in to meet Collins with two automatic pistols in his bag. Daly had woken up sweating last night, as he realized that those pistols might not only have been loaded *but intended for use*. He had not thought of that at the time, when he had failed to check. The German had been too convincing. But then he himself had been convincing the other morning, in Mountjoy Prison: he could have shot the governor if he had wanted.

This time, the German was going to meet Collins unarmed and well escorted. Daly had brought along one of his biggest men, Brendan O'Reardan, to make sure of that. The two of them waited uncomfortably in the foyer of the Lambert Hotel.

The manager, a little bald-headed man in half-moon glasses and a pepper-and-salt suit, was dealing with an enquiry from two ladies about a laundry bill. A grey-haired woman, his wife perhaps, emerged from the office behind the counter. She peered at Daly and O'Reardan doubtfully. 'If it's a delivery, the door is round the side,' she said.

Daly took his cap off respectfully. 'No, missus, we've come to see one of your guests. A Count von Hessel, it is.'

She reached past her husband for the registration book. 'Ah yes. He arrived this morning. Wheatcroft will show you up.'

It was the same room as last time, Daly saw. Count von Hessel stood up as they were shown in. He had a newspaper in his hand, and was dressed, as before, in a well-cut, slightly crumpled English suit. He clicked his heels, bowed, and held out his hand.

'Mr Daly, you are prompt.'

'You said there was only today. This is one of my soldiers, Volunteer O'Reardan.'

Andrew bowed again. 'Mr Collins received my letter?'

'He did that. He wants to meet you.'

'Good. When, and where?'

'Now. We'll take you.'

'Right.' Andrew went to the door and put on his coat.

Kee had been up until three in the morning. He had managed to persuade the military to mount a dozen raids on suspected addresses all over the city, and he had been out on two himself. The night had been full of bright lights the roaring of engines in sleeping streets, soldiers hammering on doors with rifle butts, little clusters of surly, terrified individuals clinging to each other as their homes were ransacked, the arrests of young men, the banshee screams of their wives or mothers ...

And no Sean Brennan.

Five of the young men were still waiting in police cells for interrogation. None of them appeared to be anything but minor hangers-on of Sinn Fein. One had had a revolver in his bedroom, one a Lee Enfield beneath the floorboards. All had had some kind of subversive literature. All had been sullen and defiant: all would involve Kee in a great deal of paperwork and interrogation over the next few days. None, he was almost sure, had a connection with anything as important as the murder of Bill Radford.

And if I'm not damned careful, Kee thought, half of them will bloody well escape in the next few days.

His rage against Davis still shook him. After a hurried breakfast, he went to Brunswick Street where he spent twenty minutes on the phone pleading with an army brigadier for an increase in the number of roadblocks and army patrols throughout the day. The soldier said his men were young and tired. Kee thought: Since when has that been an excuse? Two years ago they'd have been woken every dawn by an artillery barrage. He had arranged to have another hundred copies of Brennan's prison photograph printed and distributed by midday, and then wondered which addresses he could ask the army to search tonight.

The trouble was, he didn't know. Their information just

wasn't good enough. The only people with decent information in this city were the damned Shinners.

He called for Foster, and stormed downstairs to the cells where Davis was kept.

Davis had spent a long, cold, lonely night. He had spent most of it hunched on the corner of his bed furthest from the door, his knees clasped to his chin, shivering. He had lived so long with success he had come to believe himself invincible. He could point the finger at one of his colleagues and the man would die; he could bring Michael Collins right into G Division HQ; he could plant false information that would send soldiers chasing wild geese all over the city. He could set men free from Mountjoy.

And now he had no power at all.

It was the suddenness of the collapse that had shocked him. No hint of suspicion, nothing — just immediate, total arrest. And the contempt in the eyes of Kee and Foster.

He wondered if Collins would try to get him out. They said Collins valued his men above anything — look at what he had done for Brennan. And last year he had travelled over to England to free de Valera from Lincoln Gaol, had spirited thirty over the walls of Mountjoy. But those men were Collins's colleagues in Sinn Fein, in the Volunteer movement itself. Davis had none of the companionship, the sense of working in a team, that they had. Now, even if they got him out, his use as a spy was ended. Would any of them risk their lives for a man they had hardly seen?

The cell door slammed open and Foster burst in. 'On your feet, traitor!' he yelled. 'Stand to attention, damn you!'

When he got up too slowly, Foster wrenched him upright, and a uniformed man came in to snap the handcuffs on behind his back.

'That's better. Now, along this corridor – march!'

Davis knew the routine. He had used it himself. Deny your prisoner any chance of autonomy or self-respect, wake him up throughout the night so that he doesn't sleep, break him down with continued, ferocious questioning. He could resist it, he thought. But he had never seen young Foster quite so incensed.

In the interrogation room Kee sat, Davis stood. A uniformed man brought Kee a cup of tea. Kee sipped it, and stared at him.

'You're going to hang, Davis,' Kee said.

'Why? I haven't killed anyone!'

'You killed Bill Radford. You put the finger on him.'

'You can't prove that.'

'I can. I've got a magnetic recording of Brennan saying it. And two witnesses who heard it – plus the prisoner he was speaking to. He'll testify.'

'They never said my name. I didn't kill anyone.'

'I didn't kill anyone, *sir*!' Foster bawled.

Davis glared at the younger officer in disgust, then lowered his eyes. 'I didn't kill anyone, sir.'

'Oh yes, you did,' Kee said. 'You're a nasty, stinking little Judas, Davis. How much did they pay you?'

'They didn't pay me anything, sir.'

'Don't say you did it for idealism. An independent Ireland for the bog-trotters, ruled by murder. Is that what you want?'

'Sir.'

'Listen to me, Davis.' Kee stood up. He gripped Davis's ear and jerked it suddenly upwards, so that his head was tilted sideways on his neck. 'You'll hang all right, boy, just like that, if I say so. And richly you'd deserve it. But it all depends on the charge, as you know. Now you're not a stupid man, even if you are a Judas. You know what I want. I want the men who killed my friend Bill Radford, and I'm not going to leave this city until I've found them. There were two men in Harcourt Street that night. One of them was Sean Brennan, the man who you helped escape. So what I need is the name of the other man, and an address where I can I find him. You tell me that, and I'll drop the murder charge and just put you away for the other things. Understand?'

He let go of Davis's ear and sat back on the table, looking at him. Davis stared straight ahead.

'I said, do you understand?'

'Yes.'

'Yes *what*?' Foster bawled.

'Yes sir, I understand, sir.'

'Right.' Kee spoke softly. 'I've got two charge sheets here. One charges you with being an accomplice in the murder of a senior police officer. The other charges you with passing information to criminals, but it doesn't mention murder at all. You're going before a court with one of these today. Which will it be?'

No answer. Kee spread the papers out on the desk, so that Davis could see. He took out a pen, and looked up. There was a faint sheen of sweat on Davis's forehead. Kee said: 'Don't worry about your friends. They won't ever know what you said. They won't need to. Who was the other man?'

Silence. Kee waited. 'Think of the drop, Dick. That little shed at the back of Kilmainham. You've seen it. Early morning, a few weeks from now, you walk out there all alone, they put a hood over your head, a noose tightens round your throat. And you didn't even do it, you didn't pull the trigger.' He paused. There was sweat on Davis's forehead, he could see it. Little beads of sweat that grew on the pale skin. One grew too big and trickled down towards his eyebrows, gathering others as it went.

Kee said: 'They don't care about you, Dick, you know. Nobody really cares about a traitor. A traitor has to care about himself. They'll still be snoring in their beds, and you'll be alone on that trapdoor. And you didn't even pull the trigger. *Who did it?*'

Davis's lips moved. A word came out, a whisper. 'Daly.'

'Daly? First name?'

Another whisper. 'Patrick.'

'Patrick Daly. He was the other man who killed Bill Radford?'

Davis stopped staring past Kee at the wall, and his eyes looked at him for the first time. Kee saw how wide the eyes were, haunted. Davis gave a faint, almost imperceptible nod.

Kee forced himself to smile. It was vital to engage the man's sympathy at this point, make him feel valued, not scorned. 'There. That wasn't so hard, to save your life, was it? He won't know, no one'll ever know who told me. Now, where can I find them?'

'I can't tell you that. They move around all the time. I don't know where they sleep.'

'All right. Let's try it another way. Have a look at this.' He took a notebook out of his pocket. Davis recognized it as his own. 'There are some telephone numbers in here. I can check them through the exchange but that'll take time. What are they?'

Davis looked at them. He didn't speak.

'Come on now, Dick.' Kee held up the notebook so that he could see it clearly. 'I'm a man of my word, you know that. But I can only keep a promise for the whole bargain, not half of it. It's lonely on that dawn walk.' He pointed to the number at the top of the list. 'Let's take that one first.'

Davis licked his lips. His mouth felt dry, parched. There was an empty, aching feeling in his stomach. He thought of the man he had seen hung, standing straight to attention like this, his hands bound behind him, the black hood over his head. He remembered the obscenely stretched neck, the empty bowels afterwards.

He looked at the telephone number again, and began to talk.

Catherine had never been good at sitting still. Even as a student, when she was reading, she would twist a strand of hair around her finger, chew her pencil, or tap it on the table. Often she would get up and walk around with the book in her hands, trying to remember what she had read. She was a born fidget.

Now she had no books and nowhere to go. She moved around on the sofa, trying to find a more comfortable position, but with the chain on her ankle only a limited number were possible. She had read the newspaper but it was a month old, it told her nothing about Sean. She had used the bucket and it stank, so she had moved it as far as she could from where she sat. Her dirty plate was on the floor too, together with a bottle of water and a cup.

Apart from that there was nothing useful except some matches and the oil lamp, which he had topped up and relit. The lamp was both a curse and a blessing. It stood on the floor in front of her, spluttering and muttering sometimes as its flame threatened to go out. It gave out a yellowish light and a faint hint of warmth. But it also smoked, used up air, and gave her a headache.

Halfway through the morning she blew it out. At first the darkness was a relief. She wrapped herself in her coat and the blankets and lay there, waiting for her eyes to accustom themselves to the gloom. There was just a faint suggestion, a hint of grey light which seeped through the grille on the opposite wall. It must provide some ventilation, then, she thought, some link with the outside world. She listened very hard and she could hear tiny, distant noises, like those of small people far away. She tried to identify them: feet on the pavement, a cart maybe, pulled by a horse, then another, then what might have been a car. And then, for long periods, nothing at all.

Then there was a much bigger sound. A scrabbling, scratching sound, from the wall behind her. The sound was enormous. There's someone in here, she thought, a man, a dog, a cat — *what the hell is it?* She had the box of matches in her hand; quickly she struck one, fumbled with the oil lamp, lit it, held it up.

A rat stared back at her.

It was quite a big rat, about a foot long, with a scaly tail twice that length behind it. Its eyes reflected the yellow flame of the lamp and its whiskers twitched. It sniffed at her nervously and bared its teeth. Then it resumed its exploration of her lavatory bucket.

'Oh, my God,' Catherine groaned. She put the lamp down on the sofa, picked up one of her boots, and flung it at the creature. The boot struck the rat's back, and sailed away into the corner. The rat, startled, ran behind the sofa and disappeared. Catherine peered over the back of the sofa and saw the tip of its tail vanishing down a hole in the wall.

She groaned again. No rat. No boot either.

This won't do, she told herself. I've got to get out of here, I can't stand it. She tugged angrily at the chain, aggravating the sore places it had made on her ankle. I'm lucky the bloody rat didn't come in and eat my toes in the night. Anyway I've got to get out to go and see Sean before he dies.

'Sean!' she yelled. '*Sean! SEAAAN!*'

The scream echoed back at her in the cellar, making her headache worse. As the echoes died away, she listened, wondering if it had reached the ears of the distant people pattering on the pavement beyond the grille. At first she could not hear the footsteps at all, the sounds were so tiny in comparison. Then she heard them. There was no change, no evidence of interest in what was going on below the street. Why should there be? If their sounds were almost inaudible to her, they would never hear her, with the busy noise of the city street all around them. Andrew had fired a gun in here, confident that no one would hear it.

She looked at the chain again. If only he had fastened the padlock one link further down, she could have managed it. If she tried very hard she could almost slip it over her heel, but not quite. Neither the chain nor her bones would give; the only thing that could be pressured was her skin and flesh, and after four efforts that was bruised and swollen now. It couldn't be done.

The only thing was to cut the chain, or undo the lock.

She couldn't cut the chain. But she might pick the lock.

That was what burglars did, wasn't it? They were experts at it – there was a magician called Houdini who could pick any lock in a few seconds. As soon as the idea came to her she cursed herself for not thinking of it sooner. She could have done it last night; she could have lain in wait for Andrew when he came down and smashed him over the head with something.

Never mind that. How was it done?

She examined the padlock and saw a slot with two indentations in, to fit the key. Inside there must be more ridges and grooves and – what were they called? Tumblers, was it? Wheels? Anyway, things that moved. The key must push them back somehow, like the bars that stuck out of a lock in a door, and then the hasp of the padlock could be pulled out smoothly and she would be free.

Since she had no key she had to slide something into that slot and jiggle it about. What? She looked around and saw the knife and fork on the floor from her breakfast. She picked them up and tried. The knife blade was too wide; the tines of the fork might just go in if there weren't four of them. She bent one of the tines back by pressing it on the floor and tried. It went in, for about an eighth of an inch, and then . . . stuck.

That was no good. She tugged it out and threw it away. What else? A wire, a pin. She ran her hands through her hair but it was smooth and clear. No hairpins. No hatpin either, she hadn't worn a hat. She searched her coat pockets: handkerchief, train ticket, purse – nothing useful in the purse. There must be something.

She remembered the brooch on the front of her dress.

She unfastened it. It was a big, heavy brooch of an Irish queen, Maeve, riding horseback. Her mother had given it to her long ago. There was a pin in the back about two inches long.

She drew her ankle up to her knee, and bent to work.

After half an hour she had got nowhere. Nothing had moved inside the lock. Her back and legs ached, and her head throbbed when she moved it. She sat back for a rest, exhausted.

But there was nothing else to do. After a minute or two she moved the oil lamp closer, lifted her ankle, and began again.

'Yesterday morning?' Sir Jonathan said.

Over the telephone, David Ferguson's distant voice answered: 'Yes, sir. By the morning train. I drove them to the station.'

'Good Lord. I knew Major Butler was coming back, but I thought Catherine would stay on. It's very strange.'

'Yes, sir. It seemed a rather sudden decision. But I expect she'll explain it when she sees you. Weren't you home last night?'

'Well, I ... no, of course I wasn't. Bit of a flap on here with escaped Sinn Feiners, I'm afraid. We'll catch the beggars, though, don't worry.'

'Glad to hear it, sir.'

'Yes. I say, David. Just one thing.'

'Yes, sir?'

Sir Jonathan cleared his throat. 'Well, when Miss Catherine was down there, did you happen to get any impression whether she was, well, fond of Major Butler at all? I mean, you know, did they spend a lot of time together, that sort of thing?'

The distant voice sounded hesitant. 'It's hard for me to say, sir, really. They certainly rode out together most days and talked. It's hard to say with Miss Catherine. She's very forceful, you know, sir. And I wasn't with them a great deal myself.'

'All right. Thanks, David. I'll be in touch.'

Sir Jonathan put the phone down. He shouldn't have asked, really: it would show everyone what he was thinking. It didn't sound very hopeful, but it was a good sign that they had spent *some* time with each other. And they must have been on fairly good terms, to take the train back together.

But where on earth was Catherine now?

He had covered up quickly to David, but in fact Sir Jonathan *had* been in Merrion Square last night. He had come home late, true, but he had seen his butler last night and this morning. It was inconceivable that the man would not have said something about Catherine's surprise arrival, if she had been there. So she had come back to Dublin with Andrew, but she hadn't come home.

Sir Jonathan thought he ought to be appalled by this, but in fact he was not. By God, I ought to be grateful, Sir Jonathan thought. He's probably taken her to a hotel, or to that house of his, wherever it is. Good luck to you, young man. Maybe you can tame her when I could not.

The only thing that puzzled him was that Andrew should do this at the very moment when he was planning his attack on Collins. It was a hell of a risk, surely, to involve oneself in a love affair right in the middle of an operation like that. Andrew must have realized by now that the girl had sympathies with Sinn Fein. Or had he managed to cure her of that, too? he wondered.

If he has, he's a son-in-law after my own heart, he thought. He picked up the pile of intelligence reports from last night, and began to work his way through them, whistling tunelessly through his teeth. He felt more optimistic than he had done for months.

Sean woke again because there was water trickling down his face. At first it came into his dreams – he was walking in the country when it began to rain, and then a waterfall poured over his head. But a moment later he woke up, and saw Michael Collins standing above him, squeezing drops of water out of a flannel.

'Ah, is himself alive then? I was beginning to wonder, after all that high living at the King's expense. As was the good widow Casey downstairs. Will you take a look at that clock, now?'

Sean glanced at the clock on his bedside, and saw it was half past nine. 'Oh,' he grunted. It didn't seem to matter to him.

'Oh, is it?' Collins flung the wet flannel in his face and laughed. 'The wicked among us have had our breakfast and put in an hour's work already. Not that I want you to do that, Sean, but you could at least eat what the good widow's prepared before it rots.'

'Yes, right.' Sean had never been overfond of the big man's practical jokes. But he was hardly in a position to complain. He swung his legs out of bed. 'What are the orders for today?'

'For you, just keep your face out of sight. The army have been waking up half the city looking for you in the night. Don't go out at all if you don't need to. Paddy says his nerves won't stand two rescues in the same week.'

'I'll do that.' Sean pulled off his shirt, poured some water from a ewer into a bowl, and began to wash. Then he turned round and said: 'And thanks, Mr Collins. I should have said that last night. I didn't think I'd ever see daylight again.'

Collins ruffled his hair and punched him playfully on the chin. 'Did you think we'd forget you? This country won't have any more lonely martyrs, if I can help it.'

Then he was gone. Sean dressed, went down to breakfast, and began to think of Catherine.

Stay out of sight, Collins had said. The whole city is looking for you. If Sean went out and got himself captured again it would be an insult to the others who had risked their lives to set him free. And anyway Catherine didn't want him, she had taken up with another man. To go looking for her would be a waste of time. Pure emotional self-indulgence.

Seamus Kelly was in the same house. After breakfast

they sat by the fire in the living room, reading the newspaper accounts of Sean's escape. After a while Sean asked: 'What else has been happening while I've been in? Any new operations planned?'

'Not that I know of,' Kelly said. 'The British are still cut up about the death of the police commissioner. They'll be hopping mad now you've escaped. Paddy was hoping to have another crack at Lord French, but the old fool's more or less imprisoned himself in the Viceregal Lodge since Ashtown. And I heard him talking to Collins about that German officer again over breakfast. They're going to meet him in Clancy's later today, they said.'

Sean nodded. Somehow it all seemed a little distant to him. He would get back into it, of course, but just now, sitting here by the fire, he found his mind wandering. The flames reminded him of the fires in the room in the tenement. Catherine's skin had been a warm, rose colour then, as she knelt before the blaze. Did she look the same for the man in Nelson Street, he wondered; did she turn and smile at him too, and lay her head along his thigh?

There was something about that man. In his dream Sean had seen him as the hangman, but of course he was not that. He tried to remember what the man had looked like in that brief glimpse in Nelson Street. Sean had been looking at Catherine, but he had a vague impression of a tall figure in a long trenchcoat, with an upright, confident military bearing. A man of her own class. The sort of man her father might choose.

But there was something more to it than that. Sean imagined the man laughing at him, knowing he was there. Why? He had never seen Sean before. Yet there was something familiar about him, something he ought to remember. Sean had the feeling that if only the man had turned round he would have recognized the face. But in his own mind he could not picture what the face should be.

Anyway, what did it matter? He sighed, got up and began to pace the room. It was bigger than his cell, much, but the table and chairs cluttered it. Kelly looked up. 'Still feel trapped?'

Sean nodded. 'I am that. You get to wondering what it's like to walk the streets, when you're shut up in there.'

'I can believe it. But the streets are full of soldiers with your photo, Mick says.'

'If they were up all night, they'll be back in barracks sleeping, won't they?'

'Maybe. I don't know. You're not to risk it. Orders.'

Sean sat down again, and picked up a paper. He had read most of it already. He wondered what the house in Nelson Street was like. There were back alleys around there, he might be able to break in. Or he could just knock on the front door, and she would open it, and he would say: 'Hello, Catherine.'

He got up and went to his room. Paddy Daly had given him a Webley revolver last night. It was not a gun he was used to. He practised loading it, spinning the rounds in the chamber, cocking it, easing the hammer gently down again. Then he put it in his pocket, walked downstairs, and went down the garden to the privy.

When he had used the privy he unlatched the door at the end of the garden and walked through into the alley. Pulling his cap down low over his eyes, he set off briskly for Nelson Street.

Just as Catherine was a fidget, she was also impatient. Normally if she could not master a task quickly, she would leave it and go on to something else. She might come back and try again and again, but she would not sit doggedly for hours. That was not her way. She needed new interests all the time.

In the cellar, there was nothing new or interesting at all. Once the rat came back, and she crept towards it slowly and stabbed at it with the table knife. But the creature was too quick for her, and scurried away down its hole again. She spent a few minutes thinking how she might trap it next time, but could work out nothing practical. She used the bucket once, hating the squalor of it. She listened for the street noises, but there was no change there. Then she returned to the padlock.

Once or twice, she had felt something move inside it. But if the hasp was a little bit looser, it was so little as to be almost imperceptible. The second time something moved, she was terrified that she might have moved the first thing back again. If Houdini can do this sort of thing in a few seconds, he must be a genius, she thought. But then he probably understands what's inside the damn locks. Catherine hadn't got a clue.

Her leg had pins and needles from being stuck for so long in the same position, and her head throbbed unmercifully from the fumes of the oil lamp. A little longer, she told herself. Just a little longer, then I'll give up for a while and have a rest.

A third thing moved. There was a definite click, and she could feel, now, a smooth line inside the lock where there had been resistance before. She tugged eagerly at the hasp. It jiggled. It was definitely looser. But it did not come out.

She took a deep breath. Patience, she told herself. Keep plugging on. She poured herself half a cup of water from the bottle Andrew had left her, and sipped it appreciatively, in quiet celebration. Then she stretched her legs, to get rid of the pins and needles, and knocked the oil lamp over.

She had stood it just beside her on the floor in front of the sofa, where it would give her the best light. The sofa had a ragged, tattered cover, which hung down to the floor in places, and when she knocked the light over the top came off, and oil spilt all over the sofa cover. Catherine didn't see this, because the lamp had gone out, and it was immediately dark. She cursed, and struck a match to relight it.

The fumes from the hot oil caught fire.

Catherine screamed and leapt back, shielding her face with her hands. There was a sizzling, crackling sound from above her forehead, and she beat at her hair frantically with her hands to put out the flames. The sound stopped, but the sofa was blazing furiously. She hobbled away from it, as far along the cellar wall as the chain would allow her to go, but the sudden heat was nearly roasting her. The flames had not reached the end of the sofa yet, and she pushed at it, screaming and heaving to get it as far away from her as possible, out into the middle of the cellar.

She retreated to the end of the chain and thought: If I'm not burnt alive I'll be suffocated.

The sofa was burning steadily now, and the room was

filling with smoke. She tugged frantically at the hasp of the padlock, but although it was loose it did not move. Then she saw the brooch lying on the floor in front of her. She snatched it up.

I've got to do it, she thought. There's only a few minutes now and I've *got* to do it. Keep cool. Think like Houdini. Remember what the lock feels like inside.

She sat down cross-legged on the floor, choking in the smoke, and slipped the pin of the brooch carefully inside the lock.

Andrew, Daly and O'Reardan walked briskly through the busy streets. Daly walked by his side, O'Reardan a little behind and to the other side, Andrew noted. Clearly O'Reardan, the big man, was a bodyguard, there to make sure Andrew gave no trouble. A quick step to the rear, Andrew thought, a jab in his throat, a knife in his gut, and he'll have failed in that task.

But there was no call for anything like that yet. They walked down Henry Street, by the side of the General Post Office, and on to Mary Street. There were no soldiers but twice they passed tall, magnificently uniformed constables of the DMP without trouble; indeed, on the second occasion Andrew thought he saw the constable give Daly a brief nod, almost of recognition. And they say this is a civil matter that can be dealt with by the police, he thought.

They stopped outside an unremarkable shop door in Mary Street. A sign in the window said *Clancy's Joiners and Decorators*. Daly opened the door, a bell rang, and they stepped inside.

The room was largely bare, with a counter opposite th

door. Behind the counter sat a young woman, typing. There were certificates on the walls, testifying to the competence of various craftsmen, and a couple of upright chairs for customers to sit on.

The young woman glanced at Daly, unsurprised.

'Is Mick here yet?' Daly asked.

She nodded. 'Upstairs.'

'Good.' Daly turned to Andrew. 'That's all in order, then, Mr Hessel. But first it's my duty to make sure that visitors don't go armed into the office of the Finance Minister. So would you just raise your hands while I go through your pockets, please?'

Andrew glanced behind him at O'Reardan. To his dismay, he saw that the big man had already taken an automatic out of his pocket, and was pointing it calmly straight at him.

'Clancy's Joiners and Decorators,' Kee said. He sat at the table, notebook in hand, looking at Davis who stood opposite him. Davis looked pale, slumped, broken. He was still sweating but there was no resistance left. He answered questions freely in a low, hoarse whisper. The telephone number of Clancy's was the last one on the list in his notebook.

Kee asked: 'What sort of a place is that?'

'It's an office. They have planning meetings there, keep intelligence records, that sort of thing.'

'Are there people there every day?'

'During office hours, yes. It's a place you can phone.'

'Did you phone it, Dick?'

'Sometimes. Once or twice perhaps.'

'What for?'

'To tell them. Details of a raid, perhaps. Before we came.'

Kee controlled his disgust. This information was the best he had had since he came to Dublin. 'Does Collins go there?'

A slight hesitation, quickly overcome. 'Sometimes.'

'And Daly? Brennan?'

'They might do. I don't know.'

Davis was not looking at him. His eyes were fixed on the tabletop in front of him. Kee had seldom seen a man collapse so fast. He said: 'Have you been there yourself?'

Davis sighed, and nodded dully. 'Once.'

'One last question, Dick. Then you can go to your cell and sleep. Tell me about Clancy's. What's the place like inside?'

Sean took a tram to Dorset Street. It was true, the streets were unusually full of soldiers. Twice he saw a section of Tommies standing some young men up against a wall, while an officer went through their pockets and examined their papers. Women and boys stood at a safe distance, catcalling or muttering amongst themselves. It was possible the soldiers might stop a tram and search everyone on that, Sean knew, but less likely. If they did, he would just have to shoot and make a break for it. If he was caught after slipping out like this he wouldn't deserve to be rescued again. Better to die in a blaze of glory.

There were no soldiers in Dorset Street where he got out. He crossed the road and walked quickly down Eccles Street to Nelson Street. It was quite busy – there were women pushing prams, others scrubbing their doorsteps or gossiping, and a number of carts, cars and bicycles. Not rich dwellings, but the sort of place a moderately prosperous doctor or lawyer might live in.

Number 16 looked quiet, deserted. He went up the steps and rang the bell. It echoed away inside discouragingly. No one came. He rang again, then, looking round to see no one was watching, leaned forward and surreptitiously tried the door. It was locked.

This is a waste of time, he thought. There's no one here anyway, and even if there was, what would I say? But if I could get inside I could sit and wait for her. At least it would be safer than wandering around the streets.

He went down the steps and walked slowly away down the road. A few houses further on there was a gap in the terrace, leading to some small mean dwellings behind the larger ones. He went down it, and saw an alley to his left, behind the houses in Nelson Street. He walked along it, counting the houses back again as he went.

The smoke from the burning sofa was everywhere. It was thick and black and it scoured the back of her throat so that she coughed nonstop and wanted to be sick. She was dripping with sweat and coughing and despite the lurid flashes of light from the flames it was so dark that she couldn't even see the bloody lock. But she had the pin of the brooch in the keyhole and even when she was coughing her fingers moved it back and forth, searching, more quickly and desperately than ever before.

She felt as if her body were breaking up. Her lungs were choking and her eyes were streaming and her head was bursting but her fingers, they would never give up. They would go on picking and worrying at the lock when the rest of her was dead, like a chicken's feet carrying its headless body round and round a yard.

Something moved in the lock. Her fingers tugged at the hasp. It came loose.

The fingers fumbled, not knowing what to do next. She had not planned further and now her brain was too full of the futile, rasping struggle for breath. It sent no messages. Her fingers were on their own.

They pulled the hasp of the padlock free of the chain and dropped it. The chain slipped off her ankle. She moved her foot.

A message got through to her brain. She began to crawl, coughing and choking, across the floor. She kept her head down below the worst of the smoke because she did not have the strength to stand up. She was breathing in great, shuddering gasps, again and again, faster and faster. Each breath brought in less and less air and more and more smoke, so her need became greater and her strength ebbed. She reached the door.

Of course it was locked.

She got up on her knees and tugged at the handle and nothing happened. She had not thought this far. She had no plans. She had thought if she ever got the chain off there would be time to plan out the next stage. Now there was no time at all.

She rattled the door handle and then smashed both her fists against the door and screamed. There were no words to the scream and not much sound either because she had no breath and halfway through it ended in a fit of coughing and her lungs ached and her head was bursting so she gasped and drew in more smoke.

Her fists hammered at the door all by themselves for a few seconds more. Then she slumped down at the foot of the door where there was a little, a very little draught of air that came in between the foot of the door and the floor.

Each house seemed to have a different-sized wall behind it, with its own individual gate. Some were old, battered wooden ones, falling off their hinges, one or two were brightly painted, one or two were wrought iron.

The back yard of number 16 was fairly primitive. There was an unpainted wooden door bolted on the inside, and a six-foot-high brick wall. As Sean tried the door, a man opened the door of a yard a little further on. Sean moved away from the door. The man went back into his yard, and came out wheeling a bicycle. He got on it and cycled away to the far end of the alley.

Sean took a quick run at the wall, got his forearms on to the top, swung himself over, and dropped down the far side.

No one there. Two dustbins, a shed for an outside privy and another for coal, a rusty old bicycle, a window and a door. No one was looking out of the window. He tried the door. It was locked.

He glanced quickly up at the backs of the houses on either side. Some windows overlooked the yard but if he stood close up against the door like this people would have to lean out quite a way to see him. He couldn't see anyone watching at the moment.

I've got a right, he thought. I've got a right to know what

sort of a man he is. He stood back from the door and kicked it, hard, with his hobnailed boot, just beside the door handle. The door shuddered, but did not open. He kicked it again, afraid of the attention the noise might attract. This time something gave. The lock rattled, but still held.

The third kick burst it.

He stepped into the kitchen. He shut the door and stood quite still, listening. His hand fingered the revolver in his pocket. A man he could cope with; a woman, a cook or maid, coming in flustered with a dustpan and brush in her hand, would be harder to manage.

There was no sound at all.

He stepped through the scullery into the hall. There were doors on each side. It was very quiet, dusty, with an empty feel to it. The hat and coat stand was bare. There were no umbrellas, no shoes, no letters or newspapers. He caught sight of himself in a mirror. A young man in a cloth cap, wide-eyed, scowling, nervous, with his right hand in a bulging coat pocket. A burglar, certainly. If I meet anyone, that's what they're bound to think.

There was a smell of smoke, as though someone might be lighting a fire somewhere and the chimney wasn't drawing. If there was a fire, someone must be here.

If someone was here, sooner or later they would make a sound.

He waited, listening. Then he heard it.

It was not the sort of sound he expected. It sounded like a scream almost, as if someone were in pain or ill. And there was a muffled banging.

It came from behind a door to his left. When he tried the

door it was locked, but there was a key on the wall beside it. When he opened the door, there was a stairway leading down, and smoke floated out. The banging came again briefly, then stopped.

Sean waved his arms in front of his face to clear the smoke, and went down the steps. He unbolted the door at the bottom.

To be certain of success, Kee thought, I'll need the army.

He sat at his desk, sipping a cup of coffee, and thought of the detectives he could call up from G Division.

Except for Foster, Kee did not think he trusted any of them. Those whom he had seen had taken the news of Davis's arrest with shock, apparent concern and, most worrying of all, silence. Perhaps if he called a meeting now and told them they were going to raid Clancy's, the whole bunch of them would walk out in a block and phone Collins. And it would only take one.

Kee decided to use the army instead. He picked up the phone and rang Dublin Castle.

He was put through to Colonel Sir Jonathan O'Connell-Gort.

Even *his* daughter is a blasted Sinn Feiner, Kee thought. The whole town is riddled with them, like maggots in a mouldy cheese.

Nonetheless, Sir Jonathan, it appeared, was duty coordinating officer for the day, and Kee had no actual doubts about the man's loyalty. He explained what he wanted. Sir Jonathan responded briskly enough; in fact he sounded unusually cheerful.

'Right-ho, old chap. I'll get on to it right away. Usual

thing – lorries front and back, you say, street cordoned off, and a section to go in with you?'

'Yes, sir. And I don't want any new recruits, either. The place could be empty but if my information's right we might find half a dozen of them and they'll be shooting to avoid arrest.'

'I'll see to it.' Sir Jonathan seemed to hesitate as though a thought might have crossed his mind. But all he said was: 'Sounds like an interesting show. I'll try to get down there myself if you like, Inspector, make extra sure there are no cock-ups, what?'

Cock-ups by whom? Kee wondered. But the man sounded too cheerful to be intentionally malicious, and Kee had no more objection to him than to any other army officer. They agreed a time and an assembly point, and then Kee put the phone down, yawned, and rasped his hand across his bristly chin.

Perhaps I should smarten myself up, he thought. Can't be showing Davis's murderous friends any disrespect now, can we?

He lurched to his feet and strode down the corridor to the washroom, in search of hot water and a razor.

Sean was panicking. He wished desperately that he had studied the medical books more closely and that he could remember what to do, because he thought she was dying. And he blamed himself because he had nearly left her down there for good.

When he had opened the door a vast cloud of black choking smoke had poured out, and he had staggered backwards up the stairs, coughing wildly. He had already reached the door at the top and was just about to close it to keep the horrible smoke down there, when he had remembered the scream and the banging.

Even then he had retreated into the hall to suck in clean air before he thought of returning. Then he had taken off his jacket, wrapped it round his head, and plunged back down the steps.

He had trodden on the body, not seen it.

He had felt something soft, moving feebly under his boot. He had picked it up and lugged it up the stairs, letting the legs bang all the way on the steps, and only when he had got it out and into the now smoke-filled hall had he looked and seen who it was.

She had been lying slumped, face down on the floor. She was filthy, some of her hair seemed to be burnt, and her face was blackened by the smoke, but there was no doubt.

He opened one of the doors off the hall, dragged her in there, and flung the windows open. Then he turned her over and wondered if she would live, and what he would do if she did not.

She was breathing in a very strange way — great snoring gulps one minute, and then nothing at all, feebly, the next. He felt for the arterial pulse in her throat. Not steady, but something there, anyway. He tilted her head back, opened her mouth and felt inside with his finger to make sure her throat wasn't blocked.

She gagged, opened her eyes, and saw him.

He took his fingers out. She closed her eyes, took another great shuddering breath, opened them again, and sat up.

'Sean!' she said. '*Sean?*'

'Yes,' he said. 'It's me.'

'Oh, my God, we've got to get out of this place! It's on fire, Sean – quick, it's on fire!'

He looked round. There was not a lot of smoke in this room, and he could see no sign of flames coming into the hall. What worried him more was the thought that the smoke, blowing out of the windows, would attract attention. But far more important was the fact that he was here, with her, and she was alive.

He said: 'No rush, it's all right for a minute or two. Was there anyone else down there with you?'

'No. No, I was alone.' She gathered her wits. Maybe the sofa had not set light to anything else yet. 'Sean. Why are you here?'

'I came to look for you.'

'But – you're in prison! You're going to hang!'

'Not if I can help it.'

That wide, boyish grin, the smooth face, the stick-out ears – he was here, he was really here! She put her hand on his cheek to prove it. 'But how? How did you get out?'

'It's the long story you want, is it? I think we may have to save that, Caitlin. We'll be getting ourselves an audience.'

He heard some shouts, and glanced outside. A group of boys were staring at the smoke floating out of the window and a woman was coming down the steps of the house opposite.

'Look,' he said. 'I came to find you, not the whole street. Where can we go?'

'I don't care where, but I want to get out of this house,' she said. 'He might come back, any time!'

'Who?'

'Andrew, of course. Sean, *you don't know?*' She stared at him.

Sean said, carefully: 'I saw you come in here with a man. Yesterday. I didn't know who it was.'

'It was Andrew Butler. He locked me down there, the pig.' She was struggling to make sense of Sean's presence. 'Sean. Why are you here if you didn't know that?'

'Just – I had to see you. Mick Collins would thrash me if he knew.'

The mention of Collins triggered something else in her mind, but someone was hammering at the door. There were too many impressions crowding in on her. She said: 'I don't want to see these people. They may be friends of his. Is there a back way?'

'It's how I came in.' He took her hand, led her out through the smoking hall, through the kitchen, and across the back yard to the door, which he unbolted. They were halfway down the alleyway before he noticed she had no boots on. One silk stocking was in shreds, and the ankle was grazed. 'Where are your boots?'

'I threw them at a rat.' She grinned at him, her face all smudged with smoke, part of her hair crinkly where it had been burnt. My God, he thought. Mick Collins tells me to stay out of sight and here I am walking through the city with a barefoot girl in black make-up. He didn't care. *She wanted to come with him.* He didn't know why yet but it was more than he had ever expected.

He said: 'I could lend you my boots.'

They looked down together at the big, hobnailed boots and laughed. He put his arms round her and kissed her, very gently, nervously on the lips, and she didn't move away. Shakily, she stood on tiptoe and touched his nose with hers, and it was like that first moment in the tenement, the time when she had been quite naked and he had held her against his shaggy, rough outdoor clothes. He said: 'I came to say I was sorry, Cathy.'

'For what?'

'For all of it. I shouldn't have sent you away.'

Over her shoulder he saw a group of boys in long trousers and noisy boots clattering by. One looked at him curiously and said: 'There's a fire in a house in Nelson Street, mister. Our Seamus has gone for the peelers. Will you help us put it out?'

'I'll be right there,' Sean said. Then when they had gone he asked: 'How are you going to get around town without boots?'

She shrugged. 'The beggars do it.'

They hurried away, through the maze of small, one-storey houses and down an alley into Blessington Street, and then down Mountjoy Street to a square with a church in it and a school on one corner. Sean had an idea. He turned left. 'If we cross Dorset Street we can go to Parnell Square,' he said. 'At least you can get a wash there, and maybe find something for your feet.'

'That would be nice,' she said.

Then she saw the soldiers.

Andrew raised his hands and stood quietly. A small part of his mind wondered what a genuine customer might think he walked into Clancy's Joiners and Decorators now and saw O'Reardan lounging against the wall with his Mauser in his hand, Daly ransacking Andrew's pockets, and th secretary, unconcerned, feeding another sheet of paper into her typewriter behind the counter. Sorry sir, be with you in a moment.

Daly found the automatic in his coat pocket and took it out. 'You won't be needing that for negotiation, will you, Mr Hessel?'

'I need it for protection,' Andrew snapped. 'If you remember, last time the police came. I do not wish to be arrested again!'

'I'll keep it for you.' Daly slipped it into his own pocket and stood back. 'All right. You can put your hands down now.'

Andrew did so, still looking aggrieved, hiding the sigh of satisfaction that might give him away. Just a search of the pockets and a quick pat under the arms – Daly had not thought to feel along the insides of his arms, under the sleeve of his jacket. Without the gun things would be a little harder, but not impossible. If he struck first he would always be invincible. Andrew felt his anger rise, the adrenalin begin to flow as it always did before combat. Time had begun to slow down for him. He noticed everything in great detail: the way Daly turned to the door beside the counter, the brief smile the secretary gave him, the shrug with which O'Reardan uncocked his pistol and pushed on the safety catch before putting it back into his pocket.

'Through here, Mr Hessel. Mr Collins has an office upstairs.'

The soldiers were on Dorset Street, directly in between Catherine and Sean and Parnell Square. Two of them were searching some young men who had their hands raised high against a wall while other soldiers covered them with rifles. Passers-by glanced at the scene and hurried on, glad not to be troubled themselves.

Catherine took Sean's arm and turned him gently round.

'Not that way,' she said. 'The soldiers are bound to notice me like this, and then they'll look at you.'

They hurried out of sight behind the school, where the children were just coming out to play, the boys in their knee-length trousers and little jackets, the girls in long dresses and petticoats. Catherine gripped Sean's arm tightly. 'Oh God, Sean, they won't catch you again, will they?

He patted his pocket. 'Not this time, Caitlin, not alive.'

She remembered the gun Andrew had fired in the cellar. And the bombs at Ashtown and the policeman Sean had killed, half his face blown away by a bullet from a gun in that same pocket. 'For God's sake, it's all violence and killing everywhere. Why can't it stop?'

She saw him watching her quietly and thought: Such a lovely, boyish face. Why does it freeze like stone sometimes? Is this how he looked when he shot the policeman?

Sean said: 'I thought you supported the movement, at least.'

'I do. I did anyway, you know that. But I don't want you caught by men like him. I'm sick of it — I want it to end now.'

'Men like who?'

'Butler. The man who chained me in the cellar.'

'Chained you? Cathy, what do you mean?'

Catherine was dazed. She realized that things had happened so fast she had explained nothing to Sean yet. 'He chained me in the cellar so I couldn't get out. Oh, heavens, Sean, I should have told you. He's gone out to kill Collins today.'

'Cathy, I don't understand a word.' He gripped her shoulders, held her against the playground wall. 'What is all this about? Tell me.'

She glanced quickly around the square, checking that they were out of sight of the soldiers. They were.

She told him.

To Sean it was as though the man he had seen in his dreams had become real and was stalking the city. The hangman, the man with the unseen face. He had nearly killed Catherine, he was out to murder Michael Collins. And he was posing as a German, von Hessel. He remembered the face, now, briefly. Outside the Lambert Hotel – the man he had lost. What had Kelly said this morning about the German? Collins was meeting him today, somewhere.

Where? Kelly had said a place, surely.

Clancy's.

'Come on.' He took Catherine's hand and began to run, away towards Dominick Street. 'We've got to find a phone, quickly.'

Or, failing that, he realized, Clancy's itself was only ten minutes' walk. Less if they ran.

As he went through the door, Andrew noticed that O'Reardan stayed behind. O'Reardan would be a problem, then, if Andrew came down this way. But the man looked stolid, slow-thinking. When I come down I'll be moving too fast for him, Andrew thought. Behind the door were two steps down into a short passageway, then a staircase and a corridor, leading out the back, no doubt, with two bicycles parked in it. He glanced along it swiftly before following Daly up the stairs.

Time was moving very slowly and everything was very clear in his mind. Collins would be in a room at the top of the stairs. If Daly stayed outside the room and Collins was alone he could kill him immediately, with a swift thrust of the knife to the throat. If Daly came in or Collins was not alone then it would take a minute or so longer. He would have to think about movements and distances and the positions of all the people in the room, and he would begin the negotiation about the machine guns. He had a specification of the Maxim gun in his pocket – details of its range, its weight, its cooling system, the tripod, the estimated penetration of bullets at various distances – all in diagrams, with the text in German. He would show it to Collins, and Collins would say he did not understand the German. Andrew would move to his side to translate whip the knife from his sleeve, and plunge it into Collins' throat. Swift. Easy. A jab in, a tearing slash on the way out and the artery would be cut, death inevitable. He should be able to deal with Daly and anyone else in the room before they had moved from their chairs.

So Michael Collins had only a few more minutes to live.

At the top of the stairs there was a landing with baniste over the stairwell, and two doors. Daly knocked at one.

'Come in!'

Daly opened the door for Andrew to walk past him into the room. He said: 'Count von Hessel, Mick,' and followed him in.

On his first stride into the room, Andrew noticed several things. A burly dark-haired man sat behind a desk in the middle of the room, facing the door. Surely that must be Collins – the round, beefy face, the air of confidence and command, marked him out. There was a window about six feet behind him, which meant his face was slightly in shadow, and to the right of the window a small man sat at a desk facing the wall. And there was a third man lounging against the mantelpiece on Andrew's right. There was a fire burning in the grate behind him.

In his second stride Andrew noticed that the man by the fireplace had a Mauser pistol in his hand. And there was a revolver on top of a pile of papers on Collins's desk. And Daly had come into the room behind him. Not so easy, then.

He stopped in front of the desk, bowed, clicked his heels, and held out his hand. He said: 'A great honour, Mr Collins.'

To his surprise Collins did not stand up or shake his hand. Instead he drummed his fingers on the desk beside the revolver and said: 'Good morning, Mr Butler.'

How the hell does Collins know my name? Forget that, do something, this is all wrong, they know. Automatically, he said: 'I beg your pardon, Mr Collins?' And he would have moved then, snatched the revolver from Collins's desk and blown his brains out with it, if he had not seen, over Collins's shoulder, the eyes of the little man at the desk in the corner, watching him.

The eyes, behind the round pebble-lensed spectacles, were huge. Like the eyes of a scientist, peering at him like at a microbe under a microscope. Inhuman, compelling eyes. The eyes of the civil servant in Dublin Castle, Harrison.

Andrew's brain froze. His hand stopped moving. His body didn't know what to do. *Harrison?*

He stood quite still while his brain failed to take it in. Then he realized that there was something horribly familiar about the third man standing in front of the fireplace, pointing the round black snout of the Mauser directly at Andrew's heart. He had seen him before, too. Where? At Ardmore, that was it. He was the third man in the group who had come to Ardmore to demand money for the Loan; the man Andrew had expected to kill at the Blackwater Bridge along with Slaney and Rafferty. Davitt, he was called. The man whose place in the car had been taken by a young boy.

Ten seconds had passed and Andrew's brain was still frozen. Collins's hand closed on the butt of the revolver. He glanced at the man by the fireplace. He asked: 'Is that him?'

'That's the fellow,' the man said. 'That's the bastard who murdered my little brother.'

From behind Andrew, Daly said: 'What's happening, Mick?'

Collins leaned back in his chair, the revolver held casually in his right hand. 'Keep your eyes on him, Paddy. This isn't a German count. This is a British spy. Andrew Butler, from Ardmore. He murdered Slaney, Rafferty and Frank Davitt's baby brother.'

Andrew said: '*Ich verstehe nichts. Wer sind Sie?*'

Collins said: 'Don't trouble yourself with play-acting, Mr Butler. Here, perhaps you'd like to read this.'

He picked up a sheet of paper from his desk and passed it over to Andrew. Andrew took it. At the bottom was the signature of Colonel Sir Jonathan O'Connell-Gort. Above that it said:

> In my capacity as commanding officer of Military Intelligence Dublin, I confirm that a reward of £10,000 will be paid to Major Andrew Butler in the event that any action of his is the main or substantial cause of the arrest of Michael Collins, dead or alive.

It was the second copy of the contract that Sir Jonathan had signed in Dublin Castle. The one that was to be kept in Harrison's safe, Andrew remembered. Even as he held it in his hand and read it, Andrew's brain unfroze and his thoughts began to flow again. Any minute now they would kill him. But for the moment Collins held some more papers in his left hand and had the air of someone in control, who wanted to justify himself first. Collins held the revolver clumsily, not like a soldier. Daly was behind Andrew to the right. Harrison would be no problem. The first man to deal with was Davitt, who held the Mauser rock-steady, unwavering.

Collins said: 'You recognize that, Mr Butler, I suppose? Clear proof that the British government employs murderers?'

Andrew looked up and saw Collins, Harrison and Davitt watching him closely. He realized suddenly how important the sheet of paper was to them. He scrumpled it into a ball and flung it past Davitt, into the fire.

Collins rose to his feet, and yelled: 'Frank! Get it out!' Davitt turned, looked behind him, and lowered the muzzle of the gun. Andrew drew the knife from his left sleeve, stepped forward, and stabbed it into Davitt's throat.

As Davitt collapsed Andrew twisted the knife, turned and saw Collins two feet from him, raising the revolver. With his left hand Andrew grabbed Collins's right wrist, pulling the hand with the revolver up and across Collins's body, so that the gun was no longer pointing towards Andrew and Collins was pulled off balance and falling sideways towards him. With his right hand Andrew stabbed upwards with the knife, aiming to catch Collins under the ribs, below the heart.

As he stabbed, Davitt's legs, jerking in the throes of death, kicked Andrew behind the knee.

Andrew fell with Collins on top of him. The knife snagged in the thick cloth of Collins's jacket, and fell out of Andrew's hand, on to the floor somewhere, out of reach. The revolver dropped out of Collins's hand into the fire.

Collins was a big man, heavy. Andrew wrenched himself sideways and reached for Collins's throat, but at the same time Collins punched him in the ribs and a boot landed in Andrew's back and he thought: There's no time, it takes minutes to strangle a man and Daly will shoot me long before that. So he jabbed his fist into Collins's face and rolled clear, turning fast, to see Daly with a gun in his hand thumbing back the safety catch.

Andrew dived at him, catching him hard around the waist in a rugby tackle just as the gun fired above his head

He knocked Daly to the floor and grabbed his wrist before he could fire the gun again. For two or three seconds there was a tense, vicious struggle for the gun. Daly was a big strong man and wouldn't let go, and Andrew was aware of Collins getting to his feet on the other side of the room. The little man Harrison was behind him, shaking, useless.

Andrew jerked Daly's arm right back, over his shoulder, and butted him in the face. Daly loosened his grip. Andrew dragged the gun out of his hand, stumbled to his feet, lifted it, aimed it at Collins, pulled the trigger and ...

The bloody thing misfired.

Collins was on his feet, running towards Andrew, and before Andrew could pull the trigger again Collins was on him and they lurched, punching and wrestling for the gun, against the wall near the door. Collins was very powerful and Andrew could get no advantage. He saw himself being held in a bearhug until Daly was up and then the two of them would have him for sure.

Collins reached behind him, dragged open the door and yelled: 'O'Reardan!' In the moment when Collins loosened his grip Andrew forced him back, heaving him out through the door on to the landing. They reeled against the banisters, Andrew drew his knee up into Collins's stomach, and as the big man doubled up Andrew dragged his hand with the pistol free. Almost free. Collins grabbed for it again and the weight of his movement sent them both tumbling, off balance, down the stairs.

Collins hit his head on something and slumped across Andrew, stunned. The gun was gone, lost, fallen out of sight. As Andrew dragged himself to his feet, the door from the shop opened and O'Reardan came through it, his

Mauser in his hand. He was about five yards away from Andrew, halfway down the two steps leading into the shop. He glanced wildly along the passage, trying to take the scene in. 'What's happening?' he said.

Andrew lurched to his feet and stepped forward, holding out his hand and smiling. Davitt's blood was dripping from his hand but he didn't see it. 'It's all right,' he said. 'We just fell down the stairs, that's all.'

Just one more step and I'll have hold of that gun, Andrew thought. The man's confused, he'll do what he's told. Pray God his gun works, and doesn't jam like the other. 'Put down the gun and give me a hand here, will you?'

From the top of the stairs Daly yelled: 'Shoot the bugger, Brendan!'

O'Reardan backed away up the steps into the shop, waving the gun from side to side. 'Don't worry,' Andrew said. 'It's all right now.'

O'Reardan shot him in the face.

In the telephone box on Dominick Street Sean had been speaking to the secretary at Clancy's Joiners and Decorators. He told her he wanted to speak to Michael Collins, but she said he was in a meeting. 'I don't care!' Sean said. 'It's urgent. Someone's coming there to try to kill him! Get him, will you!'

The secretary said: 'All right,' and then she screamed. Sean yelled: 'Hello? Hello? What's happening there?' But there was no answer. Only a confused clattering over the crackle of the phone. And before that there had been bang, like a gunshot.

Sean put down the phone and said: 'He's there now. There's a fight going on.'

Catherine stared at him, aghast, her face still smudged with the black smoke of the fire. His face was frozen, distant. She knew what he was going to say. She gripped him tightly by the shoulders and said: 'Stay here, Sean. You can't go. It'll be all over by the time you get there. You've done what you can.'

He pushed her aside and opened the door. 'It's only in Mary Street. It's just a few minutes.' He was halfway out of the door.

'Sean, please. Stay here with me!'

He paused, looked in her eyes. 'Wait for me outside. Or if not, meet me in Parnell Square tonight.' There was a tension, a fear in his eyes, but a trace of that wide, boyish grin flickered for a second across his face, and he said: 'I love you.' He kissed her smudged nose and was away, sprinting down the street, his boots sparking on the cobbles as he ran.

After a few seconds' pause Catherine ran too, after him. Her bare feet hurt sometimes on the loose stones but she ignored the pain. Usually she could run fast but her breath came short and she had to stop and cough because of the smoke that was still in her lungs. But I have to go on, I can't lose him now, she thought. She had tried to exorcize him and she had failed; he had come back from nowhere to save her life. For better or worse this was the only boy she loved and she couldn't let him out of her sight now.

Sean turned left into Parnell Street, dodging between trams, making a grocer's delivery boy on a bicycle wobble wildly. Catherine followed. A group of soldiers passing in a lorry laughed and whistled. Catherine thought they must look like a pair of students on some prank, she madly chasing her boyfriend who had covered her with soot. If the soldiers thought it was all a game, so much the better.

As they came down Jervis Street she realized it had started to rain. Thin cold rain that blurred her vision and bit at her face. Most of the people here were well-dressed, prosperous, struggling with umbrellas. Several of them turned to look at her and then glance ahead at Sean, and she thought: If I draw attention to him, that might be the worst of all.

So she slowed to a walk, letting him get ahead. When he came to the end of Jervis Street he turned left. When she reached the corner half a minute later she saw the sign for Clancy's twenty yards away on the opposite side of the road.

Oh, God, don't let Andrew be there, she thought. I don't want Sean to murder anyone else now, not even him.

Ever since Brendan Road, Kee had been determined that there would be no more failures with Sinn Feiners slipping out of the back entrance while he was raiding the front. This time, he took young Foster round to the back with him, to survey the scene. It was not easy, from Upper Abbey Street, to determine which were the most likely rear exits from buildings in Mary Street, but they located them at last. Kee left Foster there, and promised to direct a section of the troops round to him as soon as they arrived. The raid was not to begin until Foster had sent a messenger back to Kee, to confirm that they were in position.

When they had discussed this, Kee walked back to Mar

Street to watch the front door, and wait for the army lorries to arrive.

Three minutes before he reached the front of the building, a woman came out of the front door. She glanced up and down the street, as though expecting someone to be waiting for her. When no one appeared, she went back inside, and came out almost immediately with four men, two of whom were pushing bicycles.

One of the men was limping, and another had the beginnings of a black eye. The third was very small, with a briefcase and enormous pebble glasses. He and the man with the limp got on a tram with the woman. The other two mounted their bicycles and pedalled away swiftly into the crowds, pulling down their hats and turning up their collars to shield themselves against the rain.

Catherine saw Sean open the door of Clancy's and walk in. She sheltered in the doorway of a shop on the opposite side of the road, shivering, and waited for him to come out. She wondered if she should go in after him. But she didn't want any part of it, not even revenge against Andrew, not any more. Sean had told her to wait outside and that was what she wanted to do.

She was not in the habit of praying but she prayed now, swiftly and urgently and repetitively, that Sean would not meet Andrew in there and that he would come out alive and give up killing and still love her. Oh, please, God, I'll even start going to church again and go to confession and light a hundred candles if only you'll grant me that.

She saw Kee before he saw her. He crossed the road, a sturdy determined figure with his thick neck and feet planted heavily on the ground, and stood for a moment staring at the door of Clancy's. The rain dripped off his hat and he had his collar turned up against it, hiding half his face, but it was Kee all right, there was no doubt of that. And so Catherine knew God had not listened, and it was all going to go wrong.

Kee glanced up and down the street impatiently as though he were waiting for something. She wondered if she could sneak across the road behind his back and go into Clancy's and warn Sean, but there was no way Kee could fail to see her go in because he was watching the other side of the road all the time.

Perhaps he would go away. Perhaps she could ring the number that Sean had rung and warn the people inside. But she could see no phone and she didn't know the number. Perhaps she should wait until the moment Sean came out of the door and then spring on Kee and tear his eyes out.

She was still dithering when the soldiers arrived. Two army lorries and an armoured car pulled up with a grinding of brakes about twenty yards down the road. Kee hurried across to meet them, and a moment later one of the army lorries drove away up the road and turned left. Kee came up the road with about a dozen soldiers, wearing tin hats and armed with rifles. It's worse than an execution Catherine thought. Sean's in there and I've got to stop them somehow but there's only me and all those men and I don't know what to do.

The soldiers stood on the pavement about five yards from the door as though they were thinking of checking passers-by but Catherine was sure they had not come for that. Kee stood looking at his watch and Catherine saw a single soldier running down the road towards them from the right, where the lorry had gone.

It was at that moment that Sean came out. He stood in the doorway of Clancy's, glancing up and down the street, and Kee saw him immediately. Catherine started to run. She sprinted straight out into the street between two bicycles and dodged behind a tram but it was always, always going to be too late. She saw Kee shout something to Sean and Sean hesitate and then put his hand in his pocket and start to pull out his gun *no don't do that please Sean!* and long before the gun was even half out of his pocket Kee had raised a revolver and three of the soldiers had raised their rifles and before she even heard the bangs she saw Sean jerk and twitch like a marionette and then slump down head lolling on the pavement with his back against the door.

She reached him and had his head in her arms but it was far, far too late. He opened his eyes once so perhaps he saw her but then all the life was gone from them and blood dribbled out of his mouth and down his chest where it soaked into his shirt with the rain.

Kee gave an order and the soldiers surged past, stepping over his body with their big boots, hurrying into the building.

Catherine could never remember much of the sequence of events after that but after a time she saw two bodies being carried out on a stretcher into the drumming rain. One of them was Andrew's. She didn't know if the body was dead or not, but it meant nothing to her, it wasn't Sean.

A while later her father was there, she didn't know how. He put his coat around her shoulders and led her away and she didn't resist. She didn't think she would resist anything ever again, not any more.

26

D ALY PACED UP and down the drawing room of the big Georgian house. He was furious. For once not even Michael Collins could overawe him.

'If you'd just told me, Mick!' he was saying. 'I could have had the knife off him and handcuffed him before he ever came upstairs. Why didn't you say?'

Collins looked up wearily from where he sat on the edge of a chair, his head in his hands. The room was a wreck. He had already smashed a chair and a row of ornaments against the wall in his rage and grief. His friends were used to these outbursts, but today it seemed childish, futile, even to himself.

He said: 'I asked you to search him, now, Paddy, didn't I?'

'Yes, but not for a bloody knife! And you *knew* he was an assassin all along!'

'Oh yes, I knew.' Collins drummed his fists on his knees as though he would break them. Then he stood up suddenly and put his hand on Daly's shoulder. 'It's not your fault, Paddy, it's all mine. I underestimated the man, and I wanted to see him and surprise him for myself. That's why Frank Davitt died.'

'But what was the point of it all anyway?'

'The point?' Collins sighed. 'There were two points, really. The first was to get justice for those three boys who died down in County Waterford. You knew about that, surely?' Collins explained briefly what had happened. 'The other papers that Harrison brought me – they were copies of the RIC investigation into the murders. I asked Frank Davitt to be there just to provide the final proof that Butler was the man they spoke to, and to give him the satisfaction of knowing that justice was to be done. I won't have our boys being murdered by the bloody British, damn them! That's what it's all about. And now all I do is get Frank killed as well. I wish it had been me.'

'It damn near was you,' Daly said softly. 'That's my job, Mick, remember? To keep you alive.'

'I'm sorry, Paddy. I'll tell you next time.'

'If you don't, I'll go back to Connaught and spend my time fishing. What was the the second point?'

'The second point? To prove beyond any doubt that the government are employing murderers against us. We had the evidence which the RIC had collected about the killings near Ardmore, we had Frank Davitt as a witness, and we had that document offering a reward for me dead or alive. So we would have had a brief trial, executed him, and passed on the lot to the newspapers. Can you imagine what they would have made of all that?'

'What do you mean, would have? Can't you still do it?'

'I don't think so, Paddy. The whole key to it was that contract he threw in the fire. We would have said we'd found it on him, you see. Without that, they can deny the whole thing, and we'd just blow Harrison's cover to no purpose. And before you say anything, Paddy Daly, no, you were not supposed to know about Harrison.'

'So who is he then?'

Collins flopped down on a sofa, exhausted, his arms sprawled along the back, his boots up on the cushions. 'Harrison, Mr Daly, is a top-level British civil servant who, since 1916, has been convinced of the justice of our cause and is devoted to furthering it in any way he can. Post-imperial guilt, they call it.'

'So what does he do? Pass you minutes of Cabinet meetings, that sort of thing?'

Collins grinned faintly. 'Sometimes. More often, as in this case, he helps by persuading French and his top brass to take the worst possible course of action. Such as employing assassins to murder me, for instance.'

Daly scowled. 'Sounds like a very good course of action from their point of view.'

'Only if it works, Paddy. Not if we can expose it.'

Daly's frown deepened. 'But what about the first time, Mick – in Brendan Road? Did you know about Butler then?'

'Well, now. I did that, but G Division got to him first. You remember I was late for the meeting? I'd been with Harrison that morning. He'd only just found out that Butler was impersonating a German – we hadn't expected that. I rang to ask you to keep Hessel waiting upstairs, remember, so that you and I could have a word first. I was going to tell you then.'

'I wish you had, Mick.'

'So do I, now. But when he was arrested I wanted you to keep up the contact with him in case he came back. You did well the other day at the Joy, Paddy, but they'd never take you on as an actor at the Abbey Theatre, would they now? If you'd known who he was you'd have shot the man before he opened his mouth.'

The front door slammed, and there were loud, excited voices in the hall. Seamus Kelly came in, his face red with the cold and the rain, his eyes wide, staring, distraught.

'What is it now?' Collins asked.

'Sean!' Seamus's voice was high, wild, unsteady with emotion. 'They shot Sean Brennan! Half an hour ago outside Clancy's!'

'But – what in the world was he doing there? I ordered him to stay inside with you, blast you!'

'Yes, I know, but . . .' Seamus told the story of the morning, the way Sean had suddenly disappeared. When Seamus had realized Sean had gone, he had begun his own fruitless search of the city. He had been coming to Clancy's to tell Collins he couldn't find him when the police and soldiers arrived. 'It was that other Ulsterman who did it. I saw him. I forget the name.'

'Holy Mary, Mother of God!' Collins face was white, strained, intense as that of a ghost. 'Sean Brennan as well!'

Daly walked past him and put on his coat. This at least was something he could deal with. 'Kee, they call the man,' he said over his shoulder. 'Detective Inspector Kee.'

In his office in Brunswick Street, Kee slumped in his chair and picked up the telephone.

He was exhausted. The events of the last twenty-four hours – the arrest of Davis, the shambles he had found inside Clancy's, the confusion, the unanswered questions – would have been enough to shatter any man. But in addition he had had to cope with the combined guilt and elation he had felt at shooting down Sean Brennan on the pavement in Mary Street.

Elation, because he had fulfilled half of his promise to Bill Radford. Brennan was dead – he had lived by the gun and died by it, shot down on the street in exactly the same way as he had shot down Bill. An eye for an eye, a life for a life. He would never escape or laugh about it again with his perky, choirboy smile.

But Kee felt guilt too, because although Brennan had drawn his gun Kee would have shot him anyway, even if he had been unarmed. Before the raid he had cocked his revolver, and as soon as he had seen the boy come out of the door he had taken it out of his pocket and aimed it. He had fired the first shot. The soldiers' rifles had fired the rest sending the boy jerking and twitching back into the doorway, because Kee had started it. A year ago, a few months ago, Kee would have waited and tried to arrest the boy, but today he had not cared. A red rage had seized him and when he had seen the boy fall he had felt a savage, vengeful delight. Part of him still felt that. Another part felt that he had no right, any longer, to be a policeman.

The voice on the telephone answered and he gave the number of his small terraced house in Belfast. The phone began to ring – a tinny, unreal sound, infinitely far away. He thought how it would be if he walked down those streets near his home. The yellow gaslight, the sound of his boots on the cobbles, the hard clear tones of the Belfast accent all around him. And when he opened the door, the smell of warm stew or fresh bread, the smiling face of his wife, his daughter and the three boys helping to set the table, bowing their heads around it to listen to him say grace.

The ringing stopped, a voice said: 'Hello. Belfast 358.'

'Hello, Mary.' Although he rang every few days, when it came down to it Kee could never think of very much to say. He never had that problem when he was with her.

'Tom? Oh Tom, I hoped you'd ring today. It's Ruth's ninth birthday.'

'Is it? Yes, of course.' And I'd forgotten, Kee thought. What's happening to me? 'Let me talk to her, will you?'

There was a pause, a few crackles, and then a little girl's voice came on the line. 'Daddy? When are you coming home?'

'Oh, in a few days, my dear. Just a week or two, perhaps.' It would be longer than that, Kee knew. First there was this man Daly to find, so that he could keep his promise to Bill. Then there was the prosecution of Davis, and all the details from today, before he could even think of asking for a transfer home. He sighed, and looked out of the window, where the winter rain was sweeping in. He would have a foul, lonely walk back to the Standard Hotel. But there was no hurry about that.

He smiled, and said: 'Tell me about your birthday now, Ruthie. What did you do?'

When he had taken his daughter home, Sir Jonathan went to Brunswick Street and the hospital. He stayed there some time, and then returned to the Viceregal Lodge. As he walked down the ornate corridor with his riding boots clicking on the marble floor, Sir Jonathan remembered how often he had come to knock on this door before. Half a dozen times, perhaps, since the attempt on Lord French's life. And each time he had felt a curious excitement and companionship, as though only Harrison in all the world understood him. He straightened his back, and walked faster.

He met Harrison in his grand room on the second floor. The curtains were drawn against the evening rain, and a fire crackled busily in the grate. Harrison was working quietly at his desk, his big eyes scanning the paperwork before him. He looked up calmly as Sir Jonathan entered.

'I've heard the news already,' he said. 'Butler got very close, I understand. A pity. He was a brave man.'

'Yes.' Sir Jonathan chose his words carefully. 'But I haven't got all the information. The police don't seem to know who was there.'

Harrison folded a letter in front of him carefully, and put it in an envelope as if the operation were some kind of scientific experiment. 'The police are useless,' he said. His voice was quiet, almost a whisper, like an old man's. 'The only way we can ever defeat these people is by using their own methods.'

'You said that before,' Sir Jonathan said. 'I'm not so sure now. There are some things no one should do.'

The big eyes looked up at him over the envelope, considering him curiously. There was a patronizing smile on the man's lips, Sir Jonathan noted; not the slightest sign of nerves.

'Come, come, Colonel,' Harrison said. 'The man Butler was a hero. He only killed a few bog Irishmen — that's nothing to be ashamed of. We should recruit more men like him.'

'Perhaps,' Sir Jonathan said. He felt he was holding himself unnaturally stiff, like a man on parade ground. But it was the only way he could contain his feelings. He said, slowly: 'If we do, I shall ask Major Butler to help us train them.'

There was a silence. Harrison did not move for some time. Then, very gently, he put the paper knife down on the envelope in front of him. As the soft fingers moved away from it, Sir Jonathan saw them tremble slightly.

Harrison's voice was even more of a whisper than before. He said: 'I don't understand you, Colonel. Major Butler is dead.'

'I imagine that is what the Shinners think, certainly,' Sir Jonathan answered. 'But if you had got your information from the hospital, you would know that the bullet entered his cheek, just below his left eye, and came out lower down through the back of the neck. It seems to have been fired from above. He may lose the sight of the eye, but it missed the brain. I have just spent some time with him in hospital.'

'And?'

'And for a few moments he was conscious and able to talk. He mentioned you, Mr Harrison.'

Harrison pushed his chair back and got to his feet. He stood there, a short, ineffectual figure in the grand room, framed in the window with the fine view of Phoenix Park behind. Now he had got up, he seemed uncertain where to go.

Sir Jonathan strode briskly to the door behind him, and opened it. There were two uniformed military policemen in the corridor outside. Sir Jonathan pointed to Harrison.

'That's your man, Sergeant,' he said. 'It's a hanging matter, so guard him well.'

For Andrew the nurses were like angels. Their faces were soft and kind and they had beautiful crisp white caps with high wings on either side. He could see only dimly through one eye, but he always searched their faces anxiously to see if one might look like Catherine. But in fact it didn't matter, because they brought her to him anyway, in a bottle.

They tilted up his head very gently on the pillow and fed him with a spoon from the bottle, and then Catherine would come.

She came to him in his house at Ardmore. The house had been rebuilt and gleamed with new yellow stone, and she walked with him in the early morning across the lawn by the pond, while the southwest breeze blew the mist curling up from the sea, and the tops of the hills came clear. She held his hand and walked with him into the stables, where they talked to the grooms and stroked the noses of the young racehorses he had bred.

Then, without any change of time, they were in his mother's bedroom with the Chinese carpet and silken dragons writhing over the bedspread as they had done when he was a child. But he was not a child now and Catherine was his wife, as he had wanted her to be. She lay on the bedspread with her head propped on her elbow, her short bobbed hair hanging loose as she smiled at him, her body quite smooth and naked with the small brown nipples erect as he remembered them. There was a bulge in her stomach that had not been there before, but as he came closer to touch it his eyes became bad again, and he lost sight of her altogether because of the pain in his face.

It was worse than the pain he had had in the war. It was as though the side of his face were being crushed with giant pincers, and a spike thrust in his eye. The medicine the nurses gave him took it away for a while, but when it came back he could only turn his head feebly from side to side to try to escape, and stare grimly at the cracks in the ceiling. But it brought him back to reality.

The reality was that he had failed and Collins had won. There would be no money now and no rebuilt Ardmore. If he lived, his face would be uglier than ever before. A target for every Sinn Feiner in the land. An object of revulsion for every woman.

Sir Jonathan had spoken of taking Catherine home, so

she must have escaped from the cellar. Andrew was glad of that, he had never meant to starve her. He wondered if she had got to see her young Sinn Feiner, and when the boy would be hanged. When the boy was dead at last, she might come to her senses, and forget him.

And then? Would she would want to marry a one-eyed cripple with no home or money or job and a broken face? A man who believed in an Ireland she had rejected and which didn't exist any more? A man who was prepared to murder again and again for it until he was shot in his turn?

It hardly seemed likely. But everything about the girl was unpredictable. It was that which gave him hope. Andrew turned his head from side to side, gripped by the pincers of pain, and stared at the cracked hospital ceiling with his one remaining eye. If he stared at it hard enough, he thought, he might see the vision of her face, smiling at him again as she had done in the bed at Killrath.

He had to believe in her. There was no other reason to live.

When her father told her Andrew was alive, Catherine left the house. She couldn't bear it. She didn't want to know. The words of a poem kept running through her mind and they were the only thing she had left to hold on to now.

The poem was about Christ, but Catherine did not think of it like that. It had been written by Joseph Plunkett in 1916, on the day before he had been shot as a traitor in Kilmainham Gaol. He had given it to his wife Grace whom he had married the morning before his death, in his cell. As Catherine walked alone through the rainy streets the lines echoed in her mind:

> *I see His blood upon the rose*
> *And in the stars the glory of His eyes.*
> *His body gleams amid eternal snows*
> *His tears fall from the skies.*

Catherine had stopped going to church during the war, and she was not sure if she could believe in any God after what the world had been through since her childhood. Her prayer this afternoon had sprung more from desperation than belief. Certainly she did not believe in a God who was all-powerful or all-loving. But there must still be some spirit in the universe, responsible for what happened and how people lived and felt. Catherine believed that spirit must be made up of the best and worst actions that people did; the things they gave their lives for and were remembered by. Surely that was what Grace Plunkett must have thought when she read the poem that her husband of less than a day had written. Not just that Christ was in the stars and the rain and the snow, but that the spirit of her dead husband was in them also. And that he was part of the spirit of the nation because of the nobility of the way he had lived and what he had done.

Catherine wanted to believe all that of Sean. She walked in the icy winter rain along Bachelor's Walk towards the Customs House, and watched the black water of the river glitter in gaslight. It was very late, but she could not stay at home. Only the cold and the rain and the wind were bearable. She thought of all the things she and Sean had done together, and wondered whether he had really loved her as he had said this morning.

And she wondered whether Sean's deeds could be

thought of as noble in the way that Plunkett's were, and if he would be remembered as a hero one day in Ireland, and whether that memory would make the world a better place or a worse one.

> *His body gleams amid eternal snows*
> *His tears fall from the skies.*

She had nothing else but the rain to remember him by, not even a lock of hair or a photograph. She stood alone upon O'Connell Bridge until midnight, letting the sleet drive into her face until the bones of her cheeks were quite numb.